William Alexander

The Epistles of St. John

twenty-one discourses - with Greek text, comparative versions, and notes chiefly

exegetical

William Alexander

The Epistles of St. John
twenty-one discourses - with Greek text, comparative versions, and notes chiefly exegetical

ISBN/EAN: 9783337398552

Printed in Europe, USA, Canada, Australia, Japan

Cover: Foto ©Andreas Hilbeck / pixelio.de

More available books at **www.hansebooks.com**

THE

EPISTLES OF ST. JOHN

TWENTY-ONE DISCOURSES

𝔚ith 𝔊reek 𝔗ext, 𝔠omparative 𝔙ersions, and 𝔑otes
𝔠hiefly 𝔈xegetical

BY

WILLIAM ALEXANDER

D.D., D.C.L. OXON., HON. LL.D. DUBLIN

BRASENOSE COLLEGE, OXFORD

LORD BISHOP OF DERRY AND RAPHOE

FOURTH EDITION

𝔏ondon

HODDER AND STOUGHTON

27, PATERNOSTER ROW

MDCCCXCVI

PREFACE.

IT is now many years ago since I entered upon a study of the Epistles of St. John, as serious and prolonged as was consistent with the often distracting cares of an Irish Bishop. Such fruit as my labours produced enjoyed the advantage of appearing in the last volume of the *Speaker's Commentary* in 1881.

Since that period I have frequently turned again to these Epistles—subsequent reflection or study not seldom filling in gaps in my knowledge, or leading me to modify former interpretations. When invited last year to resume my old work, I therefore embraced willingly the opportunity which was presented to me.

Let me briefly state the method pursued in this book.

I. The First Part contains four Discourses.

(1) In the first Discourse I have tried to place the reader in the historical surroundings from which (unless all early Church history is unreal, a past that never was present) these Epistles emanated.

(2) In the second Discourse I compare the Epistle with the Gospel. This is the true point of orientation for the commentator. Call the connection between the two documents what we may; be the Epistle

preface, appendix, moral and devotional commentary,
or accompanying encyclical address to the Churches,
which were " the nurslings of John " ; that connection is
constant and pervasive.   Unless this principle is firmly
grasped, we not only lose a defence and confirmation of
the Gospel, but dissolve the whole consistency of the
Epistle, and leave it floating—the thinnest cloud in the
whole cloudland of mystic idealism.

(3) The third Discourse deals with the polemical
element in these Epistles.   Some commentators indeed,
like the excellent Henry Hammond, "spy out Gnostics
where there are none."   They confuse us with uncouth
names, and conjure up the ghosts of long-forgotten
errors until we seem to hear a theological bedlam, or to
see theological scarecrows.   Yet Gnosticism, Doketism,
Cerinthianism, certainly sprang from the teeming soil
of Ephesian thought ; and without a recognition of this
fact, we shall never understand the Epistle.   Undoubtedly, if the Apostle had addressed himself only
to contemporary error, his great Epistle would have
become completely obsolete for us.   To subsequent
ages an antiquated polemical treatise is like a fossil
scorpion with a sting of stone.   But a divinely taught
polemic under transitory forms of error finds principles
as lasting as human nature.

(4) The object of the fourth Discourse is to bring
out the image of St. John's soul—the essentials of the
spiritual life to be found in those precious chapters which
still continue to be an element of the life of the Church.
Such a view, if at all accurate, will enable the

reader to contemplate the whole of the Epistle with
the sense of completeness, of remoteness, and of
unity which arises from a general survey apart from
particular difficulties. An ancient legend insisted that
St. John exercised miraculous power in blending again
into one the broken pieces of a precious stone. We
may try in an humble way to bring these fragmentary
particles of spiritual gem-dust together, and fuse them
into one.

II. The plan pursued in the second part is this.
The First Epistle (of which only I need now speak) is
divided into ten sections.

The sections are thus arranged—

(1) The *text* is given in Greek. In this matter I
make no pretence to original research; and have
simply adopted Tischendorf's text, with occasional
amendments from Dr. Scrivener or Prof. Westcott.
At one time I might have been tempted to follow
Lachmann; but experience taught me that he is
"audacior quàm limatior," and I held my hand. The
advantage to every studious reader of having the
divine original close by him for comparison is too
obvious to need a word more.

With the Greek I have placed in parallel columns
the translations most useful for ordinary readers—the
Latin, the English A.V. and R.V. The Latin text is
that of the "Codex Amiatinus," after Tischendorf's
splendid edition of 1854. In this the reader will find
the Hieronymian interpretation as it stood not more

than a hundred and twenty years after the death of St. Jerome, an interpretation more diligent and more accurate than that which is supplied by the ordinary Vulgate text. The saint felt "the peril of presuming to judge others where he himself would be judged by all; of changing the tongue of the old, and carrying back a world which was growing hoary to the initial essay of infancy." The Latin is of that form to which ancient Latin Church writers gave the name of "rusticitas." But it is a happy—I had almost said a divine—rusticity. In translating from the Hebrew of the Old Testament, St. Jerome has given a new life, a strange tenderness or awful cadence, to prophets and psalmists. The voice of the fields is the voice of Heaven also. The tongue of the people is for once the tongue of God. This Hebraistic Latin or Latinised Hebrew forms the strongest link in that mysterious yet most real spell wherewith the Latin of the Church enthrals the soul of the world. But to return to our immediate subject. The student can seldom go wrong by more than a hair's breadth when he has before him three such translations. In the first column stands St. Jerome's vigorous Latin. The second contains the English A.V., of which each clause seems to be guarded by the spirits of the holy dead, as well as by the love of the living Church; and to tell the innovator that he "does wrong to show it violence, being so majestical." The third column offers to view the scholarlike—if sometimes just a little pedantic and provoking—accuracy of the R.V. To this comparison

of versions I attach much significance. Every translation is an additional commentary, every good translation the best of commentaries.

I have ventured with much hesitation to add upon another column in each section a translation drawn up by myself for my own private use; the greater portion of which was made a year or two before the publication of the R.V. Its right to be here is this, that it affords the best key to my meaning in any place where the exposition may be imperfectly expressed.[1]

(2) One or more Discourses are attached to most of the sections. In these I may have seemed sometimes to have given myself a wide scope, but I have tried to make a sound and careful exegesis the basis of each. And I have throughout considered myself bound to draw out some great leading idea of St. John with conscientious care.

(2) The Discourses (or if there be no Discourse in

---

[1] I venture to call attention to the rendering "very." It enables the translator to mark the important distinction between two words : ἀληθής, *factually* true and real, as opposed to that which in point of fact is mendacious; ἀληθινός, *ideally* true and real, that which alone realizes the idea imperfectly expressed by something else. This is one of St. John's favourite words. In regard to ἀγάπη I have not had the courage of my convictions. The word "charity" seems to me almost providentially preserved for the rendering of that term. It is not without a purpose that ἔρως is so rigorously excluded from the New Testament. [So also from the Epp. of Ignatius.] The objection that "charity" conveys to ordinary English people the notion of mere material alms is of little weight. If "charity" is sometimes a little *metallic*, is not "love" sometimes a little *maundering?* I agree with Canon Evans that the word, strictly speaking, should be always translated "charity" when alone, "love" when in regimen. Yet I have not been bold enough to put "God is charity " for "God is love."

the section, the text and versions) are followed by short
notes, chiefly exegetical, in which I have not willingly
passed by any real difficulty.

I have not wished to cumber my pages with constant
quotations.   But in former years I have read, in some
cases with much care, the following commentators—St.
Augustine's *Tractatus*, St. John Chrysostom's Homilies
on the Gospel (full of hints upon the Epistles), Cornelius
à Lapide ; of older post-Reformation commentators, the
excellent Henry Hammond, the eloquent Dean Hardy,
the precious fragments in Pole's *Synopsis*—above all, the
inimitable Bengel ; of moderns, Düsterdieck, Huther,
Ebrard, Neander ; more recently, Professor Westcott,
whose subtle and exquisite scholarship deserves the
gratitude of every student.of St. John.   Of Haupt I
know nothing, with the exception of an analysis of
the Epistle, which is stamped with the highest praise
of so refined and competent a judge as Archdeacon
Farrar.   But having read this list fairly in past
years, I am now content to have before me nothing
but a Greek Testament, the Grammars of Winer and
Donaldson, the New Testament lexicons of Bretschneider, Grimm, and Mintert, with Tromm's "Concor-
dantia LXX."   For, on the whole, I really prefer St.
John to his commentators.   And I hope I am not
ungrateful for help which I have received from
them, when I say that I now seem to myself to understand him better without the dissonance of their
many voices.   "Johannem nisi ex Johanne ipso
non intellexeris."

III. It only remains to commend this book, such as it is, not only to theological students, but to general readers, who I hope will not be alarmed by a few Greek words here and there.

I began my fuller study of St. John's Epistle in the noonday of life; I am closing it with the sunset in my eyes. I pray God to sanctify this poor attempt to the edification of souls, and the good of the Church. And I ask all who may find it useful, to offer their intercessions for a blessing upon the book, and upon its author.

WILLIAM DERRY AND RAPHOE.

THE PALACE, LONDONDERRY,
   February 6th, 1889.

MERCIFUL GOD, we beseech Thee to cast Thy bright beams of light upon Thy Church, that it being enlightened by the doctrine of Thy blessed Apostle and Evangelist St. John, may so walk in the light of Thy truth, that it may at length attain to the light of everlasting life, through Iesus Christ our Lord. Amen.

CONTENTS.

PART II.

SECTION III. (3)

SECTION IX.

SECTION X.

SECOND EPISTLE.

THIRD EPISTLE.

PART I.

I

"JOHANNIS EPISTOLÆ, ULTIMUSQUE PRIMÆ VERSICULUS, IN EPHESUM IMPRIMIS CONVENIUNT."

(BENGEL *in Act.* xix. 21.)

DISCOURSE I.

THE SURROUNDINGS OF THE FIRST EPISTLE OF ST. JOHN.

"Little children, keep yourselves from idols."—I JOHN v. 21.

AFTER the example of a writer of genius, preachers and essayists for the last forty years have constantly applied—or misapplied—some lines from one of the greatest of Christian poems. Dante sings of St. John—

> "As he, who looks intent,
> And strives with searching ken, how he may see
> The sun in his eclipse, and, through decline
> Of seeing, loseth power of sight: so I
> Gazed on that last resplendence."[1]

The poet meant to be understood of the Apostle's spiritual splendour of soul, of the absorption of his intellect and heart in his conception of the Person of Christ and of the dogma of the Holy Trinity. By these expositors of Dante the image is transferred to the style and structure of his writings. But confusion of thought is not magnificence, and mere obscurity is never sunlike. A blurred sphere and undecided outline is not characteristic of the sun even in eclipse. Dante never intended us to understand that St. John as a writer

---

[1] Cary's *Dante, Paradiso,* xxv. 117. Stanley's *Sermons and Essays on the Apostolic Age,* 242.

was distinguished by a beautiful vagueness of sentiment, by bright but tremulously drawn lines of
dogmatic creed.   It is indeed certain that round St.
John himself, at the time when he wrote, there were
many minds affected by this vague mysticism.   For
them, beyond the scanty region of the known, there
was a world of darkness whose shadows they desired
to penetrate.   For them this little island of life was
surrounded by waters into whose depths they affected
to gaze.   They were drawn by a mystic attraction to
things which they themselves called the "shadows,"
the "depths," the "silences."   But for St. John these
shadows were a negation of the message which he
delivered that "God is light, and darkness in Him is
none."   These silences were the contradiction of the
Word who has once for all interpreted God.   These
depths were "depths of Satan."[1]   For the men who
were thus enamoured of indefiniteness, of shifting sentiments and flexible creeds, were Gnostic heretics.   Now
St. John's style, as such, has not the artful variety, the
perfect balance in the masses of composition, the
finished logical cohesion of the Greek classical writers.
Yet it can be loftily or pathetically impressive.   It can
touch the problems and processes of the moral and
spiritual world with a pencil-tip of deathless light, or
compress them into symbols which are solemnly or
awfully picturesque.[2]   Above all St. John has the
faculty of enshrining dogma in forms of statement
which are firm and precise—accurate enough to be
envied by philosophers, subtle enough to defy the
passage of heresy through their finely drawn yet
powerful lines.   Thus in the beginning of his Gospel

---

[1] Apoc. ii. 24.   [2] John xiii. 30 cf. 1 John ii. 11.

all false thought upon the Person of Him who is the
living theology of His Church is refuted by anticipation—that which in itself or in its certain consequences
unhumanises or undeifies the God Man; that which
denies the singularity of the One Person who was
Incarnate, or the reality and entireness of the Manhood of Him who fixed His Tabernacle[1] of humanity
in us. [2]

It is therefore a mistake to ·look upon the First
Epistle of St. John as a creedless composite of miscellaneous sweetnesses, a disconnected rhapsody upon
philanthropy. And it will be well to enter upon a
serious perusal of it, with a conviction that it did not
drop from the sky upon an unknown place, at an
unknown time, with an unknown purpose. We can
arrive at some definite conclusions as to the circumstances from which it arose, and the sphere in which
it was written—at least if we are entitled to say that
we have done so in the case of almost any other ancient
document of the same nature.

Our simplest plan will be, in the first instance, to
trace in the briefest outline the career of St. John after
the Ascension of our Lord, so far as it can be followed
certainly by Scripture, or with the highest probability
from early Church history.   We shall then be better

---

[1] ἐσκήνωσεν ἐν ἡμῖν.

[2] This characteristic of St. John's style is powerfully expressed by
the great hymn-writer of the Latin Church.

> " Hebet sensus exors styli ;
> Stylo scribit tam subtili,
>   Fide tam catholicâ,
> Ne de Verbo salutari
> Posset quicquam refragari
>   Pravitas hæretica."
>
> *Adam of St. Victor,*   *Seq.* xxxii.

able to estimate the degree in which the Epistle fits into the framework of local thought and circumstances in which we desire to place it.

Much of this biography can best be drawn out by tracing the contrast between St. John and St. Peter, which is conveyed with such subtle and exquisite beauty in the closing chapter of the fourth Gospel.

The contrast between the two Apostles is one of *history* and of *character*.

Historically the work done by each of them for the Church differs in a remarkable way from the other.

We might have anticipated for one so dear to our Lord a distinguished part in spreading the Gospel among the nations of the world. The tone of thought revealed in parts of his Gospel might even have seemed to indicate a remarkable aptitude for such a task. St. John's peculiar appreciation of the visit of the Greeks to Jesus, and his preservation of words which show such deep insight into Greek religious ideas, would apparently promise a great missionary, at least to men of lofty speculative thought.[1] But in the Acts of the Apostles St. John is first overshadowed, then effaced, by the heroes of the missionary epic, St. Peter and St. Paul. After the close of the Gospels he is mentioned five times only. Once his name occurs in a list of the Apostles.[2] Thrice he passes before us with Peter.[3] Once again (the first and last time when we hear of St. John in personal relation with St. Paul) he appears in the Epistle to the Galatians with two others, James and Cephas, as reputed to be pillars of the Church.[4] But whilst we read in the Acts of his taking a certain part in miracles, in preaching, in

---

[1] John xii. 20—34, especially ver. 24.   [3] Acts iii. 4, v. 13, viii. 14.
[2] Acts i. 13.   [4] Gal. ii. 9.

confirmation ; while his boldness is acknowledged by
adversaries of the faith ; not a line of his individual
teaching is recorded.   He walks in silence by the side
of the Apostle who was more fitted to be a missionary
pioneer.[1]

With the materials at our command, it is difficult
to say how St. John was employed whilst the first
great advance of the cross was in progress.   We know
for certain that he was at Jerusalem during the second
visit of St. Paul.   But there is no reason for conjecturing
that he was in that city when it was visited by St. Paul
on his last voyage [2] (A.D. 60) ; while we shall presently
have occasion to show how markedly the Church
tradition connects St. John with Ephesus.

We have next to point out that this contrast in
the *history* of the Apostles is the result of a contrast
in their *characters*.   This contrast is brought out with
a marvellous prophetic symbolism in the miraculous
draught of fishes after the Resurrection.

First as regards St. Peter.

" When Simon Peter heard that it was the Lord, he
girt his fisher's coat unto him (for he was naked), and
did cast himself into the sea." [3]   His was the warm

---

[1] Acts iii. 4, iv. 13, viii. 14.   The singular and interesting manuscript of Patmos (Αἱ περίοδοι τοῦ θεολογοῦ) attributed to St. John's
disciple, Prochorus, seems to recognise that St. John's chief mission
was not that of working miracles.   Even in a kind of duel of prodigies
between him and the sinister magician of Patmos, the following
occurs.   " Kynops asked a young man in the multitude where his
father then was.   ' My father is dead,' he replied, ' he went down
yonder in a storm.'   Turning to John, the magician said,—' Now then,
bring up this young man's father from the dead.'   ' I have not come
here,' answered the Apostle, ' to raise the dead, but to deliver the
living from their errors.' "

[2] Gal. ii. 9 ; Acts xxi. 17, *sqq.*

[3] John xxi. 7.

energy, the forward impulse of young life, the free bold plunge of an impetuous and chivalrous nature into the waters which are nations and peoples. *In* he *must; on* he *will.* The prophecy which follows the thrice renewed restitution of the fallen Apostle is as follows : "Verily, verily, I say unto thee, When thou wast young, thou girdest thyself, and walkedst whither thou wouldest : but when thou shalt be old, thou shalt stretch forth thy hands, and another shall gird thee, and carry thee whither thou wouldest not. This spake He, signifying by what death He should glorify God, and when He had spoken this, He saith unto him, Follow Me."[1] This, we are told, is obscure ; but it is obscure only as to details. To St. Peter it could have conveyed no other impression than that it foretold his martyrdom. "When thou wast young," points to the tract of years up to old age. It has been said that forty is the old age of youth, fifty the youth of old age. But our Lord does not actually define old age by any precise date. He takes what has occurred as a type of Peter's youthfulness of heart and frame—"girding himself," with rapid action, as he had done shortly before ; "walking," as he had walked on the white beach of the lake in the early dawn ; "whither thou wouldest," as when he had cried with impetuous half defiant independence, "I go a fishing," invited by the auguries of the morning, and of the water. The form of expression seems to indicate that Simon Peter was not to go far into the dark and frozen land ; that he was to be growing old, rather than absolutely old.[2] Then should he stretch forth his hands, with the

---

[1] Ibid., vers. 17, 18, 19.

[2] The beginning of old age would account sufficiently for the anticipation of death in 2 Peter i. 13, 14, 15.

dignified resignation of one who yields manfully to
that from which nature would willingly escape. "This
spake He," adds the evangelist, "signifying by what
death he shall glorify God." [1] What fatal temptation
leads so many commentators to minimise such a prediction as this? If the prophecy were the product of
a later hand added after the martyrdom of St. Peter,
it certainly would have wanted its present inimitable
impress of distance and reserve.

It is in the context of this passage that we read
most fully and truly the contrast of our Apostle's nature
with that of St. Peter. St. John, as Chrysostom has
told us in deathless words, was loftier, saw more
deeply, pierced right into and through spiritual truths,[2]
was more the lover of Jesus than of Christ, as Peter
was more the lover of Christ than of Jesus. Below
the different work of the two men, and determining it,
was this essential difference of nature, which they carried
with them into the region of grace. St. John was not
so much the great missionary with his sacred restless-
ness; not so much the oratorical expositor of prophecy
with his pointed proofs of correspondence between
prediction and fulfilment, and his passionate declamation driving in the conviction of guilt like a sting that
pricked the conscience. He was the theologian; the
quiet master of the secrets of the spiritual life; the
calm strong controversialist who excludes error by
constructing truth. The work of such a spirit as his
was rather like the finest product of venerable and

---

[1] δοξάσει ver. 19. The lifelike *shall* (not *should*) is part of the
many minute but vivid touches which make the whole of this scene
so full of motion and reality—"I go a fishing" (ver. 3); "*about* two
hundred cubits" (ver. 8); the accurate αἰγιαλός (ver. 4. See Trench,
On Parables, 57; Stanley, *Apostolic Age*, 135).

[2] διορατικώτερος. S. Joann. Chrysost.—*Hom. in Joann.*

long established Churches.   One gentle word of Jesus sums up the biography of long years which apparently were without the crowded vicissitudes to which other Apostles were exposed.   If the old Church history is true, St. John was either not called upon to die for Jesus, or escaped from that death by a miracle.   That one word of the Lord was to become a sort of motto of St. John.   It occurs some twenty-six times in the brief pages of these Epistles.   "If I will that he abide"— abide in the bark, in the Church, in one spot, in life, in spiritual communion with Me.   It is to be remembered finally, that not only spiritual, but ecclesiastical consolidation is attributed to St. John by the voice of history.   He occupied himself with the visitation of his Churches and the development of Episcopacy.[1]   So in the sunset of the Apostolic age stands before us the mitred form of John the Divine.   Early Christianity had three successive capitals—Jerusalem, Antioch, Ephesus. Surely, so long as St. John lived, men looked for a Primate of Christendom not at Rome but at Ephesus.

How different were the two deaths !   It was as if in His words our Lord allowed His two Apostles to look into a magic glass, wherein one saw dimly the hurrying feet, the prelude to execution which even the saint wills not ; the other the calm life, the gathered disciples, the quiet sinking to rest.   In the clear obscure of that prophecy we may discern the outline of Peter's cross, the bowed figure of the saintly old man.   Let us be thankful that John "*tarried.*"   He has left the Church three pictures that can never fade—in the Gospel the picture of Christ, in the Epistles the picture of his own soul, in the Apocalypse the picture of Heaven.

---

[1] *Euseb. H. E.*, iii. 23.   See other quotations in Bilson, *Government of Christ's Church*, p. 365.

So far we have relied almost exclusively upon indications supplied by Scripture. We now turn to Church history to fill in some particulars of interest.

Ancient tradition unhesitatingly believed that the latter years of St. John's prolonged life, were spent in the city of Ephesus, or province of Asia Minor, with the Virgin-Mother, the sacred legacy from the cross, under his fostering care for a longer or shorter portion of those years. Manifestly he would not have gone to Ephesus during the lifetime of St. Paul. Various circumstances point to the period of his abode there as beginning a little after the fall of Jerusalem (A.D. 67). He lived on until towards the close of the first century of the Christian era, possibly two years later (A.D. 102). With the date of the Apocalypse we are not directly concerned, though we refer it to a very late period in St. John's career, believing that the Apostle did not return from Patmos until just after Domitian's death. The date of the Gospel may be placed between A.D. 80 and 90. And the First Epistle accompanied the Gospel, as we shall see in a subsequent discourse.

The Epistle then, like the Gospel, and contemporaneously with it, saw the light in Ephesus, or in its vicinity. This is proved by three pieces of evidence of the most unquestionable solidity.

(1) The opening chapters of the Apocalypse contain an argument, which cannot be explained away, for the connection of St. John with Asia Minor and with Ephesus. And the argument is independent of the authorship of that wonderful book. *Whoever* wrote the Book of the Revelation must have felt the most absolute conviction of St. John's abode in Ephesus and temporary exile to Patmos. To have written with a special view of acquiring a hold upon the Churches

of Asia Minor, while assuming from the very first as *fact* what *they*, more than any other Churches in the world, must have known to be *fiction*, would have been to invite immediate and contemptuous rejection.   The three earliest chapters of the Revelation are unintelligible, except as the real or assumed utterance of a Primate (in later language) of the Churches of Asia Minor.   To the inhabitants of the barren and remote isle of Patmos, Rome and Ephesus almost represented the world; their rocky nest among the waters was scarcely visited except as a brief resting-place for those who sailed from one of those great cities to the other, or for occasional traders from Corinth.

(2) The second evidence is the fragment of the Epistle of Irenæus to Florinus preserved in the fifth book of the Ecclesiastical History of Eusebius.   Irenæus mentions no dim tradition, appeals to no past which was never present.   He has but to question his own recollections of Polycarp, whom he remembered in early life.   "Where he sat to talk, his way, his manner of life, his personal appearance, how he used to tell of his intimacy with John, and with the others who had seen the Lord."[1]   Irenæus elsewhere distinctly says that " John himself issued the Gospel while living at Ephesus in Asia Minor, and that he survived in that city until Trajan's time."[2]

(3) The third great historical evidence which connects St. John with Ephesus is that of Polycrates, Bishop of Ephesus, who wrote a synodical epistle to Victor and the Roman Church on the quartodeciman question, toward the close of the second century. Polycrates speaks of the great ashes which sleep in

---

[1] *Ap. Euseb. H. E.,* v. 20.   [2] *Adv. Hæres.,* lib. iii., ch. I.

Asia Minor until the Advent of the Lord, when He shall raise up His saints. He proceeds to mention Philip who sleeps in Hierapolis ; two of his daughters ; a third who takes her rest in Ephesus, and "John moreover, who leaned upon the breast of Jesus, who was a high priest bearing the radiant plate of gold upon his forehead." [1]

This threefold evidence would seem to render the sojourn of St. John at Ephesus for many years one of the most solidly attested facts of earlier Church history.

It will be necessary for our purpose to sketch the general condition of Ephesus in St. John's time.

A traveller coming from Antioch of Pisidia (as St. Paul did A.D. 54) descended from the mountain chain which separates the Meander from the Cayster. He passed down by a narrow ravine to the "Asian meadow" celebrated by Homer. There, rising from the valley, partly running up the slope of Mount Coressus, and again higher along the shoulder of Mount Prion, the traveller saw the great city of Ephesus towering upon the hills, with widely scattered suburbs. In the first century the population was immense, and included a strange mixture of races and religions. Large numbers of Jews were settled there, and seem to have possessed a full religious organisation under a High Priest or Chief Rabbi. But the prevailing super-

---

[1] ἱερεὺς τὸ πέταλον πεφορεκώς—"Pontifex ejus (sc. *Domini*) auream laminam in fronte habens." So translated by S. Hieron. *Lib. de Vir. Illust.*, xlv. The πέταλον is the LXX. rendering of צִיץ, the projecting leaf or plate of radiant gold (Exod. xxviii. 26, xxxix. 30), associated with the "mitre" (Lev. viii. 9). Whether Polycrates speaks literally, or wishes to convey by a metaphor the impression of holiness radiating from St. John's face, we probably cannot decide.

stition was the worship of the Ephesian Artemis. The great temple, the priesthood whose chief seems to have enjoyed a royal or quasi-royal rank, the affluence of pilgrims at certain seasons of the year, the industries connected with objects of devotion, supported a swarm of devotees, whose fanaticism was intensified by their material interest in a vast religious establishment. Ephesus boasted of being a theocratic city, the possessor and keeper of a temple glorified by art as well as by devotion. It had a civic calendar marked by a round of splendid festivities associated with the cultus of the goddess. Yet the moral reputation of the city stood at the lowest point, even in the estimation of Greeks. The Greek character was effeminated in Ionia by Asiatic manners, and Ephesus was the most dissolute city of Ionia. Its once superb schools of art became infected by the ostentatious vulgarity of an ever-increasing parvenu opulence. The place was chiefly divided between dissipation and a degrading form of literature. Dancing and music were heard day and night; a protracted revel was visible in the streets. Lascivious romances whose infamy was proverbial were largely sold and passed from hand to hand. Yet there were not a few of a different character. In that divine climate, the very lassitude, which was the reaction from excessive amusement and perpetual sunshine, disposed many minds to seek for refuge in the shadows of a visionary world. Some who had received or inherited Christianity from Aquila and Priscilla, or from St. Pauı himself, thirty or forty years before, had contaminated the purity of the faith with inferior elements derived from the contagion of local heresy, or from the infiltration of pagan thought. The Ionian intellect seems to have delighted in imaginative metaphysics; and foı

minds undisciplined by true logic or the training of
severe science imaginative metaphysics is a dangerous
form of mental recreation.   The adept becomes the
slave of his own formulæ, and drifts into partial insanity
by a process which seems to himself to be one of in-
disputable reasoning.   Other influences outside Christianity ran in the same   direction.   Amulets were
bought by trembling believers.   Astrological calculations
were received with the irresistible fascination of terror.
Systems of magic, incantations, forms of exorcism, traditions of theosophy, communications with demons—all that
we should now sum up under the head of spiritualism—
laid their spell upon thousands.   No Christian reader
of the nineteenth chapter of the Acts of the Apostles
will be inclined to doubt that beneath all this mass of
superstition and imposture there lay some dark reality
of evil power.   At all events the extent of these practices,
these "curious arts" in Ephesus at the time of St. Paul's
visit, is clearly proved by the extent of the local literature
which spiritualism put forth.   The value of the books
of magic which were burned by penitents of this class,
is estimated by St. Luke at fifty thousand pieces of
silver—probably about thirteen hundred and fifty
pounds of our money![1]

Let us now consider what ideas or allusions in the
Epistles of St. John coincide with, and fit into, this
Ephesian contexture of life and thought.

We shall have occasion in the third discourse to
refer to forms of Christian heresy or of semi-Christian

---

[1] Acts xix. 20, 21. In this description of Ephesus the writer has
constantly had in view the passages to which he referred in the
Speaker's Commentary, *N.T.*, iv., 274, 276. He has also studied M.
Renan's *Saint Paul*, chap. xii., and the authorities cited in the notes,
pp. 329, 350.

speculation indisputably pointed to by St. John, and prevalent in Asia Minor when the Apostle wrote. But besides this, several other points of contact with Ephesus can be detected in the Epistles before us. (1) The first Epistle closes with a sharp decisive warning, expressed in a form which could only have been employed when those who were addressed habitually lived in an atmosphere saturated with idolatry, where the social temptations to come to terms with idolatrous practices were powerful and ubiquitous. This was no doubt true of many other places at the time, but it was pre-eminently true of Ephesus. Certain of the Gnostic Christian sects in Ionia held lax views about " eating things sacrificed unto idols," although fornication was a general accompaniment of such a compliance. Two of the angels of the Seven Churches of Asia within the Ephesian group —the angels of Pergamum and of Thyatira—receive especial admonition from the Lord upon this subject. These considerations prove that the command, "Children, guard yourselves from the idols," had a very special suitability to the conditions of life in Ephesus. (2) The population of Ephesus was of a very composite kind. Many were attracted to the capital of Ionia by its reputation as the capital of the pleasures of the world. It was also the centre of an enormous trade by land and sea. Ephesus, Alexandria, Antioch and Corinth were the four cities where at that period all races and all religions of civilised men were most largely represented. Now the First Epistle of St. John has a peculiar breadth in its representation of the purposes of God. Christ is not merely the fulfilment of the hopes of one particular people. The Church is not merely destined to be the home of a handful of spiritual citizens. The Atonement is as wide as the race of man. " He is the propitiation

for the whole world;" "we have seen, and bear
witness that the Father sent the Son as Saviour of the
world."[1]   A cosmopolitan population is addressed in a
cosmopolitan epistle.   (3) We have seen that the gaiety
and sunshine of Ephesus was sometimes darkened by
the shadows of a world of magic, that for some natures
Ionia was a land haunted by spiritual terrors. He
must be a hasty student who fails to connect the
extraordinary narrative in the nineteenth chapter of
the Acts with the ample and awful recognition in the
Epistle to the Ephesians of the mysterous conflict in
the Christian life against evil intelligences, real, though
unseen.[2]   The brilliant rationalist may dispose of such
things by the convenient and compendious method
of a sneer.   "Such narratives as that" (of St. Paul's
struggle with the exorcists at Ephesus) "are dis-
agreeable little spots in everything that is done by the
people.   Though we cannot do a thousandth part of
what St. Paul did, we have a system of physiology and
of medicine very superior to his."[3]   Perhaps *he* had
a system of spiritual diagnosis very superior to ours.
In the epistle to the Angel of the Church of Thyatira,
mention is made of " the woman Jezebel, which calleth
herself a prophetess,"[4] who led astray the servants ·of
Christ.   St. John surely addresses himself to a community where influences precisely of this kind exist,
and are recognised when he writes,—" Beloved, believe

---

[1] St. John ii. 2, iv. 14.   ·

[2] "We wrestle not against flesh and blood, but against," etc.
Eph. vi. 12-17.

[3] *Saint Paul*, Renan, 318, 319.

[4] For the almost certain reference here to the Chaldean Sybil Sam-
bethe, see Apoc. ii. 20, Archdeacon Lee's note in *Speaker's Commentary*,
N.T., iv. 527, 534, 535, and Dean Blakesley (art. *Thyatira, Dict. of
the Bible*).

not every spirit, but try the spirits whether they are of God : because many false prophets are gone out into the world. . . . Every spirit that confesseth not Jesus is not of God."[1] The Church or Churches, which the First Epistle directly contemplates, did not consist of men just converted. Its whole language supposes Christians, some of whom had grown old and were "fathers" in the faith, while others who were younger enjoyed the privilege of having been born and brought up in a Christian atmosphere. They are reminded again and again, with a reiteration which would be unaccountable if it had no special significance, that the commandment "that which they heard," " the word," " the message," is the same which they " had from the *beginning*."[2] Now this will exactly suit the circumstances of a Church like the Ephesian, to which another Apostle had originally preached the Gospel many years before.[3]

---

[1] I John iv. 1, 3.

[2] I John ii. 7, ii. 24, iii. 11 ; 2 John vv. 5, 6. The passage in ii. 24 is a specimen of that simple emphasis, that presentation of a truth or duty under two aspects, which St. John often produces merely by an inversion of the order of the words. " Ye—what ye *heard* from the beginning let it abide in you. If what from the *beginning* ye heard abide in you " (ὃ ἠκούσατε ἀπ' ἀρχῆς . . . ὃ ἀπ' ἀρχῆς ἠκούσατε). The emphasis in the first clause is upon the *fact* of their having *heard* the message ; in the second upon this feature of the message—that it was given in the *beginning* of Christianity amongst them, and kept unchanged until the present time. Cf. ἐντολὴ παλαιά (ii. 7) with ἀρχαῖος = "of the early Christian time," in Polycarp, *Ep. ad Philipp.,* i.

[3] Acts xviii. 18-21. To these general links connecting our Epistles with Ephesus, a few of less importance, yet not without significance, may be added. (1) The name of Demetrius (3 John 12) is certainly suggestive of the holy city of the earth-mother (Acts xix. 24, 38). Vitruvius assigns the completion of the temple of Ephesus to an architect of the name, and calls him " servus Dianæ." (2) St. John in his Gospel adopts, as if instinctively, the computation of time which was used in Asia Minor (John iv. 6, xix. 4—Hefel. *Martyrium S. Polycarp.*

On the whole, we have in favour of assigning these
Epistles to Ionian and Ephesian surroundings a considerable amount of external evidence. The general
characteristics of the First Epistle consonant with the
view of their origin which we have advocated are
briefly these. (1) It is addressed to readers who were
encompassed by peculiar temptations to make a
compromise with idolatry. (2) It has an amplitude
and generality of tone which befitted one who wrote
to a Church which embraced members from many
countries, and was thus in contact with men of many
races and religions. (3) It has a peculiar solemnity
of reference to the invisible world of spiritual evil and
to its terrible influence upon the human mind. (4) The
Epistle is pervaded by a desire to have it recognised
that the creed and law of practice which it asserts is
absolutely one with that which had been proclaimed by
earlier heralds of the cross to the same community.
Every one of these characteristics is consistent with
the destination of the Epistle for the Christians of
Ephesus in the first instance. Its polemical element,
which we are presently to discuss, adds to an accumula-

---

xxi.). On the same principle he speaks in the Apocalypse of " day
and night " (Apoc. iv. 8, vii. 15, xii. 10, xiv. 11, xx. 10); St. Paul, on
the other hand, speaks of " night and day " (1 Tim. v. 5). It is a
very real indication of the accuracy of the report of words in the Acts
that, while St. Luke himself uses either form indifferently (Luke ii. 37,
xviii. 2), St. Paul, as quoted by him, always says " night and day " (Acts
xx. 31, xxvi. 7). (3) Is it merely fanciful to conjecture that the unusual
ἀγαθοποιῶν (3 John 11) may be an allusion to the astrological language
in which alone the term is ever used outside a very few instances in
the sacred writers? "He only is under a good star, and has beneficent
omens for his life." Balbillus, one of the most famous astrologers
of antiquity, the confidant of Nero and Vespasian, was an Ephesian,
and almost supreme in Ephesus, not long before St. John's arrival
there. Sueton., *Neron.*, 36.

tion of coincidences which no ingenuity can volatilise away.   The Epistle meets Ephesian circumstances; it also strikes at Ionian heresies.

Aïa-so-Louk,[1] the modern name of Ephesus, appears to be derived from two Greek words which speak of St. John the divine, the theologian of the Church.   As the memory of the Apostle haunts the city where he so long lived, even in its fall and long decay under its Turkish conquerors,—and the fatal spread of the malaria from the marshes of the Cayster—so a memory of the place seems to rest in turn upon the Epistle, and we read it more satisfactorily while we assign to it the origin attributed to it by Christian antiquity, and keep that memory before our minds.

---

[1] Aïa-so-Louk, a corruption of ἅγιος θεόλογος, *holy theologian* (or ἁγία θεολόγου, *holy city of the theologian*).   Some scholars, however, assert that the word is often pronounced and written *aiaslyk*, with the common Turkish termination *lyk*.   See *S. Paul* (Renan, 342, note 2).

DISCOURSE II.

THE CONNECTION OF THE EPISTLE WITH THE GOSPEL OF ST. JOHN.

Συνᾴδουσι μὲν γὰρ ἀλλήλοις τὸ εὐαγγέλιον καὶ ἡ ἐπιστολή.
Dionys. Alexandr. ap Euseb., H. E., vii., 25.

"And these things write we unto you, that your joy may be full."
—I JOHN i. 4.

FROM the wholesale burning of books at Ephesus, as a consequence of awakened convictions, the most pregnant of all commentators upon the New Testament has drawn a powerful lesson. "True religion," says the writer, "puts bad books out of the way." Ephesus at great expense burnt curious and evil volumes, and the "word of God grew and prevailed." And he proceeds to show how just in the very matter where Ephesus had manifested such costly penitence, she was rewarded by being made a sort of depository of the most precious books which ever came from human pens. St. Paul addresses a letter to the Ephesians. Timothy was Bishop of Ephesus when the two great pastoral Epistles were sent to him.[1] All St. John's writings point to the same place. The Gospel and Epistles

---

[1] Bengel, on Acts xix. 19, 20, finds a reference to manuscripts of some of the synoptical Gospels and of the Epistles in 2 Tim. iv. 13, and conjectures that, after St. Paul's martyrdom, Timothy carried them with him to Ephesus.

were written there, or with primary reference to the capital of Ionia.[1]   The Apocalypse was in all probability first read at Ephesus.

Of this group of Ephesian books we select two of primary importance—the Gospel and First Epistle of St. John.   Let us dwell upon the close and thorough connection of the two documents, upon the interpenctration of the Epistle by the Gospel, by whatever name we may prefer to designate the connection.

It is said indeed by a very high authority, that while the "whole Epistle is permeated with thoughts of the person and work of Christ," yet "direct references to facts of the Gospel are singularly rare."   More particularly it is stated that "we find here none of the foundation and (so to speak) crucial events summarised in the earliest Christian confession as we still find them in the Apostle's creed."   And among these events are placed, "the Birth of the Virgin Mary, the Crucifixion, the Resurrection, the Ascension, the Session, the Coming to Judgment."

To us there seems to be some exaggeration in this way of putting the matter.   A writing which accompanied a sacred history, and which was a spiritual comment upon that very history, was not likely to repeat the history upon which it commented, just in the same shape.   Surely the Birth is the necessary condition of having come in the flesh.   The incident of the piercing of the side, and the water and blood

---

[1] Renan's curious theory that Rom. xvi. 1-16 is a sheet of the Epistle to the Ephesians accidentally misplaced, rests upon a supposed prevalence of Ephesian names in the case of those who are greeted.   Archdeacon Gifford's refutation, and his solution of an unquestionable difficulty, seems entirely satisfactory.   (*Speaker's Commentary, in loc.,* vol. iii., New Testament.)

which flowed from it, is distinctly spoken of; and in
that the Crucifixion is implied.   Shrinking with shame
from Jesus at His Coming, which is spoken of in
another verse, has no meaning unless that Coming be
to Judgment.[1]   The sixth chapter is, if we may so say,
the section of "the Blood," in the fourth Gospel.   That
section standing in the Gospel, standing in the great
Sacrament of the Church, standing in the perpetually
cleansing and purifying efficacy of the Atonement—ever
present as a witness, which becomes personal, because
identified with a Living Personality [2]—finds its echo and
counterpart in the Epistle towards the beginning and
near the close.[3]

   We now turn to that which is the most conclusive
evidence of connection between two documents—one
historical, the other moral and spiritual—of which
literary composition is capable.   Let us suppose that
a writer of profound thoughtfulness has finished, after
long elaboration, the historical record of an eventful
and many-sided life—a life of supreme importance to
a nation, or to the general thought and progress of
humanity.   The book is sent to the representatives
of some community or school.   The ideas which its
subject has uttered to the world, from their breadth and
from the occasional obscurity of expression incident to

---

   [1] It has become usual to say that the Epistle does not advert to
John iii. or John vi.   To us it seems that *every* mention of the Birth
of God *is* a reference to John iii.   (1 John ii. 23, iii. 9, iv. 7, v. 1-4.)
The word αἷμα occurs *once* only in the fourth Gospel outside the
sixth chapter (xix. 34; for i. 13 belongs to physiology).   Four times
we find it in that chapter—vi. 53, 54, 55, 56.   Each mention of the
"Blood" in connection with our Lord *does* advert to John vi.
   [2] The masc. part. οἱ μαρτυροῦντες is surely very remarkable with the
three neuters (τὸ πνεῦμα, τὸ ὕδωρ, τὸ αἷμα) 1 John v. 7, 8.
   [3] 1 John i. 7, v. 6, 8.

all great spiritual utterances, need some elucidation. The plan is really exhaustive, and combines the facts of the life with a full insight into their relations ; but it may be missed by any but thoughtful readers. The author will accompany this main work by something which in modern language we might call an introduction, or appendix, or advertisement, or explanatory pamphlet, or encyclical letter. Now the ancient form of literary composition rendered books packed with thought doubly difficult both to read and write ; for they did not admit foot-notes, or marginal analyses, or abstracts. St. John then practically says, first to his readers in Asia Minor, then to the Church for ever—"with this life of Jesus I send you not only thoughts for your spiritual benefit, moulded round His teaching, but something more ; I send you an *abstract*, a compendium of contents, at the beginning of this letter; I also send you at its close a key to the plan on which my Gospel is conceived." And surely a careful reader of the Gospel at its first publication would have desired assistance exactly of this nature. He would have wished to have a synopsis of contents, short but comprehensive, and a synoptical view of the author's plan—of the idea which guided him in his choice of incidents so momentous and of teaching so varied.

We have in the First Epistle two synopses of the Gospel which correspond with a perfect precision to these claims.[1] We have : (1) a synopsis of the *contents* of the Gospel ; (2) a synoptical view of the *conception* from which it was written.

1. We find in the Epistle at the very outset a synopsis of the contents of the Gospel.

---

[1] See note A. at the end of this Discourse, which shows that there are, in truth, *four* such summaries.

"That which was from the beginning, that which we have heard, that which we have seen with our eyes, that which we gazed upon, and our hands handled—*I speak* concerning the Word who is the Life—that which we have seen and heard, declare we unto you also."

What are the contents of the Gospel ? (1) A lofty and dogmatic *proœmium*, which tells us of "the Word who was in the beginning with God — in Whom was life." (2) *Discourses* and utterances, sometimes running on through pages, sometimes brief and broken. (3) *Works*, sometimes miraculous, sometimes wrought into the common contexture of human life—looks, influences, seen by the very eyes of St. John and others, gazed upon with ever deepening joy and wonder. (4) *Incidents* which proved that all this issued from One who was intensely human ; that it was as real as life and humanity—historical not visionary ; the doing and the effluence of a Manhood which could be, and which was, grasped by human hands.

Such is a synopsis of the Gospel precisely as it is given in the beginning of the First Epistle. (1) The Epistle mentions *first*, "that which was from the beginning." There is the compendium of the proœmium of the Gospel. (2) One of the most important constituent parts of the Gospel is to be found in its ample preservation of dialogues, in which the Saviour is one interlocutor ; of monologues spoken to the hushed hearts of the disciples, or to the listening Heart of the Father, yet not in tones so low that their love did not find it audible. This element of the narrative is summed up by the writer of the Epistle in two words— "That which we heard." [1] (3) The *works* of bene-

---

[1] ὃ ἀκηκόαμεν.

volence or power, the doings and sufferings; the pathos or joy which spring up from them in the souls of the disciples, occupy a large portion of the Gospel. All these come under the heading, "that which we have seen with our eyes,[1] that which we gazed upon,"[2] with one unbroken gaze of wonder as so beautiful, and of awe as so divine.[3] (4) The assertion of the *reality of the Manhood*[4] of Him who was yet the Life manifested—a reality through all His words, works, sufferings—finds its strong, bold summary in this compendium of the contents of the Gospel, "and our hands have handled." Nay, a still shorter compendium follows: (1) The Life with the Father. (2) The Life manifested.[5]

2. But we have more than a synopsis which embraces the contents of the Gospel at the beginning of the

---

[1] ὃ ἑωράκαμεν τοῖς ὀφθαλμοῖς ἡμῶν.

[2] John xx. 20.

[3] ὃ ἐθεασάμεθα, 1 John i. 1. The same word is used in John i. 14.

[4] John xix. 27 would express this in the most palpable form. But it is constantly understood through the Gospel. The tenacity of Doketic error is evident from the fact that Chrysostom, preaching at Antioch, speaks of it as a popular error in his day. A little later, orthodox ears were somewhat offended by some beautiful lines of a Greek sacred poet, too little known among us, who combines in a singular degree Roman gravity with Greek grace. St. Romanus (A.D. 491) represents our Lord as saying of the sinful woman who became a penitent,

> τὴν βρέξασαν ἴχνη
> ἃ οὐκ ἔβρεξε βυθὸς
> ψιλοῖς τότε τοῖς δάκρυσιν.

> "Which with her tears, then pure,
> Wetted the feet the sea-depth wetted not."

(*Spicil. Solesmen.* Edidit T. B. Pitra, *S. Romanus*, xvi. 13, *Cant. de Passione.* 120.)

[5] 1 John i. 2. The Life with the Father = John i. 1, 14. The Life manifested = John i. 14 to end.

Epistle.   We have towards its close a *second* synopsis
of the whole framework of the Gospel ; not now the
theory of the Person of Christ, which in such a life was
necessarily placed at its beginning, but of the human
conception which pervaded the Evangelist's composition.

The second synopsis, not of the contents of the
Gospel, but of the aim and conception which it assumed
in the form into which it was moulded by St. John,
is given by the Epistle with a fulness which omits
scarcely a paragraph of the Gospel.   In the space of
six verses of the fifth chapter the word *witness*, as
verb or substantive, is repeated *ten* times.[1]   The simplicity of St. John's artless rhetoric can make no more
emphatic claim on our attention.   The Gospel is indeed
a tissue woven out of many lines of evidence human
and divine.   Compress its purpose into one single
word.   No doubt it is supremely the Gospel of the
Divinity of Jesus.   But, next to that, it may best be
defined as the Gospel of *Witness*.   These witnesses
we may take in the order of the Epistle.   St. John
feels that his Gospel is more than a book ; it is a past
made everlastingly present.   Such as the great Life
was in history, so it stands for ever.   Jesus *is* "the
propitiation, *is* righteous," "is *here*."[2]   So the great
influences round His Person, the manifold witnesses
of His Life, stand witnessing for ever in the Gospel
and in the Church.   What are these ?   (1) The Spirit
is ever *witnessing*.   So our Lord in the Gospel—
"when the Comforter is come, He shall witness of

---

[1] The A.V. (1 John v. 6-12) obscures this by a too great sensitive-
ness to monotony.   The language of the verses is varied unfortunately
by "bear record " (ver. 7), "hath testified " (ver. 9), "believeth not
the record " (ver. 10), "this is the record " (ver. 11).

[2] 1 John ii. 2-29, iii. 7, iv. 3, v. 20.

Me."[1]   No one can doubt that the Spirit is one
pre-eminent subject of the Gospel.   Indeed, teaching
about Him, above all as the witness to Christ, occupies three unbroken chapters in one place.[2]   (2) The
water is ever witnessing.   So long as St. John's
Gospel lasts, and permeates the Church with its influence, the water must so testify.   There is scarcely
a paragraph of it where water is not; almost always
with some relation to Christ.   The witness of the
Baptist[3] is, "I baptize with water."   The Jordan itself
bears witness that all its waters cannot give that which
He bestows who is "preferred before" John.[4]   Is not
the water of Cana that was made wine a witness to His
glory?[5]   The birth of "water and of the Spirit,"[6]
is another witness.   And so in the Gospel section after
section.   The water of Jacob's well; the water of the
pool of Bethesda; the waters of the sea of Galilee, with
their stormy waves upon which He walked; the water
outpoured at the feast of tabernacles, with its application
to the river of living water; the water of Siloam; the
water poured into the basin, when Jesus washed the
disciples' feet; the water which, with the blood, streamed
from the riven side upon the cross; the water of the
sea of Galilee in its gentler mood, when Jesus showed
Himself on its beach to the seven; as long as all this
is recorded in the Gospel, as long as the sacrament
of Baptism, with its visible water and its invisible
grace working in the regenerate, abides among the

---

[1] John xv. 26.
[2] John xiv., xv., xvi., Cf. vii. 39.   The witness of the Spirit in the
Apostolic ministry will be found John xx. 22.
[3] John i. 19.
[4] John i. 16, 31, 33.
[5] John ii. 9, iv. 46.
[6] John iii. 5.

faithful;—so long is the water ever witnessing.[1]   (3)
The Blood is ever "witnessing." Expiation once for
all; purification continually from the blood outpoured;
drinking the blood of the Son of Man by participation
in the sacrament of His love, with the grace and
strength that it gives day by day to innumerable souls;
the Gospel concentrated into that great sacrifice; the
Church's gifts of benediction summarised in the un-
speakable Gift; this is the unceasing witness of the
Blood.   (4) Men are ever witnessing.   "The witness
of men" fills the Gospel from beginning to end.   The
glorious series of confessions wrung from willing and
unwilling hearts form the points of division round
which the whole narrative may be grouped. Let us
think of all those attestations which lie between the
Baptist's precious testimony with the sweet yet fainter
utterances of Andrew, Philip, Nathanael, and the perfect
creed of Christendom condensed into the burning words
of Thomas—"my Lord and my God."[2]   What a range
of feeling and faith; what a variety of attestation coming
from human souls, sometimes wrung from them half
unwillingly, sometimes uttered at crisis-moments with
an impulse that could not be resisted! The witness of
men in the Gospel, and the assurance of one testimony
that was to be given by the Apostles individually and
collectively,[3] besides the evidences already named includes the following—the witness of Nicodemus, of the
Samaritan woman, of the Samaritans, of the impotent

---

[1] John iv. 5, 7, 11, 12, v. 1, 8, vi. 19, vii. 35, 37, ix. 7, xiii. 1, 14,
xix. 34, xxi. 1, 8. In the other great Johannic book water is constantly mentioned. Apoc. vii. 7, xiv. 7, xvi. 5, xxi. 6, xxii. 1, xxii. 17.
(Cf. the τὸ ὕδωρ, Acts x. 47.)

[2] John i. 19, 29, 32, 34, 35, 36, 41, 45, 47, xix. 27.

[3] John xv. 27.

man at the pool of Bethesda, of Simon Peter, of the officers of the Jewish authorities, of the blind man, of Pilate.[1] (5) The "witness of God" occupies also a great position in the fourth Gospel. That witness may be said to be given in five forms : the witness of the Father,[2] of Christ Himself,[3] of the Holy Spirit,[4] of Scripture,[5] of miracles.[6] This great cloud of witnesses, human and divine, finds its appropriate completion in another subjective witness.[7] The whole body of evidence passes from the region of the intellectual to that of the moral and spiritual life. The *evidence* acquires that *evidentness* which is to all our knowledge what the sap is to the tree. The faithful carries it in his heart; it goes about with him, rests with him day and night, is close to him in life and death. He, the principle of whose being is belief ever going out of itself and resting its acts of faith on the Son of God, has all that manifold witness in him.[8]

It would be easy to enlarge upon the verbal connection between the Epistle before us and the Gospel which it accompanied. We might draw out (as has

---

[1] John iii. 2. The Baptist's final witness (iii. 25, 33, iv. 39, 42, v. 15, vi. 68, 69, vii. 46, xix. 4, 6). Note, too, the accentuation of the idea of *witness* (John v. 31, 39). It is to be regretted that the R.V. also has sometimes obscured this important term by substituting a different English word, *e.g.*, "the word of the woman who *testified*" (John iv. 39).

[2] John viii. 18, xii. 28.

[3] Ibid. viii. 17, 18.

[4] Ibid. xv. 26.

[5] Ibid. v. 39, 46, xix. 35, 36, 37.

[6] Ibid. v. 36.

[7] This sixth witness (1 John v. 10) exactly answers to John xx. 30, 31.

[8] ὁ πιστεύων εἰς τὸν υἱόν, κτλ (v. 10). The construction is different in the words which immediately follow (ὁ μὴ πιστεύων τῷ θεῷ), not even giving Him credence, not *believing Him*, much less *believing on Him*.

often been done) a list of quotations from the Gospel, a whole common treasury of mystic language; but we prefer to leave an undivided impression upon the mind. A document which gives us a synopsis of the *contents* of another document at the beginning, and a synoptical analysis of its predominant idea at the close, covering the entire work, and capable of absorbing every part of it (except some necessary adjuncts of a rich and crowded narrative), has a connection with it which is vital and absorbing.   The Epistle is at once an abstract of the contents of the Gospel, and a key to its purport. To the Gospel, at least to it and the Epistle considered as integrally one, the Apostle refers when he says: "these things write we unto you."[1]

St. John had asserted that one end of his declaration was to make his readers hold fast "fellowship with us," *i.e.*, with the Church as the Apostolic Church; aye, and

---

[1] The view here advocated of the relation of the Epistle to the Gospel of St. John, and of the brief but complete analytical synopsis in the opening words of the Epistle, appears to us to represent the earliest known interpretation as given by the author of the famous fragment of the Muratorian Canon, the first catalogue of the books of the N. T. (written between the middle and close of the second century).   After his statement of the circumstances which led to the composition of the fourth Gospel, and an assertion of the perfect internal unity of the Evangelical narratives, the author of the fragment proceeds.   "What wonder then if John brings forward each matter, point by point, with such consecutive order (tam constanter singula), even in his Epistles saying, when he comes to write in his own person (dicens in semetipso), 'what we have seen with our eyes, and heard with our ears, and our hands have handled, these things have we written.'   For thus, in orderly arrangement and consecutive language he professes himself not only an eye-witness, but a hearer, and yet further a writer of the wonderful things of the Lord."   [So we understand the writer.   "Sic enim non solum visorem, sed et auditorem, sed et scriptorem omnium mirabilium Domini, per ordinem profitetur."   The fragment, with copious annotations, may be found in *Reliquæ Sacræ*, Routh, Tom. i., 394, 434.]

that fellowship of ours is "with the Father, and with His Son Jesus Christ;" "and these things," he continues (with special reference to his Gospel, as spoken of in his opening words), "we write unto you, that your joy may be fulfilled."

There is as truly a joy as a "patience and comfort of the Scriptures." The Apostle here speaks of "your joy," but that implied *his* also.

All great literature, like all else that is beautiful, is a "joy for ever." To the true student his books are this. But this is so only with a few really great books. We are not speaking of works of exact science. Butler, Pascal, Bacon, Shakespeare, Homer, Scott, theirs is work of which congenial spirits never grow quite tired. But to be capable of giving out joy, books must have been written with it. The Scotch poet tells us, that no poet ever found the Muse, until he had learned to walk beside the brook, and "no think long." That which is not thought over with pleasure; that which, as it gradually rises before the author in its unity, does not fill him with delight; will never permanently give pleasure to readers. He must know joy before he can say—"these things write we unto you, that your joy may be full."

The book that is to give joy must be a part of a man's self. That is just what most books are not. They are laborious, diligent, useful perhaps; they are not interesting or delightful. How touching it is, when the poor old stiff hand must write, and the overworked brain think, for bread! Is there anything so pathetic in literature as Scott setting his back bravely to the wall, and forcing from his imagination the reluctant creations which used to issue with such splendid profusion from its haunted chambers?

Of the conditions under which an inspired writer

pursued his labours we know but little.   But some
conditions are apparent in the books of St. John with
which we are now concerned.   The fourth Gospel
is a book written without *arrière pensée*, without
literary conceit, without the paralysing dread of criticism.   What verdict the polished society of Ephesus
would pronounce ;   what sneers would circulate in
philosophic quarters ;   what the numerous heretics
would murmur in their conventicles ;   what critics
within the Church might venture to whisper, missing
perhaps favourite thoughts and catch-words ;[1] St. John
cared no more than if he were dead.   He communed
with the memories of the past ; he listened for the
music of the Voice which had been the teacher of his
life.   To be faithful to these memories, to recall these
words, to be true to Jesus, was his one aim.   No one
can doubt that the Gospel was written with a full
delight.   No one who is capable of feeling, ever has
doubted that it was written as if with "a feather
dropped from an angel's wing ;" that without aiming
at anything but truth, it attains in parts at least a transcendent beauty.   At the close of the procemium, after
the completest theological *formula* which the Church
has ever possessed—the still, even pressure of a tide
of thought—we have a parenthetic sentence, like the
splendid unexpected rush and swell of a sudden wave
("we beheld the glory, the glory as of the Only-Begotten of the Father "); then after the parenthesis a

---

[1] For whatever reason, four classical terms (if we may so call
them) of the Christian religion are excluded, or nearly excluded, from
the Gospel of St. John, and from its companion document. *Church,
gospel, repentance,* occur nowhere. *Grace* only once (John i. 14; see,
however, 2 John 3; Apoc. i. 4; xxii. 21), *faith* as a substantive only
once. (1 John v. 4, but in Apoc. ii. 13-19; xiii. 10; xiv. 123.)

soft and murmuring fall of the whole great tide ("full
of grace and truth"). Can we suppose that the Apostle
hung over his sentence with literary zest? The
number of writers is small who can give us an everlasting truth by a single word, a single pencil touch;
who, having their mind loaded with thought, are wise
enough to keep that strong and eloquent silence which
is the prerogative only of the highest genius. St.
John gives us one of these everlasting pictures, oι
these inexhaustible symbols, in three little words—
"He then having received the sop, went immediately
out, and *it was night*."[1] Do we suppose that he admired the perfect effect of that powerful self-restraint?
Just before the crucifixion he writes—"Then came Jesus
forth, wearing the crown of thorns, and the purple robe,
and Pilate saith unto them, Behold the Man!"[2] The
pathos, the majesty, the royalty of sorrow, the admiration and pity of Pilate, have been for centuries the
inspiration of Christian art. Did St. John congratulate
himself upon the image of sorrow and of beauty which
stands for ever in these lines? With St. John as a
writer it is as with St. John delineated in the fresco
at Padua by the genius of Giotto. The form of the
ascending saint is made visible through a reticulation
of rays of light in colours as splendid as ever came
from mortal pencil; but the rays issue entirely from
the Saviour, whose face and form are full before him.

The feeling of the Church has always been that the
Gospel of St. John was a solemn work of faith and
prayer. The oldest extant fragment upon the canon
of the New Testament tells us that the Gospel was
undertaken after earnest invitations from the brethren
and the bishops, with solemn united fasting; not with-

[1] ἦν δὲ νύξ. John xiii. 30.   [2] John xix. 5.

out special revelation to Andrew the Apostle that John was to do the work.[1] A later and much less important document connected in its origin with Patmos embodies one beautiful legend about the composition of the Gospel. It tells how the Apostle was about to leave Patmos for Ephesus; how the Christians of the island besought him to leave in writing an account of the Incarnation, and mysterious life of the Son of God; how St. John and his chosen friends went forth from the haunts of men about a mile, and halted in a quiet spot called the gorge of Rest,[2] and then ascended the mountain which overhung it. There they remained three days. "Then," writes Prochorus, "he ordered me to go down to the town for paper and ink. And after two days I found him standing rapt in prayer. Said he to me—'take the ink and paper, and stand on my right hand.' And I did so. And there was a great lightning and thunder, so that the mountain shook. And I fell on the ground as if dead. Whereupon John stretched forth his hand and took hold of me, and said—'stand up at this spot at my right hand.' After which he prayed again, and after his prayer said unto me—'son Prochorus, what thou hearest from my mouth, write upon the sheets.' And having opened his mouth as he was standing praying, and looking up to heaven, he began to say—'in the beginning was the Word, and the Word was with God, and the Word was God.' And so following on, he spake in order, standing as he was, and I wrote sitting."[3]

---

[1] Canon. Murator. (apud Routh., *Reliq. Sacræ*, Tom. i., 394).

[2] ἐν τόπω ἡσύχῳ λεγομένῳ καταπαύσις.

[3] This passage is translated from the Greek text of the manuscript of Patmos, attributed to Prochorus, as given by M. Guérin. (*Description de l'Isle de Patmos*, pp. 25-29.)

True instinct which tells us that the Gospel of St.
John was the fruit of prayer as well as of memory ;
that it was thought out in some valley of rest, some
hush among the hills ; that it came from a solemn joy
which it breathed forth upon others ! "These things
write I unto you, that your joy may be fulfilled."
Generation after generation it has been so. In the
numbers numberless of the Redeemed, there can be
very few who have not been brightened by the joy of
that book. Still, at one funeral after another, hearts
are soothed by the word in it which says—"I am the
Resurrection and the Life." Still the sorrowful and
the dying ask to hear again and again—"let not your
heart be troubled, neither let it be afraid." A brave
young officer sent to the war in Africa, from a regiment
at home, where he had caused grief by his extravagance,
penitent, and dying in his tent, during the fatal day
of Isandula, scrawled in pencil—"dying, dear father
and mother—happy—for Jesus says, ' He that cometh
to Me I will in no wise cast out.'" Our English
Communion Office, with its divine beauty, is a texture
shot through and through with golden threads from
the discourse at Capernaum. Still are the disciples
glad when they see the Lord in that record. It is the
book of the Church's smiles ; it is the gladness of the
saints ; it is the purest fountain of joy in all the literature of earth.

Note A.

THE thorough connection of the Epistle with the Gospel may
be made more clear by the following tabulated analysis :—

The (A) *beginning* and (B) the *close* of the Epistle contain
two abstracts, longer and shorter, of the contents and bearing
of the Gospel.

A.

i.—1 John i. 1.

1. "That which was from the beginning—concerning the Word of Life "=John i. 1-15.

2. (*a*) "Which we have *heard*"=John i. 38, 39, 42, 47, 50, 51, ii. 4, 7, 8, 16, 19, iii. 3, 22, iv. 7, 39, 48, 50, v. 6, 47, vi. 5, 70, vii. 6, 39, viii. 7, 58, ix. 3, 41, x. 1, 39, xi. 4, 45, xii. 7, 50, xiii. 6, 38, xiv., xvii., xviii. 14, 37, xix. 11, 26, 27, 28, 30, xx. 15, 16, 17, 19, 21, 23, 27, 29, xxi. 5, 6, 10, 12, 22.

(*b*) "Which we have seen *with our eyes*"=John i. 29, 36, 39, ii. 11, vi. 2, 14, 19, ix., xi. 44, xiii. 4, 5, xvii. 1, xviii. 6, xix. 5, 17, 18, 34, 38, xx. 5, 14, 20, 25, 29, xxi. 1, 14.

(*c*) "Which we gazed upon "=*ibid.*

(*d*) "Which we have handled"=John xx. 27 (refers also to a synoptical Gospel, Luke xxiv. 39, 40).

ii.—1 John i. 2.

1. "The Life was manifested "=John i. 29—xxi. 25.

2. (*a*) "We have seen "=(A *i.* 2 (*b*)).

(*b*) "And bear witness"=John i. 7, 19, 37, iii. 2, 27, 33, iv. 39, vi. 69, xx. 28, 30, 31, xxi. 24.

(*c*) "And declare unto you "=John *passim.*

"The Life, the Eternal Life, which

א "Was with the Father "=John i. 1-4.

ב "And was manifested unto us "=John *passim.*

B.

i.—1 John v. 6-10.

Summary of the Gospel as a Gospel of *witness.*

1. "The Spirit beareth witness"=John i. 32, xiv., xv., xx. 22

2. "The water beareth witness"=John i. 28, ii. 9, iii. 5, iv. 13, 14, v. 1, 9, vi. 19, vii. 37, ix. 7, xiii. 5, xix. 34, xxi. 1.

3. "The blood beareth witness"=John vi. 53, 54, 55, 56, xix. 34.

4. "The witness of men "=(A. *ii.* 1 (*b*)) Also John i. 45, 49, iii. 2, iv. 39, vii. 46, xii. 12, 13, 17, 19, 20, 21, xviii. 38, xix. 35, xx. 28.

5. "The witness of God "—

(*a*) Scripture = John i. 45, v. 39, 46, xix. 36, 37.

(*b*) Christ's own — John viii. 17, 18, 46, xv. 30, xviii. 37.

(*c*) His Father's = John v. 37, viii. 18, xii. 28.

(*d*) His works — John v. 36, x. 25, xv. 24.

ii.—1 John v. 20.

We know (*i.e.*, by the Gospel) that—

1. "The Son of God is come" (ἥκεν), "has come and is here."

Note.—בָּאתִי = ἥκω, LXX. Psalm xl. 7. "*Venio* symbolum quasi Domini Jesu fuit." (Bengel on Heb. x. 7), the *Ich Dien* of the Son of the Father—ἐγὼ γάρ ἐκ τοῦ θεοῦ ἐξῆλθον καὶ ἥκω. "I came forth from God, and am here" (John viii. 4) = John i. 29—xxi. 23 (John xiv. 18, 21, 23, xvi. 16, 22, form part of the thought "is here").

2. "And hath given us an understanding"—gift of the Spirit, John xiv., xv., xvi. (especially 13, 16).

3. "This is the very God and eternal Life "—John i. 1, 4.

The whole Gospel of St. John brings out these primary principles of the Faith,—

That the Son of God has come. That He is now and ever present with His people. That the Holy Spirit gives them a new faculty of spiritual discernment. That Christ is the very God and the Life of men.

DISCOURSE III.

THE POLEMICAL ELEMENT IN THE FIRST EPISTLE OF ST. JOHN.

> " Dum Magistri super pectus
> Fontem haurit intellectûs
> Et doctrinæ flumina,
> Fiunt, ipso situ loci,
> Verbo fides, auris voci,
> Mens Deo contermina.
>
> " Unde mentis per excessus,
> Carnis, sensûs super gressus,
> *Errorumque nubila,*
> Contra veri solis lumen
> Visum cordis et acumen
> Figit velut aquila."
>
> *Adam of St. Victor,* Seq. xxxii.

" Every spirit that confesseth that Jesus Christ is come in the flesh is of God. Every spirit that confesseth not [that] Jesus Christ [is come in the flesh] is not of God."—I JOHN iv. 2, 3.

A DISCUSSION (however far from technical completeness) of the polemical element in St. John's Epistle, probably seems likely to be destitute of interest or of instruction, except to ecclesiastical or philosophical antiquarians. Those who believe the Epistle to be a *divine* book must, however, take a different view of the matter. St. John was not merely dealing with forms of human error which were local and fortuitous. In refuting *them* he was enunciating principles of universal import, of almost illimitable

application.   Let us pass by those obscure sects, those
subtle curiosities of error, which the diligence of minute
research has excavated from the masses of erudition
under which they have been buried ; which theologians,
like other antiquarians, have sometimes labelled with
names at once uncouth and imaginative.   Let us fix our
attention upon such broad and well-defined features of
heresy as credible witnesses have indelibly fixed upon
the contemporaneous heretical thought of Asia Minor ;
and we shall see not only a great precision in St. John's
words, but a radiant image of truth, which is equally
adapted to enlighten us in the peculiar dangers of our age.

Controversy is the condition under which all truth
must be held, which is not in necessary subject-matter—
which is not either mathematical or physical.   In the
case of the second, controversy is active, until the fact
of the physical law is established beyond the possibility
of rational discussion ; until self-consistent thought
can only think upon the postulate of its admission.
Now in these departments all the argument is on one
side.   We are not in a state of suspended speculation,
leaning neither to affirmation nor denial, which is *doubt.*
We are not in the position of inclining either to one side
or the other, by an almost impalpable overplus of evidence, which is *suspicion;* or by those additions to this
slender stock, which convert suspicion into *opinion.*   We
are not merely yielding a strong adhesion to one side,
while we must yet admit, to ourselves at least, that our
knowledge is not perfect, nor absolutely manifest—which
is the mental and moral position of *belief.*   In necessary
subject-matter, we know and see with that perfect intellectual vision for which controversy is impossible.[1]

---

[1] " Proprium est credentis ut cum assensu cogitet."   " The intellect
çf him who believes assents to the thing believed, not because he

The region of belief must therefore, in our present condition, be a region from which controversy cannot be excluded.

Religious controversialists may be divided into three classes, for each of which we may find an emblem in the animal creation. The first are the nuisances, at times the numerous nuisances, of Churches. These controversialists delight in showing that the convictions of persons whom they happen to dislike, can, more or less plausibly, be pressed to unpopular conclusions. They are incessant fault-finders. Some of them, if they had an opportunity, might delight in finding the sun guilty in his daily worship of the many-coloured ritualism of the western clouds. Controversialists of this class, if minute are venomous, and capable of inflicting a degree of pain quite out of proportion to their strength. Their emblem may be found somewhere in the range of "every creeping thing that creepeth upon the earth." The second class of controversialists is of a much higher nature. Their emblem is the hawk with his bright eye, with the forward throw of his pinions, his rushing flight along the woodland skirt, his unerring stroke. Such hawks of the Churches, whose delight is in pouncing upon fallacies, fulfil an important function. They rid us of tribes of mischievous winged errors. The third class of controversialists is that which embraces St. John supremely— such minds also as Augustine's in his loftiest and most

---

sees that thing either in itself or by logical reference to first self-evident principles; but because it is so far convinced by Divine authority as to assent to things which it does not see, and on account of the dominance of the will in setting the intellect in motion." This sentence is taken from a passage of Aquinas which appears to be of great and permanent value. *Summa Theolog.* 2ᵃ, 2ᵃᵉ quæst. i. art. 4. quæst. v. art. 2.

inspired moments, such as those which have endowed
the Church with the Nicene Creed. Of such the eagle
is the emblem. Over the grosser atmosphere of earthly
anger or imperfect motives, over the clouds of error,
poised in the light of the True Sun, with the eagle's
upward wing and the eagle's sunward eye, St. John
looks upon the truth. He is indeed the eagle of the
four Evangelists, the eagle of God. If the eagle could
speak with our language, his style would have something of the purity of the sky and of the brightness
of the light. He would warn his nestlings against
losing their way in the banks of clouds that lie below
him so far. At times he might show that there is a
danger or an error whose position he might indicate
by the sweep of his wing, or by descending for a
moment to strike.

There are then *polemics* in the Epistle and in the
Gospel of St. John. But we refuse to hunt down some
obscure heresy in every sentence. It will be enough
to indicate the master heresy of Asia Minor, to which
St. John undoubtedly refers, with its intellectual and
moral perils. In so doing, we shall find the very truth
which our own generation especially needs.

The prophetic words addressed by St. Paul to the
Church of Ephesus thirty years before the date of
this Epistle had found only too complete a fulfilment.
"From among their own selves," at Ephesus in particular, through the Churches of Asia Minor in general,
men *had* arisen "speaking perverse things, to draw
away the disciples after them."[1] The prediction began
to justify itself when Timothy was Bishop of Ephesus
only five or six years later. A few significant words

---

[1] Acts xx. 30.

in the First Epistle to Timothy let us see the heretical
influences that were at work. St. Paul speaks with
the solemnity of a closing charge when he warns
Timothy against what were at once [1] "profane babblings," and "antitheses of the Gnosis which is falsely
so called." In an earlier portion of the same Epistle
the young Bishop is exhorted to charge certain men
not to teach a "different doctrine," neither to give
"heed to myths and genealogies," out of whose endless
mazes no intellect entangled in them can ever find
its way. [2] Those commentators put us on a false scent
who would have us look after Judaizing error, Jewish
"stemmata." The reference is not to Judaistic ritualism,
but to semi-Pagan philosophical speculation. The
"genealogies" are systems of divine potencies which
the Gnostics (and probably some Jewish Rabbis of
Gnosticising tendency) called "æons," [3] and so the
earliest Christian writers understood the word.

Now without entering into the details of Gnosticism,
this may be said of its general method and purpose.
It aspired at once to accept and to transform the
Christian creed; to elevate its faith into a philosophy,
a *knowledge*—and then to make this knowledge cashier
and supersede faith, love, holiness, redemption itself.

This system was strangely eclectic, and amalgamated
certain elements not only of Greek and Egyptian, but
of Persian and Indian Pantheistic thought. It was

---

[1] τὰς βεβήλους κενοφωνίας, καὶ ἀντιθέσεις τῆς ψευδωνύμου γνώσεως.
1 Tim. vi. 20. The "antitheses" may either touch with slight sarcasm
upon pompous pretensions to scientific logical method; or may denote
the really self-contradictory character of these elaborate compositions;
or again, their polemical opposition to the Christian creed.

[2] μύθοις καὶ γενεαλογίαις ἀπεράντοις. 1 Tim. i. 3, 4.

[3] Irenæus quotes 1 Tim. i. 4, and interprets it of the Gnostic
'æons.' *Adv. Hæres.,* i. Proœm.

infected throughout with dualism and doketism. Dualism held that all good and evil in the universe proceeded from two first principles, good and evil. Matter was the power of evil whose home is in the region of darkness. Minds which started from this fundamental view could only accept the Incarnation provisionally and with reserve, and must at once proceed to explain it away. "The Word was made flesh;" but the Word of God, the True Light, could not be personally united to an actual material system called a human body, plunged in the world of matter, darkened and contaminated by its immersion. The human flesh in which Jesus appeared to be seen was fictitious. Redemption was a drama with a shadow for its hero. The phantom of a redeemer was nailed to the phantom of a cross. Philosophical dualism logically became theological *doketism*. Doketism logically evaporated dogmas, sacraments, duties, redemption.[1]

It may be objected that this doketism has been a mere temporary and local aberration of the human intellect; a metaphysical curiosity, with no real roots in human nature. If so, its refutation is an obsolete piece of an obsolete controversy; and the Epistle in some of its most vital portions is a dead letter.

---

[1] Few phenomena of criticism are more unaccountable than the desire to evade any acknowledgment of the historical existence of these singular heresies.   Not long after St. John's death, Polycarp, in writing to the Philippians, quotes 1 John iv. 3, and proceeds to show that doketism had consummated its work down to the last fibres of the root of the creed, by two negations—no resurrection of the body, no judgment. (Polycarp, *Epist. ad Philip.*, vii.) Ignatius twice deals with the Doketæ at length.   To the Trallians he delivers what may be called an antidoketic creed, concluding in the tone of one who was wounded by what he was daily hearing.   "Be deaf then when any man speaks unto you without Jesus Christ, who is of Mary, who truly was born, truly suffered under Pontius Pilate, truly was crucified and

Now of course literal doketism is past and gone, dead and buried. The progress of the human mind, the slow and resistless influence of the logic of common sense, the wholesome influence of the sciences of observation in correcting visionary metaphysics, have swept away æons, emanations, dualism, [1] and the rest. But a subtler, and to modern minds infinitely more attractive, doketism is round us, and accepted, as far as words go, with a passionate enthusiasm.

What is this doketism ?

Let us refer to the history and to the language of a mind of singular subtlety and power.

In George Eliot's early career she was induced to prepare for the press a translation of Strauss's mythical explanation of *the Life of Jesus.* It is no disrespect to so great a memory to say, that at that period of her career, at least, Miss Evans must have been unequal to grapple with such a work, if she desired to do so from a Christian point of view. She had not apparently studied the history or the structure of the Gospels. What she knew of their meaning she had imbibed from an antiquated and unscientific school of theologians. The faith of a sciolist engaged in a struggle for its life

---

died, truly also was raised from the dead. But if some who are un-believing say that He suffered apparently, *as if in vision, being visionary themselves,* why am I a prisoner ? why do I choose to fight with wild beasts ? " (Ignat., *Ep. ad Trall.,* iv. x.) The play upon the name doketæ cannot be mistaken (λέγουσιν τὸ δοκεῖν πεπονθέναι αὐτὸν, αὐτοὶ ὄντες τὸ δοκεῖν). Ignatius writes to another Church—"What profited it me if one praiseth me but blasphemeth my Lord, not confessing that He bears true human flesh. They abstain from Eucharist and prayer, because they confess not that the Eucharist is flesh of our Saviour Jesus Christ." (*Ep. ad Smyrn.,* v. vi. vii.)

[1] The elder Mr. Mill, however, appears to have seriously leaned to this as a conceivable solution of the contradictory phenomena of existence.

with the fatal strength of a critical giant instructed in
the negative lore of all ages, and sharpened by hatred
of the Christian religion, met with the result which was
to be expected.   Her faith expired, not without some
painful throes.   She fell a victim to the fallacy of
youthful conceit—*I* cannot answer this or that objection, *therefore* it is unanswerable.   She wrote at first
that she was "Strauss-sick."   It made her ill to dissect
the beautiful story of the crucifixion.   She took to herself a consolation singular in the circumstances.   The
sight of an ivory crucifix, and of a pathetic picture of
the Passion, made her capable of enduring the first
shock of the loss which her heart had sustained.   That
is, she found comfort in looking at tangible reminders
of a scene which had ceased to be an historical reality,
of a sufferer who had faded from a living Redeemer
into the spectre of a visionary past.   After a time,
however, she feels able to propose to herself and others
"a new starting point.   We can never have a satisfactory basis for the history of the man Jesus, but that
negation does not affect the Idea of the Christ, either
in its historical influence, or its great symbolic meanings."[1]   Yes! a Christ who has no history, of whom
we do not possess one undoubted word, of whom we
know, and can know, nothing; who has no flesh of fact,
no blood of life; an idea, not a man; this is the Christ
of modern doketism.   The method of this widely
diffused school is to separate the *sentiments* of admiration which the history inspires from the *history* itself;
to sever the *ideas* of the faith from the *facts* of the
faith, and then to present the *ideas* thus surviving the
dissolvents of criticism, as at once the refutation of
the facts and the substitute for them.

---

[1] *Life* vol. ii., 359, 360.

This may be pretty writing, though false and illogical writing is rarely even *that;* but a little consideration will show that this new starting point is not even a plausible substitute for the old belief.

(1) We question simple believers in the first instance. We ask them what is the great religious power in Christianity for themselves, and for others like-minded ? What makes people pure, good, self-denying, nurses of the sick, missionaries to the heathen ? They will tell us that the power lies, not in any doketic idea of a Christ-life which was never lived, but in " the conviction that that idea was really and perfectly incarnated in an actual career," [1] of which we have a record literally and absolutely true in all essential particulars. When we turn to the past of the Church, we find that as it is with these persons, so it has ever been with the saints. For instance, we hear St. Paul speaking of his whole life. He tells us that " whether we went out of our-selves it was unto God, or whether we be sober, it is for you ; " that is to say, such a life has two aspects, one God-ward, one man-ward. Its God-ward aspect is a noble insanity, its man-ward aspect a noble sanity ; the first with its beautiful enthusiasm, the second with its saving common sense. What is the source of this ? " *For* the love of Christ constraineth us,"—forces the whole stream of life to flow between these two banks without the deviations of selfishness— " because we thus judge, that He died for all, that they which live should no longer live unto themselves, but to Him who for their sakes died and rose again." [2] It was the real unselfish life of a real unselfish Man which

---

[1] Much use has here been made of a truly remarkable article in the *Spectator*, Jan. 31st, 1885.

[2] 2 Cor. v. 13-15.

made such a life as that of St. Paul a possibility. Or
we may think of the first beginning of St. John's love
for our Lord.   When he turned to the past, he
remembered one bright day about ten in the morning,
when the real Jesus turned to him and to another with
a real look, and said with a human voice, "what seek
ye ?" and then—"come, and ye shall see."[1]   It was
the real living love that won the only kind of love
which could enable the old man to write as he did
in this Epistle so many years afterwards—"we love
because He first loved us."[2]

(2) We address ourselves next to those who look
at Christ simply as an ideal.   We venture to put to
them a definite question.   You believe that there is no
solid basis for the history of the man Jesus; that His
life as an historical reality is lost in a dazzling mist
of legend and adoration.   Has the idea of a Christ,
divorced from all accompaniment of authentic fact,
unfixed in a definite historical form, uncontinued in an
abiding existence, been operative or inoperative for
yourselves ?   Has it been a practical power and motive,
or an occasional and evanescent sentiment ?   There
can be no doubt about the answer.   It is not a make-
belief but a belief which gives purity and power.   It
is not an ideal of Jesus but the blood of Jesus which
cleanseth us from all sin.

There are other lessons of abiding practical importance
to be drawn from the polemical elements in St. John's
Epistle.   These, however, we can only briefly indicate
because we wish to leave an undivided impression of
that which seems to be St. John's chief object *con-
troversially.*   There were Gnostics in Asia Minor for

---

[1] John i. 43.   [2] 1 John iv 19.

whom the mere *knowledge* of certain supposed spiritual truths was all in all, as there are those amongst ourselves who care for little but what are called clear views.   For such St. John writes—"and hereby we do *know* that we *know* Him, if we keep His commandments."[1]   There were heretics in and about Ephesus who conceived that the special favour of God, or the illumination which they obtained by junction with the sect to which they had "gone out" from the Church, neutralised the poison of sin, and made innocuous for *them* that which might have been deadly for others. They suffered, as they thought, no more contamination by it, than "gold by lying upon the dunghill" (to use a favourite metaphor of their own).   St. John utters a principle which cleaves through every fallacy in every age, which says or insinuates that sin subjective can in any case cease to be sin objective.   " Whosoever committeth sin transgresseth also the law, for sin is the transgression of the law.   All unrighteousness is sin."[2] Possibly within the Church itself, certainly among the sectarians without it, there was a disposition to lessen the glory of the Incarnation, by looking upon the Atonement as narrow and partial in its aim.   St. John's unhesitating statement is that " He is the propitiation for the whole world."   Thus does the eagle of the Church ever fix his gaze above the clouds of error, upon the Sun of universal truth.

Above all, over and through his negation of temporary and local errors about the person of Christ, St. John leads the Church in all ages to the true Christ. Cerinthus, in a form which seems to us eccentric and revolting, proclaimed a Jesus not born of a virgin, temporarily endowed with the sovereign power of the

---

[1] 1 John ii. 3.   [2] 1 John iii. 4, v. 17.

4

Christ, deprived of Him before his passion and resurrection, while the Christ remained spiritual and impassible.   He taught a *commonplace* Jesus.   At the
beginning of his Epistle and Gospel, John "wings his
soul, and leads his readers onward and upward."   He
is like a man who stands upon the shore and looks
upon town and coast and bay.   Then another takes the
man off with him far to sea.   All that he surveyed
before is now lost to him ; and as he gazes ever ocean-
ward, he does not stay his eye upon any intervening
object, but lets it range over the infinite azure.   So
the Apostle leads us above all creation, and transports
us to the ages before it ; makes us raise our eyes, not
suffering us to find any end in the stretch above, since
end is none.[2]   That "in the beginning," "from the
beginning," of the Epistle and Gospel, includes nothing
short of the eternal God.   The doketics of many shades
proclaimed an ideological, a misty Christ.   "Every
spirit which confesseth Jesus Christ as in flesh having
come is of God, and every spirit which confesseth not
Jesus, is not of God."   "Many deceivers have gone
out into the world, they who confess not Jesus Christ
coming in flesh."[2]   Such a Christ of mist as these
words warn us against is again shaped by more
powerful intellects and touched with tenderer lights.
But the shadowy Christ of George Eliot and of Mill is
equally arraigned by the hand of St. John.   Each
believer may well think within himself—I must die, and
that, it may be, very soon ; I must be alone with God,
and my own soul ; with that which I am, and have
been ; with my memories, and with my sins.   In that

---

[1] Every one who reads Greek should refer to the magnificent passage, *S. Joann. Chrysos.*, *in Joann.*, *Homil.* ii. 4.

[2] I John iv. 2 ; 2 John v. 7.   See notes on the passages.

hour the weird desolate language of the Psalmist will find its realisation : "lover and friend hast thou put from me, and mine acquaintance are—*darkness.*" [1] Then we want, and then we may find, a real Saviour. Then we shall know that if we have only a doketic Christ, we shall indeed be alone—for "except ye eat the flesh of the Son of Man, and drink His blood, ye have no life in you." [2]

NOTE.

THE two following extracts, in addition to what has been already said in this discourse, will supply the reader with that which it is most necessary for him to know upon the heresies of Asia Minor. 1. "Two principal heresies upon the nature of Christ then prevailed, each diametrically opposite to the other, as well as to the Catholic faith. One was the heresy of the Doketæ, which destroyed the verity of the *Human Nature* in Christ ; the other was the heresy of the Ebionites, who denied the *Divine Nature*, and the eternal Generation, and inclined to press the observation of the ceremonial law. Ancient writers allow these as heresies of the first century ; all admit that they were powerful in the age of Ignatius. Hence Theodoret (*Proœm.*) divided the books of these heresies into two categories. In the first he included those who put forward the idea of a second Creator, and asserted that the Lord had appeared illusively. In the second he placed those who maintained that the Lord was merely a man. Of the first, Jerome observed (*Adv. Lucifer.* xxiii.) 'that while the Apostles yet remained upon the earth, while the blood of Christ was almost smoking upon

---

[1] Psalm lviii. 18.   [2] John vi. 53.

the sod of Judæa, some asserted that the body of the Lord was a phantom.' Of the second, the same writer remarked that ' St. John, at the invitation of the bishops of Asia Minor, wrote his Gospel against Cerinthus and other heretics—and especially against the dogma of the Ebionites then rising into existence, who asserted that Christ did not exist before Mary.' Epiphanius notes that these heresies were mainly of Asia Minor (φημὶ δὲ ἐν τῇ 'Ασίᾳ). *Hæres.* lvi." (Pearson, *Vindic. Ignat.,* ii., c. i., p. 351.)

2. " Two of these sects or schools are very ancient, and seem to have been referred to by St. John. The first is that of the Naassenians or Ophites. The antiquity of this sect is guaranteed to us by the author of the *Philosophumena,* who represents them as the real founders of Gnosticism. " Later," he says, " they were called *Gnostics,* pretending that they only *knew the depths.*" (To this allusion is made Apoc. ii. 24, which would identify these sectaries with the Balaamites and Nicolaitans.) The second of these great heresies of Asia Minor is the doketic. The publication of the *Philosophumena* has furnished us with much more precise information about their tenets. We need not say much about the divine emanation—the fall of souls into matter, their corporeal captivity, their final rehabilitation (these are merely the ordinary Gnostic ideas). But we may follow what they assert about the Saviour and His manifestation in the world. They admit in Him the only Son of the Father (ὁ μονογενὴς παῖς ἄνωθεν αἰώνιος), who descended to the reign of shadows and the Virgin's womb, where He clothed Himself in a gross, human material body. But this was a vestment of no integrally personal and permanent character; it was, indeed, a sort of masquerade, an

artifice or fiction imagined to deceive the prince of this world. The Saviour at His baptism received a second birth, and clad Himself with a subtler texture of body, formed in the bosom of the waters—if that can be termed a body which was but a fantastic texture woven or framed upon the model of His earthly body. During the hours of the Passion, the flesh formed in Mary's womb, and it alone, was nailed to the tree. The great Archon or Demiurgus, whose work that flesh was, was played upon and deceived, in pouring His wrath only upon the work of His hands. For the soul, or spiritual substance, which had been wounded in the flesh of the Saviour, extricated itself from this as from an unmeet and hateful vesture ; and itself contributing to nailing it to the cross, triumphed by that very flesh over principalities and powers. It did not, however, remain naked, but clad in the subtler form which it had assumed in its baptismal second birth (*Philosoph.*, viii. 10). What is remarkable in this theory is, first, the admission of the reality of the terrestrial body, formed in the Virgin's womb, and then nailed to the cross. The *negation* is only of the *real* and permanent union of this body with the heavenly spirit which inhabits it. We shall, further, note the importance which it attaches to the Saviour's baptism, and the part played by water, as if an intermediate element between flesh and spirit. This may bear upon 1 John v. 8."

[This passage is from a *Dissertation—les Trois Témoins Célestes*, in a collection of religious and literary papers by French scholars (Tom. ii., Sept. 1868, pp. 388-392). The author, since deceased, was the Abbé Le Hir, M. Renan's instructor in Hebrew at Saint Sulpice, and pronounced by his pupil one of the first of European Hebraists and scientific theologians.]

DISCOURSE IV.

THE IMAGE OF ST. JOHN'S SOUL IN HIS EPISTLE.

"He that loveth pureness of heart, for the grace of his lips
the king shall be his friend."—Prov. xxii. 11.

ὁ θεμέλιος. . . . ὁ δεύτερος σάπφειρος.—Apoc. xxi. 19.

"We know that whosoever is born of God sinneth not; but he
that is begotten of God keepeth himself, and that wicked one toucheth
him not.   And we know that we are of God, and the whole world
lieth in wickedness.   And we know that the Son of God is come, and
hath given us an understanding that we may know Him that is true,
and we are in Him that is true, even in His Son Jesus Christ.   This
is the true God and eternal life."—1 John v. 18-20.

MUCH has been said in the last few years of a
series of subtle and delicate experiments in
sound. Means have been devised of doing for the
ear something analogous to that which glasses do for
another sense, and of making the results palpable by
a system of notation.   We are told that every tree
for instance, according to its foliage, its position, and
the direction of the winds, has its own prevalent note
or tone, which can be marked down, and its *timbre*
made first visible by this notation, and then audible.
So is it with the souls of the saints of God, and chiefly
of the Apostles.   Each has its own note, the prevalent
key on which its peculiar music is set.   Or we may
employ another image which possibly has St. John's
own authority.   Each of the twelve has his peculiar
emblem among the twelve vast and precious foundation
stones which underlie the whole wall of the Church.

St. John may thus differ from St. Peter, as the sapphire's azure differs from the jasper's strength and radiance. Each is beautiful, but with its own characteristic tint of beauty.[1]

We propose to examine the peculiarities of St. John's spiritual nature which may be traced in this Epistle. We try to form some conception of the key on which it is set, of the colour which it reflects in the light of heaven, of the image of a soul which it presents. In this attempt we cannot be deceived. St. John is so transparently honest ; he takes such a deep, almost terribly severe view of truth. We find him using an expression about truth which is perhaps without a parallel in any other writer. "If we say that we have fellowship with Him and walk in darkness we lie, and are not *doing the truth*."[2] The truth then for him is something co-extensive with our whole nature and whole life. Truth is not only to be *spoken*—that is but a fragmentary manifestation of it. It is to be *done*. It would have been for him the darkest of lies to have put forth a spiritual commentary on his Gospel which was not realised in himself. In the Epistle, no doubt, he uses the first person singular sparingly, modestly including himself in the simple *we* of Christian association. Yet we are as sure of the perfect accuracy of the picture of his soul, of the music in his heart which he makes visible and audible in his letter, as we are that he heard the voice of many waters, and saw the city coming down from God out of heaven ; as sure, as if at the close of this fifth chapter he had added with the

---

[1] Apoc. xxi. 19, 20.

[2] 1 John i. 6, cf. John iii. 21. In the LXX. the phrase is only found once, and is then applied to God: ἀλήθειαν ἐποίησας (Neh. ix. 33). It is characteristic of St. John's style that *doing a lie* is found in Apoc. xxi. 27, xxii. 15.

triumphant emphasis of truth, in his simple and stately way, "I John heard these things and saw them."[1] He closes this letter with a threefold affirmation of certain primary postulates of the Christian life; of its *purity*,[2] of its *privilege*[3] of its *Presence*,[4]—"we know," "we know," "we know." In each case the plural might be exchanged for the singular. He says "*we* know," because he is sure "*I* know."

In studying the Epistles of St. John we may well ask what we see and hear therein of St. John's character, (1) as a sacred writer, (2) as a saintly soul.

I.

We consider first the indications in the Epistle of the Apostle's character as a sacred writer.

For help in this direction we do not turn with much satisfaction to essays or annotations pervaded by the modern spirit. The textual criticism of minute scholarship is no doubt much, but it is not all. Aorists are made for man, not man for the aorist. He indeed who has not traced every fibre of the sacred text with grammar and lexicon cannot quite honestly claim to be an *expositor* of it. But in the case of a book like Scripture this, after all, is but an important preliminary. The frigid subtlety of the commentator who always seems to have the questions for a divinity examination before his eyes, fails in the glow and elevation necessary to bring us into communion with the spirit of St. John. Led by such guides, the Apostle passes under our review as a third-rate writer of a magnificent language in decadence, not as the greatest of theologians

---

[1] Apoc. xxii. 8.　　[3] Ibid. 19.
[2] 1 John v. 18.　　[4] ἥκει, ' has come,—and is here."—Ibid. 20.

and masters of the spiritual life—with whatever defects
of literary style, at once the Plato of the twelve in
one region, and the Aristotle in the other; the first by
his "lofty inspiration," the second by his "judicious
utilitarianism."   The deepest thought of the Church
has been brooding for seventeen centuries over these
pregnant and many-sided words, so many of which
are the very words of Christ.   To separate ourselves
from this vast and beautiful commentary is to place
ourselves out of the atmosphere in which we can best
feel the influence of St. John.

Let us read Chrysostom's description of the style
and thought of the author of the fourth Gospel.   "The
son of thunder, the loved of Christ, the pillar of the
Churches, who leaned on Jesus' bosom, makes his
entrance.   He plays no drama, he covers his head
with no mask.   Yet he wears array of inimitable beauty.
For he comes having his feet shod with the preparation
of the Gospel of peace, and his loins girt, not with
fleece dyed in purple, or bedropped with gold, but
woven through and through with, and composed of, the
truth itself.   He will now appear before us, not drama-
tically, for with him there is no theatrical effect or
fiction, but with his head bared he tells the bare truth.
All these things he will speak with absolute accuracy,
being the friend of the King Himself—aye, having the
King speaking within him, and hearing all things
from Him which He heareth from the Father; as He
saith—'you I have called friends, for all things that I
have heard from My Father, I have made known unto
you.'   Wherefore, as if we all at once saw one stooping
down from yonder heaven, and promising to tell us
truly of things there, we should all flock to listen to
him, so let us now dispose ourselves.   For it is from

up there that this man speaks down to us.   And the fisherman is not carried away by the whirling current of his own exuberant verbosity; but all that he utters is with the steadfast accuracy of truth, and as if he stood upon a rock he budges not.   All time is his witness.   Seest thou the boldness, and the great authority of his words ! how he utters nothing by way of doubtful conjecture, but all demonstratively, as if passing sentence.   Very lofty is this Apostle, and full of dogmas, and lingers over them more than over other things ! "[1]   This admirable passage, with its fresh and noble enthusiasm, nowhere reminds us of the glacial subtleties of the schools.   It is the utterance of an expositor who spoke the language in which his master wrote, and breathed the same spiritual atmosphere.   It is scarcely less true of the Epistle than of the Gospel of St. John.

Here also "he is full of dogmas," here again he is the theologian of the Church.   But we are not to estimate the amount of dogma merely by the number of words in which it is expressed.   Dogma, indeed, is not really composed of isolated texts—as pollen showered from conifers and germs scattered from mosses, accidentally brought together and compacted, are found upon chemical analysis to make up certain lumps of coal.   It is primary and structural.   The Divinity and Incarnation of Jesus pervade the First Epistle. Its whole structure is *Trinitarian*.[2]   It contains two of

---

[1] *S. Joann. Chrysost., in Johan.,* Homil. iii., Tom. viii., 25, 36, Edit. Migne.

[2] Huther, while rejecting with all impartial critics the interpolation (1 John v. 7), writes thus: "when we embrace in one survey the contents of the Epistle as a whole, it is certainly easy to *adapt the conception* of the three Heavenly witnesses to one place after another in the document.   But it does not follow that the mention of it just

the three great three-word dogmatic utterances of the
New Testament about the nature of God (the first
being in the fourth Gospel)—" God is Spirit," "God
is light," "God is love." The chief dogmatic statements of the Atonement are found in these few chapters.
"The blood of Jesus His Son cleanseth us from all
sin." "We have an Advocate with the Father, Jesus
Christ the Righteous." "He is the propitiation for the
whole world." "God loved us, and sent His Son the
propitiation for our sins." Where the Apostle passes
on to deal with the spiritual life, he once more " is full
of dogmas," *i.e.,* of eternal self-evidenced oracular
sentences, spoken as if "down from heaven," or by
one "whose foot is upon a rock,"—apparently identical
propositions, all-inclusive, the dogmas of moral and
spiritual life, as those upon the Trinity, the Incarnation,
the Atonement, are of strictly theological truth. A
further characteristic of St. John as a sacred writer in
his Epistle is, that he appears to indicate throughout
the moral and spiritual conditions which were necessary
for receiving the Gospel with which he endowed the
Church as the life of their life. These conditions are
three. The first is *spirituality*, submission to the teaching of the Spirit, that they may know by it the meaning
of the words of Jesus—the "anointing" of the Holy
Ghost, which is ever "teaching all things" that He
said.[1] The second condition is *purity*, at least, the
continuing effort after self-purification which is incum-
bent even upon those who have received the great
pardon.[2] This involves the following in life's daily

here would be in its right place." (*Handbuch über der drei Briefe des
Johannes.* Dr. J. E. Huther.)

[1] 1 John ii. 20.

[2] 1 John i. 7, iii. 3.

walk of the One perfect life-walk,[1] the imitation of that
which is supremely good,[2] "incarnated in an actual
earthly career." All must be purity, or effort after
purity, on the side of those who would read aright the
Gospel of the immaculate Lamb of God. The third
condition for such readers is love—*charity.* When he
comes to deal fully with that great theme, the eagle of
God wheels far out of sight. In the depths of His
Eternal Being, "God is love."[3] Then this truth comes
closer to us as believers. It stands completely and for
ever *manifested* in its work *in us,*[4] because "God *hath
sent*" (a mission in the past, but with abiding consequences)[5] "His Son, His only-begotten Son into the
world, that we may live through Him." Yet again, he
rises higher from the *manifestation* of this love to the
eternal and essential principle in which it stands present
for ever. "In this *is* the love, not that we loved God,
but that God loved us, and once for all sent His Son a
propitiation for our sins."[6] Then follows the manifestation of *our* love. "If God so loved us, we also are
bound to love one another." Do we think it strange
that St. John does not first draw the lesson—"if God
so loved us, we also are bound to love God"? It has
been in his heart all along, but he utters it in his own
way, in the solemn pathetic question—"he that loveth

---

[1] 1 John ii. 6.

[2] "Imitate not that which is evil, but that which is good"
(3 John 12). A comparison of this verse with John xxi. 24 would
lead to the supposition that the writer of the letter is quoting the
Gospel, and assumes an intimate knowledge of it on the part of Caius.
See Discourse XVII. Part ii. of this vol.

[3] See note A at the end of this discourse.

[4] 1 John iv. 9.

[5] ἀπέσταλκεν.

[6] ἀπέστειλεν

not his brother whom he hath seen, God whom he hath not seen how can he love ? " [1] Yet once more he sums up the creed in a few short words. "We have believed the love that God hath in us." [2] Truly and deeply has it been said that this creed of the heart, suffused with the softest tints and sweetest colours, goes to the root of all heresies upon the Incarnation, whether in St. John's time or later. That God should give up His Son by sending Him forth in humanity; that the Word made flesh should humble Himself to the death upon the cross, the Sinless offer Himself for sinners, this is what heresy cannot bring itself to understand. It is the excess of such love which makes it incredible. "We have believed the love" is the whole faith of a Christian man. It is St. John's creed in three words. [3]

Such are the chief characteristics of St. John as a sacred writer, which may be traced in his Epistle. These characteristics of the author imply corresponding characteristics of the man. He who states with such inevitable precision, with such noble and self-contained enthusiasm, the great dogmas of the Christian faith, the great laws of the Christian life, must himself have entirely believed them. He who insists upon these conditions in the readers of his Gospel, must himself have aimed at, and possessed, spirituality, purity, and love.

II.

We proceed to look at the First Epistle as a picture of the soul of its author.

(1) His was a life free from the dominion of wilful and habitual sin of any kind. "Whosover is born of

---

[1] 1 John iv. 20.

[2] 1 John iv. 16.

[3] πεπιστεύκαμεν τὴν ἀγάπην, 1 John iv. 16.

God doth not commit sin, and he cannot continue sinning." "Whosoever abideth in Him sinneth not; whosoever sinneth hath not seen Him, neither known Him." A man so entirely true, if conscious to himself of any reigning sin, dare not have deliberately written these words.

(2) But if St. John's was a life free from subjection to any form of the power of sin, he shows us that sanctity is not sinlessness, in language which it is alike unwise and unsafe to attempt to explain away. "If we say that we have no sin, we deceive ourselves." "If we say that we have not sinned and are not sinners, we make Him a liar." But so long as we do not fall back into darkness, the blood of Jesus is ever purifying us from all sin. This he has written that the fulness of the Christian life may be realised in believers; that each step of their walk may follow the blessed foot-prints of the most holy life; that each successive act of a consecrated existence may be free from sin.[1] And yet, if any fail in some such single act,[2] if he swerve, for a moment, from the "true tenour" of the course which he is shaping, there is no reason to despair. Beautiful humility of this pure and lofty soul! How tenderly, with what lowly graciousness he places himself among those who have and who need an Advocate. "Mark John's humility," cries St. Augustine; "he says not 'ye have,' nor 'ye have me,' nor even 'ye have Christ.' But he puts forward Christ, not himself; and he says

---

[1] For the aor. conj. in this place as distinguished from the pres. conj. cf. John v. 20, 23, vi. 28, 29, 30. Professor Westcott's refined scholarship corrects the error of many commentators, "that the Apostle is simply warning us not to draw encouragement for license from the doctrine of forgiveness." The tense is decisive against this, the thought is of the single *act* not of the *state*.

[2] ἐάν τις ἁμάρτῃ, I John ii. I.

'*we* have,' not '*ye* have,' thus placing himself in the rank of sinners." [1]   Nor does St. John cover himself under the subterfuges by which men at different times have tried to get rid of a truth so humiliating to spiritual pride—sometimes by asserting that they so stand accepted in Christ that no sin is accounted to them for such; sometimes by pleading personal exemption for themselves as believers.

This Epistle stands alone in the New Testament in being addressed to two generations—one of which after conversion had grown old in a Christian atmosphere, whilst the other had been educated from the cradle under the influences of the Christian Church.   It is therefore natural that such a letter should give prominence to the constant need of pardon.   It certainly does not speak so much of the great initial pardon,[2] as of the continuing pardons needed by human frailty.   In dwelling upon pardon once given, upon sanctification once begun, men are possibly apt to forget the pardon that is daily wanting, the purification that is never to cease.   We are to walk daily from pardon to pardon, from purification to purification.   Yesterday's surrender of self to Christ may grow ineffectual if it be not renewed to-day.   This is sometimes said to be a humiliating view of the Christian life.   Perhaps so—but it is the view of the Church, which places in its offices a daily confession of sin; of St. John in this Epistle; nay, of Him who teaches us, after our prayers for bread day by day, to pray for a daily forgiveness.   This may be more humiliating, but it is safer teaching than that which proclaims a pardon to be appropriated in a moment for all sins past, present, and to come.

---

[1] *In Epist. Johann.*, Tract. I.

[2] I John ii. 12, is, of course, an important exception.

This humility may be traced incidentally in other regions of the Christian life. Thus he speaks of the possibility at least of his being among those who might " shrink with shame from Christ in His coming." He does not disdain to write as if, in hours of spiritual depression, there were tests by which he too might need to lull and " persuade his heart before God." [1]

(3) St. John again has a boundless faith in prayer. It is the key put into the child's hand by which he may let himself into the house, and come into his Father's presence when he will, at any hour of the night or day. And prayer made according to the conditions which God has laid down is never quite lost. The particular thing asked for may not indeed be given ; but the substance of the request, the holier wish, the better purpose underlying its weakness and imperfection, never fails to be granted. [2]

(4) All but superficial readers must perceive that in the writings and character of St. John there is from time to time a tonic and wholesome *severity*. Art and modern literature have agreed to bestow upon the Apostle of love the features of a languid and inert tenderness. It is forgotten that St. John was the son of thunder ; that he could once wish to bring down fire from heaven ; and that the natural character is transfigured not inverted by grace. The Apostle uses great plainness of speech. For him a lie is a lie, and darkness is never courteously called light. He abhors and shudders at those heresies which rob the soul first of Christ, and then of God. [3] Those who undermine the

---

[1] I John iii. 19, 20.

[2] See Prof. Westcott's valuable note on I John v. 15. The very things literally asked for would be τὰ ἀληθέντα, not τὰ αἰτήματα.

[3] 2 John 11.

Incarnation are for him not interesting and original speculators, but "lying prophets." He underlines his warnings against such men with his roughest and blackest pencil mark. "Whoso sayeth to him 'good speed' hath fellowship with his *works*, those wicked *works*" [1]—for such heresy is not simply one work, but a series of works. The schismatic prelate or pretender Diotrephes may "babble;" but his babblings are wicked words for all that, and are in truth the "works which he is doing."

The influence of every great Christian teacher lasts long beyond the day of his death. It is felt in a general tone and spirit, in a special appropriation of certain parts of the creed, in a peculiar method of the Christian life. This influence is very discernible in the remains of two disciples of St. John, [2] Ignatius and Polycarp. In writing to the Ephesians, Ignatius does not indeed explicitly refer to St. John's Epistle, as he does to that of St. Paul to the Ephesians. But he draws in a few bold lines a picture of the Christian life which is imbued with the very spirit of St. John. The character which the Apostle loved was quiet and real; we feel that his heart is not with "him that sayeth." [3] So Ignatius writes—"it is better to keep silence, and yet to *be*, than to talk and *not to be*. It is good to teach if 'he that sayeth doeth.' He who has gotten to himself the word of Jesus truly is able to hear the silence of Jesus also, so that he may *act* through that which he *speaks*, and *be known* through the things wherein he is *silent*. Let us therefore do all things as in His presence who dwelleth in us, that we may

---

[1] 3 John 10.
[2] *Mart. Ignat.*, i.   *S. Hieron, de Script. Eccles.*, xvii.
[3] ὁ λέγων, 1 John ii. 4, 6, 9.

be His temple, and that He may be in us our God."
This is the very spirit of St. John. We feel in it at
once his severe common sense and his glorious mysticism.

We must add that the influence of St. John may be
traced in matters which are often considered alien to
his simple and spiritual piety. It seems that Episcopacy
was consolidated and extended under his fostering care.
The language of Ignatius (probably his disciple) upon
the necessity of union with the Episcopate is, after all
conceivable deductions, of startling strength. A few
decades could not possibly have removed Ignatius so
far from the lines marked out to him by St. John as
he must have advanced, if this teaching upon Church
government was a new departure. And with this conception of Church government we must associate other
matters also. The immediate successors of St. John,
who had learned from his lips, held deep sacramental
views. The Eucharist is "the bread of God, the
bread of heaven, the bread of life, the flesh of Christ."
Again Ignatius cries—"desire to use one Eucharist,
for one is the flesh of our Lord Jesus Christ, and
one cup unto oneness of His blood, one altar, as one
Bishop, with the Presbytery and deacons." [2] Hints
are not wanting that sweetness and life in public
worship derived inspiration from the same quarter.
The language of Ignatius is deeply tinged with his
passion for *music*. [3] The beautiful story, how he set

---

[1] *Ignat. Epist. ad Ephes.*, xv., cf. 1 John ii. 14, iv. 9, 17, iii. 2.

[2] *S. Ignat. Epist. ad Philad.*, iv.; cf. *Epist. ad Smyrn.*, vii.; *Epist. ad Ephes.*, xx.

[3] The most elaborate passage in the Ignatian remains is probably
this. "Your Presbytery is fitted together harmoniously with the
Bishop as chords with the cithara. Hereby in your symphonious
love Jesus Christ is sung in concord. Taking your part man by man
become one choir, that being harmoniously accordant in your like-

down, immediately after a vision, the melody to which
he had heard the angels chanting, and caused it to be
used in his church at Antioch, attests the impression
of enthusiasm and care for sacred song which was
associated with the memory of Ignatius.[1] Nor can we
be surprised at these features of Ephesian Christianity,
when we remember who was the founder of those
Churches.   He was the writer of *three* books.   These
books come to us with a continuous living interpretation of more than seventeen centuries of historical
Christianity.   From the fourth Gospel in large measure
has arisen the sacramental instinct, from the Apocalypse
the æsthetic instinct, which has been certainly exaggerated both in the East and West.   The third and
sixth chapters of St. John's Gospel permeate every
baptismal and eucharistic office.   Given an inspired
book which represents the worship of the redeemed
as one of perfect majesty and beauty, men may well
in the presence of noble churches and stately liturgies,
adopt the words of our great English Christian poet—

> "things which shed upon the outward frame
> Of worship glory and grace—which who shall blame
> That ever look'd to heaven for final rest?"

The third book in this group of writings supplies
the sweet and quiet spirituality which is the foundation
of every regenerate nature.

Such is the image of the soul which is presented to us
by St. John himself.   It is based upon a firm conviction
of the nature of God, of the Divinity, the Incarnation,

---

mindedness, having received in unity the chromatic music of God
(χρῶμα Θεοῦ λαβόντες), ye may sing with one voice through Jesus
Christ unto the Father."—*Epist. ad Ephes.*, iv.   The same image is
differently applied, *Epist. ad Philad.*, i.

[1] The story is given by Socrates.   (*H. E.*, vi. 8.)

the Atonement of our Lord. It is spiritual. It is pure, or being purified. The highest theological truth—" God is Love "—supremely *realised* in the Holy Trinity, supremely manifested in the sending forth of God's only Son, becomes the law of its common social life, made visible in gentle patience, in giving and forgiving.[1] Such a life will be free from the degradation of habitual sin. Yet it is at best an imperfect representation of the one perfect life.[2] It needs unceasing purification by the blood of Jesus, the continual advocacy of One who is sinless. Such a nature, however full of charity, will not be weakly indulgent to vital error or to ambitious schism ;[3] for it knows the value of truth and unity. It feels the sweetness of a calm conscience, and of a simple belief in the efficacy of prayer. Over every such life—over all the grief that may be, all the temptation that must be—is the purifying hope of a great Advent, the ennobling assurance of a perfect victory, the knowledge that if we continue true to the principle of our new birth we are safe. And our safety is, not that we keep ourselves, but that we are kept by arms which are as soft as love, and as strong as eternity.[4]

These Epistles are full of instruction and of comfort for us, just because they are written in an atmosphere of the Church which, in one respect at least, resembles our own. There is in them no reference whatever to a continuance of miraculous powers, to raptures, or to extraordinary phenomena. All in them which is supernatural continues even to this day, in the possession of an inspired record, in sacramental grace, in the

---

[1] 1 John iv. 7, 12.
[2] 1 John ii. 6, 9, i. 7-10, ii. 1, 2.
[3] 1 John i. 7, ii. 2, iv. 3, 6 ; 2 John 7-11 ; 3 John 9, 10.
[4] 1 John iii. 19, v. 14, 15, iv. 2, 3, v. 4, 5, 18.

pardon and holiness, the peace and strength of believers. The apocryphal "Acts of John" contain some fragments of real beauty almost lost in questionable stories and prolix declamation. It is probably not literally true that when St. John in early life wished to make himself a home, his Lord said to him, "I have need of thee, John;" that that thrilling voice once came to him, wafted over the still darkened sea—"John, hadst thou not been Mine, I would have suffered thee to marry."[1] But the Epistle shows us much more effectually that he had a pure heart and virgin will. It is scarcely probable that the son of Zebedee ever drained a cup of hemlock with impunity; but he bore within him an effectual charm against the poison of sin.[2] We of this nineteenth century may smile when we read that he possessed the power of turning leaves into gold, of transmuting pebbles into jewels, of fusing shattered gems into one; but he carried with him wherever he went that most excellent gift of charity, which makes the commonest things of earth radiant with beauty.[3]

---

[1] These sentences do not go so far as the mischievous and anti-scriptural legend of later ascetic heretics, who marred the beauty and the purpose of the miracle at Cana, by asserting that John was the bridegroom, and that our Lord took him away from his bride. *Acta Johannis,* XXI. *Act. Apost. Apoc.,* Tisch., 275).

[2] This legend no doubt arose from the promise—"if they drink any deadly thing it shall not hurt them " (Mark xvi. 18).

"Virus fidens sorbuit." Adam of St. Victor, *Seq.* XXXIII.

[3] "Aurum hic de frondibus,
   Gemmas de silicibus,
   Fractis de fragminibus,
   Fecit firmas."—*Ibid.*

There is something interesting in the persistency of legends about St. John's power over gems, when connected with the passage, flashing all over with the light of precious stones, whose exquisite disposition is the wonder of lapidaries. Apoc. xxi. 18, 22.

He may not actually have praised his Master during his last hour in words which seem to us not quite unworthy even of such lips—" Thou art the only Lord, the root of immortality, the fountain of incorruption. Thou who madest our rough wild nature soft and quiet, who deliveredst me from the imagination of the moment, and didst keep me safe within the guard of that which abideth for ever."   But such thoughts in life or death were never far from him for whom Christ was the Word and the Life ; who knew that while " the world passeth away and the lust thereof, he that doeth the will of God abideth for ever."[1]

May we so look upon this image of the Apostle's soul in his Epistle that we may reflect something of its brightness !   May we be able to think, as we turn to this threefold assertion of knowledge—"*I* know something of the security of this keeping.[2] *I* know something of the sweetness of being in the Church, that isle of light surrounded by a darkened world.[3] *I* know something of the beauty of the perfect human life recorded by St. John, something of the continued presence of the Son of God, something of the new sense which He gives, that we may know Him who is the Very God.[4]   Blessed exchange not to be vaunted loudly, but spoken reverently in our own hearts—the exchange of we, for I.   There is much divinity in these pronouns.[5]

---

[1] See note B at the end of the Discourse
[2] 1 John v. 18.
[3] Ibid. v. 19.
[4] Ibid. v. 20.
[5] Said by Luther of Psalm xxii. 1.

NOTES.

NOTE A.

1 John iv. 8, 9, 10. Modern theological schools of a Calvinistic bias have tended to overlook the conception of the nature of God as essential or substantive Love, and to consider love only as *manifested* in redemption. Socinianising interpreters understand the proposition to mean that God is simply and exclusively benevolent. (On the inadequacy of this, see Butler, *Anal.*, Part I., ch. iii., and Dissertation II. of the Nature of Virtue.) The highest Christian thought has ever recognised that the proposition ' God is Love ' necessarily involves the august truth that God if *sole* is not *solitary*. (" Credimur et confitemur omnipotentem Trinitatem—unum Deum *solum* non *solitarium*." Concil. Tolet., vi. 1.) " Let it not be supposed," said St. Bernard, "that I here account Love as an attribute or accident, but as the Divine essence—no new doctrine, seeing that St. John saith 'God is love.' It may rightly be said both that *Love* is *God*, and that love is *the gift of God*. For Love gives love; the essential Love gives that which is accidental. When Love signifies the Giver, it is the name of His essence; when it signifies His gift, it is the name of a quality or attribute." (*S. Bernard., de dil. Deo*, xii.). " This is nobly said. God is love. Thus love is the eternal law whereby all things were created and are governed—wherewith He who is the law of all things is unto Himself His own law, and that a law of love—wherewith He bindeth His Trinity into Unity." (*Thomassin. Dogm. Theol.*, lib. iii., 23.)

NOTE B.

ἡ ῥίζα τῆς ἀθανασίας καὶ ἡ πηγὴ τῆς ἀφθαρσίας· ὁ τὴν ἔρημον καὶ ἀγριωθεῖσαν φύσιν ἡμῶν ἤρεμον καὶ ἡσύχιον ποιήσας, ὁ τῆς προσκαίρου φαντασίας ῥυσάμενός με καὶ εἰς τὴν ἀεὶ μένουσαν φρουρήσας (*Acta Johannis*, 21). These sentences are surely not without freshness and power. One other passage is worth translating, because it seems to have just that imaginative cast which makes the Greek Liturgies, like so much else that is Greek, stand midway between the East and West; and because it

apparently refers to St. John's Gospel. "Jesus! Thou who hast woven this coronal with Thy plaiting, who hast blended these many flowers into the flower of Thy presence, not blown through by the winds of any storm ; Thou who hast scattered thickly abroad the seed of these words of Thine "—(*Acta Johannis*, 17).

PART II.

SOME GENERAL RULES FOR THE INTER-PRETATION OF THE FIRST EPISTLE OF ST. JOHN.

I. Subject Matter.

(1) THE *Epistle* is to be read through with constant reference to the *Gospel*. In what *precise form* the former is related to the latter (whether as a preface or as an appendix, as a spiritual commentary or an encyclical) critics may decide. But there is a vital and constant connection. The two documents not only touch each other in thought, but *interpenetrate* each other; and the Epistle is constantly *suggesting* questions which the Gospel only can answer, *e.g.*, 1 John i. 1, cf. John i. 1-14; 1 John v. 9, "witness of men," cf. John i. 15-36, 41, 45, 49, iii. 2, 27-36, iv. 29-42, vi. 68, 69, vii. 46, ix. 38, xi. 27, xviii. 38, xix. 5, 6, xx. 28.

(2) Such eloquence of *style* as St. John possesses is *real* rather than *verbal*. The interpreter must look not only at the words themselves, but at that which *precedes* and *follows*; above all he must fix his attention not only upon the *verbal expression* of the thought, but upon the *thought itself*. For the formal connecting link is not rarely omitted, and must be supplied by the devout and candid diligence of the reader. The "root

below the stream ' can only be traced by our bending over the water until it becomes translucent to us.

E.g. 1 John i. 7, 8. Ver. 7, "the root below the stream" is a question of this kind, which naturally arises from reading ver. 6—"must it be said that the sons of light need a constant cleansing by the blood of Jesus, which implies a constant guilt"? Some such thought is the latent root of connection. The answer is supplied by the following verse. ["It is so" for] "if we say that we have no sin," etc. Cf. also iii. 16, 17, xiv. 8, 9, 10, 11, v. 3 (ad. fin.), 4.

II. Language.

1. *Tenses.*

In the New Testament generally tenses are employed very much in the same sense, and with the same general accuracy, as in other Greek authors. The so-called "enallage temporum," or perpetual and convenient Hebraism, has been proved by the greatest Hebrew scholars to be no Hebraism at all. But it is one of the simple secrets of St. John's quiet thoughtful power, that he uses tenses with the most rigorous precision.

(*a*) The *Present* of continuing uninterrupted action, *e.g.*, i. 8, ii. 6, iii. 7, 8, 9.

Hence the so-called *substantized* participle with article ὁ has in St. John the sense of the continuous and constitutive temper and conduct of any man, the principle of his moral and spiritual life—*e.g.*, ὁ λέγων, he who is ever vaunting, ii. 4; πᾶς ὁ μισῶν, every one the abiding principle of whose life is hatred, iii. 15; πᾶς ὁ ἀγαπῶν, every one the abiding principle of whose life is love, iv. 7.

The Infin. Present is generally used to express an action now in course of performing or *continued* in itself

or in its results, or *frequently repeated—e.g.,* I John ii. 6,
iii. 8, 9, v. 18. (Winer, *Gr. of N. T. Diction,* Part 3,
xliv., 348.

(*b*) The *Aorist.*

This tense is generally used either of a thing occur-
ring only once, which does not admit, or at least does
not require, the notion of continuance and perpetuity ;
or of something which is brief and as it were only
momentary in duration (Stallbaum, *Plat. Enthyd.,* p.
140). This limitation or isolation of the predicated
action is most accurately indicated by the usual form
of this tense in Greek. The aorist verb is encased
between the augment ε- past time, and the adjunct σ-
future time, *i.e.,* the act is fixed off within certain limits
of previous and consequent time (Donaldson, *Gr. Gr.,*
427, B. 2). The aorist is used with most significant
accuracy in the Epistle of St. John, *e.g.,* ii. 6, 11, 27,
iv. 10, v. 18.

(*c*) The *Perfect.*

The Perfect denotes action absolutely past which
lasts on in its effects. "The idea of completeness
conveyed by the aorist must be distinguished from
that of a state consequent on an act, which is the
meaning of the perfect" (Donaldson, *Gr. Gr.,* 419).
Careful observation of this principle is the key to some
of the chief difficulties of the Epistle (iii. 9, v. 4, 18).

(2) The form of *accessional parallelism* is to be
carefully noticed. The second member is always in
advance of the first ; and a third is occasionally introduced in advance of the second, denoting the highest
point to which the thought is thrown up by the tide of
thought, *e.g.,* I John ii. 4, 5, 6, v. 11, v. 27.

(3) The *preparatory touch* upon the chord which
announces a theme to be amplified afterwards,—*e.g.,*

ii. 29, iii. 9—iv. 7, v. 3, 4; iii. 21—v. 14, ii. 20, iii. 24, iv. 3, v. 6, 8, ii. 13, 14, iv. 4—v. 4, 5.

(4) One secret of St. John's simple and solemn rhetoric consists in an *impressive change* in the order in which a leading word is used, *e.g.*, 1 John ii. 24, iv. 20.

These principles carefully applied will be the best commentary upon the letter of the Apostle, to whom not only when his subject is—

> "De Deo Deum verum
> Alpha et Omega, Patrem rerum";

but when he unfolds the principles of our spiritual life, we may apply Adam of St. Victor's powerful and untranslatable line,

> "Solers scribit idiota.'

SECTION I.

GREEK TEXT.

Ὁ ΗΝ ἀπ' ἀρχῆς, ὃ ἀκηκόαμεν, ὃ ἑωράκαμεν τοῖς ὀφθαλμοῖς ἡμῶν, ὃ ἐθεασάμεθα, καὶ αἱ χεῖρες ἡμῶν ἐψηλάφησαν περὶ τοῦ λόγου τῆς ζωῆς· καὶ ἡ ζωὴ ἐφανερώθη, καὶ ἑωράκαμεν, καὶ μαρτυροῦμεν, καὶ ἀπαγγέλλομεν ὑμῖν τὴν ζωὴν τὴν αἰώνιον, ἥτις ἦν πρὸς τὸν πατέρα, καὶ ἐφανερώθη ἡμῖν· ὃ ἑωράκαμεν καὶ ἀκηκόαμεν, ἀπαγγέλλομεν ὑμῖν, ἵνα καὶ ὑμεῖς κοινωνίαν ἔχητε μεθ' ἡμῶν· καὶ ἡ κοινωνία δὲ ἡ ἡμετέρα μετὰ τοῦ πατρὸς καὶ μετὰ τοῦ υἱοῦ αὐτοῦ Ἰησοῦ Χριστοῦ· καὶ ταῦτα γράφομεν ὑμῖν, ἵνα ἡ χαρὰ ὑμῶν ᾖ πεπληρωμένη.

LATIN.

Quod fuit ab initio, quod audivimus, et vidimus oculis nostris, quod perspeximus, et manus nostrae temptaverunt, de Verbo vitae; et vita manifestata est, et vidimus et testamur, et adnuntiamus vobis vitam aeternam, quae erat apud Patrem, et apparuit nobis: quod vidimus et audivimus, et adnuntiamus vobis, ut et vos societatem habeatis nobiscum, et societas nostra sit cum Patre, et Filio eius Iesu Christo. Et haec scripsimus vobis ut gaudium nostrum sit plenum.

AUTHORISED VERSION.

That which was from the beginning, which we have heard, which we have seen with our eyes, which we have looked upon, and our hands have handled, of the Word of Life; (for the life was manifested, and we have seen it, and bear witness, and show unto you that eternal life, which was with the Father, and was manifested unto us;) that which we have seen and heard declare we unto you, that ye also may have fellowship with us: and truly our fellowship is with the Father, and with his Son Jesus Christ. And these things write we unto you, that your joy may be full.

REVISED VERSION.

That which was from the beginning, that which we have heard, that which we have seen with our eyes, that which we beheld, and our hands handled, concerning the Word of life (and the life was manifested, and we have seen, and bear witness, and declare unto you the life, the eternal *life*, which was with the Father, and was manifested unto us); that which we have seen and heard declare we unto you also, that ye also may have fellowship with us: yea, and our fellowship is with the Father, and with his Son Jesus Christ: and these things we write, that our joy may be fulfilled.

ANOTHER RENDERING.

That which was ever from the beginning, that which we have heard, that which we have seen with our eyes, that which we gazed upon, and our hands handled — *I speak* concerning the Word who is the Life — and the Life was manifested, and we have seen, and bear witness, and declare unto you the eternal *life*, as being that which was ever with the Father, and was manifested unto us: that which we have seen and heard declare we unto you, that ye also may have fellowship with us: yea, and that fellowship, which is our *fellowship*, is with the Father and with His Son Jesus Christ. And these things write we unto you, that your joy may be fulfilled.

DISCOURSE I.

ANALYSIS AND THEORY OF ST. JOHN'S GOSPEL.

"Of the Word of Life."—1 JOHN i. 1.

IN the opening verses of this Epistle we have a sentence whose ample and prolonged prelude has but one parallel in St. John's writings.[1] It is, as an old divine says, "prefaced and brought in with more magnificent ceremony than any passage in Scripture."

The very emotion and enthusiasm with which it is written, and the sublimity of the exordium as a whole, tends to make the highest sense also the most natural sense. Of what or of whom does St. John speak in the phrase "concerning the Word of Life," or "the Word who is the Life"? The neuter "that which" is used for the masculine—"He who"—according to St. John's practice of employing the neuter comprehensively when a collective whole is to be expressed. The phrase "from the beginning," taken by itself, might no doubt be employed to signify the beginning of Christianity, or of the ministry of Christ. But even viewing it as entirely isolated from its context of language and circumstance, it has a greater claim to be looked upon as *from eternity* or *from the beginning of the creation.*

---

[1] See the noble and enthusiastic preface to the washing of the disciples' feet (John xiii. 1, 2, 3).

Other considerations are decisive in favour of the last interpretation.

(1) We have already adverted to the lofty and transcendental tone of the whole passage, elevating as it does each clause by the irresistible upward tendency of the whole sentence. The climax and resting place cannot stop short of the bosom of God. (2) But again, we must also bear in mind that the Epistle is everywhere to be read with the Gospel before us, and the language of the Epistle to be connected with that of the Gospel. The procemium of the Epistle is the subjective version of the objective historical point of view which we find at the close of the preface to the Gospel. "The Word was made flesh and dwelt among us;" so St. John begins his sentence in the Gospel with a statement of an historical fact. But he proceeds, "and·we delightedly beheld His glory;" that is a statement of the personal impression attested by his own consciousness and that of other witnesses. But let us note carefully that in the Epistle, which is in subjective relation to the Gospel, this process is exactly reversed. The Apostle begins with the personal impression; pauses to affirm the reality of the many proofs in the realm of fact of that which produced this impression through the senses upon the conceptions and emotions of those who were brought into contact with the Saviour; and then returns to the subjective impression from which he had originally started. (3) Much of the language in this passage is inconsistent with our understanding by the Word the first announcement of the Gospel preaching. One might of course speak of hearing the commencement of the Gospel message, but surely not of seeing and handling it. (4) It is a noteworthy fact that the Gospel

6

and the Apocalypse begin with the mention of the personal Word.   This may well lead us to expect that Logos should be used in the same sense in the prooemium of the great Epistle by the same author.

We conclude then that when St. John here speaks of the Word of Life, he refers to something higher again than the preaching of life, and that he has in view both the manifestation of the life which has taken place in our humanity, and Him who is personally at once the Word and the Life.[1]   The prooemium may be thus paraphrased.   "That which in all its collective influence was from the beginning as understood by Moses, by Solomon, and Micah;[2] which we have first and above all heard in divinely human utterances, but which we have also seen with these very eyes ; which we gazed upon with the full and entranced sight that delights in the object contemplated;[3] and which these hands handled reverentially at His bidding.[4]   I speak all this concerning the Word who is also the Life."

Tracts and sheets are often printed in our day with anthologies of texts which are supposed to contain

---

[1] The phrase probably means the Logos, the Personal "Word who is at once both the Word and the Life."   For the double genitive, the second almost appositional to the first, conf. John ii. 21, xi. 13. This interpretation would seem to be that of Chrysostom.   "If then the Word is the Life; and if this Christ who is at once the Word and the Life became flesh; then the Life became flesh."   (*In Joan. Evang.* v.)

[2] Gen. i. 1 ; Prov. viii. 23 ; Micah v. 2.

[3] Cf. John vi. 36, 40.   The word is applied by the angel to the disciples gazing on the Ascension, Acts i. 11.   The Transfiguration may be here referred to.   Such an incident as that in John vii. 37 attests a vivid delighted remembrance of the Saviour's very attitude.

[4] Luke xxiv. 39 ; John xx. 27.

the very essence of the Gospel.　But the sweetest scents,
it is said, are not distilled exclusively from flowers, for
the flower is but an exhalation.　The seeds, the leaf,
the stem, the very bark should be macerated, because
they contain the odoriferous substance in minute sacs.
So the purest Christian doctrine is distilled, not only
from a few exquisite flowers in a textual anthology,
but from the whole substance, so to speak, of the
message.　Now it will be observed that at the beginning of the Epistle which accompanied the fourth
Gospel, our attention is directed not to a sentiment,
but to a fact and to a Person.　In the collections of
texts to which reference has been made, we should
probably never find two brief passages which may not
unjustly be considered to concentrate the essence of
the scheme of salvation more nearly than any others.
"The Word was made flesh."　"Concerning the Word
of Life (and that Life was once manifested, and we
have seen and consequently are witnesses and announce
to you from Him who sent us that Life, that eternal
Life whose it is to have been in eternal relation with
the Father, and manifested to us); That which we have
seen and heard declare we from Him who sent us unto
you, to the end that you too may have fellowship with
us."

It would be disrespectful to the theologian of the
New Testament to pass by the great dogmatic term
never, so far as we are told, applied by our Lord to
Himself, but with which St. John begins each of his
three principal writings—THE WORD.[1]

Such mountains of erudition have been heaped over
this term that it has become difficult to discover the

---

[1] Gospel i. 1-14; 1 John i. 1 ; Apoc. i. 9.

buried thought. The Apostle adopted a word which was already in use in various quarters simply because if, from the nature of the case necessarily inadequate,[1] it was yet more suitable than any other. He also, as profound ancient thinkers conceived, looked into the depths of the human mind, into the first principles of that which is the chief distinction of man from the lower creation—language. The human word, these thinkers taught, is twofold; inner and outer—now as the manifestation to the mind itself of unuttered thought, now as a part of language uttered to others. The word as signifying unuttered thought, the mould in which it exists in the mind, illustrates the eternal relation of the Father to the Son. The word as signifying uttered thought illustrates the relation as conveyed to man by the Incarnation. "No man hath seen God at any time; the only begotten God which is in the bosom of the Father He interpreted Him." For the theologian of the Church Jesus is thus the Word; because He had His being from the Father in a way which presents some analogy to the human word, which is sometimes the inner vesture, sometimes the outward utterance of thought—sometimes the human thought in that language without which man cannot think, sometimes the speech whereby the speaker interprets it to others. Christ is the Word Whom out of the fulness of His thought and being the Father has

---

[1] " He hath a name written which *no one knoweth but He Himself,* —and His name is called THE WORD OF GOD " (Apoc. xix. 12, 13). Gibbons' adroit italics may here be noted. "The Logos, TAUGHT in the school of Alexandria BEFORE Christ 100—REVEALED to the Apostle St. John, ANNO DOMINI, 97 " (*Decline and Fall,* ch. xxi.). Just so very probably—though whether St. John ever read a page of Philo or Plato we have no means of knowing.

eternally inspoken and outspoken into personal existence.[1]

One too well knows that such teaching as this runs
the risk of appearing uselessly subtle and technical,
but its practical value will appear upon reflection. Because it gives us possession of the point of view from
which St. John himself surveys, and from which he
would have the Church contemplate, the history of the
life of our Lord.   And indeed for that life the theology
of the Word, *i.e.*, of the Incarnation, is simply necessary.

For we must agree with M. Renan so far at least
as this, that a great life, even as the world counts
greatness, is an organic whole with an underlying
vitalising idea; which must be construed as such, and
cannot be adequately rendered by a mere narration of
facts. Without this unifying principle the facts will
be not only incoherent but inconsistent.   There must
be a point of view from which we can embrace the

---

[1] The following table may be found useful :—

THE WORD IN ST. JOHN IS OPPOSED.

(A) To the Gnostic Word, created and temporal as — (A) Uncreated and Eternal. " In the beginning was the Word."

(B) To the Platonic Word, ideal and abstract as — (B) Personal and Divine. "The Word was God." "He"—"His."

(C) To the Judaistic and Philonic Word — the type and idea of God in creation . . . as — (C) Creative and First Cause. " All things were made by Him."

(D) To the Dualistic Word— limitedly and partially instrumental in creation . as — (D) Unique and Universally Creative. "Without Him was not anything made that hath been made."

(E) To the Doketic Word— impalpable and visionary as — (E) Real and Permanent. "The Word became flesh."

life as one.   The great test here, as in art, is the
formation of a living, consistent, unmutilated whole.[1]

Thus a general point of view (if we are to use modern
language easily capable of being misunderstood we
must say a theory) is wanted of the Person, the work,
the character of Christ.   The synoptical Evangelists
had furnished the Church with the narrative of His
earthly origin.   St. John in his Gospel and Epistle,
under the guidance of the Spirit, endowed it with the
theory of His Person.

Other points of view have been adopted, from the
heresies of the early ages to the speculations of our
own.   All but St. John's have failed to co-ordinate the
elements of the problem.   The earlier attempts essayed
to read the history upon the assumption that He was
merely human or merely divine.   They tried in their
weary round to unhumanise or undeify the God-Man,
to degrade the perfect Deity, to mutilate the perfect
Humanity—to present to the adoration of mankind a
something neither entirely human nor entirely divine,
but an impossible mixture of the two.   The truth on
these momentous subjects was fused under the fires of
controversy.   The last centuries have produced theories
less subtle and metaphysical, but bolder and more
blasphemous.   Some have looked upon Him as a
pretender or an enthusiast.   But the depth and sobriety
of His teaching upon ground where we are able to test
it—the texture of circumstantial word and work which
will bear to be inspected under any microscope or
cross-examined by any prosecutor — have almost
shamed such blasphemy into respectful silence.   Others
of later date admit with patronising admiration that

---

[1] *Vie de Jesus,* Int. 4.

the martyr of Calvary is a saint of transcendent excellence.   But if He who called Himself Son of God
was not much more than saint, He was something less.
Indeed He would have been something of three characters ; saint, visionary, pretender—at moments the
Son of God in His elevated devotion, at other times
condescending to something of the practice of the
charlatan, His unparalleled presumption only excused
by His unparalleled success.

Now the point of view taken by St. John is the only
one which is possible or consistent—the only one which
reconciles the humiliation and the glory recorded in
the Gospels, which harmonises the otherwise insoluble
contradictions that beset His Person and His work.
One after another, to the question, "what think ye of
Christ ?" answers are attempted, sometimes angry,
sometimes sorrowful, always confused.   The frank
respectful bewilderment of the better Socinianism, the
gay brilliance of French romance, the heavy insolence
of German criticism, have woven their revolting or
perplexed christologies.   The Church still points with
a confidence, which only deepens as the ages pass, to
the enunciation of the theory of the Saviour's Person
by St. John—in his Gospel, "The Word was made
flesh "—in his Epistle, "concerning the Word of Life."

DISCOURSE II.

ST. JOHN'S GOSPEL HISTORICAL NOT IDEOLOGICAL.

"That which we have heard."—1 JOHN i. 1.

OUR argument so far has been that St. John's Gospel is dominated by a central idea and by a theory which harmonises the great and many-sided life which it contains, and which is repeated again at the beginning of the Epistle in a form analogous to that in which it had been cast in the procemium of the Gospel—allowing for the difference between a history and a document of a more subjective character moulded upon that history.

There is one objection to the accuracy, almost to the veracity, of a life written from such a theory or point of view. It may disdain to be shackled by the bondage of facts. It may become an essay in which possibilities and speculations are mistaken for actual events, and history is superseded by metaphysics. It may degenerate into a romance or prose-poem ; if the subject is religious, into a mystic effusion. In the case of the fourth Gospel the cycles in which the narrative moves, the unveiling as of the progress of a drama, are thought by some to confirm the suspicion awakened by the point of view given in its procemium, and in the opening of the Epistle. The Gospel, it is said, is *ideological.* To us it appears that those who have entered most deeply into the spirit of St. John will most deeply feel the

significance of the two words which we place at the head of this discourse—" which we have heard," " which we have seen with our very eyes," (which we contemplated with entranced gaze) " which our hands have handled."

More truly than any other, St. John could say of this letter in the words of an American poet :

<blockquote>"This is not a book—It is I!"</blockquote>

In one so true, so simple, so profound, so oracular, there is a special reason for this prolonged appeal to the senses, and for the place which is assigned to each. In the fact that *hearing* stands first, there is a reference to one characteristic of that Gospel to which the Epistle throughout refers.   Beyond the synoptical Evangelists, St. John records the words of Jesus.   The position which *hearing* holds in the sentence, above and prior to *sight* and *handling*, indicates the reverential estimation in which the Apostle held his Master's teaching.[1]   The expression places us on solid historical ground, because it is a moral demonstration that one like St. John would not have dared to invent whole discourses and place them in the lips of Jesus.   Thus in the *"we have heard"* there is a guarantee of the sincerity of the report of the discourses, which forms so large a proportion of the narrative that it practically guarantees the whole Gospel.

On this accusation of ideology against St. John's Gospel, let us make a further remark founded upon the Epistle.

---

[1] The appeal to the senses of *seeing* and *hearing* is a trait common to *all* the group of St. John's writings (John i. 14, xix. 35 ; 1 John i. 1, 2, iv. 14 ; Apoc. i. 2).   The true reading (κἀγὼ Ἰωάννης ὁ ἀκούων καὶ βλέπων ταῦτα.   Apoc. xxi. 8, where *hearing* stands before *seeing*) is indicative of John's style.

It is said that the Gospel systematically subordinates chronological order and historical sequence of facts to the necessity imposed by the theory of the Word which stands in the forefront of the Epistle and Gospel.

But mystic ideology, indifference to historical veracity as compared with adherence to a conception or theory, is absolutely inconsistent with that strong, simple, severe appeal to the validity of the historical principle of belief upon sufficient evidence which pervades St. John's writings. His Gospel is a tissue woven of many lines of evidence. "Witness" stands in almost every page of that Gospel, and indeed is found there nearly as often as in the whole of the rest of the New Testament. The word occurs *ten* times in five short verses of the Epistle.[1] There is no possibility of mistaking this prolixity of reiteration in a writer so simple and so sincere as our Apostle. The theologian is an historian. He has no intention of sacrificing history to dogma, and no necessity for doing so. His theory, and that alone, harmonises his facts. His facts have passed in the domain of human history, and have had that evidence of witness which proves that they did so.

A few of the stories of the earliest ages of Christianity have ever been repeated, and rightly so, as affording the most beautiful illustrations of St. John's character, the most simple and truthful idea of the impression left by his character and his work. His tender love for souls, his deathless desire to promote mutual love among his people, are enshrined in two anecdotes which the Church has never forgotten. It has scarcely been noticed that a tradition of not much later date (at least

---

[1] I John v. 6-12.

as old as Tertullian, born probably about A.D. 150)
credits St. John with a stern reverence for the accuracy
of historical truth, and tells us what, in the estimation
of those who were near him in time, the Apostle thought
of the lawfulness of ideological religious romance. It
was said that a presbyter of Asia Minor confessed that
he was the author of certain apocryphal Acts of Paul
and Thecla—probably the same strange but unquestionably very ancient document with the same title which
is still preserved. The man's motive does not seem
to have been selfish. His work was apparently the
composition of an ardent and romantic nature passionately attracted by a saint so wonderful as St. Paul.[1]
The tradition went on to assert that St. John without
hesitation degraded this clerical romance-writer from
his ministry. But the offence of the Asiatic presbyter
would have been light indeed compared with that of

---

[1] That the "Acts of Paul and Thecla" are of high antiquity there
can be no rational doubt. Tertullian writes: "But if those who read
St. Paul's writings rashly use the example of Thecla, to give licence to
women to teach and baptize publicly, let them know that a presbyter
of Asia Minor, who put together that piece, crowning it with the
authority of a Pauline title, convicted by his own confession of doing
this from love of St. Paul, was deprived of his orders." (Tertullian,
De Baptismo, xvii.) On which St. Jerome remarks—"We therefore
relegate to the class of apocryphal writings, the περιοδόι of Paul
and Thecla, and the whole fable of the baptized lion. For how could
it be that the sole real companion of the Apostle" (Luke) "while so
well acquainted with the rest of the history, should have known
nothing of this? And further, Tertullian, who touched so nearly
upon those times, records that a certain presbyter in Asia Minor,
convicted before *John* of being the author of that book, and confessing that as a σπουδαστής of the Apostle Paul he had done this
from loving devotion to that great memory, was deposed from his
ministry." (St. Hieron., *de Script. Eccles.*, VII.) See the mass of
authority for the antiquity of this document, which gives a considerable degree of probability to the statement about St. John, in *Acta
Apost. Apoc.*, Edit. Tischendorf.--Proleg. xxi., xxvi.

the mendacious Evangelist, who could have deliberately
fabricated discourses and narrated miracles which he
dared to attribute to the Incarnate Son of God. The
guilt of publishing to the Church apocryphal Acts of
Paul and Thecla would have paled before the crimson
sin of forging a Gospel.

These considerations upon St. John's prolonged and
circumstantial claim to personal acquaintance with the
Word made flesh, confirmed by every avenue of communication between man and man—and first in order
by the hearing of that sweet yet awful teaching—point
to the fourth Gospel again and again. And the simple
assertion—" that which we have heard "—accounts for
one characteristic of the fourth Gospel which would
otherwise be a perplexing enigma—its *dramatic* vivid-
ness and consistency.

This dramatic truth of St. John's narrative, manifested
in various developments, deserves careful consideration.
There are three notes in the fourth Gospel which
indicate either a consummate dramatic instinct or a
most faithful record. (1) The delineation of *individual
characters*. The Evangelist tells us with no unmeaning
distinction, that Jesus " knew all men, and knew what
is in man ! " [1] For some persons take an apparently
profound view of human nature in the abstract. They
pass for being sages so long as they confine themselves
to sounding generalizations, but they are convicted on
the field of life and experience. They claim to know
what is in man ; but they know it vaguely, as one might
be in possession of the outlines of a map, yet totally
ignorant of most places within its limits. Others, who
mostly affect to be keen men of the world, refrain from
generalizations ; but they have an insight, which at

---

[1] John iii. 24, 25.

times is startling, into the characters of the individual
men who cross their path. There is a sense in which
they superficially seem to know all men, but their
knowledge after all is capricious and limited. One
class affects to know men, but does not even affect
to know man; the other class knows something about
man, but is lost in the infinite variety of the world of
real men. Our Lord knew both—both the abstract ultimate principles of human nature and the subtle distinctions which mark off every human character from every
other. Of this peculiar knowledge he who was brought
into the most intimate communion with the Great
Teacher was made in some degree a partaker in the
course of His earthly-ministry. With how few touches
yet how clearly are delineated the Baptist, Nathanael,
the Samaritan woman, the blind man, Philip, Thomas,
Martha and Mary, Pilate! (2) More particularly the
appropriateness and *consistency* of the language used by
the various persons introduced in the narrative is, in
the case of a writer like St. John, a multiplied proof
of historical veracity.[1] For instance, of St. Thomas

---

[1] Those who are perplexed by the identity in style and turn of
language between the Epistle and the discourse of our Lord in
St. John's Gospel may be referred to the writer's remarks in *The
Speaker's Commentary* (N. T. iv. 286-89). It should be added
that the Epp. to the Seven Churches (Apoc. ii., iii.)—especially to
Sardis—interweave sayings of Jesus recorded by the Synoptical
evangelists, *e.g.*, "as a thief," Apoc. iii. 3, cf. Mark xiii. 37; "book
of life," Apoc. iii. 5, cf. Luke x. 20; "confessing a name," Apoc. iii.
5, cf. Matt. x. 32; "He that hath an ear," Apoc. iii. 6, 13, 22, and
ii. 7, 11, 17, 29. This phrase, found in each of the seven Epp., occurs
nowhere in the fourth Gospel, but constantly in the Synoptics. Cf.
Matt. x. 27, xi. 15, xiii. 19, 43; Mark iv. 9, 23, vii. 16; Luke viii. 8, xiv.
35; cf. also "giving power over the nations," Apoc. ii. 26—with the
conception in Matt. xix. 28; Luke xxii. 29, 30. The word *repentance*
is nowhere in the fourth Gospel, nor given as part of our Lord's
teaching; but we find it Apoc. ii. 5, 16, iii. 3, 19. If the author of the

only one single sentence, containing seven words, is preserved,[1] outside the memorable narrative in the twentieth chapter; yet how unmistakably does that brief sentence indicate the same character—tender, impetuous, loving, yet ever inclined to take the darker view of things because from the very excess of its affection it cannot believe in that which it most desires, and demands accumulated and convincing proof of its own happiness. (3) Further, the *language* of our Lord which St. John preserves is both morally and intellectually a marvellous witness to the proof of his assertion here in the outset of his Epistle.

This may be exemplified by an illustration from modern literature. Victor Hugo, in his *Légende des Siècles*, has in one passage only placed in our Lord's lips a few words which are not found in the Evangelist.[2] Every one will at once feel that these words ring hollow, that there is in them something exaggerated and factitious—and *that* although the dramatist had the advantage of having a *type* of style already constructed for him. People talk as if the representation in detail of a perfect character were a comparatively easy performance. Yet every such representation shows some flaw when

---

fourth Gospel was also the author of the Apocalypse, his choice of the style which he attributes to the Saviour was at least decided by no lack of knowledge of the Synoptical type of expression, and by no incapacity to use it with freedom and power.

[1] John xi. 16.

[2] "Qui me suit, aux anges est pareil.
Quand un homme a marché tout le jour au soleil
Dans un chemin sans puits et sans hôtellerie,
S'il ne croit pas quand vient le soir il pleure, il crie,
Il est las; sur la terre il tombe haletant.
S'il croit en moi, qu'il prie, il peut au même instant.
Continuer sa route avec des forces triples."

(*Le Christ et le Tombeau.*) Tom. i. 44.

closely inspected.   For instance, a character in which Shakespeare so evidently delighted as Buckingham, whose end is so noble and martyr-like, is thus described, when on his trial, by a sympathising witness :

> "'How did he bear himself?'
> 'When he was bought again to the bar, to hear,
> His knell rung out, his judgment, he was struck
> With such an agony, he sweat extremely,
> And something spoke in choler, *ill and hasty;*
> But he fell to himself again, and sweetly
> In all the rest show'd a most noble patience.'"[1]

Our argument comes to this point.   Here is one man of all but the highest rank in dramatic genius, who utterly fails to invent even one sentence which could possibly be taken for an utterance of our Lord.   Here is another, the most transcendent in the same order whom the human race has ever known, who tacitly confesses the impossibility of representing a character which shall be "one entire and perfect chrysolite," without speck or flaw.   Take yet another instance.   Sir Walter Scott appeals for "the fair licence due to the author of a fictitious composition;" and admits that he "cannot pretend to the observation of complete accuracy even in outward costume, much less in the more important points of language and manners."[2]   But St. John was evidently a man of no such pretensions as these kings of the human imagination—no Scott or Victor Hugo, much less a Shakespeare.   How then

---

[1] King Henry VIII., Act 2, Sc. 1.   Contrast again our Lord before the council with St. Paul before that tribunal.   In the case of one of the chief of saints there is the touch of human infirmity, the "something spoken in choler, ill and hasty," the angry and contemptuous "whited wall"—the confession of hasty inconsiderateness (οὐκ ᾔδειν—ὅτι ἐστὶν ἀρχιερεύς) which led to a violation of a precept of the law (Exod. xxii. 28).

[2] Preface to *Ivanhoe.*

—except on the assumption of his being a faithful
reporter, of his recording words actually spoken, and
witnessing incidents which he had seen with his very
eyes and contemplated with loving and admiring reverence—can we account for his having given us long
successions of sentences, continuous discourses in
which we trace a certain unity and adaptation;[1] and a
character which stands alone among all recorded in
history or conceived in fiction, by presenting to us
an excellence faultless in every detail? We assert
that the one answer to this question is boldly given
us by St. John in the forefront of his Epistle—"That
which we have heard, which we have seen with our
eyes—concerning the Word who is the Life—declare
we unto you."

St. John's mode of writing history may profitably be
contrasted with that of one who in his own line was
a great master, as it has been ably criticised by a distinguished statesman. Voltaire's historical masterpiece
is a portion of the life of Maria Theresa, which is un-

---

[1] *How* the great sayings were accurately collected has not been
the question before us in this discourse. But it presents little difficulty. It is not absurd to suppose (if we are required to postulate
no divine assistance) that notes may have been taken in some form
by certain members of the company of disciples. The profoundly
thoughtful remark of Irenæus upon his own unfailing recollection of
early lessons from Polycarp, would apply with indefinitely greater
force to such a pupil as John, of such a teacher as Jesus. "I can
thoroughly recollect things so far back better than those which have
lately occurred ; for lessons which have grown with us since boyhood
are compacted into a unity with the very soul itself." ($\tau\hat{\eta}$ $\psi\upsilon\chi\hat{\eta}$ $\dot{\epsilon}\nu\upsilon\hat{\upsilon}\nu\tau\alpha\iota$
$\alpha\dot{\upsilon}\tau\hat{\eta}$) *Euseb.*, v. 29. But above all, whatever subordinate agency may
have been employed in the preservation of those precious words,
every Christian reverently acknowledges the fulfilment of the Saviour's
promise—"The Comforter, the Holy Ghost, He shall teach you all
things, and bring all things to your remembrance *whatsoever I have
said unto you*" (John xiv. 26).

questionably written from a partly ideological point of
view.   For, those who have patience to go back to the
"sources," and to compare Voltaire's narrative with
them, will see the process by which a literary master
has produced his effect.   The writer works as if he
were composing a classical tragedy restricted to the
unities of time and place.   The three days of the
coronation and of the successive votes are brought
into one effect, of which we are made to feel that it
is due to a magic inspiration of Maria Theresa.   Yet, as
the great historical critic to whom we refer proceeds
to demonstrate, a different charm, very much more
real because it comes from truth, may be found in
literal historical accuracy without this academic rouge.
Writers more conscientious than Voltaire would not
have assumed that Maria Theresa was degraded by a
husband who was inferior to her.   They would not
have substituted some pretty and pretentious phrases
for the genuine emotion not quite veiled under the
official Latin of the Queen.   "However high a thing
art may be, reality, truth, which is the work of God, is
higher !"[1]   It is this conviction, this entire intense
adhesion to truth, this childlike ingenuousness which
has made St. John as an historian attain the higher
region which is usually reached by genius alone—
which has given us narratives and passages whose
ideal beauty or awe is so transcendent or solemn,
whose pictorial grandeur or pathos is so inexhaustible, whose philosophical depth is so unfathomable.[2]
    He stands with spell-bound delight before his work

---

[1] Duc de Broglie. *Revue des deux Mondes.*   15 Jan. 1882.   Coxe,
House of Austria, vol. iii., chap. xcix., p. 415, sqq.
[2] John xiii. 30, xi. 35, xix. 5, xxii. 29–35.

without the disappointment which ever attends upon
men of genius; because that work is not drawn from
himself, because he can say three words—which we
have *heard*, which we have *seen* with our eyes, which
we have *gazed* upon.

NOTES.
Ch. i. 2, 4.

Ver. 2. *Us, we.*] " The nominative plural first person is not
always of *majesty* but often of *modesty*, when we share our
privilege and dignity with others " (*Grotius*). The context
must decide what shade of meaning is to be read into the
text, *e.g.*, here it is the *we* of modesty, as also (very tenderly
and beautifully) in ii. 1, 2, v. 5. It rises into *majesty* with the
majestic, " we announce."

Ver. 4. " *These things.*"] Not even the *fellowship* with the
Church and with the Father and with the Son is so much in
the Apostle's intention here as the record in the *Gospel.*

We write unto you.] In days when men's minds were still
freshly full of the privilege of free access to the Scriptures,
these words suggested (and they naturally enough do so still)
the use of the written word, and the guilt of the Church or of
individuals in neglecting it. This has been well expressed by
an old divine. " That which is able to give us full joy must
not be deficient in anything which conduceth to our happiness; but the holy Scriptures give fulness of joy, and therefore the way to happiness is perfectly laid down in them. The
major of this syllogism is so clear, that it needs no probation;
for who can or will deny, that full joy is only to be had in a
state of bliss ? The *minor* is plain from this scripture, and
may thus be drawn forth. That which the Apostles aimed at
in, may doubtless be attained to by, their writings ; for they
being inspired of God, it is no other than the end that God
purposed in inspiring which they had in writing; and either
God Himself is wanting in the means which He hath designed
for this end, or these writings contain in them what will yield
fulness of joy, and to that end bring us to a state of blessed-
ness.

" How odious is the profaneness of those Christians who

neglect the holy Scriptures, and give themselves to reading other books ! How many precious hours do many spend, and that not only on work days, but holy days, in foolish romances, fabulous histories, lascivious poems ! And why this, but that they may be cheered and delighted, when as full joy is only to be had in these holy books. Alas, the joy you find in those writings is perhaps pernicious, such as tickleth your lust, and promoteth contemplative wickedness. At the best it is but vain, such as only pleaseth the fancy and affecteth the wit ; whereas these holy writings (to use David's expression, Psalm xix. 8), are ' right, rejoicing the heart.' Again, are there not many who more set by Plutarch's morals, Seneca's epistles, and suchlike books, than they do by the holy Scriptures ? It is true, there are excellent truths in those moral writings of the heathen, but yet they are far short of these sacred books. Those may comfort against outward trouble, but not against inward fears ; they may rejoice the mind, but cannot quiet the conscience ; they may kindle some flashy sparkles of joy, but they cannot warm the soul with a lasting fire of solid consolation. And truly, if ever God give you a spiritual ear to judge of things aright, you will then acknowledge there are no bells like to those of Aaron, no harp like to that of David, no trumpet like to that of Isaiah, no pipes like to those of the Apostles." (*First Epistle of St. John, unfolded and applied* by Nathaniel Hardy, D.D., Dean of Rochester, about 1660.)

GREEK.

Καὶ αὕτη ἐστὶν ἡ ἀγγελία ἣν ἀκηκόαμεν ἀπ' αὐτοῦ, καὶ ἀναγγέλλομεν ὑμῖν, ὅτι ὁ Θεὸς φῶς ἐστιν, καὶ σκοτία ἐν αὐτῷ οὐκ ἐστιν οὐδεμία. ἐὰν εἴπωμεν ὅτι κοινωνίαν ἔχομεν μετ' αὐτοῦ, καὶ ἐν τῷ σκότει περιπατῶμεν, ψευδόμεθα, καὶ οὐ ποιοῦμεν τὴν ἀλήθειαν· ἐὰν δὲ ἐν τῷ φωτὶ περιπατῶμεν, ὡς αὐτός ἐστιν ἐν τῷ φωτὶ, κοινωνίαν ἔχομεν μετ' ἀλλήλων, καὶ τὸ αἷμα Ἰησοῦ τοῦ υἱοῦ αὐτοῦ καθαρίζει ἡμᾶς ἀπὸ πάσης ἁμαρτίας. Ἐὰν εἴπωμεν ὅτι ἁμαρτίαν οὐκ ἔχομεν, ἑαυτοὺς πλανῶμεν, καὶ ἡ ἀλήθεια ἐν ἡμῖν οὐκ ἐστιν. ἐὰν ὁμολογῶμεν τὰς ἁμαρτίας ἡμῶν, πιστός ἐστι καὶ δίκαιος, ἵνα ἀφῇ ἡμῖν τὰς ἁμαρτίας, καὶ καθαρίσῃ

LATIN.

Et haec est adnuntiatio quam audivimus ab eo, et adnuntiamus vobis, quoniam Deus lux est, et tenebrae in eo non sunt ullae. Si dixerimus quoniam societatem habemus cum eo et in tenebris ambulamus, mentimur, et non facimus veritatem: si autem in luce ambulamus sicut et ipse est in luce, societatem habemus ad invicem, et sanguis Iesu Christi, Filii eius, mundat nos ab omni peccato. Si dixerimus quoniam peccatum non habemus, ipsi nos seducimus, et veritas in nobis non est. Si confitemur peccata nostra, fidelis et iustus est, ut remittat nobis peccata nostra, et emundet nos ab omni iniqui-

AUTHORISED VERSION.

This then is the message which we have heard of Him, and declare unto you, that God is light, and in Him is no darkness at all. If we say that we have fellowship with Him, and walk in darkness, we lie, and do not the truth: but if we walk in the light, as He is in the light, we have fellowship one with another, and the blood of Jesus Christ His Son cleanseth us from all sin. If we say that we have no sin, we deceive ourselves, and the truth is not in us. If we confess our sins, He is faithful and just to forgive us our sins, and to cleanse us from all unrighteousness. If we say that we have not sinned,

REVISED VERSION.

And this is the message which we have heard from Him, and announce unto you, that God is light, and in Him is *no darkness* at all. If we say that we have fellowship with him, and walk in the darkness, welie, and do not the truth: but if we walk in the light, as He is in the light, we have fellowship one with another, and the blood of Jesus His Son cleanseth us from all sin, If we say that we have no sin, we deceive ourselves, and the truth is not in us. If we confess our sins He is faithful and righteous to forgive us our sins, and to cleanse us from all unrighteousness. If we say that we have not sinned,

ANOTHER VERSION.

And this is the message which we have heard from Him and are announcing unto you that God is light, and darkness in Him there is none. If we say that we have fellowship with Him and are walking in the darkness, we lie and are not doing the truth; but if we walk in the light as He is in the light have we fellowship one with another, and the blood of Jesus His Son is purifying us from all sin. If we say that we have not sin, we mislead ourselves and the truth in us is not. If we confess our sins He is faithful and righteous that He may forgive our sins and purify us from all unrighteous-

we make Him a liar, and His word is not in us. My little children, these things write I unto you, that ye may not sin. And if any man sin, we have an Advocate with the Father, Jesus Christ the righteous: and He is the propitiation for our sins; and not for ours only, but also for the whole world.

ness. If we say that we have not sinned a liar we are making Him, and His word is not in us. My children these things write I unto you that ye may not sin. And yet if any may have sinned, an Advocate have we with the Father Jesus Christ *who is* righteous: and He is propitiation for our sins; yea, and not for ours only but also for the whole world

we make Him a liar, and His word is not in us. My little children, these things write I unto you, that ye sin not. But if any man sin, we have an advocate with the Father, Jesus Christ the righteous: and He is the propitiation for our's sins: and not for our's only, but also for *the sins of* the whole world.

tate. Si dixerinus quoniam non peccavimus, mendacem faciemus eum, et verbum eius in nobis non est. Filioli mei, haec scribo vobis, ut non peccetis: sed et si quis peccaverit advocatum habemus apud Patrem, Iesum Christum iustum et ipse est propitiatio pro peccatis nostris, non pro nostris autem tantum sed etiam pro totius mundi.

ἡμᾶς ἀπὸ πάσης ἀδικίας. ἐὰν εἴπωμεν ὅτι οὐχ ἡμαρτήκαμεν, ψεύστην ποιοῦμεν αὐτόν, καὶ ὁ λόγος αὐτοῦ οὐκ ἔστιν ἐν ἡμῖν.

Τεκνία μου, ταῦτα γράφω ὑμῖν, ἵνα μὴ ἁμάρτητε· καὶ ἐάν τις ἁμάρτῃ, παράκλητον ἔχομεν πρὸς τὸν πατέρα, Ἰησοῦν Χριστὸν δίκαιον· καὶ αὐτὸς ἱλασμός ἐστι περὶ τῶν ἁμαρτιῶν ἡμῶν· οὐ περὶ τῶν ἡμετέρων δὲ μόνον, ἀλλὰ καὶ περὶ ὅλου τοῦ κόσμου.

DISCOURSE III.

EXTENT OF THE ATONEMENT.

"My little children, these things write I unto you, that ye sin not. And if any man sin we have an advocate with the Father, Jesus Christ the righteous: and He is the propitiation for our sins, and not for ours only, but also for the sins of the whole world."—I JOHN ii. 1, 2.

OF the Incarnation of the Word, of the whole previous strain of solemn oracular annunciation, there are two great objects. Rightly understood it at once stimulates and soothes; it supplies inducements to holiness, and yet quiets the accusing heart. (1) It urges to a pervading holiness in each recurring circumstance of life.[1] "That ye may not sin" is the bold universal language of the morality of God. Men only understand moral teaching when it comes with a series of monographs on the virtues, sobriety, chastity, and the rest. Christianity does not overlook these, but it comes first with all-inclusive principles. The morality of man is like the sculptor working line by line and part by part, partially and successively. The morality of God is like nature, and works in every part of the flower and tree with a sort of ubiquitous presence. "These things write we unto you." No dead letter— a living spirit infuses the lines; there is a deathless principle behind the words which will vitalize and

---

[1] Observe in the Greek the μὴ ἁμάρτητε, which refers to single acts, not to a continuous state—"that ye *may not sin.*"

permeate all isolated relations and developments of conduct. "These things write we unto you that ye may not sin."

(2) But further, this announcement also soothes. There may be isolated acts of sin against the whole tenor of the higher and nobler life. There may be, God forbid!—but it may be—some glaring act of inconsistency. In this case the Apostle uses a form of expression which includes himself, " we have," and yet points to Christ, not to himself, "we have an Advocate with the Father, Jesus Christ"—and that in view of His being One who is perfectly and simply righteous; "and He is the propitiation for our sins."

Then, as if suddenly fired by a great thought, St. John's view broadens over the whole world beyond the limits of the comparatively little group of believers whom his words at that time could reach. The Incarnation and Atonement havè been before his soul. The Catholic Church is the correlative of the first, humanity of the second. The Paraclete whom he beheld is ever in relation with, ever turned towards the Father.[1] His propitiation *is*, and He *is* it. It *was* not simply a fact in history which works on with unexhaustible force. As the Advocate is ever turned towards the Father, so the propitiation lives on with unexhausted life. His intercession is not verbal, temporary, interrupted. The Church, in her best days, never prayed—" Jesus, pray for me!" It is interpretative, continuous, unbroken. In time it is eternally valid, eternally present. In

---

[1] 1 John ii. 2. As a translation, "towards" seems too pedantic; yet πρός is *ad-versus* rather than *apud*, and with the accusative signifies either the direction of motion, or the relation between two objects. (Donaldson, *Greek Grammar*, 524). We may fittingly call the preposition here πρός *pictorial*.

space it extends as far as human need, and therefore takes in every place. "Not for our sins only," but for men universally, "for the whole world."[1]

It is implied then in this passage, that Christ was *intended* as a propitiation for the whole world ; and that He is *fitted* for satisfying all human wants.

(1) Christ was intended for the whole world. Let us see the Divine intention ·in one incident of the crucifixion. In that are mingling lines of glory and of humiliation. The King of humanity appears with a scarlet camp-mantle flung contemptuously over His shoulders ; but to the eye of faith it is the purple of empire. He is crowned with the acanthus wreath ; but the wreath of mockery is the royalty of our race. He is crucified between two thieves ; but His cross is a Judgment-Throne, and at His right hand and His left are the two separated worlds of belief and unbelief. All the Evangelists tell us that a superscription, a title of accusation, was written over His cross ; two of them add that it was written over Him "in letters of Greek, and Latin, and Hebrew" (or in Hebrew, Greek, Latin). In Hebrew—the sacred tongue of patriarchs and seers, of the nation all whose members were in idea and destination those of whom God said, "My prophets." In Greek—the "musical and golden tongue which gave a soul to the objects of sense and a body to the abstractions of philosophy ;" the language of a

---

[1] The various meanings of κόσμος are fully traced below on 1 John ii. 17. There is one point in which the notions of κόσμος and αἰών intersect. But they may be thus distinguished. The first signifies the world projected in *space*, the second in *time*. The supposition that the form of expression at the close of our verse is elliptical, and to be filled up by the repetition of "for the sins of the whole world" "is not justified by usage, and weakens the force of the passage." (*Epistles of St. John*, Westcott, p. 44.)

people whose mission it was to give a principle of fermentation to all races of mankind, susceptible of those subtle and largely indefinable influences which are called collectively Progress.   In Latin—the dialect of a people originally the strongest of all the sons of men.   The three languages represent the three races and their ideas—revelation, art, literature; progress, war, and jurisprudence.   Beneath the title is the thorn-crowned head of the ideal King of humanity.   `

Wherever these three tendencies of the human race exist, wherever annunciation can be made in human language, wherever there is a heart to sin, a tongue to speak, an eye to read, the cross has a message. The superscription, "written in Hebrew, Greek, and Latin," is the historical symbol translated into its dogmatic form by St. John—"He is the propitiation[1] for our sins, and not for ours only, but also for the whole world."

---

[1] As to doctrine. There are three "grand circles" or "families of images" whereby Scripture approaches from different quarters, or surveys from different sides, the benefits of our Lord's meritorious death.   These are represented by, are summed up in, three words—ἀπολύτρωσις, καταλλαγή, ἱλασμός.   The last is found in the text and in iv. 10; nowhere else precisely in that form in the New Testament. " Ἱλασμός (expiation or propitiation) and ἀπολύτρωσις (redemption) is fundamentally one single benefit, *i.e.*, the restitution of the lost sinner. Ἀπολύτρωσις is in respect of *enemies;* καταλλαγή in respect of *God.* And here again the words ἱλασμ. and καταλλ. differ.   *Propitiation* takes away offences as against *God.*   *Reconciliation* has two sides.   It takes away (*a*) God's *indignation* against *us*, 2 Cor. v. 18, 19; (*b*) *our alienation* from *God*, 2 Cor. v. 20."   (Bengel on Rom. iii. 24.   Whoever would rightly understand all that we can know on these great words must study *New Testament Synonyms, Archbp. Trench*, pp. 276-82.)

DISCOURSE IV.

"For the whole world."—1 John ii. 2.

LET us now consider the universal and ineradicable wants of man.

Such a consideration is substantially unaffected by speculation as to the theory of man's origin. Whether the first men are to be looked for by the banks of some icy river feebly shaping their arrowheads of flint, or in godlike and glorious progenitors beside the streams of Eden; whether our ancestors were the result of an inconceivably ancient evolution, or called into existence by a creative act, or sprung from some lower creature elevated in the fulness of time by a majestic inspiration, —at least, as a matter of fact, man has other and deeper wants than those of the back and stomach. Man as he is has five spiritual instincts. *How* they came to be there, let it be repeated, is not the question. It is the fact of their existence, not the mode of their *genesis*, with which we are now concerned.

(1) There is almost, if not quite, without exception the instinct which may be generally described as the instinct of the Divine. In the wonderful address where St. Paul so fully recognises the influence of geographical circumstance and of climate, he speaks of God "having made out of one blood every nation of men to seek

after their Lord, if haply at least" (as might be expected) "they would feel for Him"[1]—like men in darkness groping towards the light. (2) There is the instinct of prayer, the " testimony of the soul naturally Christian." The little child at our knees meets us half way in the first touching lessons in the science of prayer.   In danger, when the vessel seems to be sinking in a storm, it is ever as it was in the days of Jonah, when "the mariners cried every man unto his God."[2] (3) There is the instinct of immortality, the desire that our conscious existence should continue beyond death.

> " Who would lose,
> Though full of pain, this intellectual being,
> These thoughts that wander through eternity,
> To perish rather swallow'd up and lost
> In the wide womb of uncreated night ? "

(4) There is the instinct of morality, call it con- science or what we will. The lowest, most sordid, most materialised languages are never quite without witness to this nobler instinct.   Though such languages have lien among the pots, yet their wings are as the wings of a dove that is covered with silver wings and her feathers like gold. The most impoverished voca- bularies have words of moral judgment, " good " or " bad ; " of praise or blame, "truth and lie ; " above all, those august words which recognise a law paramount to all other laws, " I must," " I ought."   (5) There is the instinct of *sacrifice*, which, if not absolutely universal, is at least all but so—the sense of impurity and un- worthiness, which says by the very fact of bringing a victim.   " I am not worthy to come alone ; may my guilt be transferred to the representative which I immolate."

Acts xvii. 27.   [2] Jonah i. 5.

(1) Thus then man seeks after God. Philosophy unaided does not succeed in finding Him. The theistic systems marshal their syllogisms; they prove, but do not convince. The pantheistic systems glitter before man's eye; but when he grasps them in his feverish hand, and brushes off the mystic gold dust from the moth's wings, a death's-head mocks him. St. John has found the essence of the whole question stripped from it all its plausible disguises, and characterises Mahommedan and Judaistic Deism in a few words. Nay, the philosophical deism of Christian countries comes within the scope of his terrible proposition. "Deo erexit Voltairius," was the philosopher's inscription over the porch of a church; but Voltaire had not in any true sense a God to whom he could dedicate it. For St. John tells us—"whosoever denieth the Son, the same hath not the Father."[1] Other words there are in his Second Epistle whose full import seems to have been generally overlooked, but which are of solemn significance to those who go out from the camp of Christianity with the idea of finding a more refined morality and a more ethereal spiritualism. "Whosoever goeth forward and abideth not in the doctrine of Christ"; whosoever writes progress on his standard, and goes forward beyond the lines of Christ, loses natural as well as supernatural religion—"he hath not God."[2] (2) Man wants to pray. Poor disinherited child, what master of requests shall he find? Who shall interpret his broken language to God, God's infinite language to him? (3) Man yearns for the assurance of immortal life. This can best be given by one specimen of manhood risen from the

---

[1] 1 John ii. 28.   [2] 2 John 9.

grave, one traveller come back from the undiscovered bourne with the breath of eternity on His cheek and its light in His eye; one like Jonah, Himself the living sign and proof that He has been down in the great deeps. (4) Man needs a morality to instruct and elevate conscience. Such a morality must possess these characteristics. It must be *authoritative*, resting upon an absolute will; its teacher must say, not "I think," or "I conclude," but—"verily, verily I say unto you." It must be *unmixed* with baser and more questionable elements. It must be *pervasive*, laying the strong grasp of its purity on the whole domain of thought and feeling as well as of action. It must be *exemplified.* It must present to us a series of pictures, of object-lessons in which we may see it illustrated. Finally, this morality must be *spiritual.* It must come to man, not like the Jewish Talmud with its seventy thousand precepts which few indeed can ever learn, but with a compendious and condensed, yet all-embracing brevity—with words that are spirit and life. (5) As man knows duty more thoroughly, the instinct of sacrifice will speak with an ever-increasing intensity. "My heart is overwhelmed by the infinite purity of this law. Lead me to the rock that is higher than I; let me find God and be reconciled to Him." When the old Latin spoke of *propitiation* he thought of something which brought *near (prope)*; his inner thought was—"let God come near to me, that I may be near to God." These five ultimate spiritual wants, these five ineradicable spiritual instincts, *He* must meet, of whom a master of spiritual truth like St. John can say with his plenitude of insight—"He is the propitiation for our sins, and not for ours only, but also for the whole world."

We shall better understand the fulness of St. John's

thought if we proceed to consider that this fitness in Christ for meeting the spiritual wants of humanity is *exclusive*.

Three great religions of the world are more or less *Missionary*. Hinduism, which embraces at least a hundred and ninety millions of souls, is certainly not in any sense missionary. For Hinduism transplanted from its ancient shrines and local superstitions dies like a flower without roots. But Judaism at times has strung itself to a kind of exertion almost inconsistent with its leading idea. The very word "proselyte" attests the unnatural fervour to which it had worked itself up in our Lord's time. The Pharisee was a missionary sent out by pride and consecrated by self-will. "Ye compass sea and land to make one proselyte, and when he is made, ye make him tenfold more the child of hell than yourselves."[1] Bouddhism has had enormous missionary success from one point of view. Not long ago it was said that it outnumbered Christendom. But it is to be observed that it finds adherents among people of only one type of thought and character.[2] Outside these races it is and must ever be, non-existent. We may except the fanciful perversion of a few idle people in London, Calcutta, or Ceylon, captivated for a season or two by

---

[1] Matt. xxiii. 15.

[2] Bouddhism, it is now said, appears to be on the wane, and the period for its disappearance is gradually approaching, according to the Boden Professor of Sanscrit at Oxford. In his opinion this creed is "one of rapidly increasing disintegration and decline," and "as a form of popular religion Bouddhism is gradually losing its vitality and hold on the vast populations once loyal to its rule." He computes the number of Bouddhists at 100,000,000; not 400,000,000 as hitherto estimated; and places Christianity numerically at the head of all religions—next Confucianism, thirdly Hinduism, then Bouddhism, and last Mohammedanism. He affirms that the capacity of Bouddhism for resistance must give way before the "mighty forces which are destined to sweep the earth."

"the light of Asia." We may except also a very few more remarkable cases where the esoteric principle or Bouddhism commends itself to certain profound thinkers stricken with the dreary disease of modern sentiment. Mohammedanism has also, in a limited degree, proved itself a missionary religion, not only by the sword. In British India it counts millions of adherents, and it is still making some progress in India. In other ages whole Christian populations (but belonging to heretical and debased forms of Christianity) have gone over to Mohammedanism. Let us be just to it.[1] It once elevated the pagan Arabs. Even now it elevates the Negro above his fetisch. But it must ever remain a religion for stationary races, with its sterile God and its poor literality, the dead book pressing upon it with a weight of lead. Its merits are these—it inculcates a lofty if sterile Theism ; it fulfils the pledge conveyed in the word Moslem, by inspiring a calm if frigid resignation to destiny ; it teaches the duty of prayer with a strange impressiveness. But whole realms of thought and feeling are crushed out by its bloody and lustful grasp. It is without purity, without tenderness, and without humility.

Thus then we come back again with a truer insight to the exclusive fitness of Christ to meet the wants of mankind.

Others beside the Incarnate Lord have obtained from a portion of their fellow-men some measure of passionate enthusiasm. Each people has a hero, call him demigod, or what we will. But such men are idolised by one race alone, and are fashioned after its likeness. The very qualities which procure them an

---

[1] That modern English writers have been more than just to Mohammed is proved overwhelmingly by the living Missionary who knows Mohammedanism best.—*Mohammed and Mohammedans.* Dr. Koelle.

apotheosis are precisely those which prove how narrow the type is which they represent; how far they are from speaking to all humanity. A national type is a narrow and exclusive type.

No European, unless effeminated and enfeebled, could really love an Asiatic Messiah. But Christ is loved everywhere. No race or kindred is exempt from the sweet contagion produced by the universal appeal of the universal Saviour. From all languages spoken by the lips of man, hymns of adoration are offered to Him. We read in England the Confessions of St. Augustine. Those words still quiver with the emotions of penitence and praise; still breathe the breath of life. Those ardent affections, those yearnings of personal love to Christ, which filled the heart of Augustine fifteen centuries ago, under the blue sky of Africa, touch us even now under this grey heaven in the fierce hurry of our modern life. But they have in them equally the possibility of touching the Shanar of Tinnevelly, the Negro—even the Bushman, or the native of Terra del Fuego. By a homage of such diversity and such extent we recognise a universal Saviour for the universal wants of universal man, the fitting propitiation for the whole world.

Towards the close of this Epistle St. John oracularly utters three great canons of universal Christian consciousness—"we know," "we know," "we know." Of these three canons the second is—"we know that we are from God, and the world lieth wholly in the wicked one." "A characteristic Johannic exaggeration"! some critic has exclaimed; yet surely even in Christian lands where men lie outside the influences of the Divine society, we have only to read the Police-reports to justify the Apostle. In volumes of travels, again, in the

pages of Darwin and Baker, from missionary records in places where the earth is full of darkness and cruel habitations, we are told of deeds of lust and blood which almost make us blush to bear the same form with creatures so degraded. Yet the very same missionary records bear witness that in every race which the Gospel proclamation has reached, however low it may be placed in the scale of the ethnologist; deep under the ruins of the fall are the spiritual instincts, the affections which have for their object the infinite God, and for their career the illimitable ages. The shadow of sin is broad indeed. But in the evening light of God's love the shadow of the cross is projected further still into the infinite beyond. Missionary success is therefore sure, if it be slow. The reason is given by St. John. "He is the propitiation for our sins, and not for ours only, but for the whole world."

NOTES.
Ch. i. 5 to ii. 2.

Ver. 5. The Word, the Life, the Light, are connected in the first chapter as in John i. 3, 4, 5. Upon earth, behind all life is light; in the spiritual world, behind all light is life.

Darkness.] The schoolmen well said that there is a fourfold darkness—of nature, of ignorance, of misery, of sin. The symbol of light applied to God must designate perfect goodness and beauty, combined with blissful consciousness of it, and transparent luminous clearness of wisdom.

Ver. 7. *The blood of Jesus His Son*] Sc. poured forth. This word (the Blood) denotes more vividly and effectively than any other could do three great realities of the Christian belief—the reality of the Manhood of Jesus, the reality of His sufferings, the reality of His sacrifice. It is dogma; but dogma made pictorial, pathetic, almost passionate. It may be noted that much current thought and feeling around us is just at the opposite extreme. It is a semi-doketism which is manifested in two different forms. (1) Whilst

8

it need not be denied that there are hymns which are pervaded by an ensanguined materialism, and which are calculated to wound reverence, as well as taste ; it is clear that much criticism on hymns and sermons, where the " Blood of Jesus " is at all appealed to, has an ultra-refinement which is unscriptural and rationalistic. It is out of touch with St. Paul (Col. i. 14-20), with the author of the Epistle to the Hebrews (Heb. ix. 14) (a passage strikingly like this verse), with St. Peter (1 Pet. i. 19), with St. John in this Epistle, with the redeemed in heaven (Apoc. v. 9). (2) A good deal of feeling against representations in sacred art seems to have its origin in this sort of unconscious semi-doketism. It appears to be thought that when representation supersedes symbolism, Christian thought and feeling necessarily lose everything and gain nothing. But surely it ought to be remembered that for a being like man there are two worlds, one of ideas, the other of facts ; one of philosophy, the other of history. The one is filled with things which are conceived, the other with things which are done. One contents itself with a shadowy symbol, the other is not satisfied except by a concrete representation. So we venture respectfully to think that the image of the dead Christ is not foreign to Scripture or Scriptural thought ; simply because, *as a fact*, He died. Calvary, the tree, the wounds, were not ideal. The crucifixion was not a symbol for dainty and refined abstract theorists. The form of the Crucified was not veiled by silver mists and crowned with roses. He who realises the meaning of the " Blood of Jesus," and is *consistent*, will not be severe upon the expression of the same thought in another form.

" Note that which Estius hath upon the blood of his Son, that in them there is a confutation of three heresies at once : the Manichees, who deny the truth of Christ's human nature, since, as Alexander said of his wound, *clamat me esse hominem*, it proclaimeth me a man, we may say of His blood, for had He not been man He could not have bled, have died ; the Ebionites, who deny Him to be God, since, being God's natural Son, He must needs be of the same essence with Himself ; and the Nestorians, who make two persons, which, if true, the blood of Christ the man could not have been called the blood of Christ the Son of God."

"That which I conceive here chiefly to be taken notice of is, that our Apostle contents not himself to say the *blood of Jesus Christ*, but he addeth *His Son*, to intimate to us how this blood became available to our cleansing, to wit, as it was the blood not merely of the Son of Mary, the Son of David, the Son of Man, but of Him who was also the Son of God."

"Behold, O sinner, the exceeding love of thy Saviour, who, that He might cleanse thee when polluted in thy blood, was pleased to shed His own blood. Indeed, the pouring out of Christ's blood was a super-excellent work of charity; hence it is that these two are joined together; and when the Scripture speaketh of His love, it presently annexeth His sufferings. We read, that when Christ wept for Lazarus, John xi. 36, the standers by said, "See how He loved him." Surely if His tears, much more His blood, proclaimeth His affection towards us. The Jews were the scribes, the nails were the pens, His body the white paper, and His blood the red ink ; and the characters were love, exceeding love, and these so fairly written that he which runs may read them. I shut up this with that of devout Bernard, Behold and look upon the rose of His bloody passion, how His redness bespeaketh His flaming love, there being, as it were, a contention betwixt His passion and affection : this, that it might be hotter ; that, that it might be redder. Nor had His sufferings been so red with blood had not His heart been inflamed with love. Oh let us beholding magnify, magnifying admire, and admiring praise Him for His inestimable goodness, saying with the holy Apostle (Rev. i. 5), 'Unto Him that loved us, and washed us from our sins in His blood, be honour and glory for ever.' "— *Dean Hardy* (pp. 77, 78.) Observe on this verse its unison of thought and feeling with Apoc. i. 5, xxii. 14.[1]

Chap. ii. 1. *We have an Advocate*] literally Paraclete. One called in to aid him whose cause is to be tried or petition considered. The word is used only by St. John, four times in the Gospel, of the Holy Ghost ;[2] once here of Christ.

"And now, O thou drooping sinner, let me bespeak thee in

---

[1] The inner meaning of 1 John i. 8 exactly = ὑπακοή καὶ ῥαντισμὸς (1 Peter i. 2). It is the *obedient* who are *sprinkled*.

[2] John xiv. 16, 26, xv. 26, xvi. 7.

St. Austin's[1] language : Thou committest thy cause to an
eloquent lawyer, and art safe ; how canst thou miscarry, when
thou hast the Word to be thy advocate ? Let me put this
question to thee : If, when thou sinnest, thou hadst all the
angels, saints, confessors, martyrs, in those celestial mansions
to beg thy pardon, dost thou think they would not speed ? I
tell thee, one word out of Christ's mouth is more worth than
all their conjoined entreaties. When, therefore, thy daily
infirmities discourage thee, or particular falls affright thee,
imagine with thyself that thou heardst thy advocate pleading
for thee in these or the like expressions : O My loving Father,
look upon the face of Thine Anointed ; behold the hands, and
feet, and side of Thy crucified Christ ! I had no sins of My
own for which I thus suffered ; no, it was for the sins of this
penitent wretch, who in My name sued for pardon ! Father,
I am Thy Son, the Son of Thy love, Thy bosom, who plead
with Thee ; it is for Thy child, Thy returning penitent child,
I plead. That for which I pray is no more than what I paid
for ; I have merited pardon for all that come to Me ! Oh let
those merits be imputed, and that pardon granted to this poor
sinner ! Cheer up, then, thou disconsolate soul, Christ is an
advocate for thee, and therefore do not despair, but believe ;
and believing, rejoice; and rejoicing, triumph."—*Dean Hardy*
(pp. 128, 129). In these days, when petitions to Jesus to pray
for us have crept into hymns and are creeping into liturgies,
it may be well to note that in the remains of the early saints
and in the solemn formulas of the Christian Church, Christ is
not asked to pray for us, but to hear our prayers. The Son
is prayed to ; the Father is prayed to through the Son ; the
Son is never prayed to pray to the Father. (See Greg.
Nazianz., *Oratio* xxx., *Theologiæ* iv., *de Filio.* See Thomassin,
Dogm. Theol., lib. ix., cap. 6, Tom. iv. 220, 227.)

Ver. 2. *Not for ours only.*] This large-hearted afterthought reminds one of St. Paul's " corrective and ampliative "
addition; of his chivalrous abstinence from exclusiveness in
thought or word, when having dictated " Jesus Christ our
Lord," his voice falters, and he feels constrained to say—
" both theirs, and ours " (1 Cor. i. 2).

---

[1] Aug. *in loc.*

SECTION III. (1).

GREEK.

GREEK.

Καὶ ἐν τούτῳ γινώσκομεν ὅτι ἐγνώκαμεν αὐτόν, ἐὰν τὰς ἐντολὰς αὐτοῦ τηρῶμεν. ὁ λέγων ὅτι "Ἔγνωκα αὐτόν," καὶ τὰς ἐντολὰς αὐτοῦ μὴ τηρῶν, ψεύστης ἐστίν, καὶ ἐν τούτῳ ἡ ἀλήθεια οὐκ ἔστιν. ὃς δ' ἂν τηρῇ αὐτοῦ τὸν λόγον, ἀληθῶς ἐν τούτῳ ἡ ἀγάπη τοῦ θεοῦ τετελείωται. ἐν τούτῳ γινώσκομεν ὅτι ἐν αὐτῷ ἐσμεν. ὁ λέγων ἐν αὐτῷ μένειν, ὀφείλει, καθὼς ἐκεῖνος περιεπάτησεν, καὶ αὐτὸς οὕτως περιπατεῖν.

LATIN.

Et in hoc scimus quoniam cognovimus eum, si mandata eius observemus. Qui dicit se nosse eum et mandata eius non custodit, mendax est, et in eo veritas non est: qui autem servat verbum eius, vere in eo caritas Dei perfecta est: in hoc scimus quoniam in ipso sumus. Qui dicit se in ipso manere debet sicut ille ambulavit et ipse ambulare.

AUTHORISED VERSION.

And hereby we do know that we know Him, if we keep His commandments. He that saith, I know Him, and keepeth not His commandments, is a liar, and the truth is not in Him. But whoso keepeth His word, in him verily is the love of God perfected: hereby know we that we are in Him. He that saith he abideth in Him ought himself also so to walk, even as He walked.

REVISED VERSION.

And *hereby know* we that we *know* Him, if we keep His commandments. He that saith, I know Him, and keepeth not His commandments is a liar, and the truth is not in him: but whoso keepeth His word, in him verily hath the love of God been perfected. Hereby know we that we are in Him: he that saith he abideth in Him ought himself also to walk even as He walked.

ANOTHER VERSION.

And hereby we do know that we have knowledge of Him, if we observe His commandments. He that saith I have knowledge of Him and observeth not His commandments is a liar, and in this man the truth is not. But whoso observeth His word verily in this man the love of God is perfected. Hereby know we that we are in Him: he that saith he abideth in Him is bound, even as He walked, so also himself to be ever walking.

DISCOURSE V.

*THE INFLUENCE OF THE GREAT LIFE WALK
A PERSONAL INFLUENCE.*

"He that saith he abideth in Him, ought himself also so to walk
even as He also walked."—I JOHN ii. 6.

THIS verse is one of those in reading which we
may easily fall into the fallacy of mistaking
familiarity for knowledge.

Let us bring out its meaning with accuracy.

St. John's hatred of unreality, of lying in every form,
leads him to claim in Christians a perfect correspondence between the outward profession and the inward
life, as well as the visible manifestation of it. "He
that saith" always marks a danger to those who are
outwardly in Christian communion. It is the "take
notice" of a hidden falsity. He whose claim, possibly
whose vaunt, is that he abideth in Christ, has contracted a moral debt of far-reaching significance. St.
John seems to pause for a moment. He points to a
picture in a page of the scroll which is beside him—
the picture of Christ in the Gospel drawn by himself;
not a vague magnificence, a mere harmony of colour,
but a likeness of absolute historical truth. Every
pilgrim of time in the continuous course of his daily
walk, outward and inward, has by the possession of that
Gospel contracted an obligation to be walking by the
one great life-walk of the Pilgrim of eternity. The very
depth and intensity of feeling half hushes the Apostle's

voice.   Instead of the beloved Name which all who love
it will easily supply,[1] St. John uses the reverential *He*, the
pronoun which specially belongs to Christ in the vocabu-
larly of the Epistle.[2]   " He that saith he abideth in Him "
is bound, even as HE once walked, to be ever walking.

I.

The importance of *example* in the moral and spiritual
life gives emphasis to this canon of St. John.

Such an example as can be sufficient for creatures
like ourselves should be at once manifested in concrete
form and susceptible of ideal application.

This was felt by a great but unhappily anti-christian
thinker, the exponent of a severe and lofty morality.
Mr. Mill fully confesses that there may be an elevating
and an ennobling influence in a Divine ideal ; and thus
justifies the apparently startling precept—"be ye therefore perfect, even as your Father which is in Heaven
is perfect." [3]   But he considered that some more human
model was necessary for the moral striver.   He re-
commends novel-readers, when they are charmed or
strengthened by some conception of pure manhood or
womanhood, to carry that conception with them into
their own lives.   He would have them ask themselves in difficult positions, how that strong and lofty
man, that tender and unselfish woman, would have
behaved in similar circumstances, and so bear about
with them a standard of duty at once compendious and

---

[1] "Nomen facile supplent credentes, plenum pectus habentes
memoriâ Domini."—*Bengel.*

[2] 'Εκεῖνος in our Epistle belongs to Christ in every place but one
where it occurs (1 John ii. 6, iii. 3, 5, 7, 16, iv. 17 ; cf. John i. 18, ii. 21).
It is very much equivalent to our reverent usage of printing the
pronoun which refers to Christ with a capital letter.

[3] Matt. vi. 45.

affecting. But to this there is one fatal objection—that such an elaborate process of make-believe is practically impossible. A fantastic morality, if it were possible at all, must be a feeble morality. Surely an authentic example will be greatly more valuable.

But *example*, however precious, is made indefinitely more powerful when it is *living* example, example crowned by personal influence.

So far as the stain of a guilty past can be removed from those who have contracted it; they are improvable and capable of restoration, chiefly, perhaps almost exclusively, by personal influence in some form. When a process of deterioration and decay has set in in any human soul, the germ of a more wholesome growth is introduced in nearly every case, by the transfusion and transplantation of healthier life. We test the soundness or the putrefaction of a soul by its capacity of receiving and assimilating this germ of restoration. A parent is in doubt whether a son is susceptible of renovation, whether he has not become wholly evil. He tries to bring the young man under the personal influence of a friend of noble and sympathetic character. Has his son any capacity left for being touched by such a character; of admiring its strength on one side, its softness on another? When he is in contact with it, when he perceives how pure, how self-sacrificing, how true and straight it is, is there a glow in his face, a trembling of his voice, a moisture in his eye, a wholesome self-humiliation? Or does he repel all this with a sneer and a bitter gibe? Has he that evil attribute which is possessed only by the most deeply corrupt—" they blaspheme, rail at glories "?[1] The

---

[1] δόξας βλασφημοῦντες (2 Peter ii. 10; Jude v. 8).

Chaplain of a penitentiary records that among the most
degraded of its inmates was one miserable creature.
The Matron met her with firmness, but with a good
will which no hardness could break down, no insolence
overcome. One evening after prayers the Chaplain
observed this poor outcast stealthily kissing the shadow
of the Matron thrown by her candle upon the wall.
He saw that the diseased nature was beginning to be
capable of assimilating new life, that the victory of
wholesome personal influence had begun. He found
reason for concluding that his judgment was well
founded.

The law of restoration by living example through
personal influence pervades the whole of our human
relations under God's natural and moral government
as truly as the principle of mediation. This law
also pervades the system of restoration revealed to
us by Christianity. It is one of the chief results
of the Incarnation itself. It begins to act upon us
first, when the Gospels become something more to
us than a mere history, when we realise in some
degree how He walked. But it is not complete until
we know that all this is not merely of the past, but
of the present; that He is not dead, but living;
that we may therefore use that little word *is* about
Christ in the lofty sense of St. John—"even as He
is pure;" "in Him *is* no sin;" "even as He *is*
righteous;" "He *is* the propitiation for our sins." If
this is true, as it undoubtedly is, of all good human
influence personal and living, is it not true of the
Personal and living Christ in an infinitely higher
degree? If the shadow of Peter overshadowing the
sick had some strange efficacy; if handkerchiefs or
aprons from the body of Paul wrought upon the sick

and possessed; what may be the spiritual result of contact with Christ Himself? Of one of those men specially gifted to raise struggling natures and of others like him, a true poet lately taken from us has sung in one of his most glorious strains. Matthew Arnold likens mankind to a host inexorably bound by divine appointment to march over mountain and desert to the city of God. But they become entangled in the wilderness through which they march, split into mutinous factions, and are in danger of "battering on the rocks" for ever in vain, of dying one by one in the waste. Then comes the poet's appeal to the "servants of God":—

> "In the hour of need
> Of your fainting dispirited race,
> Ye like angels appear!
> Languor is not in your heart,
> Weakness is not in your word,
> Weariness not on your brow.
> Eyes rekindling, and prayers
> Follow your steps as ye go.
> Ye fill up the gaps in our file,
> Strengthen the wavering line,
> Stablish, continue our march—
> On, to the bound of the waste—
> On, to the City of God."[1]

If all this be true of the personal influence of good and strong men—true in proportion to their goodness and strength—it must be true of the influence of the Strongest and Best with Whom we are brought into personal relation by prayer and sacraments, and by meditation upon the sacred record which tells us what

---

[1] *Poems by Matthew Arnold* ("Rugby Chapel," Nov. 1857), vol. ii., pp. 251, 255.

His one life-walk was.   Strength is not wanting upon His part, for He is able to save to the uttermost.   Pity is not wanting; for to use touching words (attributed to St. Paul in a very ancient apocryphal ·document), "He alone sympathised with a world that has lost its way."[1]

Let it not be forgotten that in that of which St. John speaks lies the true answer to an objection, formulated by the great anti-christian writer above quoted, and constantly repeated by others.   "The ideal of Christian morality," says Mr. Mill, "is negative rather than positive ; passive rather than active ; innocence rather than nobleness; abstinence from evil, rather than energetic pursuit of good ; in its precepts (as has been well said), 'thou shalt not' predominates unduly over 'thou shalt.'"[2]   The answer is this.   (1) A true religious system must have a distinct moral code.   If not, it would be justly condemned for "expressing itself" (in the words of Mr. Mill's own accusation against Christianity elsewhere) "in language most general, and possessing rather the impressiveness of poetry or eloquence than the precision of legislation."   But the necessary formula of precise legislation is, "thou shalt not"; and without this it cannot be precise.   (2) But further.   To say that Christian legislation is negative, a mere string of "thou shalt nots," is just such a superficial accusation as might be expected from a man who should enter a church upon some rare occasion, and happen to listen to the ten commandments, but fall asleep before he could hear the Epistle and Gospel.   The philosopher

---

[1] ὃς μόνος συνεπαθήσεν πλανωμένῳ κόσμῳ.   *Acta Paul. et Thec.* 16, *Acta. Apost. Apoc.* 47.   Edit. Tischendorf.

[2] *On Liberty.*   John Stuart Mill (chap. iii.).

of duty, Kant, has told us that the peculiarity of a moral principle, of any proposition which states what duty is, is to convey the meaning of an imperative through the form of an indicative. In his own expressive if pedantic language—"its categorical form involves an epitactic meaning." St. John asserts that the Christian "ought to walk even as Christ walked." To every one who receives it, that proposition is therefore precisely equivalent to a *command*—"walk as Christ walked." Is it a negative, passive morality, a mere system of "thou shalt not," which contains such a precept as that? Does not the Christian religion in virtue of this alone enforce a great "thou shalt;" which every man who brings himself within its range will find rising with him in the morning, following him like his shadow all day long, and lying down with him when he goes to rest?

II.

It should be clearly understood that in the words "even as He walked," the Gospel of St. John is both referred to and attested.

For surely to point with any degree of moral seriousness to an example, *is* to presuppose some clear knowledge and definite record of it. No example can be beautiful or instructive when its shape is lost in darkness. It has indeed been said by a deeply religious writer, "that the likeness of the Christian to Christ is to His character, not to the particular form in which it was historically manifested." And this, of course, is in one sense a truism. But how else except by this historical manifestation can we know the character of Christ in any true sense of the word knowledge? For those who are familiar with the fourth

Gospel, the term " walk " was tenderly significant. For if it was used with a reminiscence of the Old Testament and of the language of our Lord,[1] to denote the whole continuous activity of the life of any man inward and outward, there was another signification which became entwined with it.   St. John had used the word historically [2] in his Gospel, not without allusion to the Saviour's homelessness on earth, to His itinerant life of beneficence and of teaching.[3]   Those who first received this Epistle with deepest reverence as the utterance of the Apostle whom they loved, when they came to the precept—" walk even as He walked "—would ask themselves *how* did He walk ? What do we know of the great rule of life thus proposed to us ? The Gospel which accompanied this letter, and with which it was in some way closely connected, was a sufficient and definite answer.

III.

The character of Christ in his Gospel is thus, according to St. John, the loftiest ideal of purity, peace, self-sacrifice, unbroken communion with God ; the inexhaustible fountain of regulated thoughts, high aims, holy action, constant prayer.

We may advert to one aspect of this perfection as delineated in the fourth Gospel—our Lord's way of doing small things, or at least things which in human estimation appear to be small.

The fourth chapter of that Gospel contains a marvellous record of word and work.   Let us trace that

---

[1] John viii. 12-35.   For Apostolic usage of the word, see Acts i. 21; Rom. vi. 4; Ephes. ii. 10; Col. iii. 7.

[2] John vii. 1.

[3] "Ambulando docebat."—*Bretschneider.*

record back to its beginning. There are seeds of spiritual life scattered in many hearts which were destined to yield a rich harvest in due time; there is the account of one sensuous nature, quickened and spiritualised; there are promises which have been for successive centuries as a river of God to weary natures. All these results issue from three words spoken by a tired traveller, sitting naturally over a well—" give me to drink."

We take another instance. There is one passage in St. John's Gospel which divides with the procemium of his Epistle, the glory of being the loftiest, the most prolonged, the most sustained, in the Apostle's writings.

It is the prelude of a work which might have seemed to be of little moment. Yet all the height of a great ideal is over it, like the vault of heaven; all the power of a Divine purpose is under it, like the strength of the great deep; all the consciousness of His death, of His ascension, of His coming dominion, of His Divine origin, of His session at God's right hand—all the hoarded love in His heart for His own which were in the world—passes by some mysterious transference into that little incident of tenderness and of humiliation. He sets an everlasting mark upon it, not by a basin of gold crusted with gems, nor by mixing precious scents with the water which He poured out, nor by using linen of the finest tissue, but by the absolute perfection of love and dutiful humility in the spirit and in every detail of the whole action. It is one more of those little chinks through which the whole sunshine of heaven streams in upon those who have eyes to see.[1]

---

[1] John xiii. 1-6.

The underlying secret of this feature of our Lord's character is told by Himself. " My meat is to be ever doing the will of Him that sent Me, and so when the time comes by one great decisive act to finish His work." [1] All along the course of that life-walk there were smaller preludes to the great act which won our redemption—multitudinous daily little perfect epitomes of love and sacrifice, without which the crowning sacrifice would not have been what it was. The plan of our life must, of course, be constructed on a scale as different as the human from the Divine. Yet there is a true sense in which this lesson of the great life may be applied to us.

The apparently small things of life must not be despised or neglected on account of their smallness, by those who would follow the precept of St. John. Patience and diligence in petty trades, in services called menial, in waiting on the sick and old, in a hundred such works, all come within the sweep of this net, with its lines that look as thin as cobwebs, and which yet for Christian hearts are stronger than fibres of steel— "walk even as He walked." This, too, is our only security. A French poet has told a beautiful tale. Near a river which runs between French and German territory, a blacksmith was at work one snowy night near Christmas time. He was tired out, standing by his forge, and wistfully looking towards his little home, lighted up a short quarter of a mile away, and wife and children waiting for their festal supper, when he should return. It came to the last piece of his work, a rivet which it was difficult to finish properly ; for it was of peculiar shape, intended by the contractor who

---

[1] Ἵνα ποιῶ . . . καὶ τελειώσω (John iv. 34).

employed him to pin the metal work of a bridge which he was constructing over the river. The smith was sorely tempted to fail in giving honest work, to hurry over a job which seemed at once so troublesome and so trifling. But some good angel whispered to the man that he should do his best. He turned to the forge with a sigh, and never rested until the work was as complete as his skill could make it. The poet carries us on for a year or two. War breaks out. A squadron of the blacksmith's countrymen is driven over the bridge in headlong flight. Men, horses, guns, try its solidity. For a moment or two the whole weight of the mass really hangs upon the one rivet. There are times in life when the whole weight of the soul also hangs upon a rivet; the rivet of sobriety, of purity, of honesty, of command of temper. Possibly we have devoted little or no honest work to it in the years when we should have perfected the work; and so, in the day of trial, the rivet snaps, and we are lost.

There is one word of encouragement which should be finally spoken for the sake of one class of God's servants.

Some are sick, weary, broken, paralysed, it may be slowly dying. What—they sometimes ask—have we to do with this precept? Others who have hope, elasticity, capacity of service, may walk as He walked; but we can scarcely do so. Such persons should remember what walking in the Christian sense is—all life's activity inward and outward. Let them think of Christ upon His cross. He was fixed to it, nailed hand and foot. Nailed; yet never—not when He trod upon the waves, not when He moved upward through the air to His throne—never did He walk more truly

because He walked in the way of perfect love. It is just whilst looking at the moveless form upon the tree that we may hear most touchingly the great "thou shalt" —thou shalt walk even as He walked.

IV.

As there is a literal, so there is a mystical walking as Christ walked. This is an idea which deeply pervades St. Paul's writings. Is it His birth? We are born again. Is it His life? We walk with Him in newness of life. Is it His death? We are crucified with Him. Is it His burial? We are buried with Him. Is it His resurrection? We are risen again with Him. Is it His ascension—His very session at God's right hand? " He hath raised us up and made us sit together with Him in heavenly places." They know nothing of St. Paul's mind who know nothing of this image of a soul seen in the very dust of death, loved, pardoned, quickened, elevated, crowned, throned. It was this conception at work from the beginning in the general consciousness of Christians which moulded round itself the order of the Christian year.

It will illustrate this idea for us if we think of the difference between the outside and the inside of a church.

Outside on some high spire we see the light just lingering far up, while the shadows are coldly gathering in the streets below ; and we know that it is winter. Again the evening falls warm and golden on the church-yard, and we recognise the touch of summer. But inside it is always God's weather ; it is Christ all the year long. Now the Babe wrapped in swaddling clothes, or circumcised with the knife of the law, manifested to

9

the Gentiles, or manifesting Himself with a glory that breaks through the veil; now the Man tempted in the wilderness; now the victim dying on the cross; now the Victor risen, ascended, sending the Holy Spirit; now for twenty-five Sundays worshipped as the Everlasting Word with the Father and the Holy Ghost. In this mystical following of Christ also, the one perpetual lesson is—"he that saith he abideth in Him, ought himself also so to walk even as He walked."

NOTES.

Ch. ii. 3-11.

Ver. 4. A liar.] There are many things which the "sayer" says by the language of his life rather than by his lips to others: many things which he says to himself. "We lead ourselves astray" (i. 8). We "say" I have knowledge of Him, while yet we observe not His commandments. Strange that we can lie to the one being who knows the truth thoroughly—*self*; and having lied, can get the lie believed,—

> " Like one,
> Who having, unto truth, by telling of it,
> Made such a sinner of his memory,
> To credit his own lie."
>
> *Tempest*, Act I. Sc. 2.

Ver. 7. Fresh.] There are two quite different words alike translated new in A. V.: one of these is the word used here (καινός); the other (νέος). The first always signifies *new* in quality—intellectual, ethical, spiritual *novelty*—that which is opposed to, which replaces and supersedes, the antiquated, inferior, outworn; *new* in the world of thought. (Heb. viii. 13 states this with perfect precision.) It may sometimes not inadequately be rendered *fresh* ("youngly," Shakespeare, *Coriolanus*). The other term (νέος) is simply *recent; new* chronologically in the world of time.

Which ye heard from the beginning.] Probably a recognition of St. Paul's teaching at Ephesus, and of his Epistle to the Ephesians.

Ver. 8. To many commentators this verse seems almost of insoluble difficulty. Surely, however, the meaning is clear enough for those who will place themselves within the atmosphere of St. John's thought. " Again a fresh commandment I am writing to you" [this commandment, charity, is no unreal and therefore delusive standard of duty]. Taken as one great whole (ὅ) it is true, matter of observable historical fact, because it is realised in Him who gave the commandment ; capable of realisation, and even in measure realised in you. [And this can be actually done by Christians, and recognised more and more by others], "because the shadow is drifting by from the landscape even of the world, and the light, the very light, enlighteneth by a new ideal and a new example."

Ver. 10. *Scandal.*] In Greek is the rendering of two Hebrew words. (1) That against which we trip and stumble, a stumbling-block ; (2) A hook or snare.

Ver. 11. The terrible force of this truly Hebraistic parallelism should be noted.

1. He that hateth his brother *is* in darkness.
2.   ,,   ,,   ,,   walketh in darkness.
3.   ,,   ,,   ,,   knoweth not where he goeth.
4.   ,,   ,,   ,,   darkness has blinded his eyes.

The third beat of the parallelism contains an allusion to that Cain among the nations, the Jewish people in our Lord's time. (John xii. 35.)

In illustration of the powerful expression, ("darkness has blinded his eyes") the present writer quoted a striking passage from Professor Drummond, who adduces a parallel for the Christian's loss of the spiritual faculty, by the atrophy of organs which takes place in moles, and in the fish in dark caverns. (*Speaker's Commentary, in loc.*) But as regards the mole at least, a great observer of Nature entirely denies the alleged atrophy. Mr. Buckland quotes Dr. Lee in a paper, in the Proceedings of the Royal Society, where he says, —" the eye of the mole presents us with an instance of an organ which is rudimentary, not by arrest of development, but through disuse, aided perhaps by natural selection." But Mr. Buckland asserts that "the same great Wisdom who made the mole's teeth the most beautiful set of insectivorous teeth among

animals, also made its eye fit for the work it has to do. The mole has been designed to prey upon earthworms; they will not come up to the surface to him, so he must go down into the earth to them. For this purpose his eyes are fitted." (*Life of F. Buckland*, pp. 247, 248).

SECTION III. (2)

GREEK.

Ἀγαπητοί, οὐκ ἐντολὴν καινὴν γράφω ὑμῖν, ἀλλ' ἐντολὴν παλαιὰν ἣν εἴχετε ἀπ' ἀρχῆς· ἡ ἐντολὴ ἡ παλαιά ἐστιν ὁ λόγος ὃν ἠκούσατε. πάλιν ἐντολὴν καινὴν γράφω ὑμῖν, ὅ ἐστιν ἀληθὲς ἐν αὐτῷ καὶ ἐν ὑμῖν, ὅτι ἡ σκοτία παράγεται καὶ τὸ φῶς τὸ ἀληθινὸν ἤδη φαίνει. ὁ λέγων ἐν τῷ φωτὶ εἶναι καὶ τὸν ἀδελφὸν αὐτοῦ μισῶν ἐν τῇ σκοτίᾳ ἐστὶν ἕως ἄρτι. ὁ ἀγαπῶν τὸν ἀδελφὸν αὐτοῦ ἐν τῷ φωτὶ μένει, καὶ σκάνδαλον ἐν αὐτῷ οὐκ ἔστιν. ὁ δὲ μισῶν τὸν ἀδελφὸν αὐτοῦ ἐν τῇ σκοτίᾳ ἐστὶν καὶ ἐν τῇ σκοτίᾳ περιπατεῖ, καὶ οὐκ οἶδε ποῦ ὑπάγει, ὅτι ἡ σκοτία ἐτύφλωσεν τοὺς ὀφθαλμοὺς αὐτοῦ.

LATIN.

Carissimi non mandatum novum scribo vobis, sed mandatum vetus quod habuistis ab initio: mandatum vetus est verbum quod audistis. Iterum mandatum novum scribo vobis, quod est verum et in ipso et in vobis, quoniam tenebrae transierunt et lumen verum jam lucet. Qui dicit se in luce esse et fratrem suum odit, in tenebris est usque adhuc. Qui diligit fratrem suum in lumine manet, et scandalum in eo non est: qui autem odit fratrem suum, in tenebris est, et in tenebris ambulat et nescit quo eat, quoniam tenebrae obcaecaverunt oculos eius.

AUTHORISED VERSION.

Brethren, I write no new commandment unto you, but an old commandment which ye had from the beginning. The old commandment is the word which ye have heard from the beginning. Again, a new commandment I write unto you, which thing is true in Him and in you: because the darkness is past, and the true light now shineth. He that saith he is in the light, and hateth his brother, is in darkness even until now. He that loveth his brother abideth in the light, and there is none occasion of stumbling in him. But he that hateth his brother is in darkness, and walketh in darkness, and knoweth not whither he goeth, because that darkness hath blinded his eyes.

REVISED VERSION.

Beloved, no new commandment write I unto you, but an old commandment which ye had from the beginning: the old commandment is the word which ye heard. Again, a new commandment write I unto you, which thing is true in Him and in you: because the darkness is passing away, and the true light already shineth. He that saith he is in the light, and hateth his brother, is in the darkness even until now. He that loveth his brother abideth in the light, and there is none occasion of stumbling in him. But he that hateth his brother is in the darkness, and walketh in the darkness, and knoweth not whither he goeth, because the darkness hath blinded his eyes.

ANOTHER VERSION.

Beloved, no fresh commandment I am writing unto you, but an old commandment which ye had from the beginning. The commandment, the old commandment, is the word which ye heard. Again, a fresh commandment I am writing unto you, which thing [as a whole] is true in Him and in you: because the shadow is drifting by, and the light, the very *light*, is already enlightening. He that saith he is in the light and hateth his brother, in the darkness is he hitherto. He that loveth his brother in the light abideth he, and scandal in him there is not. But he that hateth his brother in the darkness is he, and in the darkness walketh he, and he knoweth not whither he goeth because the darkness hath blinded his eyes.

SECTION III. (3)

GREEK.

Γράφω ὑμῖν, τεκνία, ὅτι ἀφέωνται ὑμῖν αἱ ἁμαρτίαι διὰ τὸ ὄνομα αὐτοῦ. γράφω ὑμῖν, πατέρες, ὅτι ἐγνώκατε τὸν ἀπ᾽ ἀρχῆς. γράφω ὑμῖν, νεανίσκοι, ὅτι νενικήκατε τὸν πονηρόν. ἔγραψα ὑμῖν, παιδία, ὅτι ἐγνώκατε τὸν πατέρα. ἔγραψα ὑμῖν, πατέρες, ὅτι ἐγνώκατε τὸν ἀπ᾽ ἀρχῆς. Ἔγραψα ὑμῖν, νεανίσκοι, ὅτι ἰσχυροί ἐστε, καὶ ὁ λόγος τοῦ Θεοῦ ἐν ὑμῖν μένει, καὶ νενικήκατε τὸν πονηρόν. μὴ ἀγαπᾶτε τὸν κόσμον, μηδὲ τὰ ἐν τῷ κόσμῳ. ἐάν τις ἀγαπᾷ τὸν κόσμον, οὐκ ἔστιν ἡ ἀγάπη τοῦ πατρὸς ἐν αὐτῷ· ὅτι πᾶν τὸ ἐν τῷ κόσμῳ, ἡ ἐπιθυμία τῆς σαρκὸς καὶ ἡ ἐπιθυμία τῶν ὀφθαλμῶν καὶ ἡ ἀλαζονία τοῦ βίου, οὐκ ἔστιν ἐκ τοῦ πατρὸς,

LATIN.

Scribo vobis, filioli, quoniam remittentur vobis, peccata propter nomen eius. Scribo vobis, patres, quoniam cognovistis eum qui ab initio est. Scribo vobis, adolescentes, quoniam vicistis malignum. Scribo vobis, infantes, quia cognovistis patrem. Scripsi vobis, iuvenes quia fortes estis et verbum Dei in vobis manet et vicistis malignum. Nolite diligere mundum ne que eaque in mundo sunt. Si quis diligit mundum, non est caritas Patris in eo : quoniam omne quod in mundo est, concupiscentia carnis est, et concupiscentia oculorum, et superbia vitæ ; quæ non est ex Patre, sed ex mundo est. Et

AUTHORISED VERSION.

I write unto you, little children, because your sins are forgiven you for His name's sake. I write unto you, fathers, because ye have known Him that is from the beginning. I write unto you, young men, because ye have overcome the wicked one. I write unto you, little children, because ye have known the Father. I have written unto you, fathers, because ye have known Him that is from the beginning. I have written unto you, young men, because ye are strong, and the word of God abideth in you, and ye have overcome the wicked one. Love not the world, neither the things that are in the

REVISED VERSION.

I write unto you, my little children, because your sins are forgiven you for His name's sake. I write unto you, fathers, because ye know Him that is from the beginning. I write unto you, young men, because ye have overcome the evil one. I have written unto you, little children, because ye know the Father. I have written unto you, fathers, because ye know Him which is from the beginning. I have written unto you, young men, because ye are strong, and the word of God abideth in you, and ye have overcome the evil one. Love not the world, neither the things that are in the world. If

ANOTHER VERSION.

I am writing unto you, children, because your sins are forgiven you for His name's sake. I am writing unto you, fathers, because ye have knowledge of Him who is from the beginning. I am writing unto you, young men, because ye are conquerors of the wicked one.

I have written unto you, little children, because ye have knowledge of the Father. I have written unto you, fathers, because ye have knowledge of Him who is from the beginning. I have written unto you, young men, because ye are strong and the word of God abideth in you, and ye are conquerors of the wicked one.

ἀλλὰ ἐκ τοῦ κόσμου ἐστίν· καὶ ὁ κόσμος παράγεται καὶ ἡ ἐπιθυμία αὐτοῦ· ὁ δὲ ποιῶν τὸ θέλημα τοῦ Θεοῦ μένει εἰς τὸν αἰῶνα.

mundus transibit et concupiscentia eius: qui autem facit voluntatem Dei, manet in eternum.

world. If any man love the world, the love of the Father is not in him. For all that is in the world, the lust of the flesh, and the lust of the eyes, and the pride of life, is not of the Father, but is of the world. And the world passeth away, and the lust thereof: but he that doeth the will of God abideth for ever.

any man love the world, the love of the Father is not in him. For all that is in the world, the lust of the flesh, and the lust of the eyes, and the vainglory of life, is not of the Father, but is of the world. And the world passeth away, and the lust thereof: but he that doeth the will of God abideth for ever.

Love not the world, neither the things that are in the world. If any man love the world the love of the Father is not in him. For all that is in the world, the lust of the flesh and the lust of the eyes and the arrogancy of living, is not from the Father, but from the world is it. And the world is drifting by, and the lust of it: but he that is doing the will of God abideth for ever.

DISCOURSE VI.

THE WORLD WHICH WE MUST NOT LOVE.

"Love not the world, neither the things that are in the world. If any man love the world, the love of the Father is not in him. For all that is in the world, the lust of the flesh, and the lust of the eyes, and the pride of life, is not of the Father, but of the world."—1 JOHN ii. 15, 16.

AN adequate development of words so compressed and pregnant as these would require a separate treatise, or series of treatises.[1] But if we succeed in grasping St. John's conception of *the world*, we shall have a key that will open to us this cabinet of spiritual thought.

I.

In the writings of St. John the world is always found in one or other of four senses, as may be decided by the context. (1) It means the creation,[2] the universe.

---

[1] After all deductions for the lack of accurate and searching textual exegesis, perhaps Bossuet's "Traité de la concupiscence, ou Exposition de ces Paroles de Saint Jean, 1 John ii. 15-17" (*Œuvres de Bossuet*, Tom. vii., 380-420), remains unrivalled.

[2] The word κόσμος originally signified ornament (chiefly perhaps of dress) ; figuratively it came to denote order. It was first applied by Pythagoras to the *universe*, from the conception of the order. which reigns in it (Plut., *de Plac. Phil.*, ii. 1). From schools of philosophy it passed into the language of poets and writers of elevated prose. It is somewhat singular that the Romans, possibly from Greek influence, came to apply "mundus" by the same process to *the world*, as it had also originally signified *ornament*, especially of female dress

So our Lord in His High-priestly prayer—"Thou lovedst Me before the foundation of the world."[1] (2) It is used for the earth *locally* as the place where man resides;[2] and whose soil the Son of God trod for awhile. . "I am no more in the world, but these are in the world."[3] (3) It denotes the chief inhabitants of the earth, they to whom the counsels of God mainly point—men universally. Such a transference is common in nearly all languages. Both the inhabitants of a building, and the material structure which contains them, are called "a house;" and the inhabitants are frequently bitterly blamed, while the beauty of the structure is passionately admired. In this sense there is a magnificent width in the word *world.* We cannot but feel indignant at attempts to gird its grandeur within the narrow rim of a human system. "The bread that I will give," said He who knew best, "is My flesh which I will give for the life of the world."[4] "He is the propitiation for the whole world," writes the Apostle at the beginning of this chapter. In this sense, if we would imitate Christ, if we would aspire to the Father's perfection, "love not the world" must be tempered by that other tender oracle—"God so loved the world."[5]

(See Richard Bentley against Boyle, *Opera Philol.*, 347-445, and Notes, Humboldt's *Cosmos*, xiii.). In the LXX. κόσμος does not appear as the translation of עוֹלָם its spiritual equivalent in Hebrew; but very often in the sense of "ornament" and "order." (See Tromm., *Concord. Gr. in LXX.*, 1, 913), but it is found as *world* several times in the Apocrypha (Wisdom vi. 26, vii. 18, ix. 3, xi. 18, xv. 14; 2 Mac. iii. 12, vii. 9-23, viii. 18, xiii. 14.

[1] John xvii. 24.
[2] In Hebrew תֵּבֵל habitable globe; translated οἰκουμένη in LXX. (see Psalm lxxxix. 11).
[3] John v. 11.
[4] John vi. 31; 1 John ii. 2.
[5] John iii. 16. It may be added that these are passages where the

In none of these senses can the world here be under-stood.[1]

There remains then (4) a fourth signification, which has two allied shades of thought. World is employed to cover the whole present existence, with its blended good and evil—susceptible of elevation by grace, susceptible also of deeper depths of sin and ruin. But yet again the indifferent meaning passes into one that is wholly evil, wholly within a region of darkness. The first creation was pronounced by God in each department "good" collectively; when crowned by God's masterpiece in man, "very good."[2] "All things," our Apostle tells us, "were made through Him (the Word), and without Him was not any thing made that was made."[3] But as that was a world wholly good, so is this a world wholly evil. This evil world is not God's creation, drew not its origin from Him. All that is *in* it came out *from* it, from nothing *higher*.[4] This wholly evil world is not the material creation; if it were, we should be landed in dualism, or Manicheism. It is not an entity, an actual tangible thing, a creation. It is not of God's world that St. John cries in that last fierce word of abhorrence which he flings at it as he sees the shadowy thing like an evil spirit made visible in an idol's arms—" the world lieth wholly in the evil one."[5]

This anti-world, this caricature of creation, this

---

world as humanity generally passes into the darker meaning of that portion of it which is actively hostile to God. John xv. 18, 19.

[1] See note on ver. 16 at the end of the next Discourse.

[2] Gen. i. 31.

[3] John i. 3.

[4] The writer does not happen to remember any commentator who has pointed out this subtle but powerful thought, $\pi\hat{a}\nu$ $\tau\grave{o}$ $\grave{e}\nu$ $\tau\hat{\omega}$ $\kappa\acute{o}\sigma\mu\hat{\omega}$—$\grave{e}\kappa$ $\tauο\hat{u}$ $\kappa\acute{o}\sigma\mu\omega$ $\grave{e}\sigma\tau\acute{\iota}\nu$ (1 John ii. 16).

[5] 1 John v. 19.

thing of negations, is spun out of three abuses of the
endowment of God's glorious gift of free-will to man ; out
of three noble instincts ignobly used. *First,* "the lust
of the flesh"—of which flesh is the seat, and supplies
the organic medium through which it works. The flesh
is that softer part of the frame which by the network
of the nerves is intensely susceptible of pleasurable
and painful sensations; capable of heroic patient submission to the higher principles of conscience and
spirit,[1] capable also of frightful rebellion. Of all
theologians St. John is the least likely to fall into the
exaggeration of libelling the flesh as essentially evil.
Is it not he who, whether in his Gospel, or in his
Epistles, delights to speak of the *flesh* of Jesus, to
record words in which He refers to it ?[2] Still the flesh
brings us into contact with all sins which are sins that
spring from, and end in, the senses. Shall we ask for
a catalogue of particulars from St. John? Nay, we
cannot expect that the virgin Apostle, who received
the virgin Mother from the Virgin Lord upon the
cross, will sully his virgin pen with words so abhorred.
When he has uttered *the lust of the flesh* his shudder
is followed by an eloquent silence. We can fill up
the blank too well—drunkenness, gluttony, thoughts
and motions which spring from deliberate, wilfully
cherished, rebellious sensuality; which fill many of
us with pain and fear, and wring cries and bitter
tears from penitents, and even from saints. The
second, abuse of free-will, the second element in this
world which is not God's world, is the desire of which
the eyes are the seat—"the lust of the eyes." To

---

[1] John xiv. 1 ; 1 John iv. 2, 3; 2 John 7.
[2] John vi. 51, 53-56; 1 John iv. 2, 3; 2 John 7.

the two sins which we instinctively associate with this phrase—voluptuousness and curiosity of the senses or the soul—Scripture might seem to add *envy*, which derives so much of its aliment from sight. In this lies the Christian's warning against wilfully indulging in evil sights, bad plays, bad books, bad pictures. He who is outwardly the spectator of these things becomes inwardly the actor of them. The eye is, so to speak, the burning-glass of the soul; it draws the rays from their evil brightness to a focus, and may kindle a raging fire in the heart. Under this department comes unregulated spiritual or intellectual curiosity. The first need not trouble us so much as it did Christians in a more believing time. Comparatively very few are in danger from the *planchette* or from astrology. But surely it is a rash thing for an ordinary mind, without a clear call of duty, without any adequate preparation, to place its faith within the deadly grip of some powerful adversary. People really seem to have absolutely no conscience about reading anything—the last philosophical Life of Christ, or the last romance; of which the titles might be with advantage exchanged, for the philosophical history is a light romance, and the romance is a heavy philosophy. The *third* constituent in the evil anti-trinity of the anti-world is "the pride" (the arrogancy, gasconade, almost swagger) "of life," of which the lower life[1] is the seat. The thought is not so much of outward pomp and ostentation as of that false pride which arises in the heart. The arrogancy is within; the gasconade plays its "fantastic tricks before high heaven." And each of these three elements (making up as they do collectively all that is "in the world" and springing out of the

---

[1] ἡ ἀλαζονία τοῦ βίου.

world) is not a substantive thing, not an original in-gredient of man's nature, or among the forms of God's world ; it is the perversion of an element which had a use that was noble, or at least innocent. For first comes "the lust of the flesh." Take those two objects to which this lust turns with a fierce and perverted passion. The possession of flesh in itself leads man to crave for the necessary support to his native weakness. The mutual craving for the love of beings so like and so unlike as man and woman, if it be a weakness, has at least a most touching and exquisite side. Again, is not a yearning for beauty gratified through the eyes ? Were they not given for the enjoyment, for the teach-ing, at once high and sweet, of Nature and of Art ? Art may be a moral and spiritual discipline. The ideas of Beauty from gifted minds by cunning hands transferred to, and stamped upon, outward things, come from the ancient and uncreated Beauty, whose beauty is as perfect as His truth and strength. Still further ; in the lower life, and in its lawful use, there was in-tended to be a something of quiet satisfaction, a certain restfulness, at times making us happy and triumphant. And lo ! for all this, not moderate fare and pure love, not thoughtful curiosity and the sweet pensiveness which is the best tribute to the beautiful—not a wise humility which makes us feel that our times are in God's hands and our means His continual gift—but degraded senses, low art, evil literature, a pride which is as grovelling as it is godless.

These three typical summaries of the evil tendencies in the exercise of free-will correspond with a remarkable fulness to the two narratives of trial which give us the compendium and general outline of all human temptation. Our Lord's three temptations answer to this division.

The lust of the flesh is in essence the rebellion of
the lower appetites, inherent to creaturely dependence,
against the higher principle or law.   The nearest and
only conceivable approach to this in the sinless Man
would be in His seeking lawful support by unlawful
means—procuring food by a miraculous exertion of
power, which only would have become sinful, or short of
the highest goodness, by some condition of its exercise
at that time and in that place.   An appeal to the desire
for beauty and glory, with an implied hint of using
them for God's greater honour, is the essence of the
second temptation ; the one possible approximation to
the " lust of the eyes " in that perfect character.   The
interior deception of some touch of pride in the visible
support of angels wafting the Son of God through the
air is Satan's one sinister way of insinuating to the
Saviour something akin to "the pride of life."

In the case of the other earlier typical trials it
will be observed that while the temptations fit into
the same threefold framework, they are placed in an
order which exactly reverses that of St. John.   For
in Eden the first approach is through " pride " ; the
magnificent promise of elevation in the scale of being,
of the knowledge that would win the wonder of the
spiritual world.   " For God doth know that in the day
ye eat thereof, then your eyes shall be opened, and ye
shall be as gods, knowing good and evil."[1]   The next
step is that which directs the curiosity both of the
senses and of the aspiring mind to the object forbidden—
" when the woman saw that the tree was good for food,
and that it was pleasant to the eyes, and a tree to be
desired to make one wise." [2]   Then seems to have come

---

[1] Gen. iii. 5.   [2] Gen. iii. 6.

some strange and sad rebellion of the lower nature, filling
their souls with shame; some bitter revelation of the
law of sin in their members; some knowledge that they
were contaminated by the "lust of the flesh."[1] The
order of the temptation in the narrative of Moses is
historical; St. John's order is moral and spiritual,
answering to the facts of life. The "lust of the flesh"
which may approach the child through childish greed,
grows apace. At first it is half unconscious; then it
becomes coarse and palpable. In the man's desire
acting with unregulated curiosity, through ambition of
knowledge at any price, searching out for itself books
and other instruments with deliberate desire to kindle
lust, the "lust of the eyes" ceases not its fatal influence.
The crowning sin of pride with its *selfishness*, which
is self apart from God as well as from the brother,
finds its place in the "pride of life."

III.

We may now be in a position to see more clearly
against *what* world the Primate of early Christendom
pronounced his anathema, and launched his interdict,
and why?

What "world" did he denounce?

Clearly *not* the world as the creation, the universe.
Not again the earth locally. God made and ordered all
things. Why should we not love them with a holy and
a blameless love? Only we should not love them in
themselves; we should not cling to them forgetting
Him. Suppose that some husband heaped beautiful
and costly presents upon his wife whom he loved. At
last with the intuition of love he begins to see what

---

[1] Gen. iii. 7.

is the secret of such cold imitation of love as that icy heart can give. She loves *him* not—his riches, not the man; his gifts, not the giver. And thus loving with that frigid love which has no heart in it, there is no true love; her heart is another's. Gifts are given that the giver may be loved in them. If it is true that "gifts are nought when givers prove unkind," it is also true that there is a sort of adultery of the heart when the taker is unkind—because the gift is valuable, not because the bestower is dear.[1] And so the world, God's beautiful world, now becomes to us an idol. If we are so lost in the procession of Nature, in the march of law, in the majestic growth, in the stars above and in the plants below, that we forget the Lawgiver, who from such humble beginnings has brought out a world of beauty and order; if with modern poets we find content, calm, happiness, purity, rest, simply in contemplating the glaciers, the waves, and the stars; then we look at the world even in this sense in a way which is a violation of St. John's rule. Yet again, the world which is now condemned is not humanity. There is no real Christianity in taking black views, and speaking bitter things, about the human society to which we belong, and the human nature of which we are 'partakers. No doubt Christianity believes that man "is very far gone from original righteousness;" that there is a "corruption in the nature of every man that naturally is engendered of the offspring of Adam." Yet the utterers of unwholesome apophthegms, the suspecters of their kind, are not Christian thinkers. The philosophic historian, whose gorge rose at the doctrine of the Fall, thought much worse of man practically

---

[1] S. Augustin., *Tract. in Joann. Epist.*

than the Fathers of the Church.   They bowed before
martyrdom and purity, and believed in them with a
child-like faith.   For Gibbon, the martyr was not quite
so true, nor the virgin quite so pure, nor the saint
quite so holy.   He Who knew human nature best, Who
has thrown that terrible ray of light into the unlit gulf
of the heart when He tells us "what proceeds out of
the heart of man,"[1] had yet the ear which was the first
to hear the trembling of the one chord that yet kept
healthful time and tune in the harlot's passionate heart.
He believed that man was recoverable; lost, but capable of being found.   After all, in this sense there is
something worthy of love in man.   "God so *loved*"
(not so *hated*) "the world, that He gave His only
begotten Son."   Shall we say that *we* are to hate the
world which He loved ?

And now we come to that world which God never
loved, never will love, never will reconcile to Himself,—
which we are not to love.

This is most important to see ; for there is always
a danger in setting out with a stricter standard than
Christ's, a narrower road than the narrow one which
leads to heaven.   Experience proves that they who
begin with standards of duty which are impossibly
high end with standards of duty which are sometimes
sadly low.   Such men have tried the impracticable, and
failed ; the practicable seems to be too hard for them
ever afterwards.   They who begin by anathematising
the world in things innocent, indifferent, or even laudable, not rarely end by a reaction of thought which
believes that the world is nothing and nowhere.

But there is such a thing as the world in St. John's
sense—an evil world brought into existence by the abuse

---

[1] Mark vii. 21.

10

of our free-will; filled by the anti-trinity, by "the lust of the flesh, the lust of the eyes, and the pride of life."

Let us not confuse " the world" with the earth, with the whole race of man, with general society, with any particular set, however much some sets are to be avoided. Look at the thing fairly. Two people, we will say, go to London, to live there. One, from circumstances of life and position, naturally falls into the highest social circle. Another has introductions to a smaller set, with an apparently more serious connection. Follow the first some evening. He drives to a great gathering. The room which he enters is ablaze with light; jewelled orders sparkle upon men's coats, and fair women move in exquisite dresses. We look at the scene and we say—" what worldly society has the man fallen into!" Perhaps so, in a sense. But about the same time the other walks to a little room with humbler adjuncts, where a grave and apparently serious circle meet together. We are able to look in there also, and we exclaim—"this is serious society, unworldly society." Perhaps so again. Yet let us read the letters of Mary Godolphin. She bore a life unspotted by the world in the dissolute court of Charles II., because the love of the Father was in her. In small serious circles are there no hidden lusts which blaze up in scandals? Is there no vanity, no pride, no hatred? In the world of Charles II.'s court Mary Godolphin lived out of the world which God hated; in the religious world not a few, certainly, live in the world which is not God's. For once more, the world is not so much a place—though at times its power seems to have been drawn into one intense focus, as in the empire of which Rome was the centre, and which may have been in the Apostle's thought in the following verse. In the truest and

deepest sense the world consists of our own spiritual
surrounding; it is the place which we make for our
own souls. No walls that ever were reared can shut
out the world from us; the " Nun of Kenmare " found
that it followed her into the seemingly spiritual retreat
of a severe Order. The world in its essence is subtler
and thinner than the most infinitesimal of the bacterian
germs in the air. They can be strained off by the
exquisite apparatus of a man of science. At a certain
height they cease to exist. But the world may be where-
ever we are; we carry it with us wherever we go, it
lasts while our lives last. No consecration can utterly
banish it even from within the church's walls; it dares
to be round us while we kneel, and follows us into the
presence of God.

(2) Why does God hate this " world "—the world in
this sense? St. John tells us. " If any man love the
world, the love of the Father is not in him." Deep in
every heart must be one or other of two loves. There
is no room for two master-passions. There is an
expulsive power in all true affection. What tenderness
and pathos, how much of expostulation, more potent
because reserved—" the love of the Father is not in
him " ! He has told all his " little ones " that he has
written to them because they " know the Father."
St. John does not use sacred names at random. Even
Voltaire felt that there was something almost awful in
hearing Newton pronounce the name of God. Such in
an incomparably higher degree is the spirit of St. John.
In this section he writes of " the love of the *Father*," [1]
and of the " will of *God*." [2] The first title has more
sweetness than majesty ; the second more majesty than

---

[1] 1 John ii. 15. 16.   [2] Ibid. ver. 17.

sweetness.[1]   He would throw into his plea some of
the winningness of one who uses this as a resistless
argument with a tempted but loving child—an argument
often successful when every other fails.   " If you do
this, your Father will not love you ; you will not be
His child."   We have but to read this with the hearts
of God's dear children.   Then we shall find that if the
"love not" of this verse contains "words of extirpa-
tion ;" [2] it ends with others which are intended to draw
us with cords of a man, and with bands of love.

[1] No portion of Prof. Westcott's Commentary is more thorough
or more exquisite than his exposition here.   (*Epistles of St. John*, 66.)
 [2] *Extirpantia verba."*   St. August (in loc.).

DISCOURSE VII.

USE AND ABUSE OF THE SENSE OF THE VANITY OF THE WORLD.

"The world passeth away, and the lust thereof: but he that doeth the will of God abideth for ever."—1 John ii. 17.

THE connection of the passage in which these words occur is not difficult to trace, for those who are used to follow those "roots below the stream," those real rather than verbal links latent in the substance of St. John's thoughts. He addresses those whom he has in view with a paternal authority, as his "sons" in the faith—with an endearing variation as "little children." He reminds them of the wisdom and strength involved in their Christian life. Theirs is the sweetest flower of knowledge—"to know the Father." Theirs is the grandest crown of victory—"to overcome the wicked one." But there remains an enemy in one sense more dangerous than the evil one—the world. By the world in this place we are to understand that element in the material and human sphere, in the region of mingled good and evil, which is external to God, to the influence of His Spirit, to the boundaries of His Church—nay, which frequently passes over those boundaries. In this sense it is, so to speak, a fictitious world, a world of wills separated from God because dominated by self; a shadowy caricature of creation; an anti-kosmos, which the Author of the kosmos has not made. What has

been well called "the great love not" rings out—"love not the world." For this admonition two reasons of ever enduring validity are given by St. John. (1) The application of the law of human nature, that two master-passions cannot co-exist in one man. "If any man love the world, the love of the Father is not in him." (2) The unsatisfactory nature of the world, its incurable transitoriness, its "visible tendency to non-existence." "The world passeth away, and the lust thereof."

It will be well to consider how far this thought of the transitoriness of the world, of its drifting by in ceaseless change, is in itself salutary and Christian, how far it needs to be supplemented and elevated by that which follows and closes the verse.[1]

I.

There can be no doubt, then, that up to a certain point this conviction is a necessary element of Christian thought, feeling, and character; that it is at least among the preliminaries of a saving reception of Christ.

There is in the great majority of the world a surprising and almost incredible levity. There is a disposition to believe in the permanency of that which we have known to continue long, and which has become habitual. There is a tale of a man who was resolved

---

[1] παράγεται. It has been said that this is not the real point; that what St. John here describes is not the general attribute of the world as transitory, but its condition at the moment when the Epistle was written, in presence of the manifestation of "the kingdom of God, which was daily shining forth." But surely the world can scarcely be so completely identified with the temporary framework of the Roman Empire; and the *universality* of the antithesis (ὁ δὲ ποιῶν κ.τ.λ.) and its intensely *individual* form, lead us to take κόσμος in that universal and inclusive signification which alone is of abiding interest to every age.

to keep from his children the knowledge of *death*.   He
was the Governor of a colony, and had lost in succession
his wife and many children.   Two only, mere infants,
were left.   He withdrew to a beautiful and secluded
island, and tried to barricade his daughters from the
fatal knowledge which, when once acquired, darkens
the spirit with anticipation.   In the ocean-island death
was to be a forbidden word.   If met with in the pages
of a book, and questions were asked, no answer was
to be given.   If some one expired, the body was to be
removed, and the children were to be told that the
departed had gone to another country.   It does not
need much imagination to feel sure that the secret could
not be kept ; that some fish lying on the coral reef, or
some bright bird killed in the tropic forest, gave the
little ones the hint of a something that touched the
splendour of the sunset with a strange presentiment ;
that some hour came when, as to the rest of us, so to
them, the mute presence would insist upon being made
known.   Ours is a stranger mode of dealing with ourselves than was the father's way of dealing with his
children.   We tacitly resolve to play a game of make-
believe with ourselves, to forget that which cannot be forgotten, to remove to an incalculable distance that which is
inexorably near.   And the fear of death with us does not
come from the nerves, but from the will.   Death ushers
us into the presence of God.   Those of whom we speak
hate and fear death because they fear God, and hate
His presence.   Now it is necessary for such persons
as these to be awakened from their illusion.   That
which is supremely important for them is to realise
that " the world " is indeed " drifting by ;" that there
is an emptiness in all that is created, a vanity in all
that is not eternal ; that time is short, eternity long.

They must be brought to see that with the world, the
"lust thereof" (the concupiscence, the lust of it, which
has the world for its object, which belongs to it, and
which the world stimulates) passes by also. The world,
which is the object of the desire, is a phantom and a
shadow; the desire itself must be therefore the phantom
of a phantom and the shadow of a shadow.

This conviction has a thousand times over led human
souls to the one true abiding centre of eternal reality.
It has come in a thousand ways. It has been said
that one heard the fifth chapter of Genesis read, with
those words eight times repeated over the close of each
record of longevity, like the strokes of a funeral bell,
"*and he died;*" and that the impression never left him,
until he planted his foot upon the rock over the tide
of the changing years. Sometimes this conviction is
produced by the death of friends—sometimes by the
slow discipline of life—sometimes no doubt it may be
begun, sometimes deepened, by the preacher's voice upon
the watch-night, by the effective ritualism of the tolling
bell, of the silent prayer, of the well-selected hymn.
And it is right that the world's dancing in, or drinking
in, the New Year, should be a hint to Christians
to pray it in. This is one of the happy plagiarisms
which the Church has made from the world. The
heart feels as it never did before the truth of St. John's
sad, calm, oracular survey of existence. " The world
passeth away, and the lust thereof."

II.

But we have not sounded the depth of the truth—
certainly we have not exhausted St. John's meaning
—until we have asked something more. Is this conviction alone always a herald of salvation ? Is it

always, taken by itself, even salutary ?   Can it never
be exaggerated, and become the parent of evils almost
greater than those which it supersedes ?

We are led by careful study of the Bible to conclude
that this sentiment of the flux of things *is* capable of
exaggeration.   For there is one important principle
which arises from a comparison of the Old Testament
with the New in this matter.

It is to be noticed that the Old Testament has indefinitely more which corresponds to the first proposition of the text, without the qualification which follows
it, than we can find in the New.

The patriarch Job's experience echoes in our ears.
"Man that is born of a woman hath but a short time to
live, and is full of misery.   He cometh up, and is cut
down, like a flower ; he fleeth as it were a shadow, and
never continueth in one stay."[1]   The Funeral Psalms
make their melancholy chant.   "Behold, Thou hast made
my days as it were a span long. . . . Verily every man
living is altogether vanity.   For man walketh in a vain
shadow, and disquieteth himself in vain. . . . O spare me
a little that I may smile again."[2]   Or we read the words of
Moses, the man of God, in that ancient psalm of his, that
hymn of time and of eternity.   All that human speech
can say is summed up in four words, the truest, the
deepest, the saddest and the most expressive, that ever
fell from any mortal pen.   "We bring our years to an end,
as a sigh."[3]   Each life is a sigh between two eternities !

Our point is, that in the New Testament there is
greatly less of this element—greatly less of this pathetic
moralising upon the vanity and fragility of human life,

---

[1] Job xiv. 1, 2.   Cf. x. 20-22.
[2] Such seems to be the meaning of אַבְלִיגָה (Ps. xxxix. 14).
[3] Ps. xc. 9.

of which we have only cited a few examples—and that
what there is lies in a different atmosphere, with
sunnier and more cheerful surroundings. Indeed, in
the whole compass of the New Testament there is
perhaps but one passage which is set quite in the same
key with our familiar declamations upon the uncertainty
and shortness of human life—where St. James desires
Christians ever to remember in all their projects to
make deduction for the will of God, "not knowing
what shall be on the morrow."[1]   In the New Testament the voice, which wails for a second about the
changefulness and misery, is lost in the triumphant
music by which it is encompassed. If earthly goods
are depreciated, it is not merely because "the load of
them troubles, the love of them taints, the loss of them
tortures;"[2] it is because better things are ready.
There is no lamentation over the change, no clinging
to the dead past. The tone is rather one of joyful
invitation.   "Your raft is going to pieces in the
troubled sea of time; step into a gallant ship.   The
volcanic isle on which you stand is undermined by
silent fires; we can promise to bring you with us to a
shore of safety where you shall be compassed about
with songs of deliverance."

It is no doubt true to urge that this style of thought
and language is partly to be ascribed to a desire that
the attention of Christians should be fixed on the return
of their Lord, rather than upon their own death.   But,

---

[1] James iv. 13-17. The passage 1 Pet. i. 25 is taken from the magnificent prophecy in which the fragility of all flesh, transitory as the
falling away of the flowers of grass into impalpable dust, is contrasted
with the eternity of the word of God. Isa. xl. 6, 7, LXX.

[2] "Possessa onerant, amata inquinant, amissa cruciant."—*St
Bernard.*

if we believe Scripture to have been written under
Divine guidance, the history of religion may supply us
with good grounds for the absence of all exaggeration
from its pages in speaking of the misery of life and the
transitoriness of the world.

The largest religious experiment in the world, the
history of a religion which at one time numerically ex-
ceeded Christendom, is a gigantic proof that it is *not*
safe to allow unlimited licence to melancholy speculation.   The true symbol for humanity is not a skull
and an hour glass.

Some two thousand five hundred years ago, towards
the end of the seventh century before Christ, at the
foot of the mountains of Nepaul, in the capital of a
kingdom of Central India, an infant was born whom
the world will never forget.   All gifts seemed to be
showered on this child.   He was the son of a powerful
king and heir to his throne.   The young Siddhârtha
was of rare distinction, brave and beautiful, a thinker and
a hero, married to an amiable and fascinating princess.
But neither a great position nor domestic happiness
could clear away the cloud of melancholy which hung
over Siddhârtha, even under that lovely sky.   His deep
and meditative soul dwelt night and day upon the
mystery of existence.   He came to the conclusion that
the life of the creature is incurably evil from three
causes—from the very fact of existence, from desire,
and from ignorance.   The things revealed by sense are
evil.   None has that continuance and fixity which is
the mark of *Law*, and the attainment of which is the
condition of happiness.   At last his resolution to leave
all his splendour and become an ascetic was irrevocably
fixed.   One splendid morning the prince drove to a
glorious garden.   On his road he met a repulsive old

man, wrinkled, toothless, bent.   Another day, a wretched
being wasted with fever crossed his path.   Yet a third
excursion—and a funeral passes along the road with a
corpse on an open bier, and friends wailing as they go.
His favourite attendant is obliged in each case to confess
that these evils are not exceptional—that old age, sickness, and death, are the fatal conditions of conscious
existence for all the sons of men.   Then the Prince
Royal takes his first step towards becoming the deliverer
of humanity.   He cries—" woe, woe to the youth which
old age must destroy, to the health which sickness
must undermine, to the life which has so few days
and is so full of evil."   Hasty readers are apt to judge
that the Prince was on the same track with the Patriarch
of Idumea, and with Moses the man of God in the
desert—nay, with St. John, when he writes from
Ephesus that " the world passeth away, and the lust
thereof."

It may be well to reconsider this; to see what contradictory principle lies under utterances which have
so much superficial resemblance.

Siddhártha became known as the Bouddha, the
august founder of a great and ancient religion.   That
religion has of later years been favourably compared
with Christianity—yet what are its necessary results,
as drawn out for us by those who have studied it most
deeply?   Scepticism, fanatic hatred of life, incurable
sadness in a world fearfully misunderstood; rejection
of the personality of man, of God, of the reality of
Nature.   Strange enigma!   The Bouddha sought to
win annihilation by good works; everlasting non-
being by a life of purity, of alms, of renunciation, of
austerity.   The prize of his high calling was not everlasting life, but everlasting death; for what else is

impersonality, unconsciousness, absorption into the universe, but the negation of human existence? The acceptance of the principles of Bouddhism is simply a sentence of death intellectually, morally, spiritually, almost physically, passed upon the race which submits to the melancholy bondage of its creed of desolation. It is the opium drunkenness of the spiritual world without the dreams that are its temporary consolation. It is enervating without being soft, and contemplative without being profound. It is a religion which is spiritual without recognising the soul, virtuous without the conception of duty, moral without the admission of liberty, charitable without love. It surveys a world without nature, and a universe without God.[1] The human soul under its influence is not so much drunken as asphyxiated by a monotonous unbalanced perpetual repetition of one half of the truth—"the world passeth away, and the lust thereof."

For let us carefully note that St. John adds a qualification which preserves the balance of truth. Over against the dreary contemplation of the perpetual flux of things, he sets a constant course of *doing*—over against the *world*, God in His deepest, truest personality, "*the will of God*"—over against the fact of our having a short time to live, and being full of misery, an everlasting *fixity*, "*he abideth for ever*"—(so well brought out by the old gloss which slipped into the Latin text, "even as God abideth for ever"). As the Lord had taught before, so the disciple now teaches, of the rock-like solidity, of the permanent abiding, under and over him who "*doeth*." Of the devotee who became in his

---

[1] The view here taken of Bouddhism follows that of M. J. Barthelemy St. Hilaire. *Le Bouddha et sa Réligion.* Prémière partie, chap. v., pp. 141-182.

turn the Bouddha, Çakhya-Mouni could not have said one word of the close of our text. "*He*"—but human personality is lost in the triumph of knowledge. "*Doeth the will of God*"—but God is ignored, if not denied.[1] "*Abideth for ever*"—but that is precisely the object of his aversion, the terror from which he wishes to be emancipated at any price, by any self-denial.

It may be supposed that this strain of thought is of little practical importance. It may be of use, indeed, in other lands to the missionary who is brought into contact with forms of Bouddhism in China, India, or Ceylon, but not to us in these countries. In truth it is not so. It is about half a century ago since a great English theologian warned his University that the central principle of Bouddhism was being spread far and wide in Europe from Berlin. This propaganda is not confined to philosophy. It is at work in literature generally, in poetry, in novels, above all in those collections of "Pensées" which have become so extensively popular. The unbelief of the last century advanced with flashing epigrams and defiant songs. With Byron it softened at times into a melancholy which was perhaps partly affected. But with Amiel, and others of our own day, unbelief assumes a sweet and dirge-like tone. The satanic mirth of the past unbelief is exchanged for a satanic melancholy in the present. Many currents of thought run into our hearts, and all are tinged with a darkness before unknown from new substances in the soil which colours the waters. There

---

[1] "These populations neither deny nor affirm God. They simply ignore Him. To assert that they are atheists would be very much the same thing as to assert that they are anti-Cartesians. As they are neither for nor against Descartes, so they are neither for nor against God. They are just children. A child is neither atheist nor deist. He is nothing."—Voltaire, *Dict. Phil.*, Art. *Athéisme.*

is little fear of our not hearing enough, great fear of
our hearing too much, of the proposition—"the world
passeth away, and the lust thereof."

All this may possibly serve as some explanation for
the fact that the Christian Church, as such, has no fast
for the last day of the year, no festival for New Year's
Day except one quite unconnected with the lessons
which may be drawn from the flight of time. The
death of the old year, the birth of the new year, have
touching associations for us. But the Church conse-
crates no death but that of Jesus and His martyrs, no
nativity but that of her Lord, and of one whose birth
was directly connected with His own—John the Baptist.[1]
A cause of this has been found in the fact that the day
had become so deeply contaminated by the abominations
of the heathen *Saturnalia* that it was impossible in the
early Church to continue any very marked observation
of it. This may well be so; but it is worth considering
whether there is not another and deeper reason. Nothing
that has now been said can be supposed to militate against
the observance of this time by Christians in private,
with solemn penitence for the transgressions of the
past year, and earnest prayer for that upon which we
enter—nothing against the edification of particular
congregations by such services as those most striking

---

[1] It is noteworthy that in the collects in the English Prayer-Book,
and indeed in its public formularies generally (outside the Funeral
Service, and that for the Visitation of the Sick), there are but two
places in which the note of the "world passeth away" is very
prominently struck, viz., the Collect for the Fourth Sunday after
Easter, and one portion of the prayer for "The Church Militant."
One of the most wholesome and beautiful expressions of the salutary
convictions arising from Christian perception of this melancholy
truth is to be found in Dr. Johnson's "Prayer for the Last Day in
the Year," as given in Mr. Stobart's *Daily Services for Christian
Households*, pp. 99, 100.

ones which are held in so many places. But some explanation is supplied why the "Watch-night" is not recognised in the calendar of the Church.

Let us take our verse together as a whole and we have something better than moralising over the flight of time and the transitoriness of the world; something better than vulgarising "vanity of vanities" by vapid iteration.

It is hard to conceive a life in which death and evanescence have nothing that enforces their recognition. Now the removal of one dear to us, now a glance at the obituary with the name of some one of almost the same age as ourselves, brings a sudden shadow over the sunniest field. Yet surely it is not wholesome to encourage the perpetual presence of the cloud. We might impose upon ourselves the penance of being shut up all a winter's night with a corpse, go half crazy with terror of that unearthly presence, and yet be no more spiritual after all.[1] We must learn to look at death in a different way, with new eyes. We all know how different dead faces are. Some speak to us merely of material ugliness, of the sweep of "decay's effacing fingers." In others a new idea seems to light up the face; there is the touch of a superhuman irradiation, of a beauty from a hidden life. We feel that we look on one who has seen Christ, and say—"we shall be like Him, for we shall see Him as He is." These two kinds of faces answer to the two different views of life.

Not the transitory, but the permanent; not the fleeting, but the abiding; not death but life, is the conclusion of the whole matter. The Christian life is not an initial spasm followed by a chronic dyspepsia. What does St. John give us as the picture of it

---

[1] The old "Memento Mori" timepiece of Mary, Queen of Scots, is a watch in the interior of a death's-head, which opens to disclose it. Surely not a symbol likely to make any soul happier or better !

exemplified in a believer? Daily, perpetual, constant
doing the will of God. This is the end far beyond—
somewhat inconsistent with—obstinately morbid meditation and surrounding ourselves with multiplied images
of mortality. Lying in a coffin half the night might
not lead to that end; nay, it might be a hindrance
thereto. Beyond the grave, outside the coffin, is the
object at which we are to look. "The current of
things temporal," cries Augustine, "sweeps along.
But like a tree over that stream has risen our Lord
Jesus Christ. He willed to plant Himself as it were
over the river. Are you whirled along by the current?
Lay hold of the wood. Does the love of the world roll
you onward in its course? Lay hold upon Christ.
For you He became temporal that you might become
eternal. For He was so made temporal as to remain
eternal. Join thy heart to the eternity of God, and
thou shalt be eternal with Him."

Those who have heard the Miserere in the Sistine
Chapel describe the desolation which settles upon the
soul which surrenders itself to the impression of the
ritual. As the psalm proceeds, at the end of each
rhythmical pulsation of thought, each beat of the alter-
nate wings of the parallelism, a light upon the altar is
extinguished. As the wail grows sadder the darkness
grows deeper. When all the lights are out and the
last echo of the strain dies away, there would be something suitable for the penitent's mood in the words—
"the world passeth away, and the lust thereof." Upon
the altar of the Christian heart there are tapers at first
unlighted, and before it a priest in black vestments. But
one by one the vestments are exchanged for others which
are white; one after another the lamps are lighted slowly
and without noise, until gradually, we know not how,

11

the whole place is full of light.   And ever sweeter and
clearer, calm and happy, with a triumph which is at first
repressed and reverential, but which increases as the
light becomes diffused, the words are heard strong and
quiet—a plain-song now that will swell into an anthem
presently—"he that doeth the will of God abideth
for ever."

NOTES.

Ch. ii. 12-17.

Ver. 12, 13, 14.   These verses cannot properly be divided
so as to embrace three departments of spiritual, answering to
three departments of natural, life.   All believers are addressed
authoritatively as "children" in the faith, *tenderly* as "little
children;" then subdivided into two classes only, "fathers,"
and "young men."   *Confirmation* is justly found implied here.

Ver. 16.   Hardy's comment is quaint, and interesting.
"These three are 'all that is in the world;' they are the
world's cursed trinity; according to that of the poet,

> Ambitiosus honos, et opes, et fœda voluptas;
> Hæc tria pro trino numine mundus habet,

which wicked men adore and worship as deities; in which
regard Lapide opposeth them to the three persons in the
blessed Trinity: the lust of the eyes to the Father, who is
liberal in communicating His essence to the Son and the
Spirit; the lust of the flesh to the Son, whose generation is
spiritual and eternal; the pride of life to the Holy Ghost,
who is the Spirit of humility.   That golden calf, which, being
made, was set up and worshipped by the Israelites in the
wilderness, is not unfitly made use of to represent these: the
calf, which is a wanton creature, an emblem of the lust of
flesh; the gold of the calf, referring to the lust of the eyes;
and the exalting it, to the pride of life.   Oh, how do the most
of men fall down before this golden calf which the world
erecteth."

In tracing the various senses of "the world" we have not
dwelt prominently upon the conception of the world as embodied

in the Roman Empire, and in the city of Rome as its seat—an empire standing over against the Church as the Kingdom of God.   The ἀλαζονία τοῦ βίου may be projected outwardly, and set in a material framework in the gorgeous description of the wealth and luxury of Rome in Apoc. xviii. 11-14.   M. Rénan finds in the Apocalypse the cry of horror of a witness who has been at Rome, seen the martyrdom of brethren, and been himself near death. (Apoc. i. 9, vi. 9, xiii. 10, xx. 4; cf. *L'Antechrist*, pp. 197, 199. Surely Apoc xviii. 20 adds a strong testimony to the martyrdom of Peter and Paul at Rome.) So early a witness as Tertullian gives the story of St. John's having been plunged into the boiling oil without injury to him before his exile at Patmos. (*De Præscr. Hær.*, 36). The Apocryphal 'Acta Iohannis' (known to Eusebius and to St. Augustine), relates at length an interview at Rome between Domitian and St. John—not without interest, in spite of some miraculous embellishment. *Acta. Apost. Apoc.* Tischendorf, 266-271.

SECTION IV.

GREEK.

Παιδία, ἐσχάτη ὥρα ἐστίν· καὶ καθὼς ἠκούσατε ὅτι ὁ ἀντίχριστος ἔρχεται, καὶ νῦν ἀντίχριστοι πολλοὶ γεγόνασιν· ὅθεν γινώσκομεν ὅτι ἐσχάτη ὥρα ἐστίν. Ἐξ ἡμῶν ἐξῆλθαν, ἀλλ᾽ οὐκ ἦσαν ἐξ ἡμῶν. εἰ γὰρ ἐξ ἡμῶν ἦσαν, μεμενήκεισαν ἂν μεθ᾽ ἡμῶν· ἀλλ᾽ ἵνα φανερωθῶσιν ὅτι οὐκ εἰσὶν πάντες ἐξ ἡμῶν. Καὶ ὑμεῖς χρίσμα ἔχετε ἀπὸ τοῦ ἁγίου, καὶ οἴδατε πάντα. οὐκ ἔγραψα ὑμῖν, ὅτι οὐκ οἴδατε τὴν ἀλήθειαν, ἀλλ᾽ ὅτι οἴδατε αὐτήν, καὶ ὅτι πᾶν ψεῦδος ἐκ τῆς ἀληθείας οὐκ ἔστιν. Τίς ἐστιν ὁ ψεύστης, εἰ μὴ ὁ ἀρνούμενος ὅτι Ἰησοῦς οὐκ ἔστιν ὁ Χριστός; οὗτός ἐστιν ὁ ἀντίχριστος, ὁ ἀρνούμενος τὸν πατέρα καὶ τὸν υἱόν, πᾶς ὁ ἀρνούμενος τὸν υἱόν, οὐδὲ τὸν πατέρα ἔχει. ὁ ὁμολογῶν τὸν υἱὸν καὶ τὸν πατέρα ἔχει. Ὑμεῖς ὃ ἠκούσατε ἀπ᾽ ἀρχῆς,

LATIN.

Filioli, novissima hora est: et sicut audistis quia antichristus venit, nunc autem antichristi multi facti sunt, unde scimus quia novissima hora est. Ex nobis prodierunt, sed non erant ex nobis, nam si fuissent ex nobis, permansissent utique nobiscum; sed ut manifesti sint quoniam non sunt omnes ex nobis. Sed vos unctionem habetis a Sancto, et nostis omnia. Non scripsi vobis quasi ignorantibus veritatem, sed quasi scientibus eam, et quoniam omne mendacium ex veritate non est. Quis est mendax, nisi qui negat quoniam Iesus non est Christus? Hic est antichristus, qui negat Patrem et Filium. Omnis qui negat Filium nec Patrem habet: qui confitetur Filium, et Patrem habet. Vos quod audistis ab initio, in vobis permaneat.

AUTHORISED VERSION.

Little children, it is the last time: and as ye have heard that antichrist shall come, even now there are many antichrists; whereby we know that it is the last time. They went out from us, but they were not of us; for if they had been of us, they would no doubt have continued with us: but they went out, that they might be made manifest that they were not all of us. But ye have an unction from the Holy One, and ye know all things. I have not written unto you be-cause ye know not the truth, but because ye know it, and that no lie is of the truth. Who is a liar but he that denieth that Jesus is the Christ? He is antichrist, that denieth the Father and the Son. Whosoever denieth the Son, the same hath not the Father: [but] he

REVISED VERSION.

Little children, it is the last hour: and as ye heard that antichrist cometh, even now have there arisen many antichrists; whereby we know that it is the last hour. They went out from us, but they were not of us; for if they had been of us, they would have continued with us: but they went out, that they might be made manifest how that they are not of us. And ye have an anointing from the Holy One, and ye know all things. I have not written unto you because ye know not the truth, but be-cause ye know it, and because no lie is of the truth. Who is the liar but he that denieth that Jesus is the Christ? This is the antichrist, even he that denieth the Father and the Son. Whosoever denieth the Son, the same hath not the

ANOTHER VERSION.

Little children, it is a last hour; and as ye heard that antichrist cometh, so now many antichrists are in exist-ence; whereby we know that it is a last hour. They went out from us, but they were not of us; for if they had been of us they would have continued with us: but that they might be made mani-fest how that all are not of us, *they all went out.* But ye have unction from the Holy One, and ye know all things. I have not written unto you *this*—"ye know not the truth"—but *this* —"ye know it," and *this*—"every lie is not from the truth." Who is the liar but he that denieth that Jesus is the Christ? The anti-christ is this, he that denieth the Father and the Son. Whosoever denieth the Son the same hath not the Father; he that con-

ἐν ὑμῖν μενέτω. ἐὰν ἐν ὑμῖν μείνῃ ὃ ἀπ᾽ ἀρχῆς ἠκούσατε, καὶ ὑμεῖς ἐν τῷ υἱῷ καὶ ἐν τῷ πατρὶ μενεῖτε. καὶ αὕτη ἐστὶν ἡ ἐπαγγελία, ἣν αὐτὸς ἐπηγγείλατο ἡμῖν, τὴν ζωὴν τὴν αἰώνιον. ταῦτα ἔγραψα ὑμῖν περὶ τῶν πλανώντων ὑμᾶς. καὶ ὑμεῖς τὸ χρῖσμα ὃ ἐλάβατε ἀπ᾽ αὐτοῦ, μένει ἐν ὑμῖν, καὶ οὐ χρείαν ἔχετε ἵνα τις διδάσκῃ ὑμᾶς· ἀλλ᾽ ὡς τὸ αὐτοῦ χρῖσμα διδάσκει ὑμᾶς περὶ πάντων, καὶ ἀληθές ἐστιν, καὶ οὐκ ἔστιν ψεῦδος, καὶ καθὼς ἐδίδαξεν ὑμᾶς, μένετε ἐν αὐτῷ. Καὶ νῦν, τεκνία, μένετε ἐν αὐτῷ· ἵνα ὅταν φανερωθῇ, σχῶμεν παρρησίαν, καὶ μὴ αἰσχυνθῶμεν ἀπ᾽ αὐτοῦ, ἐν τῇ παρουσίᾳ αὐτοῦ.

Si in vobis permanserit quod ab initio audistis, et vos in Filio et Patre manebitis. Et hæc est promissio quam ipse pollicitus est vobis, vitam æternam. Hæc scripsi vobis de his qui seducunt vos. Et vos unctionem quam accepistis ab eo, maneat in vobis; et non necesse habetis ut aliquis doceat vos, sed sicut unctio eius docet vos de omnibus, et verum est, et non est mendacium, et sicut docuit vos manete in eo. Et nunc, filioli, manete in eo, ut cum apparuerit habemus fiduciam, et non confundamur ab eo in adventu eius.

that acknowledgeth the Son hath the Father also. Let that therefore abide in you, which ye have heard from the beginning. If that which ye have heard from the beginning shall remain in you, ye also shall continue in the Son, and in the Father. And this is the promise that He hath promised us, *even* eternal life. These *things* have I written unto you concerning them that seduce you. But the anointing which ye have received of Him abideth in you, and ye need not that any man teach you: but as the same anointing teacheth you of all things, and is truth, and is no lie, and even as it hath taught you, ye shall abide in Him. And now, little children, abide in Him; that, when He shall appear, we may have confidence, and not be ashamed before Him at His coming.

Father: he that confesseth the Son hath the Father also. As for you, let that abide in you which ye heard from the beginning. If that which ye have heard from the beginning abide in you, ye also shall abide in the Son, and in the Father. And this is the promise which He promised us, *even* the life eternal. These *things* have I written unto you concerning them that would lead you astray. And as for you, the anointing which ye received of Him abideth in you, and ye need not that any one teach you; but as His anointing teacheth you concerning all things, and is true, and is no lie, and even as it hath taught you, ye abide in Him. And now, little children, abide in Him; that, when He shall appear, we may have confidence, and not be ashamed before Him at His coming.

fesseth the Son also hath the Father. As for you—that which ye heard from the beginning let it abide in you. If that abide in you which from the beginning ye heard, ye also shall abide in the Son and in the Father. And this is the promise which He promised us, the life, the eternal *life.* These things have I written unto you concerning those that would mislead you. And as for you—the anointing which ye received from Him abideth in you, and ye have no need that any be teaching you: but as His unction is teaching you continually concerning all things, and is true, and is not a lie, and as it taught you, so shall ye abide in Him. And now, children, abide in Him, that if He shall be manifested we may have boldness and not shrink in shame from Him in His coming.

DISCOURSE VIII.

KNOWING ALL THINGS.

"But ye have an unction from the Holy One, and ye know all things."—1 JOHN ii. 20.

THERE is little of the form of logical argument to which Western readers are habituated in the writings of St. John, steeped as his mind was in Hebraic influences. The inferential "therefore" is not to be found in this Epistle.[1] Yet the diligent reader

---

[1] The οὖν in ver. 24 is not recognised by the R. V. nor adopted in Professor Westcott's text. One uncial (A), however, inserts it in 1 John iv. 19. It occurs in 3 John 8. This inferential particle is found with unusual frequency in St. John's Gospel. It does not seem satisfactory to account for this by calling it "one of the beginnings of modern Greek." (B. de Xivrey.) By St. John as an *historian*, the frequent *therefore* is the spontaneous recognition of a Divine logic of events; of the necessary yet natural sequence of every incident in the life of the "Word made Flesh." The οὖν expresses something more than continuity of narrative. It indicates a connection of events so interlinked that each springs from, and is joined with, the preceding, as if it were a conclusion which followed from the premiss of the Divine argument. Now a mind which views *history* in this light is just the mind which will be *dogmatic* in theology. The inspired dogmatic theologian will necessarily write in a style different from that of the theologian of the Schools. The style of the former will be *oracular;* that of the latter will be *scholastic,* *i.e.,* inferential, a concatenation of syllogisms. The syllogistic οὖν is then naturally absent from St. John's Epistles. The one undoubted exception is 3 John 8, where a practical inference is drawn from an historical statement in ver. 7. The writer may be allowed to refer to *The Speaker's Commentary,* iv., 381.

or expositor finds it more difficult to detach any single
sentence, without loss to the general meaning, than
in any other writing of the New Testament. The
sentence may look almost as if its letters were graven
brief and large upon a block of marble, and stood out
in oracular isolation—but upon reverent study it will be
found that the seemingly lapidary inscription is one of
a series with each of which it is indissolubly connected—
sometimes limited, sometimes enlarged, always coloured
and influenced by that which precedes and follows.

It is peculiarly needful to bear this observation in
mind in considering fully the almost startling principle
stated in the verse which is prefixed to this discourse.
A kind of spiritual omniscience appears to be attributed
to believers. Catechisms, confessions, creeds, teachers,
preachers, seem to be superseded by a stroke of the
Apostle's pen, by what we are half tempted to consider
as a magnificent exaggeration. The text sounds as if
it outstripped even the fulfilment of the promise of the
new covenant contained in Jeremiah's prophecy—" they
shall teach no more every man his neighbour, and every
man his brother, saying, Know the Lord : for they shall
all know Me, from the least of them unto the greatest
of them."[1]

The passages just before and after St. John's splendid
annunciation[2] in our text are occupied with the subject
of Antichrist, here first mentioned in Scripture. In
this section of our Epistle Antichrist is (1) *revealed*,
and (2) *refuted*.

(1) Antichrist is revealed by the very crisis which
the Church was then traversing. From this especially,
from the transitory character of a world drifting by

---

[1] Jer. xxxi. 34.   [2] Vers. 18, 22.

them in unceasing mutation, the Apostle is led to consider this as one of those crisis-hours of the Church's history, each of which may be *the* last hour, and which is assuredly—in the language of primitive Christianity —*a* last hour. The Apostle therefore exclaims with fatherly affection—" Little children, it is a last hour."[1]

Deep in the heart of the Apostolic Church, because it came from those who had received it from Christ, there was one awful anticipation. St. John in this passage gives it a name. He remembers Who had told the Jews that " if another shall come in his own name, him ye will receive."[2] He can announce to them that " as ye have heard this Antichrist cometh, even so now " (precisely as ye have heard) " many antichrists have come into existence and are around you, whereby we know that it is a last hour." The *name* Antichrist occurs only in these Epistles, and seems purposely intended to denote both one who occupies the place of Christ, and one who is against Christ. In " the Antichrist " the antichristian principle is personally concentrated. The conception of representative-men is one which has become familiar to modern students of the philosophy of history. Such representative-men, at once the products of the past, moulders of the present,

---

[1] The last hour is not a date arbitrarily chosen and written down as a man might mark a day for an engagement in a calendar. It is determined by history—by the sum-total of the product of the actions of men who are not the slaves of fatality, who possess free-will, and are not forced to act in a particular way. It is supposed to derogate from the Divine mission of the Apostles if we admit that they might be mistaken as to the chronology of the closing hour of time. But to know that supreme instant would involve a knowledge of the whole plan of God and the whole predetermining motives in the appointment of that day, *i.e.*, it would constructively involve *omniscience*. Cf. Mark xiii. 32, and our Lord's profound saying, Acts i. 7.

[2] John v. 43.

and creative of the future, sum up in themselves tendencies and principles good and evil, and project them
in a form equally compacted and intensified into the
coming generations. Shadows and anticipations of
Antichrist the holiest of the Church's sons have sometimes seen, even in the high places of the Church.
But it is evident that as yet the Antichrist has not
come. For wherever St. John mentions this fearful
impersonation of evil, he connects the manifestation
of his influence with absolute denial of the true Manhood, of the Messiahship, of the everlasting sonship
of Jesus, of the Father, Who is His and our Father.[1]
In negation of the Personality of God, in the substitution
of a glittering but unreal idea of human goodness and
active philanthropy for the historical Christ, we of this
age may not improbably hear his advancing footsteps,
and foresee the advent of a day when antichristianity
shall find its great representative-man.

(2) Antichrist is also refuted by a principle common
to the life of Christians and by its result.

The principle by which he is refuted is a gift of
insight lodged in the Church at large, and partaken of
by all faithful souls.

A hint of a solemn crisis had been conveyed to the
Christians of Asia Minor by secessions from the great
Christian community. " They went out from us, but
they were not of us ; for if they had been of us, they
would have continued with us (which they did not, but
went out) that they might be made manifest that not
all are of us."[2] Not only this. " Yea further, ye yourselves have a hallowing oil from Him who is hallowed,
a chrism from the Christ, an unction from the Holy One,

---

[1] I John ii. 22, iv. 2, 3 ; 2 John 7-9.
[2] Ver. 19.

even from the Son of God." Chrism (as we are reminded
by the most accurate of scholars) is always the *material*
with which anointing is performed, never the *act* of
anointing; it points to the unction of prophets, priests
and kings under the Old Testament, in whose sacrifices
and mystic language oil symbolises the Holy Spirit as
the spirit of joy and freedom. Quite possibly there
may be some allusion to a literal use of oil in Baptism
and Confirmation, which began at a very early period;[1]
though it is equally possible that the material may have
arisen from the spiritual, and not in the reverse order.
But beyond all question the real predominant reference
is to the Holy Ghost. In the chrism here mentioned
there is a feature characteristic of St. John's style. For
there is first a faint prelusive note which (as we find
in several other important subjects[2]) is faintly struck
and seems to die away, but is afterwards taken up,
and more fully brought out. The full distinct mention
of the Holy Spirit comes like a burst of the music of
the "Veni Creator," carrying on the fainter prelude
when it might seem to have been almost lost. The first
reverential, almost timid hint, is succeeded by another,
brief but significant—almost dogmatically expressive of
the relation of the Holy Spirit to Christ as *His* Chrism,
"the Chrism of Him."[3] We shall presently have a
direct mention of the Holy Ghost. "Hereby we know

---

[1] Bingham's *Antiquities.*, i., 462-524, 565.

[2] For other instances of this characteristic, see a subject *introduced*
ii. 29, *expanded* iii. 9—another subject *introduced* iii. 21, *expanded* v.
14.

[3] τὸ αὐτοῦ χρῖσμα, ver. 27, *not* τὸ αὐτό ("the same anointing," A. V.)
"This most unusual order throws a strong emphasis on the pronoun."
(Prof. Westcott.) The writer thankfully quotes this as it seems to
him to bring out the dogmatic significance of the word, emphasised
as it is by this unusual order—the chrism, the Spirit of *Him*.

that He abideth in us, from the Spirit which He gave us."[1]

Antichrist is refuted by a result of this great principle of the life of the Holy Spirit in the living Church. "Ye have" chrism from the Christ; Antichrist shall not lay his unhallowing disanointing hand upon you. As a result of this, "ye know all things."[2]

How are we to understand this startling expression?

If we receive any teachers as messengers commissioned by God, it is evident that their message must be communicated to us through the medium of human language. They come to us with minds that have been in contact with a *Mind* of infinite knowledge, and deliver utterances of universal import. They are therefore under an obligation to use language which is capable of being misunderstood by some persons. Our Lord and His Apostles so spoke at times. Two very different classes of men constantly misinterpret words like those of our text. The rationalist does so with a sinister smile; the fanatic with a cry of hysterical triumph. The first may point his epigram with effective reference to the exaggerated promise which is belied by the ignorance of so many ardent believers; the second may advance his absurd claim to personal infallibility in all things spiritual. Yet an Apostle calmly says—" ye have an unction from the Holy One, and ye know all things." This, however, is but another

---

[1] 1 John iii. 24.

[2] The reading of the A. V. is received into Tischendorf's text and adopted by the R. V. Another reading omits καί and substitutes πάντες for πάντα so that the passage would run thus, "Ye have an unction from the Holy One. Ye all know (I have not written unto you because ye know not) the truth." As far as the difficulty of πάντα is concerned, nothing is gained by the change, as the statement recurs in a slightly varied form in ver. 27.

asterisk directing the eye to the Master's promise in
the Gospel, which is at once the warrant and the explanation of the utterance here.   " The Holy Ghost,
whom the Father will send in My name, He shall *teach
you all things*, and bring all things to your remembrance,
whatsoever I have said unto you."[1]   The express limitation of the Saviour's promise is the implied limitation
of St. John's statement.   " The Holy Ghost has been
sent, according to this unfailing pledge. He teaches
you (and, if He teaches, you know) all things which
Christ has said, as far as their substance is written
down in a true record—all things of the new creation
spoken by our Lord, preserved by the help of the Spirit
in the memories of chosen witnesses with unfading
freshness, by the same Spirit unfolded and interpreted
to you."

We should observe in what spirit and to whom St.
John speaks.

He does not speak in the strain which would be
adopted by a missionary in addressing· men lately
brought out of heathenism into the fold of Christ.   He
does not like a modern preacher or tract-writer at once
divide his observations into two parts, one for the
converted, one for the unconverted ; all are his " dear
ones" as beloved, his "sons" as brought into close
spiritual relationship with himself.   He classes them
simply as young and old, with their respective graces
of strength and knowledge.   All are looked upon as
" abiding" ; almost the one exhortation is to abide unto
the end in a condition upon which all have already
entered, and in which some have long continued.   We
feel throughout the calmness and assurance of a spiritual

---

[1] John xiv. 26.

teacher writing to Christian men who had either been
born in the atmosphere of Christian tradition, or
had lived in it for many years. They are again and
again appealed to on the ground of a common Christian
confidence—" we know." They have all the articles
of the Christian creed, the great inheritance of a faithful summary of the words and works of Christ. The
Gospel which Paul at first preached in Asia Minor
was the starting point of the truth which remained
among them, illustrated, expanded, applied, but absolutely unaltered.[1] What the Christians whom St. John
has in view really want is the revival of familiar truths,
not the impartation of new. No spiritual voyage of
discovery is needed; they have only to explore well-
known regions. The memory and the affections must
be stimulated. The truths which have become "cramped
and bed-ridden" in the dormitory of the soul must
acquire elasticity from exercise. The accumulation of
ashes must be blown away, and the spark of fire
beneath fanned into flame. This capacity of revival,
of expansion, of quickened life, of developed truth, is
in the unction common to the faithful, in the latent
possibilities of the new birth. The same verse to
which we have before referred as the best interpreter
of this should be consulted again.[2] There is an instructive distinction between the tenses—"as His
unction *is teaching*"—"as it *taught* you."[3] The teaching

---

[1] "Let that abide in you which ye heard from the beginning,"
1 John ii. 24. Cf. "Testifying that this is the true grace of God wherein ye stand," 1 Pet. v. 12. "Even as our beloved brother Paul has
written unto you," 2 Pet. iii. 15. St. Paul has thus the attestation of
St. John as well as of St. Peter.

[2] Ver. 27

[3] διδάσκει—ἐδίδαξεν.

was once for all, the creed definite and fixed, the body of truth a sum-total looked upon as one. " The unction *taught.*" Once for all the Holy Spirit made known the Incarnation and stamped the recorded words of Christ with His seal. But there are depths of thought about His person which need to be reverently explored. There is an energy in His work which was not exhausted in the few years of its doing, and which is not imprisoned within the brief chronicle in which it is written. There is a spirit and a life in His words. In one aspect they have the strength of the tornado, which advances in a narrow line ; but every foot of the column, as if armed with a tooth of steel, grinds and cuts into pieces all which resists it. Those words have also depths of tenderness, depths of wisdom, into which eighteen centuries have looked down and never yet seen the last of their meaning. Advancing time does but broaden the interpretation of the wisdom and the sympathy of those words. Applications of their significance are being discovered by Christian souls in forms as new and manifold as the claims of human need. The Church collectively is like one sanctified mind meditating incessantly upon the Incarnation ; attaining more and more to an understanding of that character as it widens in a circle of glory round the form of its historical manifestation—considering how those words may be applied not only to self but to humanity. The new wants of each successive generation bring new help out of that inexhaustible store. The Church may have " decided opinions "; but she has not the "deep slumber" which is said to accompany them. How can *she* be fast asleep who is ever learning from a teacher Who is always supplying her with fresh and varied lessons ? The Church must be ever learning,

because the anointing which "taught" once for all is also ever "teaching."

This profound saying is therefore chiefly true of Christians as a whole. Yet each individual believer may surely have a part in it. "There is a teacher in the heart who has also a chair in heaven." "The Holy Spirit who dwells in the justified soul," says a pious writer, "is a great director." May we not add that He is a great catechist? In difficulties, whether worldly, intellectual, or spiritual, thousands for a time helpless and ignorant, in presence of difficulties through which they could not make their way, have found with surprise how true in the sequel our text has become to them.

For we all know how different things, persons, truths, ideas may become, as they are seen at different times and in different lights, as they are seen in relation to God and truth or outside that relation. The bread in Holy Communion is unchanged in *substance;* but some new and glorious relation is superadded to it. It is devoted by its consecration to the noblest *use* manward and Godward, so that St. Paul speaks of it with hushed reverence as "*The Body.*"[1] It seems to be a part of the same law that some one—once perhaps frivolous, common-place, sinful—is taken into the hand of the great High Priest, broken with sorrow and penitence, and blessed; and thereafter he is at once personally the same, and yet another higher and better by that awful consecration to another use. So again with some truth of creed or catechism which we have fallen into the fallacy of supposing that we know because it is familiar. It may be a truth that is sweet

---

[1] 1 Cor. xi. 29.

or one that is tremendous.   It awaits its consecration, its blessing, its transformation into a something which in itself is the same yet which is other to us.   That is to say, the familiar truth is old, in itself, in substance and expression.   It needs no other, and can have no better formula.   To change the formula would be to alter the truth ; but to us it is taught newly with a fuller and nobler exposition by the unction which is " ever teaching," whereby we " know all things."

NOTES.

Ch. ii. 18-28.

Ver. 18. A *last hour*,] ἐσχάτη ὥρα.   "Hour" is used in all St. John's writings of a definite point of time, which is also providentially fixed. (Cf. John xvii. 1 ; Apoc. iii. 3.)   In something of this elevated signification Shakespeare appears to employ the word in *The Tempest* in relation to his own life :

> *Prospero.*   "How's the day?"
> *Ariel.*   "On the *sixth hour ;* at which time, my lord,
> You said our work should cease."

Each decade of years is here looked upon as a providentially fixed duration of time.   The poet intended to retire from the work of imaginative poetry when his life should draw on towards sixty years of age.

Ver. 19. " It doth not appear, nor is it probable, that these antichrists, when gone out from the Apostles, did still pretend to the orthodox faith ; and therefore no need for the Apostle to make any provision against it. Nay, it is plainly intimated by the following discourse, that these antichrists being gone forth, did set themselves expressly, directly, against the orthodox, denying that Jesus, whom they did profess, to be the Christ ; and therefore the design of this clause is most rationally conceived to be the prevention of that scandal which their horrid apostasy might give to weak Christians ; nor could anything more effectually prevent or remove it, than to let them know that these antichristian apostates were never

true stars in the firmament of the Church, but only blazing comets, as their falling away did evidently demonstrate."—*Dean Hardy*. 309.

Ver. 19. To use the words of a once famous controversial divine, they may be said to be "of the Church presumptively in their own, and others' opinion, but not really." (*Spalat., lib.* vii., 10, cf. on the whole subject, *St. Aug. Lib. de Bono. Persev.,* viii.)

"Let no one count that the good can go forth from the Church ; the wind cannot carry away the wheat, nor the storm overthrow the solidly rooted tree. The light chaff is tossed by the wind, the weak trees go down before the blast. 'They went out from us, but they were not of us.' "—*S. Cyp., B. de Simplic.*

Ver. 24. *Ye shall abide in the Son, and in the Father.*] "If it be asked why the Son is put before the Father, the answer is well returned. Because the Apostle had just before inveighed against those who, though they pretended to acknowledge the Father, yet deny the Son. Though withal there may besides be a double reason assigned: the one to insinuate that the Son is not less than the Father, but that they are equal in essence and dignity. Upon this account most probable it is that the apostolical benediction beginneth with 'The grace of our Lord Jesus Christ,' and then followeth 'the love of God the Father.' The other, because, as Beda well glosseth, No man cometh in, or continueth in, the Father but by the Son, who saith of Himself, 'I am the way, the truth, and the life.'

"To draw it up, lo, here *Eximia laus doctrinæ,* an high commendation of evangelical doctrine, that it leads up to Christ, and by Him to the Father. The water riseth as high as the spring from whence it floweth. No wonder if the gospel, which cometh from God through Christ, lead us back again through Christ to God; and as by hearing and believing this doctrine we are united to, so by adhering to, and persevering in it, we continue in, the Son and the Father. Suitable to this is that promise of our blessed Saviour, John xiv. 23, 'If any man love Me he will keep My word, and My Father will love him, and we will come to him and make our abode with him.' "—*Dean Hardy*, 350.

Ver. 27. The connection of the whole section is well traced by the old divine, whose commentary closes a little below.

"If you compare these three with the eight foregoing verses, you shall find them to be a summary repetition of what is there more largely delivered. There are three hinges upon which the precedent discourse turneth, namely, the peril of antichristian doctrine, the benefit of the Spirit's unction, the duty of perseverance in the Christian faith ; and these three are inculcated in these verses. Indeed, where the danger is very great, the admonition cannot be too frequent. When the benefit is of singular advantage, it would be often considered, and a duty which must be performed cannot be too much pressed. No wonder if St. John proposed them in this gemination to our second thoughts. And yet it is not a naked repetition neither, but such as hath a variation and amplification in every particular. The duty is reinforced at the eight-and-twentieth verse, but in another phrase, of 'abiding in Christ,' and with a new motive, drawn from the second coming of Christ. The benefit is reiterated, and much amplified, in the seven-and-twentieth verse, as to its excellency and energy. Finally, the danger is repeated, but with another description of those by whom they were in danger; whilst as before he had called them antichrists for their enmity against Christ, so here, for their malignity against Christians, he calleth them seducers : 'These things have I written to you concerning them that seduce you,' etc."—*Dean Hardy*, 357.

SECTION V.

AUTHORISED VERSION.

If ye know that He is righteous, ye know that every one that doeth righteousness is born of Him. Behold, what manner of love the Father hath bestowed upon us, that we should be called the sons of God: therefore the world knoweth us not, because it knew Him not. Beloved, now are we the sons of God, and it doth not yet appear what we shall be: but we know that, when He shall appear, we shall be like Him; for we shall see Him as He is. And every man that hath this hope in Him purifieth himself, even as He is pure. Whosoever committeth sin transgresseth also the law; for sin is the transgression of the

REVISED VERSION.

If ye know that He is righteous, ye know that every one also that doeth righteousness is begotten of Him. Behold, what manner of love the Father hath bestowed upon us, that we should be called children of God: and such we are. For this cause the world knoweth us not, because it knew Him not. Beloved, now are we children of God, and it is not yet made manifest what we shall be. We know that, if He shall be manifested, we shall be like Him; for we shall see Him even as He is. And every one that hath this hope set on Him purifieth himself, even as He is pure. Every one that doeth sin doeth also

ANOTHER VERSION.

If ye know that He is righteous, ye are aware that every one who is doing righteousness is born of Him. Behold what manner of love the Father hath bestowed upon us that we should be called children of God;—and we are. Because of this the world knoweth us because it knew not Him. Beloved, now are we children of God, and it never yet was manifested what we shall be; but we know that if it shall be manifested we shall be like Him; for we shall see Him as He is. And every-one that hath this hope *fixed* on Him is ever purifying himself even as He is pure. Every one that is doing sin, is

GREEK.

ἐὰν εἰδῆτε ὅτι δίκαιός ἐστιν, γινώσκετε ὅτι πᾶς ὁ ποιῶν τὴν δικαιοσύνην ἐξ αὐτοῦ γεγέννηται. Ἴδετε ποταπὴν ἀγάπην δέδωκεν ἡμῖν ὁ πατήρ, ἵνα τέκνα Θεοῦ κληθῶμεν, καὶ ἐσμεν. διὰ τοῦτο ὁ κόσμος οὐ γινώσκει ἡμᾶς, ὅτι οὐκ ἔγνω αὐτόν. Ἀγαπητοί, νῦν τέκνα Θεοῦ ἐσμεν, καὶ οὔπω ἐφανερώθη τί ἐσόμεθα· οἴδαμεν ὅτι ἐὰν φανερωθῇ ὅμοιοι αὐτῷ ἐσόμεθα, ὅτι ὀψόμεθα αὐτὸν καθὼς ἐστιν. καὶ πᾶς ὁ ἔχων τὴν ἐλπίδα ταύτην ἐπ᾽ αὐτῷ, ἁγνίζει ἑαυτὸν καθὼς ἐκεῖνος ἁγνός ἐστιν. Πᾶς ὁ ποιῶν τὴν ἁμαρτίαν καὶ τὴν ἀνομίαν ποιεῖ· καὶ ἡ ἁμαρτία ἐστὶν ἡ ἀνομία. καὶ οἴδατε ὅτι ἐκεῖνος ἐφανερώθη ἵνα τὰς ἁμαρτίας ἄρῃ, καὶ ἁμαρτία ἐν αὐτῷ οὐκ ἔστιν. πᾶς ὁ ἐν αὐτῷ μένων οὐχ ἁμαρτάνει·

LATIN.

Si scitis quoniam iustus est, scitote quoniam omnis qui facit iustitiam ex ipso natus est. Videte qualem caritatem dedit nobis Pater ut filii Dei nominemur et simus. Propter hoc mundus non novit nos, quia non novit eum. Carissimi, nunc filii .Dei sumus et nondum apparuit quid erimus. Scimus quoniam cum apparuerit similes ei erimus, quoniam videbimus eum sicuti est. Et omnis qui habet spem hanc in eo sanctificat se, sicut et ille sanctus est. Omnis qui facit peccatum et iniquitatem facit, et peccatum est iniquitas. Et scitis quoniam ille apparuit ut peccata tolerit, et peccatum in eo non est. Omnis qui in eo manet

law. And ye know that He was manifested to take away our sins; and in Him is no sin. Whosoever abideth in Him sinneth not: whosoever sinneth hath not seen Him, neither known Him. Little children, let no man deceive you: he that doeth righteousness is righteous, even as He is righteous. He that committeth sin is of the devil; for the devil sinneth from the beginning. For this purpose the Son of God was manifested, that He might destroy the works of the devil. Whosoever is born of God doth not commit sin: for His seed remaineth in him: and he cannot sin, because he is born of God

lawlessness: and sin is lawlessness. And ye know that He was manifested to take away sins; and in Him is no sin. Whosoever abideth in Him sinneth not: whosoever sinneth hath not seen Him, neither knoweth Him. *My* little children, let no man lead you astray: he that doeth righteousness is righteous, even as He is righteous; he that doeth sin is of the devil; for the devil sinneth from the beginning. To this end was the Son of God manifested, that He might destroy the works of the devil. Whosoever is begotten of God doeth no sin, because His seed abideth in him; and he cannot sin, because he is begotten of God.

also doing lawlessness; and, *indeed*, sin is lawlessness. And ye know that He was manifested that He should take away sins; and sin in Him is not. Whosoever abideth in Him is not sinning; every one that is sinning hath not seen Him neither hath known Him. Little children, let no man mislead you; he that is doing righteousness is righteous, even as He is righteous: he that is doing sin is of the devil, because the devil is continually sinning from the beginning. Unto this end the Son of God was manifested that He might destroy the works of the devil. Whosoever is born of God is not doing sin for his seed abideth in Him, and he is not able to be sinning, because he is born of God.

non peccat, et omnis qui peccat non videt eum nec cognovit eum. Filioli, nemo vos seducat. Qui facit iustitiam, iustus est, sicut et ille iustus est: qui facit peccatum, ex diabolo est quoniam ab initio diabolus peccat. In hoc apparuit Filius Dei, ut dissolvat opera diaboli. Omnis qui natus est ex Deo peccatum non facit, quoniam semen ipsius in eo manet, et non potest peccare, quoniam ex Deo natus est

πᾶς ὁ ἁμαρτάνων οὐχ ἑώρακεν αὐτὸν οὐδὲ ἔγνωκεν αὐτόν. Παιδία, μηδεὶς πλανάτω ὑμᾶς· ὁ ποιῶν τὴν δικαιοσύνην δίκαιός ἐστιν, καθὼς ἐκεῖνος δίκαιός ἐστιν· ὁ ποιῶν τὴν ἁμαρτίαν ἐκ τοῦ διαβόλου ἐστίν, ὅτι ἀπ' ἀρχῆς ὁ διάβολος ἁμαρτάνει. εἰς τοῦτο ἐφανερώθη ὁ υἱὸς τοῦ Θεοῦ, ἵνα λύσῃ τὰ ἔργα τοῦ διαβόλου. πᾶς ὁ γεγεννημένος ἐκ τοῦ Θεοῦ ἁμαρτίαν οὐ ποιεῖ, ὅτι σπέρμα αὐτοῦ ἐν αὐτῷ μένει· καὶ οὐ δύναται ἁμαρτάνειν, ὅτι ἐκ τοῦ Θεοῦ γεγέννηται.

NOTES.

III. ver. 2. "*Hope fixed in Him*" or "*on* Him."] The English reader should note the capital letter; not hope in our hearts, but hope unfastened from self. Ἐπὶ σοὶ Κύριε ἤλπισα, is the LXX. translation of Psalm xxx. 1.

Is ever purifying himself.] "See how he does not do away with freewill; for he says *purifies himself*. Who purifies us but God? Yet God does not purify you when you are unwilling; therefore in joining your will to God you purify yourself." (St. Augustine *in loc.*)

We shall be like Him; for we shall see Him as He is.] "So then we are about to see a certain sight, excelling all beauties of the earth; the beauty of gold, silver, forest, fields—the beauty of sea and air, sun and moon—the beauty of stars—the beauty of angels. Aye, excelling all these, because all these are beautiful only for *it*. What, therefore, shall we be when we shall see all these? What is promised? *We shall be like Him; for we shall see Him as He is.* The tongue hath spoken as it could; let the rest be thought over by the heart" (St. Augustine *in loc.*). Cf. 2 Cor. iii. 18. "As the whole body, face, above all eyes of those who look towards the sun are *sunnied*" (insolantur).—*Bengel.*

Ver. 3. The ample stores of English divinity contain two sermons, one excellent, one beautiful, upon this verse. The first is by Paley; it is founded upon the leading thought, which he expresses with his usual manly common sense. "There are a class of Christians to whom the admonition of the text is peculiarly necessary. Finding it an easier thing to do good than to expel sins which cleave to their hearts, their affections, or their imaginations; they set their endeavours more towards *beneficence* than *purity*. Doing good

is not the whole of our duty, nor the most difficult part of it.
In particular it is not that part of it which is insisted upon in
our text." (Paley, Sermon XLIII.) But the second sermon is
perhaps the finest which ever came from the pen of South, and
he throws into it the full power of his heart and intellect. The
bare analysis is this :—

Is it indeed possible for a man to "purify himself"?
There is a twofold work of purification. (1) The infusing of
the habit of purity into the soul (regeneration or conversion).
In this respect, no man can purify himself. (2) The other
work of purification is exercising that habit or grace of purity.
"God who made, and since new made us, without ourselves,
will not yet save us without ourselves." But again, how can
a man purify himself to that degree *even as Christ is pure*?
Even as denotes similitude of kind, not equality of degree.
We are to purify ourselves from the *power* of sin, and from
the *guilt* of sin. Purification from the *power* of sin consists in
these things. (1) A continually renewed repentance. Every
day, every hour, may afford matter for penitential sorrow.
"A fountain of sin may well require a fountain of sorrow.'
Converting repentance must be followed by daily repentance.
(2) Purifying ourselves consists in vigilant prevention of acts
of sin for the future. The means of effecting this are these.
(*a*) Opposing the very first risings of the heart to sin. "The
bees may be at work, and very busy within, though we see
none of them fly abroad." (*b*) Severe mortifying duties, such as
watchings and fastings. (*c*) Frequent and fervent prayer. "A
praying heart naturally turns into a purified heart." We are
to purify ourselves, also, from the *guilt* of sin. (1) Negatively.
No duty or work within our power to perform can take away
the guilt of sin. Those who think so, understand neither "the
fiery strictness of the law, nor the spirituality of the Gospel."
(2) That which alone can purify us from the *guilt* of sin is
applying the virtue of the blood of Christ to the soul by
renewed acts of faith. "It is that alone that is able to wash
away the deep stain, and to change the hue of the spiritual
Ethiopian." The last consideration is—how the life of heaven
and future glory has such a sovereign influence upon this work?
[This portion of the sermon falls far below the high standard
of the rest, and entirely loses the spirit of St. John's thought.]
South's *Sermons*. (Sermon 72, pp. 594-616.)

Ver. 6. *That He might destroy the works of the devil.*]
The word here used for Satan (διάβολος) is found in John vii.
70, viii. 44, xiii. 2; Apoc. ii. 10, xii. 9, 12, xx. 2, 10. One class
of miracles is not specifically recorded by St. John in his
Gospel—the dispossession of demoniacs. Probably this
terrible affliction was less common in Jerusalem than in
Galilee. But the idea of possession is not foreign to his
mode of thought. John vi. 70, viii. 44, 48, x. 20, xiii. 27.
He here points to the dispossessions, so many of which are
recorded by the Synoptics.

III. ver. 9. His *seed abideth in him.*] Of these words
only two interpretations appear to be fairly possible. (1) The
first would understand "His seed" as "*God's seed,*" the
stock or family of His children who are the true זֶרַע אֱלֹהִים, *seed
of God* (Mal. ii. 15). In favour of this intrepretation it
may be urged: first, that "seed" in the sense of "children,
posterity, any one's entire stock and filiation," in perhaps
nearly two hundred passages of the LXX., is the Greek
rendering of many different Hebrew words. (See σπέρμα in
Num. xxiv. 20; Deut. xxv. 1; Jer. l. 16; Gen. iii. 15;
Isa. xiv. 20, 30, xv. 9; Num. xxiii. 10; 2 Chron. xiv. 27.)
Secondly, no inapt meaning is given in the present text
by so understanding the word. "He is unable to go on
in sin, for *God's* true stock and family (they who are true
to the majesty of their birth) abide in Him." (2) But a
second meaning appears preferable. "Seed" (σπέρμα) would
then be understood as a metaphorical application of the grain
in the vegetable world which contains the possible germ of the
future plant or tree; and would signify the possibility, or
germinal principle, given by the Holy Spirit to the soul in
regeneration. For this signification in our passage there is
a strong argument, which we have not seen adverted to, in
St. John's mode of language and of thought. "His seed
abideth in him" (σπέρμα αὐτοῦ ἐν αὐτῷ μένει) is really a quotation
from the LXX. (οὗ τὸ σπέρμα αὐτοῦ ἐν αὐτῷ—note the repetition
of the words Gen. i. 11, 12). Now the Book of Genesis
seems to have been the part of the Old Testament which
(with the Psalms) was chiefly in St. John's mind in the Epistle.
(Cf. 1 John i. 1, Gen. i. 1.—iii. 8, Gen. ii.—iii. 12, Gen. iv. 8—
iii. 15, Gen. xxvii. 41.) St. John, also, connects the new birth
of the sons of God, as did our Lord, with the birth of the

creation, whose first germ was "the Spirit of God moving upon the face of the waters" (Gen. i. 2 ; John iii. 5). This parallel between the first creation and the second, between creation and regeneration, has always commended itself to profound Christian exegesis as being deeply set in the mind of Scripture. Witness the magnificent lines.

> Plebs ut sacra renascatur,
> Per Hunc unda consecratur,
> Cui super ferebatur
>   In rerum exordium.
> Fons, origo pietatis,
> Fons emundans a peccatis,
> Fons de fonte Deitatis,
>   Fons sacrator fontium !
>   Adam of St. Victor, Seq. xx., *Pentecoste.*

It is instructive, to study the treatment of our Lord's words (John iii. 5) by a commentator so little mystical as Professor Westcott. St. John, then, might point at this as another hint of regeneration in the parable of creation, viewed spiritually. The world of vegetation in Genesis is divided into two classes. (1) *Herbs* עֵשֶׂב = all grasses and plants which "*yield seed.*" (2) *Trees* עֵץ פְּרִי = shrubs and arboreous plants which have their seed enclosed in their fruit (Gen. i. 11, 12). Such are the plants of God's planting in His garden. Of each the "seed" from which he sprung, and which he will reproduce unless he becomes barren and blighted, "is in him." "He cannot sin." It is against the basis of his new nature. Of the new creation as of the old, the law is—"his seed is in him."

The rest of this verse is interpreted in the Discourse upon 1 John v. 4.

GREEK.

Ἐν τούτῳ φανερά ἐστιν τὰ τέκνα τοῦ Θεοῦ καὶ τὰ τέκνα τοῦ διαβόλου. Πᾶς ὁ μὴ ποιῶν δικαιοσύνην οὐκ ἔστιν ἐκ τοῦ Θεοῦ, καὶ ὁ μὴ ἀγαπῶν τὸν ἀδελφὸν αὐτοῦ· ὅτι αὕτη ἐστὶν ἡ ἀγγελία ἣν ἠκούσατε ἀπ' ἀρχῆς, ἵνα ἀγαπῶμεν ἀλλήλους· οὐ καθὼς Κάϊν ἐκ τοῦ πονηροῦ ἦν καὶ ἔσφαξε τὸν ἀδελφὸν αὐτοῦ· καὶ χάριν τίνος ἔσφαξεν αὐτόν; ὅτι τὰ ἔργα αὐτοῦ πονηρὰ ἦν, τὰ δὲ τοῦ ἀδελφοῦ αὐτοῦ δίκαια. μὴ θαυμάζετε, ἀδελφοί, εἰ μισεῖ ὑμᾶς ὁ κόσμος. Ἡμεῖς οἴδαμεν ὅτι μεταβεβήκαμεν ἐκ τοῦ θανάτου εἰς τὴν ζωήν, ὅτι ἀγαπῶμεν τοὺς ἀδελφούς· ὁ μὴ ἀγαπῶν μένει ἐν τῷ θανάτῳ· πᾶς ὁ μισῶν τὸν ἀδελφὸν αὐτοῦ ἀνθρωποκτόνος ἐστίν· καὶ

LATIN.

In hoc manifesti sunt filii Dei et filii diaboli. Omnis qui non est iustus non est ex Deo, et qui non diligit fratrem suum; quoniam haec est adnuntiatio quam audistis ab initio, ut diligamus alterutrum, non sicut Cain ex maligno erat, et occidit fratrem suum. Et propter quid occidit eum? quoniam opera eius maligna erant, fratris autem eius iusta. Nolite mirari fratres si odit nos mundus. Nos scimus quoniam translati sumus de morte in vitam, quoniam diligimus fratres: qui non diligit, manet in morte. Omnis qui odit fratrem suum homicida est, et scitis quoniam omnis homicida non habet

AUTHORISED VERSION.

In this the children of God are manifest, and the children of the devil: whosoever doeth not righteousness is not of God, neither he that loveth not his brother. For this is the message that ye heard from the beginning, that we should love one another. Not as Cain, *who* was of that wicked one, and slew his brother. And wherefore slew he him? Because his own works were evil, and his brother's righteous. Marvel not, my brethren, if the world hate you. We know that we have passed from death unto life, because we love the brethren. He that loveth not *his* brother abideth in death. Whosoever

REVISED VERSION.

In this the children of God are manifest, and the children of the devil: whosoever doeth not righteousness is not of God, neither he that loveth not his brother. For this is the message which ye heard from the beginning, that we should love one another: not as Cain was of the evil one, and slew his brother. And wherefore slew he him? Because his works were evil, and his brother's righteous. Marvel not, brethren, if the world hateth you. We know that we have passed out of death into life, because we love the brethren. He that loveth not his brother abideth in death. Whosoever hateth his

ANOTHER VERSION.

In this the children of God are manifest and the children of the devil: every one who is not doing righteousness is not of God, neither he that is not loving his brother. For this is the message that ye heard from the beginning that ye should love one another. Not as Cain was of the wicked one and slew his brother (*shall we be*). And wherefore slew he him? because his works were evil, but those of his brother righteous. Brethren, marvel not if the world hate you. We know that we have passed over from the death unto the life because we love the brethren. He who loveth not

ὥστε ὅτι πᾶς ἀνθρωποκτόνος οὐκ ἔχει ζωὴν αἰώνιον ἐν αὐτῷ μένουσαν. Ἐν τούτῳ ἐγνώκαμεν τὴν ἀγάπην, ὅτι ἐκεῖνος ὑπὲρ ἡμῶν τὴν ψυχὴν αὐτοῦ ἔθηκε· καὶ ἡμεῖς ὀφείλομεν ὑπὲρ τῶν ἀδελφῶν τὰς ψυχὰς θεῖναι. ὃς δ' ἂν ἔχῃ τὸν βίον τοῦ κόσμου καὶ θεωρῇ τὸν ἀδελφὸν αὐτοῦ χρείαν ἔχοντα καὶ κλείσῃ τὰ σπλάγχνα αὐτοῦ ἀπ' αὐτοῦ, πῶς ἡ ἀγάπη τοῦ Θεοῦ μένει ἐν αὐτῷ; τεκνία μὴ ἀγαπῶμεν λόγῳ μηδὲ γλώσσῃ, ἀλλ' ἔργῳ καὶ ἀληθείᾳ. Καὶ ἐν τούτῳ γινώσκομεν ὅτι ἐκ τῆς ἀληθείας ἐσμέν, καὶ ἔμπροσθεν αὐτοῦ πείσομεν τὰς καρδίας ἡμῶν ὅτι ἐὰν καταγινώσκῃ ἡμῶν ἡ καρδία, ὅτι μείζων ἐστὶν ὁ Θεὸς τῆς καρδίας ἡμῶν, καὶ γινώσκει πάντα. ἀγαπητοί, ἐὰν ἡ καρδία ἡμῶν μὴ καταγινώσκῃ

vitam æternam in se manentem. In hoc cognovimus caritatem Dei, quoniam ille pro nobis animam suam posuit: et nos debemus pro fratribus animas ponere. Qui habuerit substantiam mundi et viderit fratrem suum necesse habere et clauserit viscera sua ab eo, quomodo caritas Dei manet in eo? Filioli non diligamus verbo nec lingua sed opere et veritate. In hoc cognovimus quoniam ex veritate sumus: et in conspectu eius suademus corda nostra, quoniam si reprehenderit nos cor nostrum, major est Deus corde nostro et novit omnia. Carissimi si cor nostrum non reprehenderit nos, fiduciam habemus ad Deum, et quodcumque petierimus accipiemus

hateth his brother is a murderer: and ye know that no murderer hath eternal life abiding in him. Hereby perceive we the love of *God*, because He laid down His life for us: and we ought to lay down *our* lives for the brethren. But whoso hath this world's good, and seeth his brother have need, and shutteth up his bowels *of compassion* from him, how dwelleth the love of God in him? *My little children*, let us not love in word, neither in tongue; but in deed and in truth. And hereby we know that we are of the truth, and shall assure our hearts before Him. For if our heart condemn us, God is greater than our heart, and knoweth all things. Beloved, if our heart

abideth in the death. Every one who hateth his brother is a murderer: and ye know that no murderer hath eternal life abiding in him. Hereby know we The Love because He laid down His life for us: and we are bound to lay down our lives for the brethren. But whoso hath the living of the world and gazes on his brother having need and shuts out his heart from him, how doth the love of God abide in him? Children let us not love in word, nor with the tongue, but in work and truth. Hereby shall we know that we are of the truth and shall persuade our hearts before Him. For if our heart condemn us God is greater than our heart, and knoweth all things

ἡμῶν, παρρησίαν ἔχομεν πρὸς τὸν Θεόν, καὶ ὃ ἐὰν αἰτῶμεν, λαμβάνομεν παρ' αὐτοῦ, ὅτι τὰς ἐντολὰς αὐτοῦ τηροῦμεν, καὶ τὰ ἀρεστὰ ἐνώπιον αὐτοῦ ποιοῦμεν. καὶ αὕτη ἐστὶν ἡ ἐντολὴ αὐτοῦ, ἵνα πιστεύσωμεν τῷ ὀνόματι τοῦ υἱοῦ αὐτοῦ Ἰησοῦ Χριστοῦ, καὶ ἀγαπῶμεν ἀλλήλους, καθὼς ἔδωκεν ἐντολήν. καὶ ὁ τηρῶν τὰς ἐντολὰς αὐτοῦ, ἐν αὐτῷ μένει, καὶ αὐτὸς ἐν αὐτῷ. καὶ ἐν τούτῳ γινώσκομεν ὅτι μένει ἐν ἡμῖν, ἐκ τοῦ Πνεύματος οὗ ἡμῖν ἔδωκεν.

a beo, quoniam mandata eius custodemus et ea quae sunt placita coram eo facimus. Et hoc est mandatum eius ut credamus in nomine filii eius Iesu Christi et diligamus alterutrum sicut dedit mandatum nobis. Et qui servat mandata eius, in illo manet et ipse in eo: et in hoc scimus quoniam manet in nobis, de spiritu quem dedit nobis.

condemn us not, *then* have we confidence toward God. And whatsoever we ask, we receive of Him, because we keep His commandments, and do those things that are pleasing in His sight. And this is His commandment, That we should believe on the name of His Son Jesus Christ, and love one another, as He gave us commandment. And he that keepeth His commandments dwelleth in Him, and He in him. And hereby we know that He abideth in us, by the Spirit which He hath given us.

not, we have boldness toward God ; and whatsoever we ask, we receive of Him, because we keep His commandments, and do the things that are pleasing in His sight. And this is His commandment, that we should believe in the name of His Son Jesus Christ, and love one another, even as He gave us commandment. And he that keepeth His commandments abideth in Him, and He in him. And hereby we know that He abideth in us, by the Spirit which He gave us.

Beloved, if our heart condemn us not then have we boldness toward God, and whatsoever we ask we receive of Him, for we observe His commandments, and are doing those things that are pleasing in His sight. And His commandment is this, that we should believe the name of His Son Jesus Christ and love one another as He gave commandment. And he who is observing His commandments abideth in Him, and He in him. And hereby we know that He abideth in us—out of the fulness of the Spirit whereof He gave us.

DISCOURSE IX.

LOFTY IDEALS PERILOUS UNLESS APPLIED.

"Hereby perceive we the love of God, because He laid down His life for us: and we ought to lay down our lives for the brethren. But whoso hath this world's good, and seeth his brother have need, and shutteth up his bowels of compassion from him, how dwelleth the love of God in him? My little children, let us not love in word, neither in tongue, but in deed and in truth."—I JOHN iii. 16-18.

EVEN the world sees that the Incarnation of Jesus Christ has very practical results. Even the Christmas which the world keeps is fruitful in two of these results—forgiving and giving. How many of the multitudinous letters at that season contain one or other of these things—either the kindly gift, or the tender of reconciliation; the confession "I was wrong," or the gentle advance "we were both wrong."

Love, charity (as we rather prefer to say), in its effects upon all our relations to others, is the beautiful subject of this section of our Epistle. It begins with the message of love[1] itself—yet another asterisk referring to the Gospel,[2] to the very substance of the teaching which the believers of Ephesus had first received from St. Paul,[3] and which had been emphasized by St. John.

---

[1] Ver. 11.

[2] John xv. 12-17. See also the stress laid upon the unity of believers; surely including love as well as doctrine in the great High-Priestly prayer, John xvii. 21-23.

[3] "The message that ye heard *from the beginning,*" conf. I John ii. 24.

This message is announced not merely as a sounding sentiment, but for the purpose of being carried
out into action.   As in moral subjects virtues and vices
are best illustrated by their contraries[1]; so, beside the
bright picture of the Son of God, the Apostle points
to the sinister likeness of Cain.[2] After some brief
and parenthetic words of pathetic consolation, he states
as the mark of the great transition from death to
life, the existence of love as a pervading spirit effectual in operation.[3]   The dark opposite of this is then
delineated[4] in consonance with the mode of representation just above.[5]   But two such pictures of darkness
must not shadow the sunlit gallery of love.   There is
another—the fairest and brightest.   Our love can only
be estimated by likeness to it ; it is imperfect unless it
is conformed to the print of the wounds, unless it can
be measured by the standard of the great Self-sacrifice.[6]
But if this may be claimed as the one real proof of
conformity to Christ, much more is the limited partial

---

[1] "Contrariorum eadem est scientia."

[2] This is one of the few references to the Old Testament *history*
in St. John's Epistle (Gen. iv. 1-8). To the *theology* of the Old Testament there are many references; *e.g.*, light and life. 1 John i. 1-5;
John i. 4; Ps. xxxvi. 9. There is, however, another historical reference a few verses above (1 John iii. 8)—a passage of primary
importance because it recognises the whole narrative of the Fall in
Genesis, and affords a commentary upon the words of Christ (John
viii. 44). The writer has somewhere seen an interesting suggestion
that ver. 12 may contain some allusion to the visit of Apollonius of
Tyana to Ephesus. Apollonius incited the mob to kill a beggar-man
for the purpose of placing himself on a level with Chalcas and others
who caused the sacrifice of human victims. The date of this incident
would apparently coincide with the closing years of St. John's life
(*Philostrat. vita Apollon.*, Act. ii., S. 5).

[3] Ver. 14.   [5] Ver. 12.
[4] Vers. 14, 15.   [6] Ver. 16.

sacrifice of "this world's good" required.[1]   This spirit,
and the conduct which it requires in the long run, will
be found to be the test of all solid spiritual comfort,[2] of
all true self-condemnation or self-acquittal.[3]

We may say of the verses prefixed to this discourse,
that they bring before us charity in its *idea*, in its
example, in its *characteristics*—in *theory*, in *action*, in
life.

I.

We have here love in its idea, "hereby know we
love."   Rather "hereby know we *The Love*."[4]

Here the idea of charity in us runs parallel with that
in Christ.   It is a subtle but true remark,[5] that there
is here no logical inferential particle.   "Because He
laid down His life for us," is not followed by its natural
correlative "therefore we," but by a simple connective
"and we."   The reason is this, that our duty herein
is not a mere cold logical deduction.   It is all of one
piece with The Love.   "We know The Love because
He laid down His life for us; *and* we are in duty
bound for the brethren to lay down our lives."

Here, then, is the idea of love, as capable of realisation
in us.   It is continuous unselfishness, to be crowned
by voluntary death, if death is necessary.   The beautiful old Church tradition shows that this language was
the language of St. John's life.   Who has forgotten
how the Apostle in his old age is said to have gone

---

[1] Ver. 17.

[2] Vers. 18, 19.

[3] Vers. 20, 21.

[4] "For *The Love* I rather beseech thee" (Phil. v. 9).   The addition
in the A.V. (*of God*) rather impairs the sweetness and power, the
reverential reserve of the original.

[5] Of Prof. Westcott.

on a journey to find the young man who had fled from Ephesus and joined a band of robbers; and to have appealed to the fugitive in words which are the pathetic echo of these—"if needs be I would die for thee as He for us?"

II.

The idea of charity is then practically illustrated by an incident of its opposite. "But whoso hath this world's good, and gazes upon his brother in need, and shuts up his heart against him, how doth the love of God abide in him?"[1] The reason for this descent in thought is wise and sound. High abstract ideas expressed in lofty and transcendent language, are at once necessary and dangerous for creatures like us. They are necessary, because without these grand conceptions our moral language and our moral life would be wanting in dignity, in amplitude, in the inspiration and impulse which are often necessary for duty and always for restoration. But they are dangerous in proportion to their grandeur. Men are apt to mistake the emotion awakened by the very sound of these magnificent expressions of duty for the discharge of the duty itself. Hypocrisy delights in sublime speculations, because it has no intention of their costing anything. Some of the most abject creatures embodied by the masters of romance never fail to parade their sonorous generalizations. One of such characters, as the world will long remember, proclaims that sympathy is one of the holiest principles of our common nature, while he shakes his fist at a beggar.[2]

---

[1] Ver. 17.

[2] It is suggestive that on Quinquagesima Sunday, when 1 Cor. xiii. is the Epistle, St. Luke xviii. 31 sqq., is the Gospel. The lyric of love is joined with a fragment of its epic. That fragment tells us of a

Every large speculative ideal then is liable to this danger; and he who contemplates it requires to be brought down from his transcendental region to the test of some commonplace duty. This is the latent link of connection in this passage. The ideal of love to which St. John points is the loftiest of all the moral and spiritual emotions which belong to the sentiments of man. Its archetype is in the bosom of God, in the eternal relations of the Father, Son, and Holy Ghost. "God is love." Its home in humanity is Christ's heart of fire and flesh; its example is the Incarnation ending in the Cross.

Now of course the question for all but one in thousands is not the attainment of this lofty ideal—laying down his life for the brethren. Now and then, indeed, the physician pays with his own death for the heroic rashness of drawing out from his patient the fatal matter. Sometimes the pastor is cut off by fever contracted in ministering to the sick, or by voluntarily living and working in an unwholesome atmosphere. Once or twice in a decade some heart is as finely touched by the spirit of love as Father Damien, facing the certainty of death from a long slow putrefaction, that a congregation of lepers may enjoy the consolations of faith. St. John here reminds us that the ordinary test of charity is much more commonplace. It is helpful compassion to a brother who is known to be in need, manifested by giving to him something of this world's "good"—of the "living"[1] of this world which he possesses.

---

love which not only proclaimed itself ready to be sacrificed (Luke xviii. 31-33), but condescended individually to the blind importunate mendicant who sat by the wayside begging (vers. 35-43).

[1] The word here is βίος not ζωή. "Βίος period of life; hence the means by which it is sustained, means of life." (Archbp. Trench.)

III.

We have next the characteristics of love in action. "My sons, let us not love in word nor with the tongue; but in work and truth." There is love in its energy and reality; in its effort and sincerity—active and honest, without indolence and without pretence. We may wel. be reminded here of another familiar story of St. John at Ephesus. When too old to walk himself to the assembly of the Church, he was carried there. The Apostle who had lain upon the breast of Jesus; who had derived from direct communication with Him those words and thoughts which are the life of the elect; was expected to address the faithful. The light of the Ephesian summer fell upon his white hair; perhaps glittered upon the mitre which tradition has assigned to him. But when he had risen to speak, he only repeated—"little children, love one another." Modern hearers are sometimes tempted to envy the primitive Christians of the Ephesian Church, if for nothing else, yet for the privilege of listening to the shortest sermon upon record in the annals of Christianity. When Christian preachers have behind them the same long series of virgin years, within them the same love of Christ and knowledge of His mysteries; when their very presence evinces the same sad, tender, smiling, weeping, all-embracing sympathy with the wants and sorrows of humanity; they may perhaps venture upon the perilous experiment of contracting their sermons within the same span as St. John's. And when some, who like the hearers at Ephesus, are not prepared for

It is to be wished that the R. V. had either kept "the good" of the A. V., or adopted the word "living"—the translation of $\beta\iota o\varsigma$ in Mark xii. 44; Luke xxi. 4.

the repetition of an utterance so brief, begin to ask—
" why are you always saying this ? "—the answer may
well be in the spirit of the reply which the aged Apostle
is said to have made—" because it is the commandment
of the Lord, and sufficient, if it only be fulfilled indeed."

IV.

This passage supplies an argument (capable, as we
have seen in the Introduction, of much larger expansion
from the Epistle as a whole) against mutilated views,
fragmentary versions of the Christian life.

There are four such views which are widely prevalent at the present time.

(1) The *first* of these is *emotionalism ;* which makes
the entire Christian life consist in a series or bundle
of emotions. Its origin is the desire of having the
feelings touched, partly from sheer love of excitement;
partly from an idea that *if* and *when* we have worked
up certain emotions to a fixed point we are saved and
safe. This reliance upon feelings is in the last analysis
reliance upon self. It is a form of salvation by works;
for feelings are inward actions. It is an unhappy
anachronism which inverts the order of Scripture;
which substitutes peace and grace (the compendious
dogma of the heresy of the emotions) for grace and
peace, the only order known to St. Paul and St. John.[1]
The only spiritual emotions spoken of in this Epistle
are joy, confidence, assuring our hearts before Him " :[2]
the first as the result of receiving the history of Jesus
in the Gospel, the Incarnation, and the blessed communion with God and the Church which it involves ;
the second as tried by tests of a most practical kind.

---

[1] 2 John 3.
[2] 1 John i. 4, ii. 28, iii. 21, iv. 17, v. 14, iii. 19.

(2) The *second* of these mutilated views of the Christian life is *doctrinalism*—which makes it consist of a series or bundle of doctrines apprehended and expressed correctly, at least according to certain formulas, generally of a narrow and unauthorised character. According to this view the question to be answered is—has one quite correctly understood, can one verbally formulate certain almost scholastic distinctions in the doctrine of justification ? The well-known standard—"the Bible only "—must be reduced by the excision of all within the Bible except the writings of St. Paul ; and even in this selected portion faith must be entirely guided by certain portions more selected still, so that the question finally may be reduced to this shape—"am I a great deal sounder than St. John and St. James, a little sounder than an unexpurgated St. Paul, as sound as a carefully expurgated edition of the Pauline Epistles ? "

(3) The *third* mutilated view of the Christian life is *humanitarianism*—which makes it a series or bundle of philanthropic actions.

There are some who work for hospitals, or try to bring more light and sweetness into crowded dwelling-houses. Their lives are pure and noble. But the one article of their creed is humanity. Altruism is their highest duty. Their object, so far as they have any object apart from the supreme rule of doing right, is to lay hold on subjective immortality by living on in the recollection of those whom they have helped, whose existence has been soothed and sweetened by their sympathy. With others the case is different. Certain forms of this busy helpfulness—especially in the laudable provision of recreations for the poor—are an innocent interlude in fashionable life ; sometimes, alas ! a kind of work of supererogation, to atone for the want

of devotion or of purity—possibly an unthelogical survival of a belief in justification by works.

(4) The *fourth* fragmentary view of the Christian life is *observationism*, which makes it to consist in a bundle or series of observances. Frequent services and communions, perhaps with exquisite forms and in beautifully decorated churches, have their dangers as well as their blessings. However closely linked these observances may be, there must still in every life be interstices between them. How are these filled up? What spirit within connects together, vivifies and unifies, this series of external acts of devotion? They are means to an end. What if the means come to interpose between us and the end—just as a great political thinker has observed that with legal minds the forms of business frequently overshadow the substance of business, which is their end, and for which they were called into existence. And what is the end of our Christian calling? A life pardoned; in process of purification; growing in faith, in love of God and man, in quiet joyful service. Certainly a " rage for ceremonials and statistics," a long list of observances, does not infallibly secure such a life, though it may often be not alone the delighted and continuous expression, but the constant food and support of such a life. But assuredly if men trust in any of these things—in their emotions, in their favourite formulas, in their philanthropic works, in their religious observances—in anything but Christ, they greatly need to go back to the simple text—"His name shall be called Jesus, for He shall save His people from their sins."

Now, as we have said above, in distinction from all these fragmentary views, St. John's Epistle is a survey of the completed Christian life, founded upon his Gospel. It is a consummate fruit ripened in the long summers

of his experience. It is not a treatise upon the Christian affections, nor a system of doctrine, nor an essay upon works of charity, nor a companion to services.

Yet this wonderful Epistle presupposes at least much that is most precious of all these elements. (1) It is far from being a burst of emotionalism. Yet almost at the outset it speaks of an emotion as being the natural result of rightly received objective truth.[1] St. John recognises feeling, whether of supernatural or natural origin;[2] but he recognises it with a certain majestic reserve. Once only does he seem to be carried away. In a passage to which reference has just been made, after stating the dogma of the Incarnation, he suffuses it with a wealth of emotional colour. It is Christmas in his soul; the bells ring out good tidings of great joy. "These things write we unto you, that your joy may be full." (2) This Epistle is no dogmatic summary. Yet combining its prooemium with the other of the fourth Gospel, we have the most perfect statement of the dogma of the Incarnation. As we read thoughtfully on, dogma after dogma stands out in relief. The divinity of the Word, the reality of His manhood, the effect of His atonement, His intercession, His continual presence, the personality of the Holy Spirit, His gifts to us, the relation of the Spirit to Christ, the Holy Trinity—all these find their place in these few

---

[1] 1 John i. 4.

[2] τὰ σπλάγχνα (ver. 17). This however is the only occurrence of the word in St. John's writings. The substantive σπλάγχνα = *emotions*, is found in classical poets. But the verb σπλαγχνίζομαι occurs only in LXX. and New Testament—and thus, like ἀγάπη, is almost born within the circle of revealed truth. The new dispensation so rich in the mercy of God (Luke i. 78), so fruitful in mercy from man to man, may well claim a new vocabulary in the department of tenderness and pity.

pages.   If St. John is no mere doctrinalist he is yet
the greatest theologian the Church has ever seen.
(3) Once more; if the Apostle's Christianity is no mere
humanitarian sentiment to encourage the cultivation
of miscellaneous acts of good-nature, yet it is deeply
pervaded by a sense of the integral connection of
practical love of man with the love of God.   So much
is this the case, that a large gathering of the most
emotional of modern sects is said to have gone on with
a Bible reading in St. John's Epistle until they came
to the words—" we know that we have passed from
death unto life, because we love the brethren."   The
reader immediately closed the book, pronouncing with
general assent that the verse was likely to disturb the
peace of the children of God.   Still St. John puts
humanitarianism in its right place as a result of
something higher.   "This commandment have we from
Him, that he who loveth God love his brother also."
As if he would say—" do not sever the law of social life
from the law of supernatural life ; do not separate the
human fraternity from the Divine Fatherhood."   (4) No
one can suppose that for St. John religion was a mere
string of observances.   Indeed, to some his Epistle
has given the notion of a man living in an atmosphere
where external ordinances and ministries either did not
exist at all, or only in almost impalpable forms.   Yet
in that wonderful manual, " The Imitation of Christ,"
there is not more than the faintest trace of any of
these external things ; while no one could possibly argue
that the author was ignorant of, or lightly esteemed, the
ordinances and sacraments amongst which his life must
have been spent.   Certainly the fourth Gospel is deeply
sacramental.   This Epistle, with its calm, unhesitating
conviction of the sonship of all to whom it is ad-

dressed; with its view of the Christian life as in idea
a continuous growth from a birth the secret of whose
origin is given in the Gospel; with its expressive hints
of sources of grace and power and of a continual presence of Christ; with its deep mystical realisation of
the double flow from the pierced side upon the cross,
and its thrice-repeated exchange of the *sacramental*
order "*water* and blood,"[1] for the *historical* order "*blood*
and water*"; unquestionably has the sacramental
sense diffused throughout it. The Sacraments are not
in obtrusive prominence; yet for those who have eyes
to see they lie in deep and tender distances. Such is
the view of the Christian life in this letter—a life in
which Christ's truth is blended with Christ's love;
assimilated by thought, exhaling in worship, softening
into sympathy with man's suffering and sorrow. It
calls for the believing soul, for the devout heart, for the
helping hand. It is the perfect balance in a saintly
soul of feeling, creed, communion, and work.

For of work for our fellow man it is that the question
is asked half despairingly—"whoso hath this world's
good, and seeth" (gazes at)[2] "his brother have need,
and shutteth up his heart against him, how doth the
love of God[3] dwell in him?" Some can quietly look at
the poor brother; they see *him* in need, but they have
not the thoughtful eyes that see *his need*. They may
belong to "the sluggard Pity's vision-weaving tribe,"
who expend a sigh of sentiment upon such spectacles,
and nothing more. Or they may be hardened pro-
fessors of the "dismal science," who have learned to

---

[1] 1 John v. 6, conf. John xix. 34.
[2] θεωρῇ, ver. 17.
[3] "The love of which God is at once the object, and the author, and
the pattern." (Prof. Westcott.)

consider a sigh as the luxury of ignorance or of feeble-
ness.   But for all practical purposes both these classes
interpose a too effectual barrier between their heart
and their brother's need.   But true Christians are made
partakers in Christ of the mystery of human suffering.
Even when they are not actually in sight of brethren
in want, their ears are ever hearing the ceaseless moan-
ing of the sea of human sorrow, with a sympathy
which involves its own measure of pain, though a pain
which brings with it abundant compensation.   Their
inner life has not merely won for itself the partly
selfish satisfaction of personal escape from punishment,
great as that blessing may be.   They have caught
something of the meaning of the secret of all love—
" we love because He first loved us."[1]   In those words
is the romance (if we may dare to call it so) of the
divine love-tale.   Under its influence the face once
hard and narrow often becomes radiant and softened ;
it smiles, or is tearful, in the light of the love of His
face who first loved.

It is this principle of St. John which is ever at work
in Christian lands.   In hospitals it tells us that Christ
is ever passing down the wards ; that He will have no
stinted service; that He must have more for His sick
more devotion, a gentler touch, a finer sympathy ; that
where His hand has broken and blessed, every particle
is a sacred thing, and must be treated reverently.

Are there any who are tempted to think that our text
has become antiquated ; that it no longer holds true
in the light of organised charity, of economic science ?
Let them listen to one who speaks with the weight of
years of active benevolence, and with consummate
knowledge of its method and duties.[2]   " There are men

---

[1] 1 John iv. 19.   [2] Lord Meath.

who, in their detestation of roguery, forget that by a wholesale condemnation of charity, they run the risk of driving the honest to despair and of turning them into the very rogues of whom they desire so ardently to be quit. These men are unconsciously playing into the hands of the Socialists and the Anarchists, the only sections of society whose distinct interest it is that misery and starvation should increase. No doubt indiscriminate almsgiving is hurtful to the State as well as to the individual who receives the dole, but not less dangerous would it be to society if the principles of these stern political economists were to be literally accepted by any large number of the rich, and if charity ceased to be practised within the land. We cannot yet afford to shut ourselves up in the castle of philosophic indifference, regardless of the fate of those who have the misfortune to find themselves outside its walls."

NOTES.

Ch. iii. 12—21.

Ver. 12. A second reference to the Book of Genesis within a few lines (see ver. 8). It is characteristic of the historical spirit of St. John that he does not entangle himself with the luxuriant upgrowth of wild fable in which traditional Judaism has ever enveloped the simple narrative of Cain and Abel in Genesis.

Ver. 15. St. John may refer to another passage in Genesis. " And Esau said in his heart, The days of mourning for my father are at hand ; then will I slay my brother Jacob " (Gen. xxvii. 11-41).

Ver. 17. A Rabbinical saying is worth recording as an illustration of the spirit in which the " living of this world " should be held. " He that saith, Mine is thine, and thine is mine, is an idiot ; he that saith, Mine is mine, and thine is thine, is moderate ; he that saith, Mine is thine, and thine is thine, is

charitable; but he that saith, Thine is mine, and mine is mine, is wicked; even though it be only saying it in his heart, to wish it were so." Paulus Fagius. *Sentent. Heb.*

Vers. 19, 20, 21. These verses probably present more difficulties than any other portion of this Epistle. (1) For their construction. The following note from a *fasciculus* (now no longer to be procured) written by a master of sacred studies seems to us to say all that can be said for a rendering different from that of the R. V. and our own.

"Ver. 20: ὅτι ἐὰν καταγινώσκῃ ἡμῶν ἡ καρδία, ὅτι μείζων ἐστὶν ὁ Θεός. The difficulty is in the second ὅτι, which is ignored by the Vulgate and A. V. The Revisers (after Hoogeveen, *De Partic.* p. 589, ed. Schütz. and others) point ὅ,τι ἐὰν in the first clause, which they join with the preceding verse: 'and shall assure our heart before him, whereinsoever our heart condemn us; because God' etc. But this is quite inadmissible, since nothing can be plainer than that ἐὰν καταγινώσκῃ (ver. 20) and ἐὰν μὴ καταγινώσκῃ (ver. 21) are both *in protasi*, and in strict correlation with each other. Dean Alford suggests an ellipsis of the verb substantive before the second ὅτι, and would translate: 'Because if our heart condemn us, (it is) because God' etc. He instances such cases as εἴ τις ἐν Χριστῷ, (he is) καινὴ κτίσις, which are quite dissimilar; but the following from St. Chrysostom (T. X. p. 122 B) fully bears out this construction; Ὁ ζυγός μου χρηστὸς κ.τ.ἑ. εἰ δὲ οὐκ αἰσθάνῃ τῆς κουφότητος, ΟΤΙ προθυμίαν ἐρρωμένην οὐκ ἔχεις; where I have expunged δῆλον before ὅτι on the authority of three out of four MSS. collated for these Homilies, the fourth, with the old Latin version, for ὅτι προθυμίαν reading μὴ θαυμάσῃς, προθυμίαν γάρ. In my note on that place I have pointed out that the ellipsis is not of δῆλον, but of τὸ αἴτιον, *causa est, quia.* So in the present instance we might translate: 'For if our heart condemn us, (the reason is) because God is greater,' etc., were it not for the difficulty of explaining how the fact of God's being greater than our heart can be a valid reason for our heart condemning us. I would, therefore, take the second ὅτι for *quod*, not *quia*, and suppose an ellipsis of δῆλον, as in 1 Tim. vi. 7, where see note."—*Otium Norvicense*, by Frederic Field, M.A., LL.D. (pp. 153, 15).

Dr. Field's rendering then is: "For if our heart condemn us, (it is evident) that God is greater than our heart."

(2) For the meaning of these verses. All interpretations appear to fall into two classes; as St. John is supposed to aim at (*a*) *soothing* conscience, or (*b*) *awakening* it. But may he not really intend to leave people to think over a something which he has purposely omitted, and to apply it as required? The saying " God is greater than our hearts, and knoweth all things," probably cuts two ways. If my heart condemn me justly, and with truth, much more so does God who is greater than my heart. But, if my conscience is tenderly sensitive, scrupulous because full of love, God's knowledge of my heart tells in this case on the brighter side, as truly as in the other case it told on the darker side. We may lull our heart. " A tranquil God tranquillises all things, and to see His peacefulness is to be at peace." (*St. Bernard in Cant.*)

SECTION vll.

GREEK.

Ἀγαπητοί, μὴ παντὶ πνεύματι πιστεύετε, ἀλλὰ δοκιμάζετε τὰ πνεύματα, εἰ ἐκ τοῦ Θεοῦ ἐστιν· ὅτι πολλοὶ ψευδοπροφῆται ἐξελη-λύθασιν εἰς τὸν κόσμον. ἐν τούτῳ γινώσκετε τὸ Πνεῦμα τοῦ Θεοῦ· πᾶν πνεῦμα ὃ ὁμολογεῖ Ἰησοῦν Χριστὸν ἐν σαρκὶ ἐληλυθότα, ἐκ τοῦ Θεοῦ ἐστι. καὶ πᾶν πνεῦμα ὃ μὴ ὁμο-λογεῖ τὸν Ἰησοῦν Χριστὸν, ἐκ τοῦ Θεοῦ οὐκ ἔστι· καὶ τοῦτό ἐστι τὸ τοῦ ἀν-τιχρίστου, ὃ ἀκηκόατε ὅτι ἔρχεται, καὶ νῦν ἐν τῷ κόσμῳ ἐστὶν ἤδη. Ὑμεῖς ἐκ τοῦ Θεοῦ ἐστε, τεκνία, καὶ νενικήκατε αὐτούς· ὅτι μείζων ἐστὶν ὁ ἐν ὑμῖν ἢ ὁ ἐν τῷ κόσμῳ. Αὐτοὶ ἐκ τοῦ κόσμου εἰσι· διὰ τοῦτο ἐκ τοῦ κόσμου λαλοῦσι,

LATIN.

Carissimi, nolite omni spiritui credere, sed probate spiritus si ex Deo sint, quoniam multi pseudoprophetæ ex-ierunt in mundum. In hoc cognoscitur spiritus Dei. Omnis spiritus qui confitetur Iesum Christum in carne venisse, ex Deo est: et omnis spiritus qui solvit Iesum Christum ex Deo non est; et hic est Antichristus quod audistis quoniam venit et nunc iam in mundo est. Vos ex Deo estis, filioli, et vicistis eum, quoniam maior est qui in vobis est quam qui in mundo. Ipsi de mundo sunt: ideo de mundo locuntur, et mundus eos audit. Nos ex Deo sumus: qui novit Deum audit nos; qui non est ex Deo,

AUTHORISED VERSION.

Beloved, believe not every spirit, but try the spirits whether they are of God: because many false prophets are gone out into the world. Hereby know ye the Spirit of God: Every spirit that con-fesseth that Jesus Christ is come in the flesh is of God: and every spirit that con-fesseth not that Jesus Christ is come in the flesh is not of God: and this is that *spirit* of antichrist, whereof ye have heard that it should come; and even now already is it in the world. Ye are of God, little children, and have overcome them: be-cause greater is He that is in you, than he that is in the world. They are of the world: there-

REVISED VERSION.

Beloved, believe not every spirit, but prove the spirits whether they are of God; be-cause many false pro-phets are gone out into the world. Hereby know ᵧe the Spirit of God: every spirit which confesseth that Jesus Christ is come in the flesh is of God: and every spirit which confesseth not Jesus is not of God: and this is the *spirit* of the anti-christ, whereof ye have heard that it cometh; and now it is in the world already. Ye are of God, *my* little chil-dren, and have over-come them: because greater is He that is in you, than he that is in the world. They are of the world, there-fore speak they *as* of

ANOTHER VERSION.

Beloved, believe not any spirit, but try the spirits whether they are of God: because many false prophets are gone out into the world. Hereby know ye the Spirit of God: every spirit that con-fesseth Jesus Christ come in the flesh is of God: and every spirit which confesseth not Jesus is not of God: and this is that *power* of the antichrist where-of ye have heard that it cometh, and even now it is in the world al-ready. Ye are of Goᵈ, children, and have con-quered them: because greater is He that is in you, than he that is in the world. They are of the world, there-fore of the world is their manner of speech,

καὶ ὁ κόσμος αὐτῶν ἀκούει. ἡμεῖς ἐκ τοῦ Θεοῦ ἐσμεν· ὁ γινώσκων τὸν Θεόν, ἀκούει ἡμῶν· ὃς οὐκ ἔστιν ἐκ τοῦ Θεοῦ, οὐκ ἀκούει ἡμῶν. Ἐκ τούτου γινώσκομεν τὸ πνεῦμα τῆς ἀληθείας καὶ τὸ πνεῦμα τῆς πλάνης.

non audit nos. In hoc cognoscimus spiritum veritatis et spiritum erroris.

fore speak they of the world, and the world heareth them. We are of God: he that knoweth God heareth us: he that is not of God heareth not us. Hereby know we the spirit of truth, and the spirit of error.

and the world heareth them. We are of God; he that knoweth God heareth us, he who is not of God heareth not us. From this we know the spirit of The Truth, and the spirit of the error.

NOTES.

Ch. iv. 1, 7.

Ver. 1. *Believe not any spirit*] μὴ παντὶ πνεύματι πιστεύετε.
The different constructions of πιστεύειν in St. John must be
carefully noted. (*a*) With *dative* as here—" believe not such
an one; " take him not upon trust, at his own word; credit
him not with veracity. So in the Gospel, our Lord continually
complains that the Jews did not even believe Him on His
word—strong and clear as that word was with all the freshness
of Heaven, and all the transparency of truth. John v. 38,
46, viii. 45, 46, x. 37.

(*b*) πιστεύειν εἰς=to make an act of faith in, to repose in as
divine. John iii. 36, iv. 39, vi. 35, xi. 25; 1 John v. 10.

(*c*) With an *accusative*=to be persuaded of the thing—to
believe it with an implied conviction of permanence in the
persuasion—as in the beautiful verse (iv. 16)—" we are fully
persuaded of the love of God," we make it the creed of our
heart. πεπιστεύκαμεν τὴν ἀγάπην.

GREEK.

Ἀγαπητοί, ἀγαπῶμεν ἀλλήλους, ὅτι ἡ ἀγάπη ἐκ τοῦ Θεοῦ ἐστι, καὶ πᾶς ὁ ἀγαπῶν ἐκ τοῦ Θεοῦ γεγέννηται καὶ γινώσκει τὸν Θεόν· ὁ μὴ ἀγαπῶν οὐκ ἔγνω τὸν Θεόν, ὅτι ὁ Θεὸς ἀγάπη ἐστίν. Ἐν τούτῳ ἐφανερώθη ἡ ἀγάπη τοῦ Θεοῦ ἐν ἡμῖν, ὅτι τὸν υἱὸν αὐτοῦ τὸν μονογενῆ ἀπέσταλκεν ὁ Θεὸς εἰς τὸν κόσμον, ἵνα ζήσωμεν δι' αὐτοῦ. ἐν τούτῳ ἐστὶν ἡ ἀγάπη, οὐχ ὅτι ἡμεῖς ἠγαπήσαμεν τὸν Θεόν, ἀλλ' ὅτι αὐτὸς ἠγάπησεν ἡμᾶς καὶ ἀπέστειλε τὸν υἱὸν αὐτοῦ ἱλασμὸν περὶ τῶν ἁμαρτιῶν ἡμῶν. ἀγαπητοί, εἰ οὕτως ὁ Θεὸς ἠγάπησεν ἡμᾶς, καὶ ἡμεῖς ὀφείλομεν ἀλλήλους ἀγαπᾶν. Θεὸν οὐδεὶς πώποτε τεθέαται· ἐὰν ἀγαπῶμεν ἀλλήλους, ὁ Θεὸς ἐν ἡμῖν μένει,

LATIN.

Carissimi, diligamus invicem, quoniam caritas ex Deo est, et omnis qui diligit ex Deo natus est et cognoscit Deum. Qui non diligit non novit Deum, quoniam Deus caritas est. In hoc apparuit caritas Dei in nobis, quoniam Filium Suum unigenitum misit Deus in mundum, ut vivamus per Eum. In hoc est caritas, non quasi nos dilexerimus Deum, sed quoniam ipse dilexit nos et misit Filium suum propitionem pro peccatis nostris. Carissimi, si sic Deus dilexit nos, et nos debemus alterutrum diligere. Deum nemo vidit unquam: si diligamus invicem, Deus in nobis manet, et caritas eius in nobis perfecta est. In hos

SECTION VIII.

AUTHORISED VERSION.

Beloved, let us love one another: for love is of God; and every one that loveth is born of God, and knoweth God. He that loveth not knoweth not God; for God is love. In this was manifested the love of God toward us, because that God sent His only begotten Son into the world, that we might live through Him. Herein is love, not that we loved God, but that He loved us, and sent His Son to be the propitiation for our sins. Beloved, if God so loved us, we ought also to love one another. No man hath seen God at any time. If we love one another, God dwelleth in us, and His love is perfected in us. Hereby

REVISED VERSION.

Beloved, let us love one another: for love is of God; and every one that loveth is begotten of God, and knoweth God. He that loveth not knoweth not God; for God is love. Herein was the love of God manifested in us, that God hath sent His only begotten Son into the world, that we might live through Him. Herein is love, not that we loved God, but that He loved us, and sent His Son to be the propitiation for our sins. Beloved, if God so loved us, we also ought to love one another. No man hath beheld God at any time: if we love one another, God abideth in us, and His love is perfected in us: here-

Beloved, let us love one another, for love is of God, and every one that loveth is born of God, and knoweth God. He that loveth not knoweth not God, for God is love. In this was manifested the love of God in us, because that God hath sent His Son His only begotten Son into the world that we might live through Him. In this is The Love, not that we loved God, but that He loved us, and sent His Son as propitiation for our sins. Beloved, if God so loved us, we also are bounden to love one another. God no one hath ever yet beholden: if we love one another God abideth in us and His love is perfected in us. Here-

in know we that we abide in Him, and He in us, because He hath given us out of the *fulness* of His Spirit. And we have beheld and are bearing witness that the Father hath sent the Son *to be* the Saviour of the world. Whosoever shall confess that Jesus is the Son of God, God abideth in him and he in God. And we know and have believed the love which God hath in us. God is love; and he that abideth in love, abideth in God, and God in him. Herein hath The Love been perfected with us that we may have boldness in the Day of the Judgment: because as He is so are we in this world. Fear is not in love: but the perfect love casteth out fear, because fear bringeth punishment with it. He that is fearing is

by know we that we abide in Him, and He in us, because He hath given us of His Spirit. And we have beheld and bear witness that the Father hath sent the Son *to be* the Saviour of the world. Whosoever shall confess that Jesus is the Son of God, God abideth in him, and he in God. And we know and have believed the love which God hath in us. God is love; and he that abideth in love abideth in God, and God abideth in him. Herein is love made perfect with us, that we may have boldness in the day of judgment; because as He is, even so are we in this world. There is no fear in love: but perfect love casteth out fear, because fear hath punishment; and he that feareth is not made perfect in love.

know we that we dwell in Him, and He in us, because He hath given us of His Spirit. And we have seen and do testify that the Father sent the Son *to be* the Saviour of the world. Whosoever shall confess that Jesus is the Son of God, God dwelleth in him, and he in God. And we have known and believed the love that God hath to us. God is love: and he that dwelleth in love dwelleth in God, and God in him. Herein is our love made perfect, that we may have boldness in the day of judgment: because as He is, so are we in this world. There is no fear in love; but perfect love casteth out fear: because fear hath torment. He that feareth is not made perfect in love. We love Him, because He

intelligimus quoniam in cum manemus et ipse in nobis, quoniam de Spiritu Suo dedit nobis. Et nos vidimus et testificamur quoniam Pater misit Filium salvatorem mundi. Quicunque confessus fuerit quoniam Iesus est Filius Dei, Deus in eo manet, et ipse in Deo. Et nos cognovimus et credimus, caritati Dei quam habet Deus in nobis. Deus caritas est, et qui manet in caritate in Deo manet, et Deus in eo. In hoc perfecta est nobiscum caritas ut fiduciam habeamus in die iudicii quia sicut ille est et nos sumus in hoc mundo. Timor non est in caritate, sed perfecta caritas foras mittit timorem; quoniam timor poenam habet, qui autem timet non est perfectus in caritate. Nos ergo diligamus invicem quo-

καὶ ἡ ἀγάπη αὐτοῦ τετελειωμένη ἐστὶν ἐν ἡμῖν. ἐν τούτῳ γινώσκομεν ὅτι ἐν αὐτῷ μένομεν καὶ αὐτὸς ἐν ἡμῖν, ὅτι ἐκ τοῦ Πνεύματος αὐτοῦ δέδωκεν ἡμῖν. Καὶ ἡμεῖς τεθεάμεθα καὶ μαρτυροῦμεν ὅτι ὁ πατὴρ ἀπέσταλκε τὸν υἱὸν σωτῆρα τοῦ κόσμου. ὃς ἂν ὁμολογήσῃ ὅτι Ἰησοῦς ἐστιν ὁ υἱὸς τοῦ Θεοῦ, ὁ Θεὸς ἐν αὐτῷ μένει καὶ αὐτὸς ἐν τῷ Θεῷ. Καὶ ἡμεῖς ἐγνώκαμεν καὶ πεπιστεύκαμεν τὴν ἀγάπην ἣν ἔχει ὁ Θεὸς ἐν ἡμῖν. ὁ Θεὸς ἀγάπη ἐστί, καὶ ὁ μένων ἐν τῇ ἀγάπῃ ἐν τῷ Θεῷ μένει, καὶ ὁ Θεὸς ἐν αὐτῷ. Ἐν τούτῳ τετελείωται ἡ ἀγάπη μεθ' ἡμῶν, ἵνα παρρησίαν ἔχωμεν ἐν τῇ ἡμέρᾳ τῆς κρίσεως· ὅτι καθὼς ἐκεῖνός ἐστι καὶ ἡμεῖς ἐσμεν ἐν τῷ κόσμῳ τούτῳ. φόβος οὐκ ἔστιν ἐν τῇ ἀγάπῃ, ἀλλ' ἡ τελεία ἀγάπη ἔξω βάλλει τὸν φόβον, ὅτι ὁ φόβος

We love, because He first loved us. If a man say, I love God, and hateth his brother, he is a liar: for he that loveth not his brother whom he hath seen, cannot love God whom he hath not seen. And this commandment have we from Him, That he who loveth God love his brother also.

Whosoever believeth that Jesus is the Christ is born of God: and every one that loveth Him that begat loveth Him also that is begotten of Him. By this we know that we love the children of God, when we love God, and keep His commandments. For this is the love of God, that we keep His commandments.

not made perfect in his love. We love Him because He first loved us. If a man say, I love God, and hateth his brother, he is a liar: for he that loveth not his brother whom he hath seen, God whom he hath not seen how can he love? And this commandment have we from Him, that he who loveth God love his brother also.

Whosoever believeth that Jesus is the Christ is begotten of God, and every one who loveth Him that begat loveth also Him that is begotten of Him. Herein we know that we love the children of God, when we love God and do His commandments: for this is the love of God, that we observe His commandments.

niam Deus prior dilexit nos. Si quis dixerit quoniam diligo Deum, et fratrem suum oderit, mendax est: qui enim non diligit fratrem suum quem videt, Deum quem non videt quomodo potest diligere? Et hoc mandatum habemus a Deo, ut qui diligat Deum diligat et fratrem suum.

Omnis qui credit quoniam Iesus Christus, ex Deo natus est; et omnis qui diligit eum qui genuit, diligit eum qui natus est ex eo. In hoc cognoscimus quoniam diligimus natos Dei, cum Deum diligamus et mandata eius faciamus. Hæc est enim caritas Dei, ut mandata eius custodiamus.

κόλασιν ἔχει, ὁ δὲ φοβούμενος οὐ τετελείωται ἐν τῇ ἀγάπῃ. ἡμεῖς ἀγαπῶμεν αὐτόν, ὅτι αὐτὸς πρῶτος ἠγάπησεν ἡμᾶς. Ἐάν τις εἴπῃ, Ὅτι ἀγαπῶ τὸν Θεόν, καὶ τὸν ἀδελφὸν αὐτοῦ μισῇ, ψεύστης ἐστίν· ὁ γὰρ μὴ ἀγαπῶν τὸν ἀδελφὸν αὐτοῦ ὃν ἑώρακε τὸν Θεὸν ὃν οὐχ ἑώρακε πῶς δύναται ἀγαπᾶν; καὶ ταύτην τὴν ἐντολὴν ἔχομεν ἀπ' αὐτοῦ, ἵνα ὁ ἀγαπῶν τὸν Θεὸν ἀγαπᾷ καὶ τὸν ἀδελφὸν αὐτοῦ.

Πᾶς ὁ πιστεύων ὅτι Ἰησοῦς ἐστιν ὁ Χριστὸς ἐκ τοῦ Θεοῦ γεγέννηται· καὶ πᾶς ὁ ἀγαπῶν τὸν γεννήσαντα ἀγαπᾷ καὶ τὸν γεγεννημένον ἐξ αὐτοῦ. ἐν τούτῳ γινώσκομεν ὅτι ἀγαπῶμεν τὰ τέκνα τοῦ Θεοῦ, ὅταν τὸν Θεὸν ἀγαπῶμεν καὶ τὰς ἐντολὰς αὐτοῦ τηρῶμεν. αὕτη γάρ ἐστιν ἡ ἀγάπη τοῦ Θεοῦ, ἵνα τὰς ἐντολὰς αὐτοῦ τηρῶμεν.

DISCOURSE X.

BOLDNESS IN THE DAY OF JUDGMENT.

"Herein is our love made perfect, that we may have boldness in the Day of Judgment: because as He is, so are we in this world."— I JOHN iv. 17.

IT has been so often repeated that St. John's eschatology is idealized and spiritual, that people now seldom pause to ask what is meant by the words. Those who repeat them most frequently seem to think that the idealized means that which will never come into the region of historical fact, and that the spiritual is best defined as the unreal. Yet, without postulating the Johannic authorship of the Apocalypse—where the Judgment is described with the most awful accompaniments of outward solemnity[1]—there are two places in this Epistle which are allowed to drop out of view, but which bring us face to face with the visible manifestations of an external Advent. It is a peculiarity of St. John's style (as we have frequently seen) to strike some chord of thought, so to speak, before its time; to allow the prelusive note to float away, until suddenly, after a time, it surprises us by coming back again with a fuller and bolder resonance. "And now, my sons,"[2] (had the Apostle said) "abide in Him, that if He shall be manifested, we may have confidence, and not be

---

[1] Apoc. xx. 12, 13.   [2] I John ii. 28.

ashamed shrinking from Him [1] at His coming." [2]   In
our text the same thought is resumed, and the reality
of the Coming and Judgment in its external manifestation as emphatically given as in any other part of the
New Testament. [3]

We may here speak of the conception of the Day of
the Judgment : of the fear with which that conception
is encompassed ; and of the sole means of the removal
of that fear which St. John recognises.

I.

We examine the general conception of " the Day of
the Judgment," as given in the New Testament.

As there is that which with terrible emphasis is
marked off as *"the* Judgment," [4] *"the* Parousia," so
there are other judgments or advents of a preparatory
character.   As there are phenomena known as mock
suns, or haloes round the moon, so there are fainter
reflections ringed round the Advent, the Judgment. [5]

---

[1] αἰσχυνθῶμεν ἀπ' αὐτοῦ, see Jerem. xii. 13 (for בֹּשׁ מִן).   Prof.
Westcott happily quotes, " as a guilty thing surprised."

[2] *Coming,* ἐν τῇ παρουσία αὐτοῦ.   The word is not found elsewhere in the Johannic group of writings.   But by his use of it here,
St. John falls into line with the whole array of apostolic witnesses—
with St. Matthew (xxiv. 3-27, 37, 39) ; with St. Paul (*passim*) ; with
St. James (v. 7, 8) ; with St. Peter (2 Peter i. 16, iii. 4-12).   This
fact may well warn critics of the precarious character of theories
founded upon " the negative phenomena of the books of the New
Testament."   (See Professor Westcott's excellent note, *The Epistles
of St. John,* 80.)

[3] (ἐν τῇ ἡμέρᾳ τῆς κρίσεως)—"in the Day of the Judgment"—
cf. Apoc. xiv. 7.   We have "in THE Judgment" (Matt. xii. 41, 42;
Luke x. 14, xi. 31, 32)—the indefinite "day of judgment" (Matt. x.
15, xi. 22, 24 ; Mark vi. 11).

[4] 2 Pet. ii. 9, iii. 7—but " *The* Day of *The* Judgment," here only.

[5] Cf. our Lord's words—" *henceforth* (ἀπ' ἄρτι) ye shall see the Son
of Man *coming.*"   Matt. xxvi. 64.)

Thus, in the development of history, there are successive cycles of continuing judgment; preparatory advents; less completed *crises*, as even the world calls them.

But against one somewhat widely-spread way of blotting the Day of the Judgment from the calendar of the future—so far as believers are concerned—we should be on our guard. Some good men think themselves entitled to reason thus—" I am a Christian. I shall be an assessor in the judgment. For me there is, therefore, no judgment day." And it is even held out as an inducement to others to close with this conclusion, that they " shall be delivered from the bugbear of judgment."

The origin of this notion seems to be in certain universal tendencies of modern religious thought.

The idolatry of the immediate—the prompt creation of effect—is the perpetual snare of *revivalism. Revivalism* is thence fatally bound at once to follow the tide of emotion, and to increase the volume of the waters by which it is swept along. But the religious emotion of this generation has one characteristic by which it is distinguished from that of previous centuries. The revivalism of the past in all Churches rode upon the dark waves of fear. It worked upon human nature by exaggerated material descriptions of hell, by solemn appeals to the throne of Judgment. Certain schools of biblical criticism have enabled men to steel themselves against this form of preaching. An age of soft humanitarian sentiment—superficial, and inclined to forget that perfect Goodness may be a very real cause of fear—must be stirred by emotions of a different kind. The infinite sweetness of our Father's heart—the conclusions, illogically but effectively drawn from this, of

an Infinite good-nature, with its easy-going pardon, reconciliation all round, and exemption from all that is unpleasant—these, and such as these, are the only available materials for creating a great volume of emotion. An invertebrate creed; punishment either annihilated or mitigated; judgment, changed from a solemn and universal assize, a bar at which every soul must stand, to a splendid, and—for all who can say I *am saved*—a triumphant pageant in which they have no anxious concern; these are the readiest instruments, the most powerful leverage, with which to work extensively upon masses of men at the present time. And the seventh article of the Apostles' Creed must pass into the limbo of exploded superstition.

The only appeal to Scripture which such persons make, with any show of plausibility, is contained in an exposition of our Lord's teaching in a part of the fifth chapter of the fourth Gospel.[1] But clearly there are three Resurrection scenes which may be discriminated in those words. The first is spiritual, a present awakening of dead souls,[2] in those with whom the Son of Man is brought into contact in His earthly ministry. The second is a department of the same spiritual resurrection. The Son of God, with that mysterious gift of Life in Himself,[3] has within Him a perpetual spring of rejuvenescence for a faded and dying world. A renewal of hearts is in process during all the days of time, a passage for soul after soul out of death into life.[4] The third scene is the general Resurrection and general Judgment.[5] The first was the resurrection of comparatively few; the second is the resurrection of many;

---

[1] John v. 21, 29.   [2] Ver. 21.   [3] Ver. 26.
[4] Ver. 24.   [5] Ver. 28, 29.

the third will be the resurrection of all.   If it is said
that the believer "cometh not into *judgment*," the word
in that place plainly signifies *condemnation.*[1]

Clear and plain above all such subtleties ring out the
awe-inspiring words: "it is appointed unto men once
to die, but after this the Judgment;" "we must all
appear before the judgment-seat of Christ."[2]

Reason supplies us with two great arguments for the
General Judgment.   One from the conscience of history,
so to speak; the other from the individual conscience.

1. General history points to a general judgment.
If there is no such judgment to come, then there is
no one definite moral purpose in human society.
Progress would be a melancholy word, a deceptive
appearance, a stream that has no issue, a road that
leads nowhere.   No one who believes that there is a
Personal God, Who guides the course of human affairs,
can come to the conclusion that the generations of man
are to go on for ever without a winding-up, which shall
decide upon the doings of all who take part in human
life.   In the philosophy of nature, the affirmation or
denial of purpose is the affirmation or denial of God.
So in the philosophy of history.   Society without the

---

[1] The writer ventures to lament the substitution of "judgment"
for "condemnation," ver. 24. R.V.   It is a verbal consistency, or
minute accuracy, purchased at the heavy price of a false thought,
suggested to many readers who are not scholars.   "In John's
language κρίσις is, (*a*) that *judgment* which came in pain and misery
to those who rejected the salvation offered to mankind by Christ,
iii. 19, κ.τ.λ., ἔρχεσθαι εἰς κρίσιν, to *fall into the state of one thus
condemned*, v. 24.   (*b*) Judgment of condemnation to the wicked,
with ensuing rejection, v. 29."   Grimm. Lex. N.T. 247.   Between
this passage of the fourth Gospel and Apoc. xx., there is a marvellous
inner harmony of thought.   "The first resurrection" (ver. 6) =
John v. 21, 26; then vv. 11, 12, 13 = John v. 28, 29.

[2] Heb. ix. 27; 2 Cor. v. 10, cf. Rom. xiv. 10; Apoc. xx. 11, 12, 13.

General Judgment would be a chaos of random facts, a thing without rational retrospect or definite end—*i.e.,* without God. If man is under the government of God, human history is a drama, long-drawn, and of infinite variety, with inconceivably numerous actors. But a drama must have a last act. The last act of the drama of history is "The Day of the Judgment."

2. The other argument is derived from the individual conscience.

Conscience, as a matter of fact, has two voices. One is *imperative ;* it tells us what we are to do. One is *prophetic,* and warns us of something which we are to receive. If there is to be no Day of the General Judgment, then the million prophecies of conscience will be belied, and our nature prove to be mendacious to its very roots.

There is no essential article of the Christian creed like this which can be isolated from the rest, and treated as if it stood alone. There is a *solidarity* of each with all the rest. Any which is isolated is in danger itself, and leaves the others exposed. For they have an internal harmony and congruity. They do not form a hotch-pot of credenda. They are not so many *beliefs* but one *belief.* Thus the isolation of articles is perilous. For, when we try to grasp and to defend one of them, we have no means left of measuring it but by terms of comparison which are drawn from ourselves, which must therefore be finite, and by the inadequacy of the scale which they present, appear to render the article of faith thus detached incredible. Moreover, each article of our creed is a revelation of the Divine attributes, which meet together in unity. To divide the attributes by dividing the form in which they are revealed to us is to belie and falsify the attribute ; to

give a monstrous development to one by not taking into account some other which is its balance and compensation. Thus, many men deny the truth of a punishment which involves final separation from God. They glory in the legal judgment which "dismisses hell with costs." But they do so by fixing their attention exclusively upon the one dogma which reveals one attribute of God. They isolate it from the Fall, from the Redemption by Christ, from the gravity of sin, from the truth that all whom the message of the Gospel reaches may avoid the penal consequences of sin. It is impossible to face the dogma of eternal separation from God without facing the dogma of Redemption. For Redemption involves in its very idea the intensity of sin, which needed the sacrifice of the Son of God; and further, the fact that the offer of salvation is so free and wide that it cannot be put away without a terrible wilfulness.

In dealing with many of the articles of the creed, there are opposite extremes. Exaggeration leads to a revenge upon them which is, perhaps, more perilous than neglect. Thus, as regards eternal punishment, in one country ghastly exaggerations were prevalent. It was assumed that the vast majority of mankind "are destined to everlasting punishment"; that "the floor of hell is crawled over by hosts of babies a span long." The inconsistency of such views with the love of God, and with the best instincts of man, was victoriously and passionately demonstrated. Then unbelief turned upon the dogma itself, and argued, with wide acceptance, that "with the overthrow of this conception goes the whole redemption-plan, the Incarnation, the Atonement, the Resurrection, and the grand climax of the Church-scheme, the General Judgment." But the alleged article

of faith was simply an exaggeration of that faith, and the objections lay altogether against the exaggeration of it.

II.

We have now to speak of the removal of that terror which accompanies the conception of the Day of the Judgment, and of the sole means of that emancipation which St. John recognises.   For terror there is in every point of the repeated descriptions of Scripture—in the surroundings, in the summons, in the tribunal, in the trial, in one of the two sentences.

"God is love," writes St. John, "and he that abideth in love abideth in God : and God abideth in him.   In this [abiding], love stands perfected *with us*,[1] and the object is nothing less than this," not that we may be exempted from judgment, but that "we may have boldness in the Day of the Judgment."   Boldness !   It is the splendid word which denotes the citizen's right of free speech, the masculine privilege of courageous liberty.[2]   It is the tender word which expresses the child's unhesitating confidence, in "saying all out" to the parent.   The ground of the boldness is conformity to Christ.   Because "as He *is*," with that vivid idealizing sense, frequent in St. John when he uses it of our Lord—"as He is," delineated in the fourth Gospel, seen

---

[1] · μεθ' ἡμῶν—God's love in itself is perfected.   It might be made as perfect as man's nature will admit by an instantaneous act; but God works jointly, in companionship with us.   The grace of God "preventing us that we may will, *works with us* when we will."   The essential idea of μετά is *companionship* or *connexion*.   (See Donaldson, *Gr. Gr.*, 50, 52 *a*.)

[2] ἐλευθερίας ἡ πόλις μεστὴ καὶ παρρησίας γίγνεται.   (Plat., *Rep.*, 557 B).   The word is derived from πᾶν and ῥῆσις.

by "the eye of the heart"[1] with constant reverence in the soul, with adoring wonder in heaven, perfectly true, pure, and righteous—"even so" (not, of course, with any equality in degree to that consummate ideal, but with a likeness ever growing, an aspiration ever advancing[2])—"so are we in this world," purifying ourselves as He is pure.

Let us draw to a definite point our considerations upon the Judgment, and the Apostle's sweet encouragement for the "day of wrath, that dreadful day."

It is of the essence of the Christian faith to believe that the Son of God, in the Human Nature which He assumed, and which He has borne into heaven, shall come again, and gather all before Him, and pass sentence of condemnation or of peace according to their works. To hold this is necessary to prevent terrible doubts of the very existence of God ; to guard us against sin, in view of that solemn account ; to comfort us under affliction.

What a thought for us, if we would but meditate upon it ! Often we complain of a commonplace life, of mean and petty employment. How can it be so, when at the end we, and those with whom we live, must look upon that great, overwhelming sight ! Not an eye that shall not see Him, not a knee that shall not bow, not an ear that shall not hear the sentence. The heart might sink and the imagination quail under the burden of the supernatural existence which we cannot escape. One of two looks we must turn upon the Crucified—one willing as that which we cast on some glorious picture, or on the enchantment of the sky ; the other unwilling and abject. We should weep first with

---

[1] Ephes. i. 18.   [2] Cf. Matt. v. 48.

Zechariah's mourners, with tears at once bitter because they are for sin, and sweet because they are for Christ.

But, above all things, let us hear how St. John sings us the sweet low hymn that breathes consolation through the terrible fall of the triple hammer-stroke of the rhyme in the *Dies iræ.* We must seek to lead upon earth a life laid on the lines of Christ's. Then, when the Day of the Judgment comes; when the cross of fire (so, at least, the early Christians thought) shall stand in the black vault; when the sacred wounds of Him who was pierced shall stream over with a light beyond dawn or sunset; we shall find that the discipline of life is complete, that God's love after all its long working with us stands perfected, so that we shall be able, as citizens of the kingdom, as children of the Father, to say out all. A Christlike character in an un-Christlike world—this is the cure of the disease of terror. Any other is but the medicine of a quack. " There is no fear in love; but the perfect love casteth out fear, because fear brings punishment; and he that feareth is not made perfect in love." [1]

We may well close with that pregnant commentary on this verse which tells us of the four possible conditions of a human soul—" without either fear or love; with fear, without love; with fear and love; with love, without fear." [2]

NOTES.

Ch. iv. 7, v. 3.

Ver. 3. This verse should divide about the middle.

---

[1] Ver. 18.

[2] Bengel. The writer must acknowledge his obligation to Professor Westcott, whose exposition gives us a peculiar conception of the depth of St. John's teaching here. (*The Epistles of St. John,* 149-153).

SECTION IX.

ANOTHER VERSION.

And His commandments are not heavy, for whatsoever is born of God conquereth the world: and this is the conquest that hath conquered the world—the Faith of us. Who is he that is conquering the world, but he that is believing that Jesus is the Son of God? This is He that came by water and blood—Jesus Christ: not with the water only, but with the water and with the blood. And the Spirit is that which is ever witnessing that the Spirit is the truth. For three are they who are ever witnessing, the Spirit and the water and the blood: and the three agree in one. If we receive the witness of men the wit-

REVISED VERSION.

And His commandments are not grievous. For whatsoever is begotten of God overcometh the world: and this is the victory that hath overcome the world, *even* our faith. And who is he that overcometh the world, but he that believeth that Jesus is the Son of God? This is He that came by water and blood, *even* Jesus Christ; not with the water only, but with the water and with the blood. And it is the Spirit that beareth witness, because the Spirit is the truth. For there are three who bear witness, the Spirit, and the water, and the blood: and the three agree in one. If we receive the witness

AUTHORISED VERSION.

And His commandments are not grievous. For whatsoever is born of God overcometh the world: and this is the victory that overcometh the world, *even* our faith. Who is he that overcometh the world, but he that believeth that Jesus is the Son of God? This is He that came by water and blood, not by water only, but by water and blood. And it is the Spirit that beareth witness, because the Spirit is truth. For there are three that bear record in heaven, the Father, the Word, and the Holy Ghost: and these three are one. And there are three that bear witness in earth, the spirit, and

LATIN.

Et mandata eius gravia non sunt. Quoniam omne quod natum est ex Deo vincit mundum: et hæc est victoria quæ vincit mundum, fides nostra. Quis est qui vincit mundum nisi qui credit quoniam Iesus est Filius Dei? Hic est qui venit per aquam et sanguinem, Iesus Christus: non in aqua solum, sed in aqua et sanguine. Et Spiritus est qui testificatur quoniam Christus est veritas. Quia tres sunt qui testimonium dant, Spiritus et aqua et sanguis, et tres unum sunt. Si testimonium hominum accipimus, testimonium Dei maius est: quoniam hoc est testimonium Dei quod maius est, quia testi-

GREEK.

Καὶ αἱ ἐντολαὶ αὐτοῦ βαρεῖαι οὐκ εἰσίν· ὅτι πᾶν τὸ γεγεννημένον ἐκ τοῦ Θεοῦ νικᾷ τὸν κόσμον· καὶ αὕτη ἐστὶν ἡ νίκη ἡ νικήσασα τὸν κόσμον, ἡ πίστις ἡμῶν. τίς ἐστιν ὁ νικῶν τὸν κόσμον, εἰ μὴ ὁ πιστεύων ὅτι Ἰησοῦς ἐστιν ὁ υἱὸς τοῦ Θεοῦ; Οὗτός ἐστιν ὁ ἐλθὼν δι' ὕδατος καὶ αἵματος, Ἰησοῦς ὁ Χριστός· οὐκ ἐν τῷ ὕδατι μόνον, ἀλλ' ἐν τῷ ὕδατι καὶ ἐν τῷ αἵματι· καὶ τὸ πνεῦμά ἐστι τὸ μαρτυροῦν, ὅτι τὸ πνεῦμά ἐστιν ἡ ἀλήθεια. ὅτι τρεῖς εἰσιν οἱ μαρτυροῦντες, τὸ πνεῦμα, καὶ τὸ ὕδωρ, καὶ τὸ αἷμα· καὶ οἱ τρεῖς εἰς τὸ ἕν εἰσιν. Εἰ τὴν μαρτυρίαν τῶν ἀνθρώπων λαμβάνομεν, ἡ μαρτυρία τοῦ Θεοῦ μείζων ἐστίν· ὅτι αὕτη ἐστὶν ἡ μαρτυρία

ness of God is greater; because the witness of God is this, because (*I say*) He hath witnessed concerning His Son. He that is believing on the Son of God hath the witness in him, he that is not believing God hath made Him a liar: because he is not a believer in the witness that God witnessed concerning His Son. And this is the witness, that God gave unto us eternal life, and this life is in His Son. He that hath the Son hath the life, he that hath not the Son of God hath not the life. These things have I written unto you that ye may know that ye have eternal life—ye that are believing in the name of the Son of God! And this is the boldness which we have to Himward, that

of men, the witness of God is greater: for the witness of God is this, that He hath borne witness concerning His Son. He that believeth on the Son of God hath the witness in him: he that believeth not God hath made Him a liar: because he hath not believed in the witness that God hath borne concerning His Son. And the witness is this, that God gave unto us eternal life, and this life is in His Son. He that hath the Son hath the life; he that hath not the Son of God hath not the life. These things have I written unto you, that ye may know that ye have eternal life, *even* unto you that believe on the name of the Son of God. And this is the boldness which we have toward Him, that,

the water, and the blood: and these three agree in one. If we receive the witness of men, the witness of God is greater: for this is the witness of God which He hath testified of His Son. He that believeth on the Son of God hath the witness in himself: he that believeth not God hath made Him a liar; because he believeth not the record that God gave of His Son. And this is the record, that God hath given to us eternal life, and this life is in His Son. He that hath the Son hath life; *and he* that hath not the Son of God hath not life. These things have I written unto you that believe on the name of the Son of God; that ye may know that ye have eternal life, and

ficatus est de Filio suo. Qui credit in Filio Dei, habet testimonium Dei in se: qui non credit mendacem facit eum: quoniam non credidit in testimonio quod testificatus est Deus de Filio suo. Et hoc est testimonium, quoniam vitam aeternam dedit nobis Deus, et haec vita in Filio eius. Qui habet Filium habet vitam: qui non habet filium vitam non habet. Haec scripsi vobis ut sciatis quoniam vitam habetis aeternam, qui creditis in nomine Filii Dei. Et haec est fiducia quam habemus ad eum quia quodcumque petierimus secundum voluntatem eius audit nos. Et scimus quoniam audit nos quicquid petierimus, scimus quoniam habemus petitiones quas postulamus ab eo.

τοῦ Θεοῦ, ὅτι μεμαρτύρηκεν περὶ τοῦ υἱοῦ αὐτοῦ. ὁ πιστεύων εἰς τὸν υἱὸν τοῦ Θεοῦ, ἔχει τὴν μαρτυρίαν ἐν αὐτῷ. ὁ μὴ πιστεύων τῷ Θεῷ ψεύστην πεποίηκεν αὐτόν, ὅτι οὐ πεπίστευκεν εἰς τὴν μαρτυρίαν, ἣν μεμαρτύρηκεν ὁ Θεὸς περὶ τοῦ υἱοῦ αὐτοῦ. Καὶ αὕτη ἐστὶν ἡ μαρτυρία ὅτι ζωὴν αἰώνιον ἔδωκεν ἡμῖν ὁ Θεὸς, καὶ αὕτη ἡ ζωὴ ἐν τῷ υἱῷ αὐτοῦ ἐστιν. ὁ ἔχων τὸν υἱὸν ἔχει τὴν ζωήν. ὁ μὴ ἔχων τὸν υἱὸν τοῦ Θεοῦ, τὴν ζωὴν οὐκ ἔχει. Ταῦτα ἔγραψα ὑμῖν ἵνα εἰδῆτε ὅτι ζωὴν ἔχετε αἰώνιον, οἱ πιστεύοντες εἰς τὸ ὄνομα τοῦ υἱοῦ τοῦ Θεοῦ. Καὶ αὕτη ἐστὶν ἡ παρρησία ἣν ἔχομεν πρὸς αὐτόν, ὅτι ἐάν τι αἰτώμεθα κατὰ τὸ θέλημα αὐτοῦ, ἀκούει ἡμῶν. καὶ ἐὰν οἴδαμεν ὅτι ἀκούει ἡμῶν ὃ ἂν αἰτώμεθα, οἴδαμεν ὅτι

if we ask any thing according to His will, He is hearing us; and if we know that He is hearing us, we know that we have the desires that we have desired from Him. If any man see his brother sinning sin not unto death, he shall ask, and *God* shall give him life—(I *mean* for those who are not sinning unto death). Not concerning this *sin* am I saying that he should make request. All unrighteousness is sin, and there is sin not unto death.

if we ask any thing according to His will, He heareth us: and if we know that He heareth us whatsoever we ask, we know that we have the petitions which we have asked of Him. If any man see his brother sinning a sin not unto death, he shall ask, and *God* will give him life for them that sin not unto death. There is a sin unto death; not concerning this *sin* am I saying that he should make request. All unrighteousness is sin, and there is sin not unto death.

that ye may believe on the name of the Son of God. And this is the confidence that we have in Him, that, if ask any thing according to His will, He heareth us: and if we know that He hear us, whatsoever we ask, we know that we have the petitions that we desired of Him. If any man see his brother sin a sin *which is* not unto death, he shall ask, and He shall give him life for them that sin not unto death. There is a sin unto death: I do not say that he shall pray for it. All unrighteousness is sin: and there is a sin not unto death.

Qui scit fratrem suum peccare peccatum non ad mortem, petit, et dabit ei vitam, peccantibus non ad mortem. Est peccatum ad mortem: non pro illo dico ut roget quis. Omnis iniquitas peccatum est: et est peccatum ad mortem.

ἔχομεν τὰ αἰτήματα ἃ ᾐτήκαμεν παρ' αὐτοῦ. Ἐάν τις ἴδῃ τὸν ἀδελφὸν αὐτοῦ ἁμαρτάνοντα ἁμαρτίαν μὴ πρὸς θάνατον, αἰτήσει, καὶ δώσει αὐτῷ ζωὴν τοῖς ἁμαρτάνουσι μὴ πρὸς θάνατον. ἔστιν ἁμαρτία πρὸς θάνατον· οὐ περὶ ἐκείνης λέγω ἵνα ἐρωτήσῃ· πᾶσα ἀδικία ἁμαρτία ἐστίν, καὶ ἔστιν ἁμαρτία οὐ πρὸς θάνατον.

DISCOURSE XI.

BIRTH AND VICTORY.

"And His commandments are not grievous. For whatsoever is born of God overcometh the world : and this is the victory that overcometh the world, even our faith. Who is he that overcometh the world, but he that believeth that Jesus is the Son of God ?"— I JOHN v. 3, 4, 5.

ST. JOHN here connects the Christian birth with victory. He tells us that of the supernatural life the destined and (so to speak) natural end is conquest.

Now in this there is a *contrast* between the law of nature and the law of grace. No doubt the first is marvellous. It may even, if we will, in one sense be termed a victory ; for it is the proof of a successful contest with the blind fatalities of natural environment. It is in itself the conquest of a something which has conquered a world below it. The first faint cry of the baby is a wail no doubt ; but in its very utterance there is a half triumphant undertone. Boyhood, youth, opening manhood—at least in those who are physically and intellectually gifted—generally possess some share of "the rapture of the strife" with nature and with their contemporaries.

"Youth hath triumphal mornings ; its days bound
From night as from a victory."

But sooner or later that which pessimists style "the martyrdom of life" sets in. However brightly the

drama opens, the last scene is always tragic. Our natural birth inevitably ends in defeat.

A birth and a defeat is thus the epitome of each life which is naturally brought into the field of our present human existence. The defeat is sighed over, sometimes consummated, in every cradle; it is attested by every grave.

But if birth and defeat is the motto of the natural life, birth and victory is the motto of every one born into the city of God.

This victory is spoken of in our verses as a victory along the whole line. It is the conquest of the collective Church, of the whole mass of regenerate humanity, so far as it has been true to the principle of its birth[1]— the conquest of the Faith which is "The Faith of *us*,"[2] who are knit together in one communion and fellowship in the mystical body of the Son of God, Christ our Lord. But it is something more than that. The general victory is also a victory in detail. Every true individual believer shares in it.[3] The battle is a battle of soldiers. The abstract ideal victory is realised and made concrete in each life of struggle which is a life of enduring faith. The triumph is not merely one of a school, or of a party. The question rings with a triumphant challenge down the ranks—" who is the ever-conqueror of the world, but the ever-believer that Jesus is the Son of God ?"

We are thus brought to two of St. John's great master-conceptions, both of which came to him from *hearing* the Lord who is the Life—both of which are

---

[1] This is expressed, after St. John's fashion, by the neuter, πᾶν τὸ γεγεννημένον ἐκ τοῦ Θεοῦ. ver. 4.

[2] ἡ πίστις ἡμῶν, ver. 4.

[3] ὁ νικῶν τὸν κόσμον, ὁ πιστεύων, ver. 5.

to be read in connection with the fourth Gospel—the Christian's *Birth* and his *victory*.

I.

The Apostle introduces the idea of the birth which has its origin from God precisely by the same process to which attention has already been more than once directed.

St. John frequently mentions some great subject; at first like a musician who with perfect command of his instrument, touches what seems to be an almost random key, faintly, as if incidentally and half wandering from his theme. But just as the sound appears to be absorbed by the purpose of the composition, or all but lost in the distance, the same chord is struck again more decidedly; and then, after more or less interval, is brought out with a music so full and sonorous, that we perceive that it has been one of the master's leading ideas from the very first. So, when the subject is first spoken of, we hear—" every one that doeth righteousness is born of Him."[1] The subject is suspended for a while; then comes a somewhat more marked reference. " Whosoever is born of God is not a doer of sin; and he cannot continue sinning, because of God he is born." There is yet one more tender recurrence to the favourite theme—" every one that loveth is born of God."[2] Then, finally here at last the chord, so often struck, grown bolder since the prelude, gathers all the music round it. It interweaves with itself another strain which has similarly been gaining amplitude of volume in its course, until we have a great *Te Deum*, dominated by two chords of

---

[1] 1 John ii. 29.   [2] 1 John iv. 7.

15

Birth and Victory. "This *is* the conquest that has *conquered* the world—the Faith which is of us."

We shall never come to any adequate notion of St. John's conception of the Birth of God, without tracing the place in his Gospel to which his asterisk in this place refers. To one passage only can we turn—our Lord's conversation with Nicodemus. " Except a man be born again, he cannot see the kingdom of God—except a man be born of water and of the Spirit, he cannot enter into the kingdom of God."[1] The germ of the idea of entrance into the city, the kingdom of God, by means of a new birth, is in that storehouse of theological conceptions, the psalter. There is one psalm of a Korahite seer, enigmatical it may be, shadowed with the darkness of a divine compression,[2] obscure from the glory that rings it round, and from the gush of joy in its few and broken words. The 87th Psalm is the psalm of the font, the hymn of regeneration. The nations once of the world are mentioned among them that know the Lord. They are counted when He writeth up the peoples. Glorious things are spoken of the City of God. Three times over the burden of the song is the new birth by which the aliens were made free of Sion.

This one was born there,

This one and that one was born in her,

This one was born there.[3]

All joyous life is thus brought into the city of the new-born. " The singers, the solemn dances, the fresh

---

[1] John iii. 5.

[2] σφόδρα αἰνιγματώδης καὶ σκοτεινῶς εἰρημένος.   Euseb.

[3]   עֶה יֻלַּד־שָׁם.   Ver. 4.

אִישׁ וְאִישׁ יֻלַּד־בָּהּ.   Ver. 5.

עֶה יֻלַּד־שָׁם.   Ver. 6.   Psalm lxxxvii.

and glancing springs, are in thee."[1]   Hence, from the
notification of men being born again in order to see and
enter into the kingdom, our Lord, as if in surprise,
meets the Pharisee's question—"how can these things
be ?"—with another—" art thou that teacher in Israel,[2]
and understandest not these things ? "   Jesus tells His
Church for ever that every one of His disciples must
be brought into contact with two worlds, with two influences—one outward, the other inward ; one material,
the other spiritual ; one earthly, the other heavenly ;
one visible and sacramental, the other invisible and
divine.   Out of these he must come forth new-born.

Of course it may be said that "the water" here
coupled with the Spirit is *figurative*.   But let it be
observed first, that from the very constitution of St.
John's intellectual and moral being things outward and
visible were not annihilated by the spiritual transparency which he imparted to them.   Water, literal water,
is everywhere in his writings.   In his Gospel more
especially he seems to be ever seeing, ever hearing it.
He loved it from the associations of his own early life,
and from the mention made of it by his Master.   And
as in the Gospel water is, so to speak, one of the three
great factors and centres of the book ;[3] so now in the
Epistle, it still seems to glance and murmur before
him.   " The water " is one of the three abiding

---

[1] " Both they who sing and they who dance,
     With sacred song are there ;
   In thee fresh brooks and soft streams glance,
     And all my fountains clear."

                    MILTON, Paraphrase Ps. lxxxvii. 7.

This, on the whole, seems to be considered the most tenable interpretation.

[2] Σὺ εἶ ὁ διδάσκαλος τοῦ Ἰσραὴλ ; John iii. 10.

[3] John i. 26, ii. 6, 9, iii. 5-22, iv. 6-16, v. 3, vii. 37, 39, ix. 7, xiii. 1-5, xix. 34

witnesses in the Epistle also.   Surely, then, our
Apostle would be eminently unlikely to express " the
Spirit of God " *without* the outward water by " water
and the Spirit."   But above all, Christians should be-
ware of a " licentious and deluding alchemy of interpretation which maketh of anything whatsoever it
listeth."   In immortal words—" when the letter of the
law hath two things plainly and expressly specified,
water and the Spirit; water, as a duty required on our
part, the Spirit, as a gift which God bestoweth ; there
is danger in so presuming to interpret it, as if the
clause which concerneth ourselves were more than
needed.   We may by such rare expositions attain
perhaps in the end to be thought witty, but with ill
advice."[1]

But, it will further be asked, whether we bring the
Saviour's saying—" except any one be born again of
water and the Spirit "—into direct connection with the
baptism of infants ?   Above all, whether we are not
encouraging every baptised person to hold that some-
how or other he will have a part in the victory of the
regenerate ?

We need no other answer than that which is implied
in the very force of the word here used by St. John—
" all that is born of God conquereth the world."
" That is born " is the participle perfect.[2]   The force
of the perfect is not simply past action, but such action
lasting on in its effects.   Our text, then, speaks only

---

[1] Hooker, *E. P.,* V. lix. (4).
[2] So the perfect is used throughout. γεγέννηται. ii. 29, iii. 9, iv. 7.
πᾶν τὸ γεγεννημένον. v. 4.   Very remarkably below, πᾶς ὁ γεγεννημένος
—ἀλλὰ ὁ γεννηθεὶς ἐκ τοῦ Θεοῦ; the first of the regenerate man who
continues in that condition of grace, the second of the Begotten Son
of God who keeps His servant. 1 John v. 18.

of those who having been born again into the kingdom
continue in a corresponding condition, and unfold the
life which they have received. The Saviour spoke first
and chiefly of the initial act. The Apostle's circumstances, now in his old age, naturally led him to look
on from that. St. John is no "idolater of the immediate."
Has the gift received by his spiritual children worn
long and lasted well ? What of the new life which
should have issued from the New Birth ? Regenerate
in the past, are they renewed in the present ?

This simple piece of exegesis lets us at once perceive
that another verse in this Epistle, often considered of
almost hopeless perplexity, is in truth only the perfection
of sanctified (nay, it may be said, of moral) common-
sense ; an intuition of moral and spiritual instinct.
"Whosoever is born of God doth not commit sin: for his
seed remaineth in him ; and he cannot sin, because he is
born of God." We have just seen the real significance of
the words " he that is born of God "—he for whom his
past birth lasts on in its effects. " He *doeth* not sin," is
not a sin-doer, makes it not his "trade," as an old commentator says. Nay, " he is not able to be " (to keep
on) " sinning." " He cannot sin." He cannot! There
is no physical impossibility. Angels will not sweep
him away upon their resistless pinions. The Spirit
will not hold him by the hand as if with a mailed grasp,
until the blood spirts from his finger-tips, that he may
not take the wine-cup, or walk out to the guilty assigna-
tion. The compulsion of God is like that which is
exercised upon us by some pathetic wounded-looking
face that gazes after us with a sweet reproach. Tell the
honest poor man with a large family of some safe and
expeditious way of transferring his neighbour's money
to his own pocket. He will answer, " I cannot steal: "

that is, " I cannot steal, however much it may physically be within my capacity, without a burning shame, an agony to my nature worse than death." On some day of fierce heat, hold a draught of iced wine to a total abstainer, and invite him to drink. " I cannot," will be his reply. Cannot ! He can, so far as his hand goes ; he cannot, without doing violence to a conviction, to a promise, to his own sense of truth. And he who continues in the fulness of his God-given Birth "does not *do* sin," "cannot be sinning." Not that he is sinless, not that he never fails, or does not sometimes fall ; not that sin ceases to be sin to him, because he thinks that he has a standing in Christ. But he cannot go on in sin without being untrue to his birth ; without a stain upon that finer, whiter, more sensitive conscience, which is called " spirit " in a son of God ; without a convulsion in his whole being which is the precursor of death, or an insensibility which is death actually begun.

How many such texts as these are practically useless to most of us ! The armoury of God is full of keen swords which we refrain from handling, because they have been misused by others. None is more neglected than this. The fanatic has shrieked out—"sin in my case !" I *cannot* sin. *I* may hold a sin in my bosom ; and God may hold me in His arms for all that. At least, I may hold that which would be a sin in you and most others ; but to *me* it is *not* sin." On the other hand, stupid goodness maunders out some unintelligible paraphrase, until pew and reader yawn from very weariness. Divine truth in its purity and plainness is thus discredited by the exaggeration of the one, or buried in the leaden winding-sheet of the stupidity of the other.

In leaving this portion of our subject we may com-

pare the view latent in the very idea of infant baptism
with that of the leader of a well-known sect upon the
beginnings of the spiritual life in children.

"May not children grow up into salvation, without
knowing the exact moment of their conversion?" asks
"General" Booth.   His answer is—"yes, it may be
so; and we trust that in the future this will be the
usual way in which children may be brought to Christ."
The writer goes on to tell us how the New Birth will
take place in future.   "When the conditions named in
the first pages of this volume are complied with—when
the parents are godly, and the children are surrounded
by holy influences and examples from their birth, and
trained up in the spirit of their early dedication—they
will *doubtless come to know and love and trust their
Saviour in the ordinary course of things.*   The Holy
Ghost will take possession of them from the first.
Mothers and fathers will, as it were, put them into the
Saviour's arms in their swaddling clothes, and He will
take them, and bless them, and sanctify them from the
very womb, and make them His own, without their
knowing the hour or the place when they pass from the
kingdom of darkness into the kingdom of light.   In
fact, with such little ones it shall never be very dark,
for their natural birth shall be, as it were, in the
spiritual twilight, which begins with the dim dawn, and
increases gradually until the noonday brightness is
reached; so answering to the prophetic description,
'The path of the just is as the shining light, that
shineth more and more unto the perfect day.'" [1]

No one will deny that this is tenderly and beautifully

----

[1] *Training of children; or How to Make the Children into Saints
and Soldiers of Jesus Christ.*   By the General of the Salvation Army.
London : Salvation Army Book Stores, pp. 162, 163.

written.   But objections to its teaching will crowd
upon the mind of thoughtful Christians.   It seems to
defer to a period in the future, to a new era incalculably
di tant, when Christendom shall be absorbed in Salva-
tionism, that which St. John in his day contemplated
as the normal condition of believers, which the Church
has always held to be capable of realization, which has
been actually realized in no few whom most of us must
have known.   Further ; the fountain-heads of thought,
like those of the Nile, are wrapped in obscurity.   By
what process grace may work with the very young is
an insoluble problem in psychology, which Christianity has not revealed.   We know nothing further
than that Christ blessed little children.   That blessing
was *impartial,* for it was communicated to all who were
brought to Him ; it was *real,* otherwise He would not
have blessed them at all.   That He conveys to them
such grace as they are capable of receiving is all that
we can know.   And yet again ; the Salvationist theory
exalts parents and surroundings into the place of Christ.
It deposes His sacrament, which lies at the root of St.
John's language, and boasts that it will secure Christ's
end, apparently without any recognition of Christ's
means.

II.

The second great idea in the verses at the head of
this discourse is *Victory.*   The intended issue of the
new birth is conquest—"all that is born of God con-
quers the world."

The idea of victory is almost[1] exclusively confined

---

[1] Not quite, cf. Rom. viii. 37, xii. 21 ; 1 Cor. xv. 55, 57.   The substantive νίκη occurs only 1 John v. 4.   A slightly different form (νῖκος)
is in Matt. xii. 20 ; 1 Cor. xv. 54, 55, 57.

to St. John's writings.   The idea is first expressed by
Jesus—"be of good cheer: I have conquered the
world."[1]   The first prelusive touch in the Epistle,
hints at the fulfilment of the Saviour's comfortable word
in one class of the Apostle's spiritual children.   " I
write unto you, young men, because ye have conquered
the wicked one.   I have written unto you, young men,
because ye have conquered the wicked one."[2]   Next,
a bolder and ampler strain—"ye are of God, little
children, and have conquered them : because greater is
He that is in you, than he that is in the world."[3]   Then
with a magnificent persistence, the trumpet of Christ
wakens echoes to its music all down and round the
defile through which the host is passing—" all that is
born of God conquereth the world: and this is the
conquest that has conquered the world—the Faith
which is ours."[4]   When, in St. John's other great book,
we pass with the seer into Patmos, the air is, indeed,
" full of noises and sweet sounds."   But dominant over
all is a storm of triumph, a passionate exultation of
victory.   Thus each epistle to each of the seven Churches
closes with a promise " to him that *conquereth*."

The text promises *two* forms of victory.

1. A victory is promised to the Church universal.
" *All that* is born of God conquereth the world."   This
conquest is concentrated in, almost identified with " the
Faith."   Primarily, in this place, the term (here alone

---

[1] John xvi. 33.

[2] 1 John ii. 13, 14.

[3] 1 John iv. 4.

[4] It does not seem possible to convey to the English reader the fourfold harping upon the word (1 John v. 4, 5) by any other rendering.
" The *victory* that hath *overcome* the world " (R.V.) fails in this.   The
noble translation of ὑπερνικῶμεν (Rom. viii. 37), happily retained by
the Revisers, is rendered consistent by the translation here proposed.

found in our Epistle) is not the faith by *which we believe*, but the Faith *which is* believed—as in some other places;[1] not faith subjective, but The Faith objectively.[2] Here is the dogmatic principle. The Faith involves definite knowledge of definite principles. The religious know-ledge, which is not capable of being put into definite propositions, we need not trouble ourselves greatly about. But we are guarded from over-dogmatism. The word "of us" which follows "the Faith" is a mediating link between the objective and the subjective. First, we possess this Faith as a common heritage. Then, as in the Apostle's creed we begin to individualise this common possession by prefixing "I believe" to every article of it. Then the victory contained in the creed, the victory which the creed *is* (for more truly again than of Duty may it be said of Faith, "thou who *art victory*"[3]), is made over to each who believes. Each, and each alone, who in soul is ever believing, in practice is ever victorious.

This declaration is full of promise for missionary work. There is no system of error, however ancient, subtle, or highly organised, which must not go down before the strong collective life of the regenerate. No less en-couraging is it at home. No form of sin is incapable of being overthrown. No school of anti-Christian thought is invulnerable or invincible. There are other apostates besides Julian who will cry—"Galilæe, vicisti!"

2. The second victory promised is individual, for each of us. Not only where cathedral-spires lift high the triumphant cross; on battle-fields which have added kingdoms to Christendom ; by the martyr's stake, or in the arena of the Coliseum, have these words proved

---

[1] Apoc. ii. 13, xiv. 12.

[2] Fides *quæ creditur*, not *quâ creditur*.

[3] "Thou who art victory!"   Wordsworth, *Ode to Duty.*

true.   The victory comes down to us.   In hospitals, in
shops, in courts, in ships, in sick-rooms, they are fulfilled
for us.   We see their truth in the patience, sweetness, resignation, of little children, of old men, of weak
women.   They give a high consecration and a glorious
meaning to much of the suffering that we see.   What,
we are sometimes tempted to cry—is *this* Christ's
Army? are these His soldiers, who can go anywhere
and do anything? Poor weary ones! with white
lips, and the beads of death-sweat on their faces, and
the thorns of pain ringed like a crown round their
foreheads; so wan, so worn, so tired, so suffering, that
even our love dares not pray for them to live a little
longer yet.   Are these the elect of the elect, the van-
guard of the regenerate, who carry the flag of the cross
where its folds are waved by the storm of battle; whom
St. John sees advancing up the slope with such a burst
of cheers and such a swell of music that the words—
"this is the conquest"—spring spontaneously from his
lips? Perhaps the angels answer with a voice which
we cannot hear—"whatsoever is born of God conquereth the world." May we fight so manfully that
each may render if not his "pure" yet his purified

> "soul unto his captain Christ,
> Under whose colours he hath fought so long:"

—that we may know something of the great text in the
Epistle to the Romans, with its matchless translation
—"we are more than conquerors through Him who
loved us"[1]—that arrogance of victory which is at once
so splendid and so saintly.

---

[1] ὑπερνικῶμεν.   Rom. viii. 37.

DISCOURSE XII.

"It is the Spirit that beareth witness, because the Spirit is truth.
For there are three that bear witness, the Spirit, and the water, and
the blood ; and these three agree in one. If we receive the witness
of men, the witness of God is greater, for this is the witness of God
which He hath testified of His Son. He that believeth on the Son
of God hath the witness in himself."—1 JOHN v. 6-10.

IT has been said that Apostles and apostolic men
were as far as possible removed from common-
sense, and have no conception of evidence in our
acceptation of the word. About this statement there is
scarcely even superficial plausibility. Common-sense
is the measure of ordinary human tact among palpable
realities. In relation to human existence it is the balance
of the estimative faculties ; the instinctive summary of
inductions which makes us rightly credulous and
rightly incredulous, which teaches us the supreme
lesson of life, when to say " yes," and when to say
"no." Uncommon sense is superhuman tact among no
less real but at present impalpable realities ; the spiritual
faculty of forming spiritual inductions aright. So St.
John among the three great canons of primary truth
with which he closes his Epistle writes—"we know
that the Son of God hath come and is present, and hath
given us understanding, that we know Him who is

true."[1]   So with *evidences*.   Apostles did not draw
them out with the same logical precision, or rather not
in the same logical form, which the modern spirit demands.   Yet they rested their conclusions upon the
same abiding principle of evidence, the primary axiom
of our entire social life—that there is a degree of human
evidence which practically cannot deceive.   " If we receive the witness of men."   The form of expression
implies that we certainly do.[2]

Peculiar difficulty has been felt in understanding the
paragraph.   And one portion of it remains difficult
after any explanation.   But we shall succeed in ap-
prehending it as a whole only upon condition of taking
one guiding principle of interpretation with us.

The word *witness* is St. John's central thought here.
He is determined to beat it into the minds of his readers
by the most unsparing iteration.   He repeats it ten
times over, as substantive or verb, in six verses.[3]   His
object is to turn our attention to his Gospel, and to this
distinguishing feature of it—its being from beginning
to end a Gospel of *witness*.   This witness he declares
to be fivefold.   (1) The witness of the Spirit, of which
the fourth Gospel is pre-eminently full.   (2) The witness of the Divine Humanity, of the God-Man who is

---

[1] δέδωκεν ἡμῖν διάνοιαν ἵνα γινώσκομεν κ.τ.λ.   1 John v. 20.   N. T.
lexicographers give as its meaning *intelligentia* (*einsicht*).   See
Grimm. *Bretschn.*, s.v.   Prof. Westcott remarks that "generally
nouns which express intellectual powers are rare in St. John's
writings."   But διάνοια is the word by which the LXX. translate the
Hebrew לֵב, and has thus a moral and emotional tinge imparted to it.
We may compare the sense in which Aristotle uses it in his Poetics
for the cast of thought, or general sentiment.   (*Poet.*, vi.)

[2] εἰ τὴν μαρτυρίαν τῶν ἀνθρώπων λαμβάνομεν.   1 John v. 9.

[3] The A. V. (very unhappily) tried to minimise this reiteration
by the introduction of synonyms in four places—"bear record,"
"record" (vv. 7, 10, 11), "hath testified" (ver. 9).

not man deified, but God humanified.   This verse is no doubt partly polemical, against heretics of the day, who would clip the great picture of the Gospel, and force it into the petty frame of their theory.   This is He (the Apostle urges) who came on the stage of the world's and the Church's history[1] as the Messiah, under the condition, so to speak, of water and blood;[2] bringing with Him, accompanied by, not the water only, but the water and the blood.[3]   Cerinthus separated the Christ, the divine Æon, from Jesus the holy but mortal man.   The two, the divine potency and the human existence, met at the waters of Jordan, on the day of the Baptism, when the Christ united Himself to Jesus.   But the union was brief and unessential.   Before the crucifixion, the divine ideal Christ withdrew.   The man suffered.   The impassible immortal potency was far away in heaven. St. John denies the fortuitous juxta-position of two accidentally-united existences.   We worship one Lord Jesus Christ, attested not only by Baptism in Jordan, the witness of water, but by the death on Calvary, the witness of blood.   He came by water and blood, as the means by which His office was manifested ; but with the water and with the blood, as the sphere in which He exercises that office.   When we turn to the Gospel, and look at the pierced side, we read of blood and water, the order of actual history and physiological fact.   But here St. John takes the ideal, mystical, sacramental order, water and blood—cleansing and redemption—and the sacraments which perpetually symbolise and convey them.   Thus we have Spirit, water, blood. Three are they who are ever witnessing.[4]   These are

---

[1] ὁ ἐλθών.

[2] δι᾽ ὕδατος καὶ αἵματος.

[3] οὐκ ἐν τῷ ὕδατι μόνον, ἀλλ᾽ ἐν τῷ ὕδατι καὶ ἐν τῷ αἵματι.

[4] τρεῖς εἰσὶν οἱ μαρτυροῦντες, ver. 7.

three great centres round which St. John's Gospel turns.[1] These are the three genuine witnesses, the trinity of witness, the shadow of the Trinity in heaven. (3) Again the fourth Gospel is a Gospel of human witness, a tissue woven out of many lines of human attestation. It records the cries of human souls overheard and noted down at the supreme crisis-moment of life, from the Baptist, Philip, and Nathanael, to the everlasting spontaneous creed of Christendom on its knees before Jesus, the cry of Thomas ever rushing molten from a heart of fire—"my Lord and my God." (4) But if we receive, as we assuredly must and do receive, the overpowering and soul-subduing mass of attesting human evidence, how much more must we receive the Divine witness, the witness of God so conspicuously exhibited in the Gospel of St. John! "The witness of God is greater, because *this*" (even the history in the pages to which he adverts) "is the witness; because" (I say with triumphant reiteration) "He hath witnessed concerning His Son."[2] This witness of God in the last Gospel is given in four forms—by Scripture,[3] by the Father,[4] by the Son Himself,[5] by His works.[6] (5) This great volume of witness is consummated and brought home by another. He who not merely coldly assents to the word of Christ, but lifts the whole burden of his

---

[1] The *Water*, John iii. 5, cf. i. 26-33, ii. 9, iii. 23, iv. 13, v. 4, ix. 7. The *Blood*, vi. 53, 54, 56, xix. 34. The *Spirit*, vii. 39, xiv., xv., xvi., xx. 22. The water centres in *Baptism* (iii. 5); the blood is symbolised, exhibited, in Holy *Communion* (vi.): the Spirit is perpetually making them effective, and especially by the appointed ministry (xx. 22).

[2] ὅτι αὕτη ἐστὶν ἡ μαρτυρία τοῦ Θεοῦ, ὅτι μεμαρτύρηκεν περὶ τοῦ υἱοῦ αὐτοῦ, ver. 9.

[3] v. 39, 46, etc.

[4] viii. 18.

[5] viii. 17, 18.

[6] ver. 36, x. 25.

belief on to the Son of God,[1] hath the witness in him. That which was logical and external becomes internal and experimental.

In this ever-memorable passage, all scholars know that an interpolation has taken place. The words— " in heaven the Father, the Word, and the Holy Ghost ; and these three are one. And there are three that bear witness in earth "—are a gloss. A great sentence of one of the first of critics may well reassure any weak believers who dread the candour of Christian criticism, or suppose that it has impaired the evidence for the great dogma of the Trinity. " If the fourth century knew that text, let it come in, in God's name ; but if that age did not know it, then Arianism in its height was beaten down without the help of that verse ; and, let the *fact* prove as it will, the *doctrine* is unshaken."[2] The human material with which they have been clamped should not blind us to the value of the heavenly jewels which seemed to be marred by their earthly setting.

It is constantly said—as we think with considerable misapprehension—that in his Epistle St. John may imply, but does not refer directly to any particular incident in, his Gospel. It is our conviction that St. John very specially includes the Resurrection—the central point of the evidences of Christianity—among the things attested by the witness of men. We propose in another discourse to examine the Resurrection from St. John's point of view.

---

[1] ὁ πιστεύων εἰς τὸν υἱὸν τοῦ Θεοῦ, ver. 10. (See Bihs Ellicott on the force of various prepositions with πιστεύω. *Comment. on Pastoral Epistles.*)

[2] Bentley. Letter of January 1st, 1717.

DISCOURSE XIII.

THE WITNESS OF MEN (APPLIED TO THE RESURRECTION).

"If we receive the witness of men."—I JOHN v. 9.

AT an early period in the Christian Church the passage in which these words occur, was selected as a fitting Epistle for the First Sunday after Easter, when believers may be supposed to review the whole body of witness to the risen Lord and to triumph in the victory of faith. A consideration of the unity of essential principles in the narratives of the Resurrection will afford the best illustration of the comprehensive canon—" if we receive the witness of men."
if we consider the unity of essential principles in the narratives of the Resurrection, and draw the natural conclusions from them.

I.

Let us note the unity of essential principles in the narratives of the Resurrection.

St. Matthew hastens on from Jerusalem to the appearance in Galilee. "Behold! He goeth before you *into Galilee*," is, in some sense, the key of the 28th chapter. St. Luke, on the other hand, speaks only of manifestations in Jerusalem or its neighbourhood.

Now St. John's Resurrection history falls in the 20th chapter into four pieces, with three manifestations in Jerusalem. The 21st chapter (the appendix-chapter)

16

also falls into four pieces, with one manifestation to the seven disciples in Galilee.

St. John makes no profession of telling us all the appearances which were known to the Church, or even all of which he was personally cognisant. In the treasures of the old man's memory there were many more which, for whatever reason, he did not write. But these distinct continuous specimens of a permitted communing with the eternal glorified life (supplemented on subsequent thought by another in the last chapter) are as good as three or four hundred for the great purpose of the Apostle. "These are written that ye might believe that Jesus is the Christ, the Son of God."[1]

Throughout St. John's narrative every impartial reader will find delicacy of thought, abundance of matter, minuteness of detail. He will find something more. While he feels that he is not in cloudland or dreamland, he will yet recognise that he walks in a land which is wonderful, because the central figure in it is One whose name is Wonderful. The fact is fact, and yet it is something more. For a short time poetry and history are absolutely coincident. Here, if anywhere, is Herder's saying true, that the fourth Gospel seems to be written with a feather which has dropped from an angel's wing.

The unity in essential principles which has been claimed for these narratives taken together is not a lifeless identity in details. It is scarcely to be worked out by the dissecting-maps of elaborate harmonies. It is not the imaginative unity which is poetry ; nor the mechanical unity, which is fabrication ; nor the

---

[1] The writer is entirely persuaded that St. John in chap. xx. 30, 31, refers to the *Resurrection* "signs," and not to miracles generally.

passionless unity, which is commended in a police-report.   It is not the thin unity of plain-song; it is the rich unity of dissimilar tones blended into a fugue.

This unity may be considered in two essential agreements of the four Resurrection histories.

1. All the Evangelists agree in reticence on one point—in abstinence from one claim.

If any of us were framing for himself a body of such evidence for the Resurrection as should almost extort acquiescence, he would assuredly insist that the Lord should have been seen and recognised after the Resurrection by miscellaneous crowds—or, at the very least, by hostile individuals.   Not only by a tender Mary Magdalene, an impulsive Peter, a rapt John, a Thomas through all his unbelief nervously anxious to be convinced.   Let Him be seen by Pilate, by Caiaphas, by some of the Roman soldiers, of the priests, of the Jewish populace.   Certainly, if the Evangelists had simply aimed at effective presentation of evidence, they would have put forward statements of this kind.

But the apostolic principle—the apostolic canon of Resurrection evidence—was very different.   St. Luke has preserved it for us, as it is given by St. Peter. "Him God raised up the third day, and gave Him to be made manifest after He rose again from the dead, not to all the people, but unto witnesses chosen before of God, even to us."[1]   He shall, indeed, appear again

---

[1] Acts x. 41, 42.   It is to be regretted that the R. V. has not boldly given us such an arrangement of the words in this important passage as would at once connect "made manifest" with "after He rose again from the dead," and avoid making the Apostle state that the chosen witnesses ate and drank with Christ after the Resurrection.   St. Peter mentions that particular characteristic of the Apostles which made them judges not to be gainsayed of the identity of the Risen One with Him with whom they used to eat and drink.

to all the people, to every eye; but that shall be at the great Advent. St. John, with his ideal tenderness, has preserved a word of Jesus, which gives us St. Peter's canon of Resurrection evidence, in a lovelier and more spiritual form. Christ as He rose at Easter should be visible, but only to the eye of love, only to the eye which life fills with tears and heaven with light—"yet a little while, and the world seeth Me no more; but ye see Me. . . He that loveth Me shall be loved of My Father, and I will manifest Myself to Him."[1] Round that ideal canon St. John's Resurrection-history is twined with undying tendrils. Those words may be written by us with our softest pencils over the 20th and 21st chapters of the fourth Gospel. There is—very possibly there can be—under our present human conditions, no manifestation of Him who was dead and now liveth, except to belief, or to that kind of doubt which springs from love.

That which is true of St. John is true of all the Evangelists.

They take that Gospel, which is the life of their life. They bare its bosom to the stab of Celsus,[2] to the bitter sneer plagiarised by Renan—"why did He not appear to all, to His judges and enemies? Why only to one excitable woman, and a circle of His initiated?"

---

[1] John xiv. 19-21.

[2] Τίς τοῦτο εἶδεν; γυνὴ πάροιστρος, καὶ εἴ τις ἄλλος τῶν ἐκ τῆς αὐτῆς γοητείας. Ὅτε μὲν ἠπιστεῖτο ἐν σώματι πᾶσιν ἀνίδην (freely, without restraint) ἐκήρυττεν, ὅτε δὲ πίστιν ἂν ἰσχυρὰν παρεῖχεν ἐκ νεκρῶν ἀναστὰς ἑνὶ μόνῳ γυναίῳ καὶ τοῖς ἑαυτοῦ θεασιώταις (adepts, initiated) κρύβδην παρεφαίνετο . . . ἐχρῆν εἴπερ ὄντως θείαν δύναμιν ἐκφῆναι ἤθελεν ὁ Ἰησοῦς αὐτοῖς τοῖς ἐπηρεάσι καὶ τῷ καταδικάσαντι καὶ ὅλως πᾶσιν ὀφθῆναι. [Celsus, *ap. Orig.*, 2, 55, 59, 70, 63.] The passage is given in Rudolph Anger's invaluable *Synopsis Evang. cum locis qui supersunt parallelis litterarum et traditionum Evang. Irenæo. antiquiorum.* p. 254.

"The hallucination of a hysterical woman endowed
Christendom with a risen God."[1] An apocryphal Gospel
unconsciously violates this apostolic, or rather divine
canon, by stating that Jesus gave His grave-clothes to
one of the High Priest's servants.[2] There was every
reason but one why St. John and the other Evangelists
should have narrated such stories. There was only one
reason why they *should not*, but that was all-sufficient.
Their Master was the Truth as well as the Life. They
dared not lie.

Here, then, is one essential accordance in the narratives of the Resurrection. They record no appearances
of Jesus to enemies or to unbelievers.

2. A second unity of essential principle will be found
in the impression produced upon the witnesses.

There was, indeed, a moment of terror at the sepulchre, when they had seen the angel clothed in the long
white garment. " They trembled, and were amazed ;
neither said they anything to any man ; for they were
afraid." So writes St. Mark.[3] And no such word ever
formed the close of a Gospel ! On the Easter Sunday
evening there was another moment when they were
"terrified and affrighted, and supposed that they had
seen a spirit."[4] But this passes away like a shadow. For
man, the Risen Jesus turns doubt into faith, faith into joy.
For woman, He turns sorrow into joy. From the sacred
wounds joy rains over into their souls. " He showed

---

[1] γυνὴ πάροιστρος, Celsus. "Moments sacrés ou la passion d'une
hallucinée donne au monde un Dieu ressuscité." Renan, *Vie de
Jesus*, 434.
[2] " Post Resurrectionem . . . Dominus quum dedisset sindonem servo
sacerdotis "—Evang. ad Heb.—Matt. xxvii. 59.—R. Anger, *Synopsis
Evang.*, 288.
[3] Mark xvi. 8.
[4] Luke xxiv. 37.

them His hands and His feet . . . while they yet believed not for joy and wondered." " He showed unto them His hands and His side. Then were the disciples glad when they saw the Lord."[1] Each face of those who beheld Him wore after that a smile through all tears and forms of death. "Come," cried the great Swedish singer, gazing upon the dead face of a holy friend, "come and see this great sight. Here is a woman who has seen Christ." Many of us know what she meant, for we too have looked upon those dear to us who have seen Christ. Over all the awful stillness—under all the cold whiteness as of snow or marble—that strange soft light, that subdued radiance, what shall we call it? wonder, love, sweetness, pardon, purity, rest, worship, discovery. The poor face often dimmed with tears, tears of penitence, of pain, of sorrow, some perhaps which we caused to flow, is looking upon a great sight. Of such the beautiful text is true, written by a sacred poet in a language of which so many verbs are pictures. " They looked unto Him, and *were lightened.*"[2] That meeting of lights without a name it is which makes up what angels call joy. There remained some of that light on all who had seen the Risen Lord. Each might say—" have I not seen Jesus Christ our Lord ? "

This effect, like every effect, had a cause.

Scripture implies in the Risen Jesus a form with all heaviness and suffering lifted off it—with the glory, freshness, elasticity, of the new life, overflowing with beauty and power. He had a voice with some of the pathos of affection, making its sweet concession to human sensibility: saying, " Mary," " Thomas," " Simon, son of

---

[1] Luke xxiv. 41 ; John xx. 20.   [2] Ps. xxxiv. 15.

Jonas." He had a presence at once so majestic that they durst not question Him, yet so full of magnetic attraction that Magdalene clings to His feet, and Peter flings Himself into the waters when he is sure that it is the Lord.[1]

Now let it be remarked that this consideration entirely disposes of that afterthought of critical ingenuity which has taken the place of the base old Jewish theory— "His disciples came by night, and stole Him away."[2] That theory, indeed, has been blown into space by Christian apologetics. And now not a few are turning to the solution that He did not really die upon the cross, but was taken down alive.

There are other, and more than sufficient refutations. One from the character of the august Sufferer, who would not have deigned to receive adoration upon false pretences. One from the minute observation by St. John of the physiological effect of the thrust of the soldier's lance, to which he also reverts in the context.

But here, we only ask what effect the appearance of the Saviour among His disciples, supposing that He had not died, must unquestionably have had.

He would only have been taken down from the cross something more than thirty hours. His brow punctured with the crown of thorns; the wounds in hands, feet, and side, yet unhealed; the back raw and torn with scourges; the frame cramped by the frightful tension of six long hours—a lacerated and shattered man, awakened to agony by the coolness of the sepulchre and by the pungency of the spices ; a spectral, trembling, fevered, lamed, skulking thing—could that have seemed the Prince of Life, the Lord of Glory, the Bright and

---

[1] John xxi. 12, cf. 7.   [2] Matt. xxviii. 13.

Morning Star ?   Those who had seen Him in Gethse-
mane and on the cross, and then on Easter, and during
the forty days, can scarcely speak of His Resurrection
without using language which attains to more than
lyrical elevation.   Think of St. Peter's anthemlike burst.
"Blessed be the God and Father of our Lord Jesus
Christ, who hath begotten us again to a lively hope,
by the Resurrection of Jesus Christ from the dead."
Think of the words which St. John heard Him utter.
"I am the First and the Living, and behold! I became
dead, and I am, living unto the ages of ages."[1]

Let us, then, fix our attention upon the unity of
all the Resurrection narratives in these two essential
principles.   (1) The appearances of the Risen Lord to
belief and love only.   (2) The impression common to
all the narrators of glory on His part, of joy on theirs.

We shall be ready to believe that this was part of the
great body of proof which was in the Apostle's mind,
when pointing to the Gospel with which this Epistle
was associated, he wrote of this human but most convincing testimony—"if we receive," as assuredly we
do, "the witness of men"—of evangelists among the
number.

II.

Too often such discussions as these end unpractically
enough.   Too often

> " When the critic has done his best,
> The pearl of price at reason's test
> On the Professor's lecture table
> Lies, dust and ashes levigable."

But, after all, we may well ask : can we afford to
dispense with this well-balanced probability ?   Is it

---

[1] 1 Pet. i. 3, 4; Apoc. i. 17, 18.

well for us to face life and death without taking it,
in some form, into the account ?

Now at the present moment, it may safely be said
that, for the best and noblest intellects imbued with
the modern philosophy, as for the best and noblest of
old who were imbued with the ancient philosophy, external to Christian revelation, immortality is still, as
before, a fair chance, a beautiful "perhaps," a splendid
possibility. Evolutionism is growing and maturing
somewhere another Butler, who will write in another,
and possibly more satisfying chapter, than that least
convincing of any in the *Analogy*—" of a Future State."

What has Darwinism to say on the matter ?

Much. Natural selection seems to be a pitiless
worker; its instrument is *death*. But, when we
broaden our survey, the sum-total of the result is
everywhere advance—what is mainly worthy of notice,
in man the advance of goodness and virtue. For of
goodness, as of freedom,

> "The battle once begun
> Though baffled oft, is always won."

Humanity has had to travel thousands of miles, inch
by inch, towards the light. We have made such progress
that we can see that in time, relatively short, we shall
be in noonday. After long ages of strife, of victory
for hard hearts and strong sinews, goodness begins to
wipe away the sweat of agony from her brow; and will
stand, sweet, smiling, triumphant in the world. A
gracious life is free for man; generation after generation a softer ideal stands before us, and we can conceive a day when " the meek shall inherit the earth."
Do not say that evolution, if proved *à outrance*, brutalises
man. Far from it. It lifts him from below out of the

brute creation. What theology calls original sin, modern philosophy the brute inheritance—the ape, and the goat, and the tiger—is dying out of man. The perfecting of human nature and of human society stands out as the goal of creation. In a sense, all creation waits for the manifestation of the sons of God. Nor need the true Darwinian necessarily fear materialism. "Livers secrete bile—brains secrete thought," is smart and plausible, but it is shallow. Brain and thought are, no doubt, connected—but the connection is of simultaneousness, of two things in concordance indeed, but not related as cause and effect. If cerebral physiology speaks of annihilation when the brain is destroyed, she speaks ignorantly and without a brief.

The greatest thinkers in the Natural Religion department of the new philosophy seem then to be very much in the same position as those in the same department of the old. For immortality there is a sublime probability. With man, and man's advance in goodness and virtue as the goal of creation, who shall say that the thing so long provided for, the goal of creation, is likely to perish? Annihilation is a hypothesis; immortality is a hypothesis. But immortality is the more likely as well as the more beautiful of the two. We may believe in it, not as a thing demonstrated, but as an act of faith that "God will not put us to permanent intellectual confusion." [1]

But we may well ask whether it is wise and well to refuse to intrench this probability behind another. Is it likely that He who has so much care for us as to make us the goal of a drama a million times more complex than our fathers dreamed of; who lets us see that

---

[1] See *The Destiny of Man, viewed in the light of his origin,* by John Fiske, especially the three remarkable chapters pp. 96-119.

He has not removed us out of his sight; will leave Himself, and with Himself our hopes, without witness in history? History is especially human; human evidence the branch of moral science of which man is master—for man is the best interpreter of man. The primary .axiom of family, of social, of legal, of moral life, is, that there is a kind and degree of human evidence which we ought not to refuse; that if credulity is voracious in belief, incredulity is no less voracious in negation; that if there is a credulity which is simple, there is an incredulity which is unreasonable and perilous. Is it then safe to grope for the keys of death in darkness, and turn from the hand that holds them out; to face the ugly realities of the pit with less consolation than is the portion of our inheritance in the faith of Christ ?

"The disciples," John tells us, "went away again unto their own home. But Mary was standing without at the sepulchre weeping."[1] Weeping! What else is possible while we are *outside*, while we *stand*— what else until we *stoop* down from our proud grief to the sepulchre, humble our speculative pride, and condescend to gaze at the death of Jesus face to face ? When we do so, we forget the hundred voices that tell us that the Resurrection is partly invented, partly imagined, partly ideally true. We may not see angels in white, nor hear their "why weepest thou?" But assuredly we shall hear a sweeter voice, and a stronger than theirs; and our name will be on it, and His name will rush to our lips in the language most expressive to us—as Mary said unto Him in *Hebrew*,[2] Rabboni.

---

[1] John xx. 10, 11.

[2] The word Ἑβραϊστί had unfortunately dropped out of the T. R. John xx. 16.

Then we shall find that the grey of morning is passing ;
that the thin thread of scarlet upon the distant hills is
deepening into dawn ; that in that world where Christ
is the dominant law the ruling principle is not natural
selection which works through death, but supernatural
selection which works through life ; that "because He
lives, we shall live also." [1]

.With the reception of the witness of men then, and
among them of such men as the writer of the fourth
Gospel, all follows.   For Christ,

> "Earth breaks up—time drops away ;—
> In flows Heaven with its new day
> Of endless life, when He who trod,
> Very Man and very God,
> This earth in weakness, shame, and pain,
> Dying the death whose signs remain
> Up yonder on the accursèd tree ;
> Shall come again, no more to be
> Of captivity the thrall—
> But the true God all in all,
> King of kings, and Lord of lords,
> As His servant John received the words—
> 'I died, and live for evermore.'"

For us there comes the hope in Paradise—the connection with the living dead—the pulsation through the
isthmus of the Church, from sea to sea, from us to
them—the tears not without smiles as we think of the
long summer-day when Christ who is our life shall
appear—the manifestation of the sons of God, when
"them that sleep in Jesus will God bring with Him."
Our resurrection shall be a fact of history, because His
is a fact of history ; and we receive it as such—partly
from the reasonable motive of reasonable human belief
on sufficient evidence for practical conviction.

All the long chain of manifold witness to Christ is

---

[1] John xiv. 19.

consummated and crowned when it passes into the inner world of the individual life. " He that believeth on the Son of God, hath the witness in him," *i.e.*, in himself![1] Correlative to this, stands a terrible truth. He of whom we must conceive that he believes not God,[2] has made Him a liar—nothing less, because his time for receiving Christ came and went, and with this crisis his unbelief stands a completed present act as the result of his past;[3] unbelief stretching over to the completed witness of God concerning His Son ;[4]— human unbelief co-extensive with divine witness.

But that sweet witness in a man's self is not merely in books or syllogisms.   It is the creed of a living soul. It lies folded within a man's heart, and never dies— part of the great principle of victory[5] fought and won over again in each true life[6]—until the man dies, and ceasing then only because he sees that which is the object of its witness.

---

[1] ἐν ἑαυτῷ, ver. 10.

[2] ὁ μὴ πιστεύων τῷ Θεῷ, *Ibid.*

[3] οὐ πεπίστευκεν, *Ibid.*

[4] εἰς τὴν μαρτυρίαν ἣν μεμαρτύρηκεν ὁ Θεὸς περὶ τοῦ υἱοῦ αὐτοῦ. *Ibid.*

[5] πᾶν τὸ γεγεννημένον ἐκ τοῦ Θεοῦ νικᾳ τὸν κόσμον. ver. 4.

[6] With the neuter in ver. 4, contrast the individualising masculine in ver. 5, τίς ἐστιν ὁ νικῶν.

DISCOURSE XIV.

SIN UNTO DEATH.

"There is a sin unto death."—1 JOHN v. 17.

THE Church has ever spoken of seven deadly sins. Here is the ugly catalogue. Pride, covetousness, lust, envy, gluttony, hatred, sloth. Many of us pray often "from fornication and all other deadly sin, Good Lord deliver us." This language rightly understood is sound and true; yet, without careful thought, the term may lead us into two errors.

1. On hearing of *deadly* sin we are apt instinctively to oppose it to *venial.* But we cannot define by any *quantitative* test what venial sin may be for any given soul. To do that we must know the complete history of each soul; and the complete genealogy, conception, birth, and autobiography of each sin. Men catch at the term *venial* because they love to minimise a thing so tremendous as sin. The world sides with the casuists whom it satirises; and speaks of a "white lie," of a foible, of an inaccuracy, when "the 'white lie' may be that of St. Peter, the foible that of David, and the inaccuracy that of Ananias!"

2. There is a second mistake into which we often fall in speaking of deadly sin. Our imagination nearly always assumes some one definite outward act; some single individual sin. This may partly be due to a

seemingly slight mistranslation in the text. It should not run "there is *a* sin," but "there is sin unto" (*i.e.*, in the direction of, towards) "death."

The text means something deeper and further-reaching than any single sin, deadly though it may be justly called.

The author of the fourth Gospel learned a whole mystic language from the life of Jesus. Death, in the great Master's vocabulary, was more than a single action. It was again wholly different from bodily death by the visitation of God. There are two realms for man's soul co-extensive with the universe and with itself. One which leads towards God is called *Life;* one which leads from Him is called *Death.* There is a radiant passage by which the soul is translated from the death which is death indeed, to the life which is life indeed. There is another passage by which we pass from life to death ; *i.e.*, fall back towards *spiritual* (which is not necessarily eternal) death.

There is then a general condition and contexture ; there is an atmosphere and position of soul in which the true life flickers, and is on the way to death. One who visited an island on the coast of Scotland has told how he found in a valley open to the spray of the north-west ocean a clump of fir trees. For a time they grew well, until they became high enough to catch the prevalent blast. They were still standing, but had taken a fixed set, and were reddened as if singed by the breath of fire. The island glen might be " swept on starry nights by balms of spring ;" the summer sun as it sank might touch the poor stems with a momentary radiance. The trees were still *living*, but only with that cortical vitality which is the tree's death in life. Their doom was evident ; they could have but a

few more seasons. If the traveller cared some years hence to visit that islet set in stormy waters, he would find the firs blanched like a skeleton's bones. Nothing remained for them but the sure fall, and the fated rottenness.

The analogy indeed is not complete. The tree in such surroundings *must* die; it can make for itself no new condition of existence; it can hear no sweet question on the breeze that washes through the grove, " why will ye die ? " It cannot look upward—as it is scourged by the driving spray, and tormented by the fierce wind—and cry, " O God of my life, give me life." It has no will; it cannot transplant itself. But the human tree can root itself in a happier place. Some divine spring may clothe it with green again. As it was passing from life toward death, so by the grace of God in prayers and sacraments, through penitence and faith, it may pass from death to life.

The Church then is not wrong when she speaks of " deadly sin." The number *seven* is not merely a mystic fancy. But the *seven* " deadly sins " are seven attributes of the whole character ; seven master-ideas ; seven general conditions of a human soul alienated from God ; seven forms of aversion from true life, and of reversion to true death. The style of St. John has often been called " senile ; " it certainly has the oracular and sententious quietude of old age in its almost lapidary repose. Yet a terrible light sometimes leaps from its simple and stately lines. Are there not a hundred hearts among us who know that as years pass they are drifting further and further from Him who is the Life ? Will they not allow that St. John was right when, looking round the range of the Church, he asserted that there is such a thing as " sin unto death ? "

It may be useful to take that one of the seven deadly sins which people are the most surprised to find in the list.

How and why is sloth deadly sin?

There is a distinction between sloth as *vice* and sloth as *sin*. The deadly *sin* of *sloth* often exists where the *vice* has no place. The sleepy music of Thomson's "Castle of Indolence" does not describe the slumber of the spiritual sluggard. Spiritual sloth is want of care and of love for all things in the spiritual order. Its conceptions are shallow and hasty. For it the Church is a department of the civil service; her worship and rites are submitted to, as one submits to a minor surgical operation. Prayer is the waste of a few minutes daily in concession to a sentiment which it might require trouble to eradicate. For the slothful Christian, saints are incorrigibly stupid; martyrs incorrigibly obstinate; clergymen incorrigibly professional; missionaries incorrigibly restless; sisterhoods incorrigibly tender; white lips that can just whisper Jesus incorrigibly awful. For the slothful, God, Christ, death, judgment have no real significance. The Atonement is a plank far away to be clutched by dying fingers in the article of death, that we may gurgle out "yes," when asked "are you happy"? Hell is an ugly word, Heaven a beautiful one which means a sky or an Utopia. Apathy in all spiritual thought, languor in every work of God, fear of injudicious and expensive zeal; secret dislike of those whose fervour puts us to shame, and a miserable adroitness in keeping out of their way; such are the signs of the spirit of sloth. And with this a long series of sins of omission— "slumbering and sleeping while the Bridegroom tarries"—"unprofitable servants."

17

We have said that the *vice* of sloth is generally
distinct from the *sin*. There is, however, one day of
the week on which the *sin* is apt to wear the drowsy
features of the *vice—Sunday.* If there is any day on
which we might be supposed to do something towards
the spiritual world it must be Sunday. Yet what have
any of us done for God on any Sunday ? Probably
we can scarcely tell. We slept late, we lingered over
our dressing, we never thought of Holy Communion ;
after Church (if we went there) we loitered with
friends ; we lounged in the Park ; we whiled away
an hour at lunch ; we turned over a novel, with secret
dislike of the benevolent arrangements which give
the postman some rest. Such have been in the main
our past Sundays. Such will be those which remain,
more or fewer, till the arrival of a date written in a
calendar which eye hath not seen. The last evening
of the closing year is called by an old poet, " the
twilight of two years, nor past, nor next." What shall
we call the last Sunday of our year of life ?

Turn to the first chapter of St. Mark. Think of
that day of our Lord's ministry which is recorded more
fully than any other. What a day ! First that teaching
in the Synagogue, when men " were astonished," not
at His volubility, but at His " doctrine," drawn from
depths of thought. Then the awful meeting with the
powers of the world unseen. Next the utterance of
the words in the sick room which renovated the fevered
frame. Afterwards an interval for the simple festival
of home. And then we see the sin, the sorrow, the
sufferings crowded at the door. A few hours more,
while yet there is but the pale dawn before the meteor
sunrise of Syria, He rises from sleep to plunge His
wearied brow in the dews of prayer. And finally the

intrusion of others upon that sacred solitude, and the
work of preaching, helping, pitying, healing closes in
upon Him again with a circle which is of steel, because
it is duty—of delight, because it is love. O the divine
monotony of one of those golden days of God upon
earth ! And yet we are offended because He who is
the same for ever, sends from heaven that message
with its terrible plainness—" because thou art lukewarm,
I will spue thee out of my mouth."   We are angry that
the Church classes sloth as deadly sin, when the
Church's Master has said—"thou wicked and *slothful*
servant."

DISCOURSE XV.

THE TERRIBLE TRUISM WHICH HAS NO EXCEPTION.

"All unrighteousness is sin : and there is a sin not unto death."—
᷉ JOHN v. 17.

LET us begin by detaching awhile from its context this oracular utterance : " all unrighteousness is sin." Is this true universally, or is it not ?

A clear consistent answer is necessary, because a strange form of the doctrine of indulgences (long whispered in the ears) has lately been proclaimed from the housetops, with a considerable measure of apparent acceptance.

Here is the singular dispensation from St. John's rigorous canon to which we refer.

Three such indulgences have been accorded at various times to certain favoured class᷉s or persons. (1) "The moral law does not exist for the elect." This was the doctrine of certain Gnostics in St. John's day ; of certain fanatics in every age. (2) "Things absolutely forbidden to the mass of mankind, are allowable for people of commanding rank." Accommodating Prelates, and accommodating Reformers have left the burden of defending these ignoble concessions to future generations. (3) A yet baser dispensation has been freely given by very vulgar casuists. "The chosen of

Fortune "—the men at whose magic touch every stock seems to rise—may be allowed unusual forms of en-joying the unusual success which has crowned their career.

Such are, or such *were*, the dispensations from St. John's canon permitted to themselves, or to others, by the elect of *Heaven*, by the elect of *station*, and by the elect of *fortune*.

Another election hath obtained the perilous exception now—the election of *genius*. Those who endow the world with music, with art, with romance, with poetry, are entitled to the reversion. "All unrighteousness is sin "—except for *them*. (1) The indulgence is no longer valid for those who affect intimacy with heaven (partly perhaps because it is suspected that there is no heaven to be intimate with). (2) The indulgence is not extended to the men who apparently rule over nations, since it has been discovered that nations rule over them. (3) It is not accorded to the constructors of fortunes ; they are too many, and too uninteresting, though possibly figures could be conceived almost capable of buying it. But (generally speaking) men of these three classes must pace along the dust of the narrow road by the signpost of the law, if they would escape the censure of society.

For genius alone there is no such inconvenient restriction. Many men, of course, deliberately prefer the "primrose path," but they can no more avoid indignant hisses by the way than they can extinguish the "everlasting bonfire" at the awful close of their journey. With the man of genius it seems that it is otherwise. He shall "walk in the ways of his heart, and in the sight of his eyes ;" but, "for all these things" the tribunals of certain schools of a delicate criticism

(delicate criticism can be so indelicate!) will never allow him "to be brought into judgment." Some literary oracles, biographers, or reviewers, are not content to keep a reverential silence, and to murmur a secret prayer. They will drag into light the saddest, the meanest, the most selfish doings of genius. Not the least service to his generation, and to English literature, of the true poet and critic lately taken from us,[1] was the superb scorn, the exquisite wit, with which his indignant purity transfixed such doctrines. A strange winged thing, no doubt, genius sometimes is; alternately beating the abyss with splendid pinions, and eating dust which is the "serpent's meat." But for all that, we cannot see with the critic when he tries to prove that the reptile's crawling is part of the angel's flight; and the dust on which he grovels one with the infinite purity of the azure distances.

The arguments of the apologists for moral eccentricity of genius may be thus summed up:—The man of genius bestows upon humanity gifts which are on a different line from any other. He enriches it on the side where it is poorest; the side of the Ideal. But the very temperament in virtue of which a man is capable of such transcendent work makes him passionate and capricious. To be *imaginative* is to be *exceptional;* and these exceptional beings live for mankind rather than for themselves. When their conduct comes to be discussed, the only question is whether that conduct was adapted to forward the superb self-development which is of such inestimable value to the world. If the gratification of any desire was necessary for that self-development, genius itself being the judge,

---

[1] Mr. Matthew Arnold.

the cause is ended. In winning that gratification hearts may be broken, souls defiled, lives wrecked. The daintiest songs of the man of genius may rise to the accompaniment of domestic sobs, and the music which he seems to warble at the gates of heaven may be trilled over the white upturned face of one who has died in misery. What matter! Morality is so icy, and so intolerant; its doctrines have the ungentlemanlike rigour of the Athanasian Creed. Genius breaks hearts with such supreme gracefulness, such perfect wit, that they are arrant Philistines who refuse to smile.

We who have the text full in our mind answer all this in the words of the old man of Ephesus. For all that angel-softness which he learned from the heart of Christ, his voice is as strong as it is sweet and calm. Over all the storm of passion, over all the babble of successive sophistries, clear and eternal it rings out—"*all* unrighteousness is sin." To which the apologist, little abashed, replies—" of course we all know *that*—quite true as a general rule, but then men of genius have bought a splendid dispensation by paying a splendid price, and so *their* inconsistencies are not sin."

There are two assumptions at the root of this apology for the aberrations of genius which should be examined. (1) The temperament of men of genius is held to constitute an excuse from which there is no appeal. Such men indeed are sometimes not slow to put forward this plea for themselves. No doubt there are trials peculiar to every temperament. Those of men of genius are probably very great. They are children of the sunshine and of the storm ; the grey monotony of ordinary life is distasteful to them. Things which others find it easy to accept convulse their sensitive organisation. Many can produce their finest

works only on condition of being sheltered where no bills shall find their way by the post; where no sound, not even the crowing of cocks, shall break the haunted silence. If the letter comes in one case, and if the cock crows in the other, the first may possibly never be remembered, but the second is never forgotten.

For this, as for every other form of human temperament—that of the dunce, as well as of the genius—allowance must in truth be made. In that one of the lives of the English Poets, where the great moralist has gone nearest to making concessions to this fallacy of temperament, he utters this just warning. "No wise man will easily presume to say, had I been in Savage's condition I should have lived better than Savage." But we must not bring in the temperament of the man of genius as the standard of his conduct, unless we are prepared to admit the same standard in every other case. God is no respecter of persons. For each, conscience is of the same texture, law of the same material. As all have the same cross of infinite mercy, the same judgment of perfect impartiality, so have they the same law of inexorable *duty*.

(2) The necessary *disorder* and *feverishness* of high literary and artistic inspiration is a *second* postulate of the pleas to which I refer. But, is it true that disorder *creates inspiration*; or is a condition of it?

All great work is ordered work; and in producing it the faculties must be exercised harmoniously and with order. True inspiration, therefore, should not be caricatured into a flushed and dishevelled thing. Labour always precedes it. It has been prepared for by education. And that education would have been painful but for the glorious efflorescence of materials collected and assimilated, which is the compensation

for any toil. The very dissatisfaction with its own performances, the result of the lofty ideal which is inseparable from genius, is at once a stimulus and a balm. The man of genius apparently writes, or paints, as the birds sing, or as the spring colours the flowers; but his subject has long possessed his mind, and the inspiration is the child of thought and of ordered labour. Destroying the peace of one's own family or of another's, being flushed with the preoccupation of guilty passion, will not accelerate, but retard the advent of those happy moments which are not without reason called creative. Thus, the inspiration of genius is akin to the inspiration of prophecy. The prophet tutored himself by a fitting education. He became assimilated to the noble things in the future which he foresaw. Isaiah's heart grew royal; his style wore the majesty of a king, before he sang the King of sorrow with His infinite pathos, and the King of righteousness with His infinite glory. Many prophets attuned their spirits by listening to such music as lulls, not inflames passion. Others walked where "beauty born of murmuring sound" might pass into their strain. Think of Ezekiel by the river of Chebar, with the soft sweep of waters in his ear, and their cool breath upon his cheek. Think of St. John with the shaft of light from heaven's opened door upon his upturned brow, and the boom of the Ægean upon the rocks of Patmos around him. "The note of the heathen seer" (said the greatest preacher of the Greek Church) "is to be contorted, constrained, excited, like a maniac; the note of a prophet is to be wakeful, self-possessed, nobly self-conscious."[1] We may apply this test to the distinction

---

[1] This is true as a general rule; but there were exceptions.

between genius, and the dissipated affectation of genius.

Let us then refuse our assent to a doctrine of indulgences applied to genius on the ground of *temperament* or of literary and artistic *inspiration*. "Why," we are often asked, "why force your narrow judgment upon an angry or a laughing world?" What have you to do with the conduct of gifted men? Genius means exuberance. Why "blame the Niagara River" because it will not assume the pace and manner of "a Dutch canal"? Never indeed should we force that judgment upon any, unless they force it upon us. Let us avoid as far as we may posthumous gossip over the grave of genius. It is an unwholesome curiosity which rewards the blackbird for that bubbling song of ecstasy in the thicket, by gloating upon the ugly worm which he swallows greedily after the shower. The pen or pencil has dropped from the cold fingers. After all its thought and sin, after all its toil and agony, the soul is with its Judge. Let the painter of the lovely picture, the writer of the deathless words, be for us like the priest. The washing of regeneration is no less wrought through the unworthy minister; the precious gift is no less conveyed when a polluted hand has broken the bread and blessed the cup. But if we are forced to speak, let us refuse to accept an *ex post facto* morality invented to excuse a worthless absolution. Especially so when the most sacred of all rights is concerned. It is not enough to say that a man of genius dissents from the received standard of conduct. He cannot make fugitive inclination the only principle of a connection which he promised to recognise as paramount. A passage in the Psalms,[1] has been called "The catechism of Heaven."

---

[1] See Ps. xv. Cf. Ps. xxiv. 3-7.

"The catechism of Fame" differs from "the catechism of Heaven." "Who shall ascend unto the hill of Fame?" "He that possesses genius." "Who shall ascend unto the hill of the Lord?" "He that hath clean hands, and a pure heart; He that hath sworn to his neighbour and disappointeth him not" (or disappointeth *her* not) "though it were to his own hindrance" —aye, to the hindrance of his self-development. Strange that the rough Hebrew should still have to teach us chivalry as well as religion! In St. John's Epistle we find the two great axioms about sin, in its two essential aspects. "Sin is the transgression of the law:" there is its aspect chiefly *Godward.* "All unrighteousness" (mainly injustice, denial of the rights of others) "is sin:" there is its aspect chiefly *manward.*

Yes, the principle of the text is rigid, inexorable, eternal. Nothing can make its way out of those terrible meshes. It is without favour, without exception. It gives no dispensation, and proclaims no indulgences, to the man of genius, or to any other. If it were otherwise, the righteous God, the Author of creation and redemption, would be dethroned. And *that* is a graver thing than to dethrone even the author of "Queen Mab," and of "The Epipsychidion." Here is the jurisprudence of the "great white Throne" summed up in four words: "*all unrighteousness is sin.*"

So far, in the last discourse, and in this, we have ventured to isolate these two great principles from their context. But this process is always attended with peculiar loss in St. John's writings. And as some may think perhaps that the promise[1] just succeeding is falsified we must here run the risk of bringing in another

---

[1] 1 John v. 15.

thread of thought. Yet indeed the whole paragraph [1] has its source in an intense faith in the *efficacy of prayer*, specially as exercised in *intercessory prayer*.

(1) The efficacy of prayer.[2] This is the very sign of contrast with, of opposition to, the modern spirit, which is the negation of *prayer*.

What is the real value of prayer ?

Very little, says the modern spirit. Prayer is the stimulant, the Dutch courage of the moral world. Prayer is a power, not because it *is* efficacious, but because it is *believed* to be so.

A modern Rabbi, with nothing of his Judaism left but a rabid antipathy to the Founder of the Church, guided by Spinoza and Kant, has turned fiercely upon the Lord's prayer.[3] He takes those petitions which stand alone among the liturgies of earth in being capable of being translated into every language. He cuts off one pearl after another from the string. Let us look at two speci-mens. "Our Father which art in Heaven." Heaven ! the very name has a breath of magic, a suggestion of beauty, of grandeur, of purity in it. It moves us as nothing else can. We instinctively lift our heads ; the brow grows proud of that splendid home, and the eye is wetted with a tear and lighted with a ray, as it looks into those depths of golden sunset which are full for the young of the radiant mystery of life, for the old of the pathetic mystery of death.[4] Yes, but for modern science Heaven means air, or atmosphere, and the address itself

---

[1] I John v. 14, 18.

[2] Vv. 14, 15.

[3] *Historical and Critical Commentary on Leviticus.* By M. M. Kalisch. Part I. Theology of the Past and Future, 431, 438.

[4] This is denied by De Wette (*Ueber die Religion,* Vorlesungen, 106).

is contradictory. "Forgive us." But surely the guilt cannot be forgiven, except by the person against whom it is committed. There is no other forgiveness. A mother (whose daughter went out upon the cruel London streets) carried into execution a thought bestowed upon her by the inexhaustible ingenuity of love. The poor woman got her own photograph taken, and a friend managed to have copies of it hung in several halls and haunts of infamy with these words clearly written below—"come home, I forgive you." The tender subtlety of love was successful at last ; and the poor haggard outcast's face was touched by her mother's lips. " But the heart of God," says this enemy of prayer, " is not as a woman's heart." (Pardon the words, O loving Father ! Thou who hast said "Yea, she may forget, yet will I not forget thee." Pardon, O pierced Human Love ! who hast graven the name of every soul on the palms of Thy hands with the nails of the crucifixion.) Repentance subjectively seems a reality when mother and child meet with a burst of passionate tears, and the polluted brow feels purified by their molten downfall ; but repentance *objectively* is seen to be an absurdity by every one who grasps the conception of law. The penitential Psalms may be the *lyrics* of repentance, the Gospel for the third Sunday after Trinity its *idyll*, the cross its *symbol*, the wounds of Christ its *theology* and *inspiration*. But the course of Nature, the hard logic of life is its refutation—the flames that burn, the waves that drown, the machine that crushes, the society that condemns, and that neither can, nor will forgive.

Enough, and more than enough of this. The monster of ignorance who has never learnt a prayer, has hitherto been looked upon as one of the saddest of sights. But

there is something sadder—the monster of over-cultiva-
tion, the wreck of schools, the priggish fanatic of god-
lessness. Alas! for the nature which has become like
a plant artificially trained and twisted to turn away from
the light. Alas! for the heart which has hardened itself
into stone until it cannot beat faster, or soar higher,
even when men are saying with happy enthusiasm,
or when the organ is lifting upward to the heaven of
heavens the cry which is at once the creed of an everlasting dogma and the hymn of a triumphant hope—
"with Thee is the well of Life, and in Thy light shall
we see light." Now having heard the answer of the
modern spirit to the question "what is the real value
of prayer?" think of the answer of the spirit of the
Church as given by St. John in this paragraph. That
answer is not drawn out in a syllogism. St. John
appeals to our consciousness of a divine life. "That ye
may know that ye have eternal life." This *knowledge*
issues in *confidence, i.e.,* literally the sweet possibility
of saying out all to God. And this confidence is never
disappointed for any believing child of God. "If we
know that He hear us, we know that we have the
petitions that we desired of Him."[1]

On the 16th verse we need only say, that the greatness of our brother's spiritual need does not cease to
be a title to our sympathy. St. John is not speaking
of all requests, but of the fulness of brotherly intercession.

One question and one warning in conclusion ; and that
question is this. Do we take part in this great ministry
of love ? Is our voice heard in the full music of the

---

[1] The form of expression indicates *not* necessarily the very things
asked, but the spiritual essence and substance.

prayers of intercession that are ever going up to the
Throne, and bringing down the gift of life ? Do *we*
pray for others ?

In one sense all who know true affection and the
sweetness of *true* prayer do pray for others. We have
never loved with supreme affection any for whom we
have not interceded, whose names we have not baptized in the fountain of prayer. Prayer takes up a
tablet from the hand of love written over with names ;
that tablet death itself can only break when the heart
has turned Sadducee.

Jesus (we sometimes think) gives one strange proof
of the love which yet passeth knowledge. "Now Jesus
loved Martha and her sister and Lazarus ; " " when He
had heard therefore " [O that strange therefore !] " that
Lazarus was sick, He abode *two days* still in the same
place where He was." Ah ! sometimes not two days,
but two years, and sometimes evermore, He seems to
remain. When the income dwindles with the dwindling
span of life ; when the best beloved must leave us for
many years, and carries away our sunshine with him ;
when the life of a husband is in danger—then we pray ;
" O Father, for Jesu's sake spare that precious life ;
enable me to provide for these helpless ones ; bless
these children in their going out and coming in, and let
me see them once again before the night cometh, and
my hands are folded for the long rest." Yes, but have
we prayed at our Communion " because of that Holy
Sacrament in it, and with it," that He would give them
the grace which they need—the life which shall save
them from sin unto death ? Round us, close to us in
our homes, there are cold hands, hearts that beat feebly.
Let us fulfil St. John's teaching, by praying to Him
who is the life that He would chafe those cold hands

with His hand of love, and quicken those dying hearts by contact with that wounded heart which is a heart of fire.

NOTES

Ch. v. 3-17.

Ver. 3. This section should begin with the words "And His commandments are not heavy"—and should not be separated from what follows, because they give one reason of the victory whereof he proceeds to speak. "His commandments are not heavy, for all that is born of God conquereth the world." What a picture of the sweetness of a life of service! What a gentle smile must have been on the old man's face as he said, "His commandments are not grievous!"

Vers. 7, 8. This passage with its apparent obscurity, and famous interpolation, demands some additional notice. As to *criticism* and *interpretation*.

(1) *Critically*. Since the publication of J. J. Griesbach's celebrated work (*Diatribe in locum* 1 John v. 7, 8, Tom. ii., N.T. Halle: 1806), first German, and latterly English, opinion has become absolutely unanimous in agreeing with Griesbach that "the words included between brackets are spurious, and should therefore be eliminated from the Sacred Text." Even the famous Roman Catholic scholar, Scholts, in his great critical edition of the New Testament, in two volumes (Bonn: 1836), boldly dropped the disputed passage from the text. The interpolated passage has certainly no support in any uncial manuscript, or ancient version, or Greek Father of the four first centuries. (2) As to *interpretation*, the faith has lost nothing by the honesty of her wisest defenders. The whole of the genuine passage is intensely Trinitarian. The interpolation is nothing but an exposition written into the text. The three genuine witnesses do really point to the Three Witnesses in Heaven. Bengel's saying expresses the permanent feeling of Christendom, which no criticism can do away with: "This trine array of witnesses on earth is supported by, and has above and beneath it the Trinity, which is Heavenly, archetypal, fundamental, everlasting." The whole context recognizes three special works of the Three Persons of the Blessed Trinity. "This is the

witness of God," *i.e.* of the Father (ver. 9); "this is He that came by water and blood," *i.e.* the Son (ver. 6); "it is the Spirit that witnesseth," *i.e.* the Holy Ghost (*ibid.*).

A fuller examination of this passage, from a polemical point of view, will be found in the third of the introductory discourses. It will be well, however, to indicate here the immediate controversial reference in the Spirit, the water, and the blood. There is abundant proof that the popular heretical philosophy of Asia Minor struck Christianity precisely in three vital places. It denied—

(1) The Incarnation—consequently

(2) The Redemption—consequently

(3) The Sacraments.

But the mention of the water and the blood in connection with the Person of the Son Incarnate and Crucified established exactly these three points.   Narrated as it was by an eyewitness, it established :—

(1) The reality of the Incarnation—consequently

(2) The reality of Redemption—for the blood of Jesus cleanses from all sin (1 John i. 7)—consequently

(3) The reality of Sacraments.

We have articulate evidence of the denial of the two sacraments by the Docetic idealists of Asia Minor. The *Philosophumena* tells us of the view of baptism held by one of their principal sects. "According to them the promise of the laver of regeneration is nothing more than the introduction into the 'unfading pleasure' of him that is washed (as they say) with living water, and anointed with 'chrism that speaketh not.'"[1] The testimony of Ignatius is express as to the other sacrament. "From Eucharist and prayer they abstain on account of not confessing that the Eucharist is flesh of our Saviour Jesus Christ which suffered for our sins." ["Water and blood" should be noted in Heb. ix. 19. Water is not mentioned in Exod. xxiv. 6.]—(*Ep. ad Smyrn.* vii.)

---

[1] Ἡ γὰρ ἐπαγγελία τοῦ λουτροῦ οὐκ ἄλλη τίς ἐστι κατ᾽ αὐτούς, ἢ τὸ εἰσαγαγεῖν εἰς τὴν ἀμάραντον ἡδονὴν τὸν λουόμενον κατ᾽ αὐτοὺς ζῶντ ὕδατι καὶ χριόμενον ἀλάλῳ χρίσματι.—(*Philosoph.*, p. 140, de Naassenis.)

18

SECTION X.

GREEK.

Οἴδαμεν ὅτι πᾶς ὁ γεγεννημένος ἐκ τοῦ Θεοῦ οὐχ ἁμαρτάνει, ἀλλ᾽ ὁ γεννηθεὶς ἐκ τοῦ Θεοῦ τηρεῖ αὐτόν, καὶ ὁ πονηρὸς οὐχ ἅπτεται αὐτοῦ. οἴδαμεν ὅτι ἐκ τοῦ Θεοῦ ἐσμεν, καὶ ὁ κόσμος ὅλος ἐν τῷ πονηρῷ κεῖται. οἴδαμεν δὲ ὅτι ὁ υἱὸς τοῦ Θεοῦ ἥκει, καὶ δέδωκεν ἡμῖν διάνοιαν, ἵνα γινώσκωμεν τὸν ἀληθινόν· καὶ ἐσμὲν ἐν τῷ ἀληθινῷ, ἐν τῷ υἱῷ αὐτοῦ Ἰησοῦ Χριστῷ. οὗτός ἐστιν ὁ ἀληθινὸς Θεὸς καὶ ἡ ζωὴ αἰώνιος. Τεκνία, φυλάξατε ἑαυτοὺς ἀπὸ τῶν εἰδώλων. ἀμήν.

LATIN.

Scimus quoniam omnis qui natus est ex Deo non peccat, sed generatio Dei conservat eum et malignus non tangit eum. Scimus quoniam ex Deo sumus et mundus totus in maligno positus est. Et scimus quoniam Filius Dei venit, et dedit nobis sensum ut cognoscamus verum Deum et simus in vero, Filio eius; hic est verus et vita æterna. Filioli custodite vos a simulachris.

AUTHORISED VERSION.

We know that whosoever is born of God sinneth not; but he that is begotten of God keepeth himself, and that wicked one toucheth him not. *And* we know that we are of God, and the whole world lieth in wickedness. And we know that the Son of God is come, and hath given us an understanding, that we may know Him that is true, and we are in Him that is true, *even* in His Son Jesus Christ. This is the true God, and eternal life. Little children, keep yourselves from idols. Amen.

REVISED VERSION.

We know that whosoever is begotten of God sinneth not; but He that was begotten of God keepeth him, and the evil one toucheth him not. We know that we are of God, and the whole world lieth in the evil one. And we know that the Son of God is come, and hath given us an understanding that we know Him that is true, and we are in Him that is true, *even* in His Son Jesus Christ. This is the true God, and eternal life. *My* little children, guard yourselves from idols.

ANOTHER VERSION.

WE KNOW that whosoever is born of God sinneth not: but the Begotten of God keepeth him, and the evil one toucheth him not. WE KNOW that we are from God and the world lieth wholly in the evil one.

WE KNOW moreover that the Son of God hath *come and* is here, and hath given us understanding that we know Him that is the Very God: and in His Son Jesus Christ (this is the Very God and eternal life), we are in the Very (*God*). Children, guard yourselves from the idols.

NOTES.

Ch. v. 18-21.

Ver. 18, 19, 20. Three seals are affixed to the close of this Epistle—three postulates of the spiritual reason ; three primary canons of spiritual perception and knowledge. Each is marked by the emphatic "we know," which is stamped at the opening of its first line. The first "we know," is of a sense of purity made possible to the Christian through the keeping by Him Who is the one Begotten of God. The evil one cannot touch him with the contaminating touch which implies connection. The second "we know" involves a sense of *privilege ;* the true conviction that by God's power, and love, we are brought into a sphere of light, out of the darkness in which a sinful world has become as if cradled on the lap of the evil one. The third "we know" is the deep consciousness of the very Presence of the Son of God in and with His Church. And with this comes all the inner life—supremely a new way of looking at things, a new possibility of thought, a new cast of thought and sentiment, "understanding" (διάνοια). Words denoting intellectual faculties and processes are rare in St. John. This word is used in the sense just given in Plat., *Rep.*, 511, and Arist., *Poet.*, vi. (in the last, however, rather of the *senti-ment* of the piece than of the author), "He hath given us understanding that we know continuously the very [God]." And in "His Son Jesus Christ [this is the very God and eternal life] we are in the very God." This interpretation of the passage is supported by the position of the pronoun which cannot be referred naturally to any subject but Jesus Christ. Waterland quotes Irenæus. "No man can know God unless God has taught him ; that is to say, that without God, God cannot be known."[1]

Ver. 21. The Epistle closes with a short, sternly affectionate exhortation. "Children, guard yourselves" (the aorist impera-tive of immediate final decision) "from the idols." These words are natural in the atmosphere of Ephesus (Acts xix. 26, 27). The Author of the Apocalypse has a like hatred of idols. (Apoc. ii. 14, 15, ix. 20, xx. 1-8, xxii. 15.)

---

[1] Moyer Lecture, vi.

It would appear that the Gnostics allowed people to eat freely things sacrificed to idols. Modern, like ancient unbelief, has sometimes attributed to St. John a determination to exalt the Master whom he knew to be a man to an equality with God. But this is morally inconsistent with the Apostle's unaffected shrinking from idolatry in every form. (See *Speaker's Commentary, N. T.,* iv., 347).

THE SECOND EPISTLE OF ST. JOHN.

II. EPISTLE.

GREEK.

Ὁ πρεσβύτερος ἐκλεκτῇ κυρίᾳ καὶ τοῖς τέκνοις αὐτῆς, οὓς ἐγὼ ἀγαπῶ ἐν ἀληθείᾳ, καὶ οὐκ ἐγὼ μόνος ἀλλὰ καὶ πάντες οἱ ἐγνωκότες τὴν ἀλήθειαν, διὰ τὴν ἀλήθειαν τὴν μένουσαν ἐν ἡμῖν, καὶ μεθ᾽ ἡμῶν ἔσται εἰς τὸν αἰῶνα. ἔσται μεθ᾽ ἡμῶν χάρις, ἔλεος, εἰρήνη, παρὰ Θεοῦ πατρὸς καὶ παρὰ Κυρίου Ἰησοῦ Χριστοῦ τοῦ υἱοῦ τοῦ πατρός, ἐν ἀληθείᾳ καὶ ἀγάπῃ. Ἐχάρην λίαν ὅτι εὕρηκα ἐκ τῶν τέκνων σου περιπατοῦντας ἐν ἀληθείᾳ, καθὼς ἐντολὴν ἐλάβομεν παρὰ τοῦ πατρός. καὶ νῦν ἐρωτῶ σε, κυρία, οὐχ ὡς ἐντολὴν γράφων σοι καινὴν, ἀλλὰ ἣν εἴχομεν ἀπ᾽ ἀρχῆς, ἵνα ἀγαπῶμεν ἀλλήλους. καὶ αὕτη ἐστὶν ἡ ἀγάπη, ἵνα περιπατῶμεν κατὰ τὰς ἐντολὰς αὐτοῦ. αὕτη

LATIN.

Senior electae dominae et natis eius, quos ego diligo in veritate, et non ego solus sed et omnes qui cognoverunt veritatem, propter veritatem, propter veritatem quae permanet in nobis et nobis cum erit in aeternum. Sit nobiscum gratia misericordia pax a Deo Patre et Christo Iesu Filio Patris in veritate et caritate. Gavisus sum valde quoniam inveni de filii tuis ambulantes in veritate sicut mandatum accepimus a Patre. Et nunc rogo te, domina, non tamquam mandatum novum scribens tibi, sed quod habuimus ab initio, ut diligamus alterutrum. Et haec est caritas, ut ambulemus secundum mandata eius. Hoc mandatum est ut quem-

AUTHORISED VERSION.

The elder unto the elect lady and her children, whom I love in the truth; and not I only, but also all they that have known the truth; for the truth's sake, which dwelleth in us, and shall be with us for ever. Grace be with you, mercy, and peace, from God the Father, and from the Lord Jesus Christ, the Son of the Father, in truth and love. I rejoiced greatly that I found of thy children walking in truth, as we have received a commandment from the Father. And now I beseech thee, lady, not as though I wrote a new commandment unto thee, but that which we had from the beginning, that we love

REVISED VERSION.

The elder unto the elect lady and her children, whom I love in truth; and not I only, but also all they that know the truth; for the truth's sake which abideth in us, and it shall be with us for ever: Grace, mercy, peace shall be with us, from God the Father, and from Jesus Christ, the Son of the Father, in truth and love. I rejoice greatly that I have found certain of thy children walking in truth, even as we received commandment from the Father. And now I beseech thee, lady, not as though I wrote to thee a new commandment, but that which we had from the beginning, that we love one

ANOTHER VERSION.

The Elder unto the excellent Kyria and her children whom I love in truth, (and not I only, but also all they that know the truth) for the truth's sake which abideth in us—yea, and with us it shall be for ever. There shall be with you grace, mercy, peace from God the Father, and from Jesus Christ the Son of the Father, in truth and love. I was exceeding glad that I found of thy children walking in truth even as we received commandment from the Father. And now I beseech thee Kyria, not as though writing a fresh commandment unto thee, but that which we had from the beginning,

ἐστὶν ἡ ἐντολὴ, καθὼς ἠκουσατε ἀπ' ἀρχῆς, ἵνα ἐν αὐτῇ περιπατῆτε· ὅτι πολλοὶ πλάνοι εἰσῆλθον εἰς τὸν κόσμον, οἱ μὴ ὁμολογοῦντες Ἰησοῦν Χριστὸν ἐρχόμενον ἐν σαρκί· οὗτός ἐστιν ὁ πλάνος καὶ ὁ ἀντίχριστος· βλέπετε ἑαυτοὺς, ἵνα μὴ ἀπολέσωμεν ἃ εἰργασάμεθα, ἀλλὰ μισθὸν πλήρη ἀπολάβωμεν. πᾶς ὁ παραβαίνων καὶ μὴ μένων ἐν τῇ διδαχῇ τοῦ Χριστοῦ Θεὸν οὐκ ἔχει· ὁ μένων ἐν τῇ διδαχῇ οὗτος καὶ τὸν πατέρα καὶ τὸν υἱὸν ἔχει. εἴ τις ἔρχεται πρὸς ὑμᾶς καὶ ταύτην τὴν διδαχὴν οὐ φέρει, μὴ λαμβάνετε αὐτὸν εἰς οἰκίαν, καὶ χαίρειν αὐτῷ μὴ λέγετε· ὁ γὰρ λέγων αὐτῷ χαίρειν κοινωνεῖ τοῖς ἔργοις αὐτοῦ τοῖς πονηροῖς. Πολλὰ ἔχων ὑμῖν γράφειν οὐκ ἠβουλήθην διὰ χάρτου καὶ μέλανος· ἀλλὰ ἐλπίζω ἐλθεῖν πρὸς

admodum audistis ab initio in eo ambuletis. Quoniam multi seductores exierunt in mundum qui non confitentur Iesum Christum venientem in carne. Hic est seductor et antichristus. Videte vosmet ipsos, ne perdatis quæ operati estis, sed ut mercedam plenum accipiatis. Omnis qui præcedit et non manet in doctrina Christi, Deum non habet: qui permanet in doctrina, hic et Filium et Patrem habet. Si quis venit ad vos, et hanc doctrinam non adfert, nolite recipere eum in domum nec ave ei dixeritis: qui enim dicit illi ave, communicat operibus illius malignis. Plura habens vobis scribere, nolui per cartam et atramentum: spero enim me futurum apud vos et os ad os loqui, ut

one another. And this is love, that we walk after His commandments. This is the commandment, That, as ye have heard from the beginning, ye should walk in it. For many deceivers are entered into the world, who confess not that Jesus Christ is come in the flesh. This is a deceiver and an antichrist. Look to yourselves, that we lose not those things which we have wrought, but that we receive a full reward. Whosoever transgresseth, and abideth not in the doctrine of Christ, hath not God. He that abideth in the doctrine of Christ, he hath both the Father and the Son. If there come any unto you, and bring not this doctrine, receive him not into *your* house,

another. And this is love, that we should walk after His commandments. This is the commandment, even as ye heard from the beginning, that ye should walk in it. For many deceivers are gone forth into the world, even they that confess not that Jesus Christ cometh in the flesh. This is the deceiver and the antichrist. Look to yourselves, that ye lose not the things which we have wrought, but that ye receive a full reward. Whosoever goeth onward and abideth not in the teaching of Christ, hath not God: he that abideth in the teaching, the same hath both the Father and the Son. If any one cometh unto you, and bringeth not this teaching, receive

that we love one another. And this is the love, that we should walk according to His commandments. This is the commandment as ye heard from the beginning that ye should walk in it. For many deceivers are gone out into the world, *even* they who are not confessing Jesus Christ coming in the flesh. This the deceiver, and the antichrist. Look to yourselves that ye lose not the things which ye have worked, but that ye receive reward in full. Every one leading forward and not abiding in the doctrine which is Christ's hath not God: he that abideth in the doctrine, the same hath both the Son and the Father. If there come unto you any and bringeth not the doc-

ὑμᾶς καὶ στόμα πρὸς στόμα λαλῆσαι, ἵνα ἡ χαρὰ ἡμῶν ᾖ πεπληρωμένη. Ἀσπάζεταί σε τὰ τέκνα τῆς ἀδελφῆς σου τῆς ἐκλεκτῆς. ἀμήν.

gaudium vestrum sit plenum. Salutant te filii sororis tuæ electæ.

neither bid him God speed: For he that biddeth him God speed is partaker of his evil deeds. Having many things to write unto you, I would not write with paper and ink: but I trust to come unto you, and speak face to face, that our joy may be full. The children of thy elect sister greet thee. Amen.

him not into your house, and give him no greeting: for he that giveth him greeting partaketh in his evil works. Having many things to write unto you, I would not write them with paper and ink: but I hope to come unto you, and to speak face to face, that your joy may be fulfilled. The children of thine elect sister salute thee.

trine, receive him not into your house, and no good speed wish him. For he that wisheth him good speed partaketh in his works which are evil. Having many things to write unto you I would not write with paper and ink, but I hope to be with you and to speak face to face, that our joy may be fulfilled. The children of thine elect sister greet thee.

DISCOURSE XVI.

THEOLOGY AND LIFE IN KYRIA'S LETTER.

"The elder unto the elect lady and her children, whom I love in the truth . . . Grace be with you, mercy and peace, from God the Father and from the Lord Jesus Christ, the Son of the Father, in truth and love."—2 JOHN, 3.

OF old God addressed men in tones that, were so to speak, distant. Sometimes He spoke with the stern precision of law or ritual; sometimes in the dark and lofty utterances of prophets; sometimes through the subtle voices of history, which lend themselves to different interpretations. But in the New Testament He whom no man hath seen at any time, "interpreted,"[1] Himself with a sweet familiarity. It is of a piece with the dispensation of condescension, that the mysteries of the kingdom of heaven should come to us in such large measure through epistles. For a letter is just the result of taking up one's pen to converse with one who is absent, a familiar talk with a friend.

Of the epistles in our New Testament, a few are addressed to *individuals*. The effect of three of these letters upon the Church, and even upon the world, has been great. The Epistles to Timothy and Titus, according to the most prevalent interpretation of them, have been felt in the outward organization of the Church. The Epistle to Philemon, with its eager

---

[1] John i. 18.

tenderness, its softness as of a woman's heart, its chivalrous courtesy, has told in another direction. With all its freedom from the rashness of social revolution; its almost painful abstinence (as abolitionists have sometimes confessed to feeling) from actual invective against slavery in the abstract; that letter is yet pervaded by thoughts whose issue can only be worked out by the liberty of the slave. The word emancipation may not be pronounced, but it hovers upon the Apostle's lips.

The second Epistle is, in our judgment, a letter to an individual. Certainly we are unable to find in its whole contents any probable allusion to a Church personified as a lady.[1] It is, as we read it, addressed to Kyria, an Ephesian lady, or one who lived in the circle of Ephesian influence. It was sent by the Apostle during an absence from Ephesus. That absence might have been for the purpose of one of the visitations of the Churches of Asia Minor, which (as we are told by ancient Church writers) the Apostle was in the habit of holding. Possibly, however, in the case of a writer so brief and so reserved in the expression of personal sentiment as St. John, the gush and sunshine of anticipated joy at the close of this note might tempt us to think of a rift

---

[1] There is no doubt a large amount of authority for this view that St. John addresses a Church personified. It has the support of sacred critics so different as Bishop Wordsworth and Bishop Lightfoot. (*Ep. to Colossians and Philemon*, 305), and Professor Westcott seems (with some hesitation) to lean to it. But there is also a great body of support, ancient and modern, for the literal view. (Clem. Alex., *Adunbr. ad ii. Joan.*, *Op.*, iii. 1011.) So Athanasius, or the author of "Synopsis S.S." in Athanasius, *Opp.*, iv. 410. See also the heading of the A. V. ("He exhorteth a certain honourable matron, with her children.") For reasons for accepting Kyria rather than Electa as the name, see *Speaker's Commentary*, iv. 335.

in some sky that had been long darkened; of the close of some protracted separation, soon to be forgotten in a happy meeting. "Having many things to write unto you, I would not do so by means of paper and ink; but I hope to come unto you, and to speak face to face that our joy may be fulfilled."[1] The expression might not seem unsuitable for a return from exile. Several touches of language and feeling in the latter point to the conclusion that Kyria was a widow. There is no mention of her husband, the father of her children. In the case of a writer who uses the names of God with such subtle and tender suitability, the association of Kyria's " children walking in truth" with " even as we received commandment *from the Father*," may well point to Him who was for them the Father of the fatherless. We need not with some expositors draw the sad conclusion that St. John affectionately hints that there were others of the family who could not be included in this joyful message. But it would seem highly probable from the language used that there were several sons, and also that Kyria had no daughters. Over these sons who had lost one earthly parent, the Apostle rejoices with the heart of a father in God. He bursts out with his *eureka*, the *eureka* not of a philosopher, but of a saint. " I rejoiced exceedingly that I found[2] certain of the number of thy children walking in truth."

While we may not trace in this little Epistle the same fountain of wide-spreading influence as in others to which we have referred; while we feel that, like its author, its work is deep and silent rather than commanding, reflection will also lead us to the conclusion

---

[1] Ver. 12.   [2] εὔρηκα, ver. 4.

that it is worthy of the Apostle who was looked upon as one of the "pillars" of the faith. [1]

1. Let us reflect that this letter is addressed by the aged Apostle to a widow, and concerns her family.

It is significant that Kyria was, in all probability, a widow of Ephesus.

Too many of us have more or less acquaintance with one department of French literature. A Parisian widow is too often the questionable heroine of some shameful romance, to have read which is enough to taint the virginity of the young imagination. Ephesus was the Paris of Ionia. Petronius was the Daudet or Zola of his day. An Ephesian widow is the heroine of one of the most cynically corrupt of his stories.

But "where sin abounded, grace did more than abound." Strange that first in an epistle to a Bishop of the Church of Ephesus, St. Paul should have presented us with that picture of a Christian widow— "she that is a widow, indeed, and desolate, who hath her hope set on God, and continueth in prayer night and day"—yet who, if she has the devotion, the almost entire absorption in God, of Anna, the daughter of Phanuel, [2] leaves upon the track of her daily road to heaven the trophies of Dorcas—"having brought up children well, used hospitality to strangers, washed the saints' feet, relieved the afflicted, diligently followed every good work." [3] Such widows are the leaders of the long procession of women, veiled or unveiled, with vows or without them, who have ministered to Jesus through the ages. Christ has a beautiful art of turning the affliction of His daughters into the consolation

---

[1] "James, Cephas, and JOHN, who seemed to be *pillars.*" Gal. ii. 9.
[2] Luke ii. 36.
[3] 1 Tim. v. 3, 5, 10.

of suffering. When life's fairest hopes are disappointed by falsehood, by cruel circumstances, by death; the broken heart is soothed by the love of Christ, the only love which is proof against death and change. The consolation thus received is the most unselfish of gifts. It overflows, and is lavishly poured out upon the sick and weary. With St. Paul's picture of a widow of this kind, contrast another by the same hand which hangs close beside it. The younger Ephesian widow, such as Petronius described, was known by St. Paul also. If any count the Apostle as a fanatic, destitute of all knowledge of the world because he lived above it, let them look at those lines, which are full of such caustic power, as they hit off the characteristics of certain idle and wanton affecters of a sorrow which they never felt.[1] What a distance between such widows and Kyria, "beloved for the truth's sake which abideth in us!"[2]

But the short letter of St. John is addressed to Kyria's *family* as well as to herself. "The elder to the excellent Kyria and her children."[3]

There is one question which we naturally ask about every school and form of religion. It is the question which a great English Professor of Divinity used to ask his pupils to put in a homely form about every religious scheme and mode of utterance—" will it *wash* well?" Is it an influence which seems to be productive and lasting? Does it abide through time and trials? Is it capable of being passed on to another generation? Are plans, services, organizations, preachings, classes, vital or showy? Are they fads to meet fancies, or works to supply wants? Is that which we hold such sober, solid truth, that wise piety can say

---

[1] 1 Tim. v. 6-11, 12, 13. [2] 2 John 2. [3] Ver. 1.

of it, half in benediction, half in prophecy [1]—" the truth which abideth in us; yea, and with us it shall be for ever ? "

2. We turn to the *contents* of the Epistle.

We shall be better able to appreciate the value of these, if we consider the state of Christian literature at that time.

What had Christians to read and carry about with them ? The excellent work of the Bible Society was physically impossible for long centuries to come. No doubt the LXX. version of the Old Testament was widely spread. In every great city of the Roman Empire there was a vast population of Jews. Many of these were baptized into the Church, and carried into it with them their passionate belief in the Old Testament. The Christians of the time and place to which we refer could, probably, with little trouble, if not read, yet hear the Old Covenant and able expositions of it. But they had not copies of the entire New Testament. Indeed, if all the New Testament was then written, it certainly was not collected into one volume, nor constituted one supreme authority. " Many barbarous nations," says a very ancient Father, "believe in Christ without written record, having salvation impressed through the Spirit in their hearts, and diligently preserving the old tradition." [2] Possibly a Church or single believer had one synoptical Gospel. At Ephesus Christians had doubtless been catechised in, and were deeply imbued with, St. John's view of the Person, work, and teaching of our Lord. This had now been moulded into shape, and definitely committed to writing in that

---

[1] διὰ τὴν ἀλήθειαν τὴν μένουσαν ἐν ἡμῖν, καὶ μεθ' ἡμῶν ἔσται εἰς τὸν αἰῶνα. 2 John ver. 2.

[2] Irenæus, *Hær.*, iii. 4.

glorious Gospel, the Church's Holy of Holies, St. John's Gospel. For them and for their contemporaries there was a living realization of the Gospel. They had heard it from eye-witnesses. They had passed into the wonderland of God. The earth on which Jesus trod had blossomed into miracle. The air was haunted by the echoes of His voice. They had, probably, also a certain number of the Epistles of St. Paul. The Christians of Ephesus would have a special interest in their own Epistle to the Ephesians, and in the two which were written to their first Bishop, Timothy. They had also (whether written or not) impressed upon their memories by their weekly Eucharist, the liturgical Canon of consecration according to the *Ephesian usage* —from which, and not from the Roman, the Spanish and Gallican seem to be derived. The Ephesian Christians had also the first Epistle of St. John, which in some form accompanied the Gospel, and is, indeed, a picture of spiritual life drawn from it. But let us remember that the Epistle is not of a character to be very quickly or readily learned by heart. Its subtle, latent links of connection do not present many grappling hooks for the memory to fasten itself to. Copies also must have been comparatively few.

Now let us see how the second Epistle may well have been related to the first.

Supremely, and above all else, the first Epistle contained *three* warnings, very necessary for those times. (1) There was a danger of *losing the true Christ*, the Word made Flesh, Who for the forgiveness of our sins did shed out of His most precious side both water and blood—in a false, because shadowy and ideal Christ. (2) There was danger of *losing true love*, and therefore spiritual life, with truth. (3) With the true Christ and

true love there was a danger of losing *the true commandment*—love of God and of the brethren. Now in the second Epistle these very three warnings were written on a leaflet in a form more calculated for circulation and for remembrance. (1) Against the peril of faith, of *losing the true Christ.* " Many deceivers are gone out into the world—they who confess not Jesus Christ coming in flesh. This is the deceiver and the antichrist." [1] With the true Christ, the true doctrine of Christ would also vanish, and with it all living hold upon *God. Progress* was the watchword ; but it was in reality *regress.* " Every one who abideth not in the doctrine of Christ hath not God." [2] (2) Against the peril of *losing love.* " I beseech thee, Kyria . . . that we love one another." [3] (3) Against the peril of losing *the true commandment* (the great spiritual principle of charity), or the true commandments [4] (that principle in the details of life). " And this is love, that we walk after His *commandments.* This is the *commandment,* that even as ye heard from the beginning ye should walk in it." [5]

Here then were the chief practical elements of the first Epistle contracted into a brief and easily remembered shape.

Easily remembered, too, was the stern, practical prohibition of the intimacies of hospitality with those who came to the home of the Christian, in the capacity of emissaries of the antichrist above indicated. " Re-

---

[1] Ver. 7. [2] Ver. 9. [3] Ver. 5.
[4] *Commandments* and *commandment*—Love strives to realise in detail every separate expression of the will of God." (Prof. Westcott, *Epistles of St. John,* 217).
[5] Ver. 6.

19

ceive him not into your house, and good speed salute him not with." [1]

Many are offended with this. No doubt Christianity is the religion of love—"the epiphany of the sweet-naturedness and philanthropy of God." [2] We very often look upon heresy or unbelief with the tolerance of curiosity rather than of love. At all events, the Gospel has its intolerance as well as tolerance. St. John certainly had this. It is not a true conception in art which invests him with the mawkish sweetness of perpetual youth. There is a sense in which he was a son of Thunder to the last. He who believes and knows must formulate a dogma. A dogma frozen by formality, or soured by hate, or narrowed by stupidity, makes a bigot. In reading the Church History of the first four centuries we are often tempted to ask, why all this subtlety, this theology-spinning, this dogma-hammering? The answer stands out clear above the mists of controversy. Without all this the Church would have lost the conception of Christ, and thus finally Christ Himself. St. John's denunciations have had a function in Christendom as well as his love.

---

[1] It is, probably, the existence of these verses (vv. 10, 11) which acts as a stimulus to many liberal Christian commentators in favour of the ultra-mystical view, that the lady addressed in this Epistle is a Church personified. It should be carefully noted that St. John speaks of a *formal* summons, so to speak, from an emissary of anti-christ as such. (εἴ τις ἔρχεται πρὸς ὑμᾶς, ver. 10). St. John, also, must have detected a danger in the very gentleness of Kyria's character, or in the disposition of some of her children. So much, indeed, might seem implied in the sudden, solemn, and rather startling warning, which entreated constant continuous care (βλέπετε ἑαυτούς), so that they should not in some momentary impulse, under the charm of some deceiver, lose what they had wrought, and with it reward in fulness (ἵνα μὴ απολέσητε, ver. 10).

[2] Titus iii. 4.

3. There are two most precious indications of the highest Christian truth with which we may conclude.

We have prefixed to this Epistle that beautiful Apostolic salutation which is found in two only among the Epistles of St. Paul.[1] After that simple, but exquisite expression of blessing merged in prophecy—"the truth which abideth in us—yes! and with us it shall be for ever"[2]—there comes another verse set in the same key. "There shall be with us grace, mercy, peace, from God the Father, and from Jesus Christ the Son of the Father, in truth" of thought, "and love" of life.[3]

This rush and reduplication of words is not very like the usual reserve and absence of emotional excitement in St. John's style. Can it be that something (possibly the glorious death of martyrdom by which Timothy died) led St. John to use words which were probably familiar to Ephesian Christians?

However this may be, let us live by and learn from those lovely words. Our poverty wants *grace*, our guilt wants *mercy*, our misery wants *peace*. Let us ever keep the Apostle's order. Do not let us put *peace*, our feeling of peace, first. The emotionalists' is a topsy-turvy theology. Apostles do not say "peace and grace," but "grace and peace."

One more—in an age which substitutes an ideal something called the spirit of Christianity for Christ, let us hold fast to that which is the essence of the Gospel and the kernel of our three creeds. "To confess Jesus Christ coming in flesh."[4] Couple with this a

---

[1] 1 Tim. i. 1; 2 Tim. i. 2.

[2] The construction altered to bring out the meaning more strikingly than a uniform structure could have done.—Winer, *Gr. Gr.*, Part III., § 3.

[3] Ἔσται μεθ' ὑμῶν χάρις, ἔλεος, εἰρήνη, κ.τ.λ. 2 John ver. 3.

[4] Ἰησοῦν Χριστὸν ἐρχόμενον ἐν σαρκί. 2 John ver. 7.

canon of the First Epistle—"confesseth Jesus Christ *come* in flesh."[1] The second is the Incarnation *fact* with its abiding consequences; the first, the Incarnation *principle* ever living in a Person, Who will also be personally manifested. This is the substance of the Gospels; this the life of prayers and sacraments; this the expectation of the saints.

NOTES.

Ver. 1. *The Elder.*] This word has played a great part in an important controversy. It is argued that the Elder of this and of the Third Epistle is the author indeed of the first Epistle and of the Gospel, but cannot be the Apostle St. John, who would not, (it is alleged,) call himself ὁ πρεσβύτερος. And Eusebius (*H.E.*, lib. iii., cap. ult.) preserves a fragment from Papias, which he misunderstands to indicate that there were two Johns (see Riggenbach, *Leben Jesu*, 59, 60). But even if the word be Presbyter, and points to an ecclesiastical title, it might stand precisely on the same footing as St. Peter's language—"the elders among you I exhort, who am a *fellow elder*" (1 Pet. v. 1). The Elder at the opening of the Second and Third Epistles of St. John, may well signify the aged Apostle, the oldest of the company of Jesus, the one living representative of the traditions of Galilee and Jerusalem.

Ver. 7. *The seducer.*] ὁ πλάνος. The almost technical force of this word would be adequately appreciated only by readers more or less imbued with Jewish ideas. It was indeed the really strong motive in the terrible game which the Jewish priests played in bringing about the death of our Lord. The process against the *Mesith*, "seducer," is drawn out in the Talmud with an effrontery at once puerile and revolting. The man accused of *seduction* was to be drawn into conversation, while two witnesses were hidden in the next room,—and candles were to be lighted, as if accidentally, close by him, that the witnesses might be sure that they had seen, as well as heard the heretic. He was to be called upon to retract his

---

[1] Ἰησοῦν Χριστὸν ἐν σαρκὶ ἐληλυθότα. 1 John iv. 2.

heretical pravity. If he refused, he was to be brought before the Council, and stoned if the verdict was against him. The Talmudists add that this was the legal process carried out against Jesus : that He was condemned upon the testimony of two witnesses; and that the crime of "misleading" was the only one which was thus formally dealt with. (See references to the Talmud of Jerusalem, and that of Babylon, *Vie de Jesus*, Renan, 394, N. 1). The Gospels tell us that the accusation against our Lord was "misleading :" and the terrible word in the verse which we are examining was actually applied to Him (ἐκεῖνος ὁ πλάνος, Matt. xxvii. 63 ; πλανᾷ τὸν ὄχλον, John vii. 12 ; μὴ καὶ ὑμεῖς πεπλάνησθε, John vii. 47).

"Excepting some minutiæ, which were the product of the Rabbinical imagination, the narrative of the Evangelists answers, point by point, to the process actually laid down by the Talmud " (Renan, ut sup.).

Ver. 9. *Every one who leadeth forward.*] πᾶς ὁ προάγων is certainly the true reading here ; the commander himself pushing boldly onward, and also carrying others with him. The allusion is polemical to the vaunted *progress* of the Gnostic teachers.

" *The doctrine which is Christ's.*"] What is that ? John vii. 16, 17. The doctrine which Christ emphatically called " *My doctrine*," " *the doctrine.*" No doubt the word (διδαχή) sometimes means the *act*, sometimes the *mode, of teaching* (Mark xii. 38 ; 1 Cor. xiv. 6); but "it underwent a transformation which converted it into a term synonymous with dogmatic teaching," with the body of faithful doctrine which was the ultimate type and norm to which all statements must be conformed. (Acts vi. 42 ; Tit. i. 9 ; Rom. vi. 17, xvi. 17 ; see also Matt. xvi. 12 ; Acts v. 28, xvii. 19 ; Heb. xiii. 9.) It is much to be regretted that in the R.V. the word " doctrine " has disappeared from all these passages, Romans xvi. 17 alone excepted. St. John's language in this verse seems quite decisive.

THE THIRD EPISTLE OF ST. JOHN.

III. EPISTLE.

GREEK.

Ὁ πρεσβύτερος Γαΐῳ τῷ ἀγαπητῷ, ὃν ἐγὼ ἀγαπῶ ἐν ἀληθείᾳ. Ἀγαπητέ, περὶ πάντων εὔχομαί σε εὐοδοῦσθαι καὶ ὑγιαίνειν, καθὼς εὐοδοῦταί σου ἡ ψυχή. ἐχάρην γὰρ λίαν ἐρχομένων ἀδελφῶν καὶ μαρτυρούντων σου τῇ ἀληθείᾳ, καθὼς σὺ ἐν ἀληθείᾳ περιπατεῖς. μειζοτέραν τούτων οὐκ ἔχω χαράν, ἵνα ἀκούω τὰ ἐμὰ τέκνα ἐν ἀληθείᾳ περιπατοῦντα. Ἀγαπητέ, πιστὸν ποιεῖς ὃ ἐὰν ἐργάσῃ εἰς τοὺς ἀδελφοὺς καὶ εἰς τοὺς ξένους, οἳ ἐμαρτύρησάν σου τῇ ἀγάπῃ ἐνώπιον ἐκκλησίας, οὓς καλῶς ποιήσεις προπέμψας ἀξίως τοῦ Θεοῦ. ὑπὲρ γὰρ τοῦ ὀνόματος ἐξῆλθον μηδὲν λαμβάνοντες ἀπὸ τῶν ἐθνῶν. ἡμεῖς οὖν ὀφείλομεν

LATIN.

Senior Gaio carissimo, quem ego diligo in veritate. Carissime, de omnibus orationem facio prosper te ingredi et valere, sicut prospere agit anima tua. Gavisus sum valde venientibus fratribus et testimonium perhibentibus veritati tuæ, sicut tu in veritate ambulas. Maiorem horum non habeo gratiam quam ut audiam filios meos in veritate ambulantes. Carissime, fideliter facias quidquid operaris in fratres, et hoc in peregrinos; qui testimonium reddiderunt caritati tuæ in conspectu ecclesiæ; quos bene facies ducens digna Deo. Pro nomine enim profecti sunt nihil accipientes a gentibus. Nos ergo debemus sus-

AUTHORISED VERSION.

The elder unto the well beloved Gaius, whom I love in the truth. Beloved, I wish above all things that thou mayest prosper and be in health, even as thy soul prospereth. For I rejoiced greatly, when the brethren came and testified of the truth that is in thee, even as thou walkest in the truth. I have no greater joy than to hear that my children walk in truth. Beloved, thou doest faithfully whatsoever thou doest to the brethren, and to strangers; which have borne witness of thy charity before the church: whom if thou bring forward on their journey after a godly sort, thou shalt do well:

REVISED VERSION.

The elder unto Gaius the beloved, whom I love in truth. Beloved, I pray that in all things thou mayest prosper and be in health, even as thy soul prospereth. For I rejoiced greatly, when brethren came and bare witness unto thy truth, even as thou walkest in truth. Greater joy have I none than this, to hear of my children walking in the truth. Beloved, thou doest a faithful work in whatsoever thou doest toward them that are brethren and strangers withal; who bare witness to thy love before the church: whom thou wilt do well to set forward on their journey worthily of God: because that for the sake of the

ANOTHER VERSION.

The Elder unto Gaius the beloved, whom I love in truth. Beloved, in all things I pray that thou mayest prosper, and be in health, even as thy soul prospereth. For I was exceeding glad of brethren coming and witnessing to thy truth, even as thou truly walkest. Greater joy than these joys I have not, that I should hear of my own children walking truly. Beloved, thou doest in faithful wise whatsoever thou art working towards the brethren who are moreover strangers; which witness to thy charity before the Church; whom thou wilt do well to speed forward on their journey worthily of God: because

because that for His name's sake they went forth, taking nothing of the Gentiles. We therefore ought to welcome such, that we may be fellowhelpers to the truth. I wrote unto the Church: but Diotrephes, who loveth to have the pre-eminence among them, receiveth us not. Wherefore, if I come, I will remember his deeds which he doeth, prating against us with malicious words: and not content therewith, neither doth he himself receive the brethren, and forbiddeth them that would, and casteth them out of the church. Beloved, follow not that which is evil, but that which is good. He that doeth good is of God: but he that doeth evil hath not seen God. Demetrius hath good

that for the sake of the Name they went out taking nothing of the Gentiles. We therefore are bound to take up such that we may become fellow-workers with the truth. I wrote somewhat unto the Church: but Diotrephes, who loveth to have primacy over them receiveth us not. Wherefore if I come I will bring to remembrance his works which he is doing, prating against us with wicked words: and not contented herewith he himself neither doth he upon neither doth he himself receive the brethren, and them that would he hindereth, and casteth them out of the Church. Beloved, imitate not that which is evil, but that which is good. He who is doing good is from God; he that is doing evil hath not

cipere huiusmodi ut cooperatores simus veritatis. Scripsissem sitan ecclesiae: sedis qui amat primatum gerere in eis Diotripes non recipit nos. Propter hoc, si venero, commoneam eius opera quae facit verbis malignis garriens in nos, et quasi non ei ista sufficiant, nec ipse suscipit fratres, et eos quo cupiunt prohibet et de ecclesia eicit. Carissime, noli imitari malum, sed quod bonum est. Qui bene facit, ex Deo est: qui male facit, non videt Deum. Demetrio testimonium redditur ab omnibus et ab ipsa veritate: et nos testimonium perhibemus, et nosti quoniam testimonium nostrum verum est. Multa habui scribere tibi, sed nolui per atramentum et calamum scribere tibi:

ἀπολαμβάνειν τοὺς τοιούτους, ἵνα συνεργοὶ γινώμεθα τῇ ἀληθείᾳ. Ἔγραψά τι τῇ ἐκκλησίᾳ· ἀλλ' ὁ φιλοπρωτεύων αὐτῶν Διοτρεφὴς οὐκ ἐπιδέχεται ἡμᾶς. διὰ τοῦτο, ἐὰν ἔλθω, ὑπομνήσω αὐτοῦ τὰ ἔργα ἃ ποιεῖ λόγοις πονηροῖς φλυαρῶν ἡμᾶς, καὶ μὴ ἀρκούμενος ἐπὶ τούτοις οὔτε αὐτὸς ἐπιδέχεται τοὺς ἀδελφούς, καὶ τοὺς βουλομένους κωλύει καὶ ἐκ τῆς ἐκκλησίας ἐκβάλλει. Ἀγαπητέ, μὴ μιμοῦ τὸ κακόν, ἀλλὰ τὸ ἀγαθόν. ὁ ἀγαθοποιῶν ἐκ τοῦ Θεοῦ ἐστιν· ὁ δὲ κακοποιῶν οὐχ ἑώρακεν τὸν Θεόν. Δημητρίῳ μεμαρτύρηται ὑπὸ πάντων καὶ ὑπ' αὐτῆς τῆς ἀληθείας· καὶ ἡμεῖς δὲ μαρτυροῦμεν, καὶ οἴδατε ὅτι ἡ μαρτυρία ἡμῶν ἀληθής ἐστι. Πολλὰ εἶχον γράφειν, ἀλλ' οὐ θέλω διὰ μέλανος καὶ καλάμου σοι

γράψαι· ἐλπίζω δὲ εὐθέως ἰδεῖν σε, καὶ στόμα πρὸς στόμα λαλήσομεν. Εἰρήνη σοι. Ἀσπάζονταί σε οἱ φίλοι· ἀσπάζου τοὺς φίλους κατ' ὄνομα.

spero autem protinus te videre, et os ad os loquimur. Pax tibi. Salutant te amici. Saluta amicos per nomen.

report of all *men*, and of the truth itself: yea, and we *also* bear record; and ye know that our record is true. I had many things to write, but I will not with ink and pen write unto thee: but I trust I shall shortly see thee, and we shall speak face to face. Peace *be* to thee. *Our* friends salute thee. Greet the friends by name.

witness of all *men*, and of the truth itself: yea, we also bear witness; and thou knowest that our witness is true. I had many things to write unto thee, but I am unwilling to write *them* to thee with ink and pen: but I hope shortly to see thee, and we shall speak face to face. Peace *be* unto thee. The friends salute thee. Salute the friends by name.

seen God. To Demetrius witness stands given of all men and of the truth itself: yea, and we also are witnessing, and ye know that our witness is true. Many things I had to have written, but I am not willing to be writing unto thee with ink and pen: but I am hoping straightway to see thee, and we shall speak face to face. Peace unto thee. The friends greet thee. Greet the friends by name,

DISCOURSE XVII.

THE QUIETNESS OF TRUE RELIGION.

"The elder unto the well beloved Gaius. . . . He that doeth good is of God; but he that doeth evil hath not seen God."—3 JOHN I, II.

THE mere analysis of this note must necessarily present a meagre outline. There is a brief expression of pleasure at the tidings of the sweet and gracious hospitality of Gaius which was brought by certain missionary brethren to Ephesus, coupled with the assurance of the truth and consistency of his whole walk. The haughty rejection of Apostolic letters of communion by Diotrephes is mentioned with a burst of indignation. A contrast to Diotrephes is found in Demetrius, with the threefold witness to a life so worthy of imitation. A brief greeting—and we have done with the last written words of St. John which the Church possesses.

I.

Let us *first* see whether, without passing over the bounds of historical probability, we can fill up this bare outline with some colouring of circumstance.

To two of the three individuals named in this Epistle we seem to have some clue.

The *Gaius* addressed is, of course, *Caius* in Latin, a very common prænomen, no doubt.

Three persons of the name appear in the New Testament [1]—unless we suppose St. John's Caius to be a fourth. But the generous and beautiful hospitality adverted to in this note is entirely of a piece with the character of him of whom St. Paul had written, "Gaius, mine host, and of the whole Church." [2] We know further, from one of the most ancient and authentic documents of Christian literature, that the Church of Corinth (to which this Caius belonged) was, just at the period when St. John wrote, in a lamentable state of schismatic confusion. Diotrephes may, at such a period, have been aspiring to put forward his claim at Corinth; and may, in his ambitious proceedings, have rejected from communion the brethren whom St. John had sent to Caius. [3] A yet more interesting reflection is suggested by a writing of considerable authority. The writer of the "Synopsis of Holy Scripture," which stands amongst the Works of Athanasius, says—"the Gospel according to John was both dictated by John the Apostle and beloved when in exile at Patmos, and by him was published in Ephesus, through Caius the beloved and friend of the Apostles, of whom Paul also writing to the Romans

---

[1] Caius, a Macedonian (Acts xix. 29); Caius of Derbe (Acts xx. 4); Caius of Corinth (Rom. xvi. 23; I Cor. i. 14).

[2] Rom. xvi. 23.

[3] No doubt ver. 10 presents some difficulty. Voyages between Corinth were regularly and easily performed. Still it is scarcely probable that the aged Apostle should have contemplated such a voyage. But the form (ἐὰν ἔλθω) purposely expresses possibility rather than probability—the smallest amount of presumption—if I shall come, which is not quite impossible. (Donaldson, *Gr. Gr.*, "Conditional Propositions." 501.) The hope of seeing Caius "face to face" (ver. 14) contains no objection, as it may refer to a visit of Caius to Ephesus.

saith, *Caius mine host, and of the whole Church.*" [1]   This
would give a very marked significance to one touch
in this Third Epistle of St. John.   The phrase here
"and we bear witness also, *and ye know that our
witness is true*"—clearly points back to the closing
attestation of the Gospel—"*and we know that his witness
is true.*" [2]   He counts upon a quick recognition of a
common memory. [3]

Demetrius is, of course, a name redolent of the
worship of Demeter the Earth-Mother, and of
Ephesian surroundings.   No reader of the New Testament needs to be reminded of the riot at Ephesus,
which is told at such length in the history of St. Paul's
voyages by St. Luke.   The conjecture that the agita-
tor of the turbulent guild of silversmiths who made
silver shrines of Diana may have become the Demetrius, the object of St. John's lofty commendation, is
by no means improbable.   There is a peculiar fulness
in the narrative of the Acts, and an amplitude and
exactness in the reports of the speeches of Demetrius
and of the town-clerk which betray both unusually
detailed information, and a feeling on the part of the
writer that the subject was one of much interest for
many readers. [4]   The very words of Demetrius about
Paul evince that uneasy sense of the powers of
fascination possessed by the Apostle which is often

---

[1] "Synopsis S.S." '76.   (S. Athanas., *Opp.*, iv. 433.   Edit. Migne.)

[2] Read together 3 John 12, and John xxi. 24.

[3] The writer had worked out his conclusions about Caius indepen-
dently before he happened to read Bengel's note.   "Caius *Corinthi* de
quo Rom. xvi. 23, vel huic Caio, Johannis amico, fuit *simillimus* in
hospitalite—vel *idem ;*—si idem, ex Achaia in Asiam migravit, vel
Corinthum Johannes hanc epistolam misit."

[4] Acts xix. 23-41.

the first timid witness of reluctant conviction.[1] The whole story would be of thrilling interest to those who, knowing well what Demetrius had become, were here told what he once had been. In a very ancient document (the so-called "Apostolic Constitutions")[2] we read that "Demetrius was appointed Bishop of Philadelphia by me," *i.e.*, by the Apostle John. To the Bishop of a city so often shaken by the earthquakes of that volcanic soil came the commendation—"I know thy works that thou didst keep My word;" and the assuring promise that he should, when the victory was won, have the solidity and permanence of "a pillar" in a "temple"[3] that no convulsion could shake down. The witness then, which stands on record for the Bishop of Philadelphia, is threefold; the threefold witness of the First Epistle on a reduced scale—the witness of the world;[4] the witness of the Truth itself, even of Jesus;[5] the witness of the Church—including John.[6]

II.

We may now advert to the *contents* and *general style* of this letter.

I. As to its *contents*.

1. It supplies us with a valuable test of Christian life, in

---

[1] "Almost throughout all Asia this Paul hath persuaded and turned away much people, saying, that they be no gods, which are made with hands."—Acts xix. 26.

[2] vii. 46.

[3] Apoc. iii. 7, 8, 12.

[4] "All men."

[5] Καὶ ὑπ' αὐτῆς τῆς ἀληθείας, *i.e.*, Jesus (Apoc. iii. 7, 12). This type of expression marks the "Asiatic school." So Papias; 'απ' αὐτῆς τῆς 'αληθείας (Ap. Euseb. *H. E.*, iii. 39). Cf. John xiv. 6.

[6] "And we also bear witness." 3 John 12.

what may be called the Christian instinct of *missionary affection*, possessed in such full measure by Caius.[1]

This, indeed, is an ingredient of Christian character. Do we admire and feel attracted by missionaries ? They are knight-errants of the Faith ; leaders of the "forlorn hope" of Christ's cause; bearers of the flag of the cross through the storms of battle. Do we wish to honour and to help them, and feel ennobled by doing so ? He who has no almost enthusiastic regard for missionaries has not the spirit of primitive Christianity within his breast.

2. The Church is beset with different dangers from very different quarters. The second Epistle of St. John has its bold unmistakable warning of danger from the philosophical atmosphere which is not only round the Church, but necessarily finds its way within. Those who assume to be leaders of intellectual and even of spiritual progress sometimes lead away from Christ. The test of scientific truth is accordance with the proposition which embodies the last discovery ; the test of religious truth is accordance with the proposition which embodies the first discovery, *i.e.*, "the doctrine of Christ." Progress outside this is regress ; it is desertion first of Christ, ultimately of God.[2] As the second Epistle warns the Church of peril from *speculative ambition*, so the third Epistle marks a danger from *personal ambition*,[3] arrogating to itself undue authority within the Church. Diotrephes in all probability was a bishop.[4] At Rome there has been a permanent Diotrephes in the office of the Papacy ; how much this

---

[1] 3 John 5, 6, 7.
[2] 2 John 9.
[3] 3 John 9, 10.
[4] See authorities quoted by Archdeacon Lee (*Speaker's Commentary*, Tom. ii., N.T., p. 512).

has had to say to the dislocation of Christendom, God knows. But there are other smaller and more vulgar continuators of Diotrephes, who occupy no Vatican. Priests! But there are priests in different senses. The priest who stands to minister in holy things, the true *Leitourgos,* is rightly so-called. But there is an arrogant priestship which would do violence to conscience, and interpose rudely between God and the soul. Priests in this sense are called by different names. They are clad in different dresses—some in chasubles, some in frock-coats, some in petticoats. "Down with priestcraft," is even the cry of many of them. The priest who stands to offer sacrifice may or may not be a priest in the evil sense; the priest (who abjures the name) who is a master of religious small-talk of the popular kind, and winds people to his own ends round his little finger by using them deftly, is often the modern edition of Diotrephes.

3. This brief Epistle contains one of those apparently mere spiritual *truisms,* which make St. John the most powerful and comprehensive of all spiritual teachers. He had suggested a warning to Caius, which serves as the link to connect the example of Diotrephes which he has denounced, with that of Demetrius which he is about to commend. "Beloved!" he cries, "imitate not that which is evil, but that which is good." A glorious little " Imitation of Christ," a compression of his own Gospel, the record of the Great Example in three words![1] Then follows this absolutely exhaustive division, which covers the whole moral and spiritual world. "He that doeth good," (the whole principle of whose moral life is this,) "is of," has his origin from, " God;" " he that doeth evil hath not seen God," sees Him not as a consequence of having

---

[1] μιμοῦ . . . τὸ ἀγαθόν, 3 John 11.

spiritually looked upon Him.   Here, at last, we have the
flight of the eagle's wing, the glance of the eagle's eye.
Especially valuable are these words, almost at the close
of the Apostolic age and of the New Testament Scripture.   They help us to keep the delicate balance of
truth ; they guard us against all abuse of the precious
doctrines of grace.   Several texts are *mutilated;* more
are conveniently *dropped out.*   How seldom does one see
the whole context quoted, in tracts and sheets, of that
most blessed passage—"if we walk in the light, as
He is in the light, *the blood of Jesus, His Son, cleanseth
us from all sin ?* "   How often do we see these words
at all—"he that doeth good is of God, but he that doeth
evil hath not seen God ? "   Perhaps it may be a lingering suspicion that a text which comes out of a very
short Epistle is worth very little.   Perhaps doctrinalism
à outrance considers that the sentiment " savours of
works."   But, at all events, there is terrible decisive-
ness about these antithetic propositions.   For each life
is described in section and in plan by one or other of the
two.   The whole complicated series of thought, actions,
habits, purposes, summed up in the words *life* and
character, is a continuous stream issuing from the man
who necessarily is *doing* every moment of his existence.
The stream is either pure, bright, cleansing, gladdening,
capable of being tracked by a thread of emerald wherever it flows; or it carries with it on its course blackness
bitterness, and barrenness.   Men must be plainly dealt
with.   They may hold any creed, or follow any round of
religious practices.   There are creeds which are nobly
true, others which are false and feeble—practices which
are beautiful and elevating, others which are petty and
unprofitable.   They may repeat the shibboleth ever so
accurately ; and follow the observances ever so closely.

They may sing hymns until their throats are hoarse, and beat drums until their wrists are sore. But St. John's propositions ring out, loud and clear, and syllable themselves in questions, which one day or other the conscience will put to us with terrible distinctness. Are you one who is ever doing good; or one who is not doing good? "God be merciful to me a sinner!" may well rush to our lips. But *that*, when opportunity is given, must be followed by another prayer. Not only—"wash away my sins." Something more. "Fill and purify me with Thy Spirit, that, pardoned and renewed, I may become good, and be doing good." It is sometimes said that the Church is full of souls "dying of their morality." Is it not at least equally true to say that the Church is full of souls dying of their spirituality? That is— souls dying in one case of unreal morality; in the other of unreal spirituality, which juggles with spiritual words, making a sham out of them. Morality which is not spiritual, is imperfect; spirituality which is not moralized through and through is of the spirit of evil.

It is a great thing that in these last sentences, written with a trembling hand, which shrank from the labour of pen and ink,[1] the Apostle should have lifted a word (probably current in the atmosphere of Ephesus among spiritualists and astrologers[2]), from the low applications with which it was undeservedly associated; and should have rung out high and clear the Gospel's everlasting justification, the final harmony of the teaching of grace—" he that doeth good is of God."

---

[1] 3 John 13.

[2] The verb ἀγαθοποιεῖν is found in a few places in the LXX. and New Testament. "Amongst profane writers, astrologers only used this verb. They signified by it, *I offer a good omen.* So in Proclus and others." See Bretsch. and Grimm, s. v. ἀγαθοποιέω.

III.

The style of the third Epistle of St. John is certainly
that of an old man.   It is reserved in language and in
doctrine.   God is thrice and thrice only mentioned.[1]
Jesus is not once expressly uttered.   But

> ". . . They are not empty-hearted whose low sound
> Reverbs no hollowness."

In religion, as in everything else, we are earnest, not
by aiming at earnestness, but by aiming at an object.
Religious language should be deep and real, rather
than demonstrative.   It is not safe to play with sacred
names.   To pronounce them at random for the purpose
of being effective and impressive is to take them in
vain.   What a wealth of reverential love there is in that
—"for the sake of the Name !"[2]   Old copyists sometimes thought to improve upon the impressiveness of
Apostles by cramming in sacred names.   They only
maimed what they touched with clumsy hand.   A
deeper sense of the Sacramental Presence is in the
hushed, awful, reverence of "not discerning the Body,"
than in the interpolated "not discerning of the Lord's
Body."   Even so "The Name," perhaps, speaks more
to the heart, and implies more than "His Name."
It is, indeed, the "beautiful Name," by the which
we are called.   And sometimes in sermons, or in
Eucharistic "Gloria in Excelsis," or in hymns that
have come from such as St. Bernard, or in sick
rooms, it shall go up with our sweetest music, and
waken our tenderest thoughts, and be "as ointment

---

[1] "Worthily of God" ver. 6; "is of God—hath not seen God"
ver. 11.

[2] Ver. 7.

poured forth." But what an underlying Gospel, what an intense suppressed flame there is behind these quiet words! This letter says nothing of rapture, of prophecy, of miracle. It lies in the atmosphere of the Church, as we find it even now. It has a word for *friendship*. It seeks to *individualise* its benediction.[1] A hush of evening rests upon the note. May such an evening close upon our old age!

NOTES.

Ver. 2 . . . *thy soul*.] Strange difficulty seems to be felt in some quarters about the word ψυχή, as used by our Lord and the Apostles. The difficulty arises from a singular argument advanced by M. Renan. He maintains that Christ and His first followers knew nothing of "the soul" as the immortal principle in man—that in him which is capable of being saved or lost. It was simply, according to him, *either* the animal natural life[2] (Matt. ii. 20; John xii. 25); *or* at most the vague Greek immortality of the shadows, as opposed to the later Hebrew Resurrection-life. But there are very numerous passages in the New Testament where "soul" *can* only be used for "life as created by God;" for the thinking substance, different from the body and indestructible by death, created with possibilities of eternal happiness or misery. (The following passages are decisive—Matt. x. 28, xi. 29; Acts ii. 27; 2 Cor. xii. 13; Heb. xiii. 17; 1 Pet. i. 9, 22, ii. 11, 25; Jas. i. 21, v. 20; 3 John 2; Apoc. vi. 9, xx. 4.

---

[1] "The friends salute thee: salute the friends by name," ver. 14 The mention of friendship is not common in the New Testament. Beautiful exceptions will be found in Luke xii. 4; John xi. 11, xv. 14, 15; cf. Acts xxvii. 3.

[2] As indicated by breathing—from ψύχω.

Printed by Hazell, Watson, & Viney, Ld., London and Aylesbury

27, PATERNOSTER ROW,
LONDON.

HODDER AND STOUGHTON'S
New and Recent Publications.

The Expositor's Bible.

EDITED BY,
REV. W. ROBERTSON NICOLL, M.A., LL.D.

Crown 8vo, 7s. 6d. each volume.

THE OLD TESTAMENT.

GENESIS. Rev. Professor MARCUS DODS, D.D.

EXODUS. Very Rev. DEAN CHADWICK, D.D.

LEVITICUS. Rev. S. H. KELLOGG, D.D.

NUMBERS. Rev. R. A. WATSON, D.D.

DEUTERONOMY. Rev. Professor A. HARPER, B.D.

JOSHUA. Rev. Professor W. G. BLAIKIE, D.D., LL.D.

JUDGES AND RUTH. Rev. R. A. WATSON, D.D.

1 **SAMUEL.** Rev. Professor W. G. BLAIKIE, D.D., LL.D.

2 **SAMUEL.** By the same Author.

1 **KINGS.** Very Rev. DEAN FARRAR, D.D., F.R.S.

2 **KINGS.** By the same Author.

1 & 2 **CHRONICLES.** Rev. Prof. W. H. BENNETT, M.A.

EZRA—ESTHER. Rev. Professor W. F. ADENEY, M.A.

JOB. Rev. R. A. WATSON, D.D.

PSALMS. Rev. ALEX. MACLAREN, D.D. 3 Vols.

PROVERBS. Rev. R. F. HORTON, M.A.

ECCLESIASTES. Rev. SAMUEL COX, D.D.

ISAIAH. Rev. Professor G. ADAM SMITH, D.D. 2 Vols.

JEREMIAH, THE PROPHECIES OF. Rev. C. J. BALL, M.A.

JEREMIAH (Chaps. xxi.—lii.). Rev. W. H. BENNETT, M.A.

EZEKIEL. Rev. Professor SKINNER, M.A.

DANIEL. Very Rev. DEAN FARRAR, D.D., F.R.S.

THE TWELVE PROPHETS. Rev. Prof. G. A. SMITH, D.D. 2 Vols.

I

The Expositor's Bible.

EDITED BY

REV. W. ROBERTSON NICOLL, M.A., LL.D.

Crown 8vo, 7s. 6d. each volume.

THE NEW TESTAMENT.

ST. MATTHEW. Rev. J. MONRO GIBSON, D.D.
ST. MARK. Very Rev. DEAN CHADWICK, D.D.
ST. LUKE. Rev. HENRY BURTON, M.A.
ST. JOHN. Pev. Professor MARCUS DODS, D.D. 2 Vols.
THE ACTS. Rev. Professor G. T. STOKES, D.D. 2 Vols.
ROMANS. Rev. H. C. G. MOULE, M.A., D.D.
1 CORINTHIANS. Rev. Professor MARCUS DODS, D.D.
2 CORINTHIANS. Rev. JAMES DENNEY, D.D.
GALATIANS. Rev. Professor G. G. FINDLAY, B.A.
EPHESIANS. By the same Author.
PHILIPPIANS. Rev. Principal RAINY, D.D.
COLOSSIANS. Rev. A. MACLAREN, D.D.
THESSALONIANS. Rev. J. DENNEY, D.D.
PASTORAL EPISTLES. Rev. A. PLUMMER, D.D.
HEBREWS. Rev. Principal T. C. EDWARDS, D.D.
SS. JAMES AND JUDE. Rev. A. PLUMMER, D.D.
EPISTLES OF ST. PETER. Rev. Professor LUMBY, D.D.
EPISTLES OF ST. JOHN. The Right Rev. W. ALEXANDER. D.D.
REVELATION. Rev. Professor W. MILLIGAN, D.D.

THE CLERICAL LIBRARY. Complete in Twelve Volumes.
Crown 8vo, cloth, 6s. each.

1. Three Hundred Outlines of Sermons on the New Testament.
2. Outlines of Sermons on the Old Testament.
3. Pulpit Prayers. By Eminent Preachers.
4. Outline Sermons to Children. With numerous Anecdotes.
5. Anecdotes Illustrative of New Testament Texts.
6. Expository Sermons and Outlines on the Old Testament.
7. Expository Sermons on the New Testament.
8. Platform Aids.
9. New Outlines of Sermons on the New Testament. By Eminent Preachers. Hitherto unpublished.
10. Anecdotes Illustrative of the Old Testament Texts.
11. New Outlines of Sermons on the Old Testament By Eminent Preachers. Hitherto unpublished.
12. Outlines of Sermons for Special Occasions.

2

ST. PAUL THE TRAVELLER AND THE ROMAN
CITIZEN. By W. M. RAMSAY, D.C.L., LL.D., Professor
of Humanity, Aberdeen ; Author of " The Church in the
Roman Empire," etc. Second Thousand. 8vo, cloth, with
Map, 10s. 6d.

"Professor Ramsay brings not only his great experience as a traveller
and archæologist, but the resources of an ingenious mind, and a lively
style. The book is, like everything Professor Ramsay does, extra-
ordinarily alive. It shows everywhere personal learning, personal impression ; it has the sharp touch of the traveller and the eye-witness."—
Times.

" His book is at once a critical reconstruction of the narrative in 'Acts.'
A new reading of the life of the Apostle of the Gentiles, a fresh explanation
of the relation between first-century Christianity and the social and
political conditions amid which it developed, and an announcement of the
discovery of an historical star of the first magnitude. The light thrown
by Professor Ramsay on the career of the Apostle Paul is often startling
in its freshness. There is, indeed, scarcely a single incident in the
Apostle's life upon which he has not something new to say."—*Glasgow
Herald.*

THE CHURCH IN THE ROMAN EMPIRE BEFORE
A.D. 170. By W. M. RAMSAY, M.A., D.C.L., Professor of
Humanity in the University of Aberdeen. Fourth Edition.
With Maps and Illustrations, 8vo, cloth, 12s.

" This volume is the most important contribution to the study of early
Church history which has been published in this country since the great
work of Bishop Lightfoot on the Apostolic fathers. It is, too, unless our
memory fails us, without a rival in any foreign country."—*Guardian.*

THE HISTORICAL GEOGRAPHY OF THE HOLY
LAND. By GEORGE ADAM SMITH, D.D., Professor of
Hebrew and Old Testament Exegesis, Free Church College,
Glasgow. With Six Maps, specially prepared. Fifth Thousand.
8vo, cloth, 15s.

" Professor Smith is well equipped at all points for this work. He is
abreast of the latest findings of Scripture exegesis, and of geographical
survey, and of archæological exploration ; and he has himself travelled
widely over Palestine. The value of the work is incalculably increased by
the series of geographical maps, the first of the kind representing the
whole lift and lie of the land by gradations of colour."—*Scotsman.*

" A very noteworthy contribution to the study of sacred history, based
upon the three indispensable conditions of personal acquaintance with the
land, a study of the explorations, discoveries, and decipherments . . . and
the employment of the results of Biblical criticism."—*Times.*

THE ASCENT OF MAN. By HENRY DRUMMOND.

Twenty-first Thousand. Net, 7s. 6d.

"Worked out with characteristic ardour and courage. The technical quality of the book is of a high order. In none of his works is Mr. Drummond's literary skill more strikingly manifested. The style—metaphorical, allusive, picturesque—has even more of the writer's wonted grace and facility, and his command of analogy has never been employed with better effect, and productive of more varied and suggestive illustrations."—*Saturday Review.*

BY THE SAME AUTHOR.

NATURAL LAW IN THE SPIRITUAL WORLD.

Thirty-second Edition, completing 119,000. Crown 8vo, cloth, 3s. 6d.

"We have no hesitation in saying that this is one of the most able and interesting books on the relations which exist between natural science and spiritual life that has appeared. Mr. Drummond writes perfect English; his ideas are fresh, and expressed with admirable felicity. His book is one to fertilise the mind, to open it to fresh fields of thought, and to stimulate its activity."—*Literary Churchman.*

TROPICAL AFRICA. Seventh Edition, completing 34,000.

Crown 8vo, cloth, 3s. 6d.

"Professor Drummond is a clear and accurate observer, and as he has had a sound scientific training, and has a real interest in the human side of African life, he is able to present us with pictures of a distinctness and originality not often met with in books of African travel."—*Times.*

THE PERMANENT MESSAGE OF THE EXODUS;

or, The Mission of Moses. By Rev. JOHN SMITH, D.D., of Broughton Place Church, Edinburgh. Crown 8vo, cloth, 3s. 6d.

"The discourses are of a high order; their author is evidently a man thoroughly in earnest, pulsing with a life which he is eager to communicate. Fresh, fervent, and eloquent, full of interesting information and suggestive statement, they must have produced a deep impression when they were delivered, though for their true appreciation they require quiet, careful, and thoughtful perusal."—*Scotsman.*

THE PROBLEM OF THE AGES. A Book for Young

Men. By the Rev. J. B. HASTINGS, M.A., of Edinburgh. Crown 8vo, cloth, 3s. 6d.

"He puts the main broad arguments in favour of belief in God and Christianity with admirable lucidity, and generally in a terse and telling fashion. The book is well calculated to serve the purpose with which it has been written, and contains in a handy form a great many modern arguments and evidences which can be got at only by a rather extended course of reading."—*Glasgow Herald.*

4

5

THE DAYS OF AULD LANG SYNE. By IAN MAC-LAREN. Third Edition, completing **50,000.** Crown 8vo, gilt top, 6s.

"There is, we think, a sense in which the new volume is not merely an addition but a supplement to its predecessor. In 'Beside the Bonnie Brier Bush' were passages, and indeed whole stories, which were master-strokes or masterpieces of a fine poignant pathos, or a dry yet genial humour, but the former preponderated, and gave tone and expression to the book. It may be doubted whether the humorous quality of that Scots canniness which stands out most conspicuously in a difficult nego-tiation has ever been rendered with happier fineness of observation or intimacy of touch than in the opening study, 'A Triumph in Diplomacy.'"—*Daily Chronicle.*

BESIDE THE BONNIE BRIER BUSH. By the same Author. Ninth Edition, completing **60,000.** Art linen, crown 8vo, gilt top, 6s.

"As an artist in Scotch character of the sort that is found at its best in country villages he has no superior among his contemporaries, ambitious and able as several of these are."—*Spectator.*

STRANGERS AT LISCONNEL. A second Series of "Irish Idylls." By JANE BARLOW. Second Thousand. Crown 8vo, cloth, 6s.

"In 'Strangers at Lisconnel' Miss Barlow returns to her early love, and has produced a second series of 'Irish Idylls' which are in every way as delightful as the sketches of peasant life that at one bound brought her into the very front rank of delineators of Irish character. The sketches possess in a high degree all the charm, simplicity, and tenderness of the original series, while revealing the same fidelity to nature as well as the rich humour and pathos characteristic of the people which Miss Barlow so admirably describes."—*Scotsman.*

"Only the nature of a genuine artist, combined with the skill of a master of language, could lend so powerful and vivid an interest to the section of barren Irish bogland where the scenes are laid, and only one who had a tender interest and affection for the people could weave such a truthful yet fascinating web of romance around their simple lives."—*Derry Standard.*

BY THE SAME AUTHOR.

1. **IRISH IDYLLS.** Sixth Edition. Crown 8vo, cloth, 6s.

"The 'Irish Idylls' are delightful reading, and afford a truer insight into Irish peasant character, and ways of light and thought, than any book that it has been our fortune to read for a long time."—*Athenæum.*

2. **KERRIGAN'S QUALITY.** Third Thousand. Crown 8vo, art linen, gilt top, 6s.

"A book to touch the hearts of all who read it. Miss Barlow's sketches of the Irish peasantry are the work of close and sympathetic observation, combined with great literary dexterity."—*The Daily Chronicle.*

3. **BOGLAND STUDIES.** Third Edition. Crown 8vo, cloth, 6s.

"Rarely has it been our fortune to find between a couple of covers more humanity wedded to such vivid lines. Miss Barlow is remarkably observant; she has a gift of concentration, a power of showing us a scene in one line."—*Literary World.*

6

LITERARY ANECDOTES OF THE NINETEENTH CENTURY : Contributions towards the Literary History of the Period. Edited by W. ROBERTSON NICOLL, M.A., LL.D., and THOMAS J. WISE. Volume I., 20s. net.

PREFACE.—The work, of which this is the first volume, has been suggested by Nichols's well-known *Literary Anecdotes of the Eighteenth Century*. The editors hope to provide in it a considerable amount of fresh matter, illustrating the Life and work of British Authors in the Nineteenth Century. To a large extent they rely upon manuscript material, but use will be made of practically inaccessible texts, and of fugitive writings. While leading authors will receive due attention, much space will be devoted to the less-known writers of the period. It is intended to supply Biographies, Letters hitherto unpublished, additions from Manuscript sources to published works, together with a series of full Bibliographies of the writings of the greater authors. Every precaution has been taken to avoid the infringement of copyright, and the editors hope that they will be forgiven any involuntary transgression. Illustrations and numerous fac-similes will be provided in each volume. While only one thousand copies are to be printed, of which two hundred and fifty are for America, in no circumstances will a reprint be undertaken. The editors, however, reserve the right to issue separately any section of the work.

It is hoped that the second volume will be published in October, 1896.

SONGS OF REST. Edited by W. ROBERTSON NICOLL, M.A., LL.D. Presentation Edition. Second Edition. Elegantly bound in Buckram, gilt top, 5s. This volume includes the First and Second Series. They have been thoroughly revised, and increased by one-third. The Bijou Edition is still on sale, First and Second Series, 1s. 6d. each.

"He has collected many beautiful things."—*Daily Chronicle*.

"We are not surprised that this new and dainty edition, in one handsome volume, is demanded. . . . Some of the most exquisite verses in this book are by singers whose praise is certainly not in all the churches, but there is, nevertheless, a deep and impressive unison in all the music."—*The Speaker*.

7

A WINDOW IN THRUMS. By J. M. Barrie. Fourteenth Edition. Crown 8vo, buckram, gilt top, 6s.

"We think that this is the very best of the many good sketches of Scottish peasant life which we have ever read "—*Standard*.

"This remarkable little book. We follow the homely record with an interest which the most sensational drama could not surpass."—*Blackwood's Magazine*.

BY THE SAME AUTHOR.

1. MY LADY NICOTINE. Sixth Edition. Crown 8vo, buckram, gilt top, 6s.

"Humour refined, irresistible, characteristic."—*Echo*.

"A very delightful book. The book should be read straight through, and then picked up at intervals and opened anywhere. Wherever it is opened it will please."—*Speaker*.

2. AULD LICHT IDYLLS. Tenth Edition. Crown 8vo, buckram, gilt top, 6s.

"Racy, humorous, and altogether delightful."—*Truth*.

"At once the most successful, the most truly literary, and the most realistic attempt that has been made for years—if not for generations—to reproduce humble Scottish life."—*Spectator*.

An Édition de Luxe of

AULD LICHT IDYLLS. With Eighteen Etchings by William Hole, R.S.A. Handsomely printed by Messrs. R. & R. Clark, Edinburgh, on English hand-made paper. Large post 4to, 31s. 6d.

*** *A few Copies at £3 3s., signed by Author and Artist, with Etchings printed on Japanese Paper.*

3. WHEN A MAN'S SINGLE. A Tale of Literary Life. Ninth Edition. Crown 8vo, buckram, gilt top, 6s.

"The best one-volume novel of the year."—*Daily News*.

"Mr. Barrie is a man with a style. From one end to the other the story is bright, cheerful, amusing."—*Saturday Review*.

LOVE AND QUIET LIFE. Somerset Idylls. By Walter Raymond, Author of "Gentleman Upcott's Daughter," "Young Sam and Sabina," etc. Second Edition. Crown 8vo, gilt top, 6s.

LONDON IDYLLS. By W. J. Dawson. Second Thousand. Crown 8vo, cloth, 5s.

"A collection of stories of much promise. Mr. Dawson has a pleasant style, an easy command of effective expression, and he passes lightly from pathos to humour, or rather he can blend the two with no sensible transition."—*Times.*

"In 'London Idylls' W. J. Dawson has written a book that will be treasured. The poem, in which the author seeks to express the indefinable poetry of London, could only have been written by one very nearly attuned to the spirit, to the loves and passions, joys and sorrows of the world's greatest centre of romance. Of the idylls themselves little may be written to convey any real sense of their charm. The themes on which they turn are such as only London could have supplied. Than the first exquisitely rendered story—infinitely simple and tender—it is not too much to say that nothing more heartsearching has been written since the historian of Joe, the crossing-sweeper, laid down his pen. Dickens himself might have wept over it."—*Dundee Advertiser.*

BY THE SAME AUTHOR.

1. **THE REDEMPTION OF EDWARD STRAHAN:** A Social Story. Third Edition. Paper covers, 1s.

"A powerful story."—*Times.*

"A powerful book, with a pure and high aim."—Right Hon. W. E. Gladstone.

2. **QUEST AND VISION.** Second Edition. Crown 8vo, cloth, 3s. 6d.

"The marks of wide reading pervade the volume, and Mr. Dawson is in the main singularly adroit in his allusions."—*Speaker.*

3. **THE MAKERS OF MODERN ENGLISH:** A Popular Handbook to the Greater Poets of the Century. Fifth Edition. Crown 8vo, cloth, 5s.

4. **THE MAKING OF MANHOOD.** Fourth Thousand. Crown 8vo, cloth, 3s. 6d.

"There is a manly outspokenness in this book as well as vision and sympathy, and an evident understanding of the needs and aspirations which determine the point of view in youth towards religion and literature, work and play, and the give and take of society."—*Speaker.*

5. **THE THRESHOLD OF MANHOOD.** A Young Man's Words to Young Men. Eighth Thousand. Crown 8vo, cloth, 3s. 6d.

"They are full of force, penetrated with Christian manliness, unsparing in their denunciations of vice, and throb with desire for the salvation of the young. These are sermons for the times, which should nerve many young soldiers for the good fight of faith."—*London Quarterly Review.*

The Lord Bishop of Winchester says: "I consider Dr. Dale to be one of the most enlightened and profound theologians of the time. My shelves contain nearly all—if not all—of his books, and we are friends."

THE EPISTLE OF JAMES AND OTHER DIS-COURSES. Third Thousand. Crown 8vo, cloth, 6s.

CHRIST AND THE FUTURE LIFE Fourth Thousand. Elegantly bound in cloth, 1s. 6d.

CHRISTIAN DOCTRINE. A Series of Discourses. Fifth Thousand. Crown 8vo, cloth, 6s.

FELLOWSHIP WITH CHRIST, and Other Discourses Delivered on Special Occasions. Fifth Thousand. Crown 8vo, cloth, 6s.

THE LIVING CHRIST AND THE FOUR GOSPELS. Eighth Thousand. Crown 8vo, cloth, 6s.

LAWS OF CHRIST FOR COMMON LIFE. Eighth Thousand. Crown 8vo, cloth, 6s.

NINE LECTURES ON PREACHING. Eighth Edition. Crown 8vo, cloth, 6s.

THE JEWISH TEMPLE AND THE CHRISTIAN CHURCH. A Series of Discourses on the Epistle to the Hebrews. Ninth Edition. Crown 8vo, cloth, 6s.

THE EPISTLE TO THE EPHESIANS. Its Doctrines and Ethics. Eighth Edition. Crown 8vo, cloth, 7s. 6d.

WEEK-DAY SERMONS. Sixth Edition. Crown 8vo, cloth, 3s. 6d.

THE TEN COMMANDMENTS. Seventh Edition. Crown 8vo, cloth, 5s.

A. M. MACKAY, Pioneer Missionary of the Church Missionary Society to Uganda. By his SISTER. With Etched Portrait by H. Manesse. Fifteenth Thousand. Crown 8vo, cloth, 7s. 6d.

"Even for lay readers a fascinating book of African exploration and adventure."—*St. James's Gazette.*

THE LIFE OF MACKAY FOR BOYS.

THE STORY OF THE LIFE OF MACKAY OF UGANDA. Told for Boys. By his SISTER. The whole of the matter in this volume is fresh, and is not found in the larger book, "A M. Mackay." With Portrait and Illustrations. Eleventh Thousand. Handsomely bound in cloth, 8vo, gilt edges, 5s.

A. MACKAY RUTHQUIST ; Or, Singing the Gospel among the Hindus and Gonds. By the Author of "A. M. Mackay, Pioneer Missionary of the C.M.S. to Uganda," etc. With Portrait and Illustrations. Crown 8vo, cloth, 6s.

TWENTY YEARS IN KHAMA'S COUNTRY, And Pioneering among the Batauana of Lake Ngami. By the Rev. J. D. HEPBURN. With Photographic Illustrations. Third Edition. Crown 8vo, cloth, 6s.

CHARACTERISTICS AND CHARACTERS OF WILLIAM LAW. Selected and arranged with an Introduction by ALEXANDER WHYTE, D.D. Crown 8vo, cloth, 9s.

W. P. LOCKHART, Merchant and Preacher. His Life and Letters. Compiled by his WIFE. With an Introduction by the Rev. ALEXANDER MACLAREN, D.D., of Manchester, and Portrait. Second Edition. Crown 8vo, cloth, 3s. 6d.

THE BRONTES IN IRELAND ; or, Facts Stranger than Fiction. By Dr. WILLIAM WRIGHT, Author of "The Hittites," etc. With Illustrations. Third Edition. Crown 8vo, cloth, 6s.

CHARLES G. FINNEY. An Autobiography. With Steel Portrait. Crown 8vo, cloth, 3s. 6d.

LETTERS AND SKETCHES FROM THE NEW HEBRIDES. By MAGGIE WHITECROSS PATON (Mrs. John G. Paton of Aniwa). Edited by her Brother-in-Law, Rev. JAMES PATON, B.A. With Portrait, Map, and 23 Illustrations. Third Edition. Sixth Thousand. Crown 8vo, cloth, 6s.

"A very attractive piece of missionary literature, full of vivid descriptions of nature and life."—*Times.*

"A peculiar charm undoubtedly characterises these letters. They were written for members of Mrs. Paton's family and personal friends, without any thought of publication; and their literary grace is evidently natural and of the uncommon kind. They abound in homely touches and in hearty humour, while the unrestrained personal and domestic allusions afford valuable illustrations of a side of missionary life the existence of which is sometimes strangely ignored, and the value of which to the work is by some utterly denied."—*Church Missionary Intelligencer.*

JOHN G. PATON, D.D., Missionary to the Hebrides. An Autobiography. Edited by his Brother, the Rev. JAMES PATON, B.A. Popular Edition. Complete in One Volume. Twentieth Thousand. Crown 8vo, cloth, 6s.

"One of the best autobiographies we have ever read. It is candour itself, and bears the impress of truth on every page. It would take a very incorrigible Agnostic all his time not to fall in love with Dr. Paton and his noble work."—*Daily Chronicle.*

THE STORY OF JOHN G. PATON. Told for Young Folks. By the Rev. JAMES PATON, B.A. With Forty-five Full-page Illustrations by J. Finnemore. With Map. Fifteenth Thousand. 8vo, cloth, 5s.

"In the record of thirty years' good work amongst the South Sea cannibals, we have before us one of those missionary enterprises which read almost more strangely than fiction itself. . . . There are enough hairbreadth escapes and deeds of cool, if unostentatious, courage in these pages to stock half-a-dozen ordinary books, and the forty-five graphic illustrations add much to the attraction of the text."—*Daily Telegraph.*

LIFE OF ST. FRANCIS OF ASSISI. By PAUL SABATIER. Translated from the French. Gilt top. New Edition. Price 9s. net.

"M. Paul Sabatier is one of those men of letters, unhappily rare in France, in whom ripe learning and fine critical sagacity are not divorced from a reasonable Christian faith. Trained in the 'Faculté de Théologie Protestante de Paris,' he has grown into the most brilliant scholar of his Church. No commentary on the *Didache*, for instance, is more illuminating than the edition of that treasure-trove which he published in 1885. And now he has given us a 'Life of St. Francis' which may stand on the same shelf with Villari's 'Life of Savonarola.'"—*The Expositor.*

"We may cordially commend this translation. It is thoroughly well done, fluent and accurate, and nowhere betraying by idiomatic faultiness or even stiffness, that insufficient mastery of one or the other language which mars too many versions."—*Glasgow Herald.*

THE PEOPLE'S BIBLE. Discourses upon Holy Scripture, forming a Pastoral Commentary. By JOSEPH PARKER, D.D. Demy 8vo, each; 8s.

THE OLD TESTAMENT.

Vol.   I.   GENESIS.
Vol.   II. EXODUS.
Vol. III. LEVITICUS—NUMBERS XXVI.
Vol. IV. NUMBERS XXVI.—DEUTERONOMY.
Vol. V. JOSHUA—JUDGES V.
Vol. VI. JUDGES VI.—1 SAMUEL XVIII.
Vol. VII. 1 SAMUEL XVIII.—1 KINGS XIII.
Vol. VIII. 1 KINGS XV.—1 CHRONICLES IX.
Vol. IX. 1 CHRONICLES X.—2 CHRONICLES XX.
Vol. X. 2 CHRONICLES XXI.—ESTHER.
Vol. XI. THE BOOK OF JOB.
Vol. XII. THE BOOK OF PSALMS.
Vol. XIII. THE BOOK OF PROVERBS.
Vol. XIV. ECCLESIASTES—ISAIAH XXVI.
Vol. XV. ISAIAH XXVII.—JEREMIAH XIX.
Vol. XVI. JEREMIAH XX.—DANIEL.
Vol. XVII. HOSEA—MALACHI.

THE NEW TESTAMENT.

Vol. XVIII. ST. MATTHEW.
Vol. XIX. ,,   ,,
Vol. XX. ST. MARK and ST. LUKE.
Vol. XXI. ST. JOHN.
Vol. XXII. THE ACTS OF THE APOSTLES.
Vol. XXIII. ,,   ,,   ,,
Vol. XXIV. ROMANS—GALATIANS.
Vol. XXV. EPHESIANS—REVELATION.

THE UNKNOWN GOD; Or, Inspiration Among Pre-Christian Races. By C. LORING BRACE. In 8vo, cloth, 12s.

BY THE SAME AUTHOR.

GESTA CHRISTI: A History of Human Progress under Christianity. Fifth Edition. Large crown 8vo, cloth, 7s. 6d.

THE ANGLICAN PULPIT LIBRARY. Sermons, Out-
lines, Illustrations for the Sundays and Holy Days of the
Year, Original and Selected. The most complete collection
of materials for Sermons on the Church Year, providing an
average of Fifty Sermons for every Sunday of the Church
Year, the subjects being chosen from the Epistle, the Gospel,
the Lessons, and from passages bearing on the subjects of
the Day.

> Vol. I.—Advent to Christmastide.
> Vol. II.—Epiphany to Septuagesima.
> Vol. III.—Sexagesima to Passiontide.

Subscription 24s. in advance for the first three volumes, in large
8vo, of about 500 pages each. To non-subscribers, 15s. each
volume.

. Full Prospectus, with Specimen pages, may be had on
application.

Church Bells says:—"A volume of the very highest use to preachers
and teachers."

The Expositor says :—"This work, when complete, will form not merely
an aid to preachers, but a repertory of all the best sermons in the
language."

OLD FARM FAIRIES. A Summer Campaign in Brownie-
land against King Cobweaver's Pixies. By HENRY CHRISTO-
PHER McCOOK, D.D. With 150 Illustrations. Crown 8vo,
cloth, 5s.

"The story tells of a war between the Brownies and the spiders, and
will interest a child by the oddity and strangeness (greater than a purely
imaginative writer could conceive) of the devices of strategy and warfare
to which the spiders resort. The illustrations to the book are partly
fanciful, partly true to the nature of spider life. . . . A story so fresh in
its idea, and so well worked out, is sure to please a young reader, and to
lend a peculiar attraction to the study of natural history."—*Scotsman.*

BY THE SAME AUTHOR.

1. TENANTS OF AN OLD FARM : Leaves from the Note-
Book of a Naturalist. With Introduction by Sir JOHN
LUBBOCK, M.P. With Illustrations. Second Edition. Crown
8vo, cloth, 6s.

"Dr. McCook deals with friends of mine—with insects, and particularly
ants, to which I have paid special attention. I have much pleasure in
bearing testimony to the fidelity and skill which Dr. McCook has devoted
to the study of these interesting atoms; and those who read his work may
safely depend on the accuracy of what he says."—From the Introduction
by Sir JOHN LUBBOCK, M.P., D.C.L., F.R.S.

2. WOMEN FRIENDS OF JESUS; or, Lives and Charac-
ters of the Holy Women of Gospel History. Second Edition.
Crown 8vo, cloth, 5s.

14

THE VISIONS OF A PROPHET. Studies in Zechariah. By the Rev. Professor MARCUS DODS, M.A., D.D. Third Thousand. Elegantly bound in cloth, price 1s. 6d.

BY THE SAME AUTHOR.

1. **THE PARABLES OF OUR LORD (MATTHEW).** Ninth Thousand. Crown 8vo, cloth, 3s. 6d.

2. **THE PARABLES OF OUR LORD (LUKE).** Seventh Thousand. Crown 8vo, cloth, 3s. 6d.

3. **ISRAEL'S IRON AGE.** Sketches from the Period of the Judges. Seventh Edition. Crown 8vo, cloth, 3s. 6d.

4. **ERASMUS AND OTHER ESSAYS.** Second Edition. Crown 8vo, cloth, 5s.

5. **THE PRAYER THAT TEACHES TO PRAY.** Eighth Edition. Crown 8vo, 2s. 6d.

6. **MOHAMMED, BUDDHA, AND CHRIST:** Four Lectures on Natural and Revealed Religion. Eighth Edition. Crown 8vo, cloth, 3s. 6d.

THE GOD-MAN. By THOMAS CHARLES EDWARDS, D.D., of Lincoln College, Oxford, Principal of Theological College, Bala. Being the "Davies" Lecture for 1895. Crown 8vo, cloth, 3s. 6d.

BY THE SAME AUTHOR.

1. **A COMMENTARY ON THE FIRST EPISTLE TO THE CORINTHIANS.** Second Edition, 8vo, cloth, 14s.

2. **THE EPISTLE TO THE HEBREWS.** Crown 8vo, 7s. 6d.

IS GOD KNOWABLE? By the Rev. Professor J. IVERACH, D.D. Fourth Thousand. Crown 8vo, cloth, 3s. 6d.

THE MIRACLES OF OUR LORD. By the Rev. Professor LAIDLAW, D.D. Third Edition. Crown 8vo, cloth, 7s. 6d.

CHRISTIAN MINISTRY: Its Origin, Constitution, Nature, Work. By the Very Rev. WILLIAM LEFROY, D.D., Dean of Norwich. 8vo, cloth, 14s.

LITTLE BOOKS ON RELIGION. Edited by the Rev. W. ROBERTSON NICOLL, LL.D. Elegantly bound in cloth, 1s. 6d. each.

1. Christ and the Future Life. By the Rev. R. W. DALE, LL.D.

2. The Seven Words from the Cross. By the Rev. W. ROBERTSON NICOLL, LL.D.

3. The Visions of a Prophet: Studies in Zechariah. By the Rev. Professor MARCUS DODS, D.D.

4. The Four Temperaments. By the Rev. ALEXANDER WHYTE, D.D.

5. The Upper Room. By the Rev. JOHN WATSON, M.A., Author of " Beside the Bonnie Brier Bush."

THE NEWBERRY BIBLE. By THOMAS NEWBERRY. Comprising the English-Hebrew Bible and the English-Greek Testament, designed to give, as far as practicable, the Accuracy, Precision, and Certainty of the Original Hebrew and Greek Scriptures on the Page of the Authorised Version. Large Type Handy Reference Edition, Gilt Edges, 21s., 25s., 35s., 60s. ; Bible Marking Edition, 15s., 25s., 30s. ; New Pocket Edition, 6s., 9s., 12s. 6d., 7s. 6d., 15s., 20s.

UNION WITH GOD. A Series of Addresses. By Professor J. RENDEL HARRIS, M.A., Fellow of Clare College, Cambridge. Second Edition. Crown 8vo, cloth, 4s. 6d.

SOCIAL CHRISTIANITY. West Central Mission Sermons. Delivered in St. James's Hall, London. By HUGH PRICE HUGHES, M.A. Eighth Thousand. Crown 8vo, cloth, 3s. 6d.

ARE MIRACLES CREDIBLE? By the Rev. J. J. LIAS, M.A. Second Edition. Crown 8vo, cloth, 3s. 6d.

TALES OF THE WARRIOR KING. Life and Times of David, King of Israel. By the Rev. J. R. MACDUFF, D.D. With Eight Illustrations. Second Thousand. Large crown 8vo, cloth, gilt top, 6s.

BY THE SAME AUTHOR.

1. **THOUGHTS FOR THE QUIET HOUR.** Second Edition. Crown 8vo, cloth, 3s. 6d.

2. **THE PILLAR IN THE NIGHT.** Crown 8vo, cloth, 3s. 6d.

THE MYSTERY OF GRACE, and other Sermons. By the Rev. HUGH MACMILLAN, D.D. Second Edition. Crown 8vo, cloth, 6s.

EARTH'S EARLIEST AGES, and their connection with Modern Spiritualism and Theosophy. By G. H. PEMBER, M.A. Eighth Edition. Crown 8vo, cloth, 7s. 6d.

BY THE SAME AUTHOR.

1. **THE GREAT PROPHECIES OF THE CEN-TURIES CONCERNING ISRAEL AND THE GENTILES.** With Two Coloured Diagrams. Fourth Edition. Crown 8vo, cloth, 7s. 6d.

2. **THE ANTI - CHRIST, BABYLON, AND THE COMING OF THE KINGDOM.** Second Edition. Crown 8vo, cloth, 3s. 6d.

TOKIWA, and other Poems. By Mrs. ASHLEY CARUS-WILSON, *née* MARY L. G. PETRIE, B.A., Lond. Crown 8vo, cloth, 6s.

CLEWS TO HOLY WRIT; or, the Chronological Scripture Cycle. By the same Author. Ninth Thousand. Crown 8vo, cloth, 3s. 6d.

THE KEY WORDS OF THE BIBLE. By A. T. PIERSON, D.D. Fourth Edition. Crown 8vo, cloth, 2s. 6d.

BY THE SAME AUTHOR.

THE DIVINE ENTERPRISE OF MISSIONS. Second Edition. Crown 8vo, cloth, 4s. 6d.

LESSONS IN THE SCHOOL OF PRAYER AS TAUGHT BY THE LORD JESUS CHRIST HIMSELF. Crown 8vo, 3s. 6d.

CLASSIFIED GEMS OF THOUGHT. From the Great Writers of all Ages. In Convenient Form for Use as a Dictionary of Ready Reference on Religious Subjects. By the Rev. F. B. PROCTOR, M.A., Vicar of Tadcaster. Cheap Edition. Royal 8vo, cloth, 7s. 6d.

THE APOSTLE PAUL : a Sketch of the Development of his Doctrine. By M. A. SABATIER. Crown 8vo, cloth, 7s. 6d.

THE DIVINE UNITY OF SCRIPTURE. By Dr. ADOLPH SAPHIR. Crown 8vo, cloth, 3s. 6d.

THE IMPERFECT ANGEL, and other Sermons. By Rev. T. G. SELBY. Fifth Edition. Crown 8vo, cloth, 3s. 6d.

BY THE SAME AUTHOR.

THE LESSON OF A DILEMMA, and other Sermons. Third Thousand. Crown 8vo, 6s.

THE SAINT AND HIS SAVIOUR. The Progress of the Soul in the Knowledge of Jesus. By C. H. SPURGEON. With Steel Portrait. A New Edition. Crown 8vo, cloth, 3s. 6d.

COMPLETE IN CHRIST AND LOVE'S LOGIC. Extracted from "The Saint and his Saviour." Fourth Thousand. 32mo, 1s.

THE TRIAL AND DEATH OF JESUS CHRIST. A Devotional History of our Lord's Passion. By JAMES STALKER, M.A., D.D. Seventh Thousand. Crown 8vo, cloth, 5s.

BY THE SAME AUTHOR.

IMAGO CHRISTI : The Example of Jesus Christ. Twenty-seventh Thousand. Crown 8vo, cloth, 5s. Presentation Edition, handsomely bound in padded leather, net, 7s. 6d.

THE PREACHER AND HIS MODELS. Yale Lectures on Preaching, 1891. Seventh Thousand. Crown 8vo, cloth, 5s.

THE FOUR MEN. Eighth Thousand. Crown 8vo, cloth, 2s. 6d.

GARDEN GRAITH; or, Talks among my flowers. By SARAH F. SMILEY. Eighth Edition. Crown 8vo, cloth, 3s. 6d.

BY THE SAME AUTHOR.

WHO IS HE? or, the Anxious Inquiry Answered. Third Thousand. Choicely bound in cloth with gilt edges, 9d.

THE NEW ERA. By the Rev. JOSIAH STRONG, D.D. Crown 8vo, cloth, 5s.

THE LIMITATIONS OF LIFE, and other Sermons. By Rev. W. M. TAYLOR, D.D., Author of "The Ministry of the Word," etc. With Portrait of the Author. Crown 8vo, cloth, 7s. 6d.

THE PARABLES OF OUR SAVIOUR EXPOUNDED AND ILLUSTRATED. Fourth Edition. Crown 8vo, cloth, 7s. 6d.

THE MIRACLES OF OUR SAVIOUR EXPOUNDED AND ILLUSTRATED. Third Edition. Crown 8vo, cloth, 7s. 6d.

SUNLIGHT AND SHADOW; or, Gleanings from my Life Work. By J. B. GOUGH. Comprising—Personal Experiences, Anecdotes, Incidents, and Reminiscences; gathered from Thirty-seven Years' Experience on the Platform and among the People at Home and Abroad. Twelfth Edition. Crown 8vo, cloth, 3s. 6d.

"Mr. Gough has gathered together a large number of most interesting and stirring incidents, experiences, and reminiscences from his thirty-seven years' work at home and abroad."—*Record.*

BY THE SAME AUTHOR.

PLATFORM ECHOES. Leaves from my Note Book of Forty Years Illustrated by Anecdotes, Incidents, Personal Experiences, Facts, and Stories, drawn from the Humour and Pathos of Life. Seventeenth Thousand. Demy 8vo, 3s. 6d.

"These chapters abound in apt illustrations and in anecdotes both humorous and pathetic."—*Daily News.*

"Teeming with thrilling incidents, experiences, and facts."—*Methodist Times.*

1. **A GOOD START.** Sixth Thousand. Crown 8vo, cloth, 3s. 6d.

" Books which are confessedly and designedly ' improving ' without being dull, are not very common. Such books Dr. Davidson has already proved his capacity to write, and these ' homely talks ' with young men are not inferior to his previous efforts. Earnest and plain, and strictly adapted to the understanding of the ordinary man, they are never careless or meaningless."—*Academy.*

2. **SURE TO SUCCEED.** Eighth Thousand. Crown 8vo, cloth, 3s. 6d.

" An excellent present for a youth just going into business or coming up to London. It consists of twenty pithy and practical lectures to young men."—*Record.*

3. **FOREWARNED — FOREARMED.** Eighth Thousand. Crown 8vo, cloth, 3s. 6d.

" Weighty counsels. Dr. Davidson is remarkably at home in talks with young men. His words glow with an intense earnestness which demands and obtains attention from his readers."—*Sword and Trowel.*

4. **THE CITY YOUTH.** Seventh Thousand. Crown 8vo, cloth, 3s. 6d.

" A volume well worthy to rank with his previous works on kindred subjects. Dr. Davidson's matter and manner are alike excellent. About the former there is no suspicion of what hasty people might call cant, while the latter is serious but not heavy. Dr. Davidson aims at no impossible standard ; he is as sympathetic as he is acute, as kind as he is firm."—*Globe.*

5. **TALKS WITH YOUNG MEN.** Fifteenth Thousand. Crown 8vo, cloth, 3s. 6d.

" For sterling common-sense combined with true spiritual feeling, they have not been surpassed for many a day. The addresses bristle with telling metaphors and illustrations, and the book can be read from cover to cover with profitable interest."—*Literary World.*

THE CATACOMBS OF ROME, and their Testimony Relative to Primitive Christianity. By the Rev. W. H. WITHROW, M.A. Sixth Edition. 134 Illustrations. Crown 8vo, cloth, 6s.

" Mr. Withrow's account of the catacombs of Rome is an exceedingly painstaking and thorough-going work, and whether or not the writer may be correct in all his inferences, they have evidently been founded upon diligent information. He could not have very much that was absolutely new to tell on the subject ; but as a convenient account of the most remarkable and interesting monuments of primitive Christianity, of those excavations which furnished the persecuted Church with refuges during life and in death, which formed her places of worship in times of peril, and received the remains of martyrs, the present volume is perhaps inferior to none of its predecessors."—*Saturday Review.*

THE HISTORY OF THE CHRISTIAN CHURCH.
By GEORGE P. FISHER, D.D., LL.D. With Seven Coloured
Maps. New Edition. Fifteenth Thousand. 8vo, 712 pp.,
12s.

"We are sincerely thankful to Dr. Fisher for having collected with so
much labour, and sifted with so much clearness, a perfectly overwhelming
mass of facts, and we are certain that his book will be frequently referred
to by students of Church History, as a trustworthy compendium and
outline of the main events in the history of the Church."—*Guardian.*

BY THE SAME AUTHOR.

THE GROUNDS OF THEISTIC AND CHRISTIAN
BELIEF. 8vo, cloth, 10s. 6d.

"The book, which we have frequently recommended, is an able defence
of both natural and supernatural religion, and forms practically a modern
appendix to Butler's 'Analogy.' The work is not merely an 'apology';
it pursues the attack with considerable vigour, and hence it provides an
ample armoury whence to draw weapons for use against the arguments of
unbelieving scientists and philosophers."—*Church Times.*

IRELAND AND THE ANGLO-NORMAN CHURCH:
A History of Ireland and Irish Christianity from the Anglo-
Norman Conquest to the Dawn of the Reformation. By Rev.
Preb. G. T. STOKES, D.D., Professor of Ecclesiastical History
in the University of Dublin. Crown 8vo, cloth, 6s.

"Dr. Stokes's brilliant lectures."—*Athenæum.*

"His narrative, enlivened by anecdotes, and by information of a most
recondite sort, is throughout brimful of interest."—*Academy.*

BY THE SAME AUTHOR.

IRELAND AND THE CELTIC CHURCH : A History of
Ireland from St. Patrick to the English Conquest in 1172.
Third Edition. Crown 8vo, cloth, 6s.

"Any one who can make the dry bones of ancient Irish history live
again may feel sure of finding an audience sympathetic, intelligent, and
ever-growing. Dr. Stokes has this faculty in a high degree."—*Westminster
Review.*

1. **CHRISTIANITY IN THE HOME.** Second Thousand. Handsomely bound, half parchment cloth, 3*s.* 6*d.*

   "Bright and helpful."—*London Quarterly Review.*

   "The homely simplicity of Dr. Cuyler's style, his shrewdness, and the inexhaustible abundance of fresh and familiar illustrations are strongly marked."—*Literary World.*

   "Short, terse, practical papers."—*Primitive Methodist Magazine.*

   "The contents of this book are as beautiful and practical as the binding is tasteful. Herein is sound, common-sense counsel on religious matters, always thorough and always wise, and given sometimes in the form of a brief and suggestive exposition of a Scriptural phrase."—*Methodist Recorder.*

2. **NEWLY ENLISTED.** A Series of Talks with Young Converts. Tenth Thousand. Square 16mo, 160 pp., cloth, 1*s.* 6*d.*

   "Stirring and stimulative ; . . . wise and weighty."—*Word and Work.*

   "It is brimful of good advice and sanctified common-sense. There is a manly robustness about it which will make it acceptable to all readers."—*Rock.*

3. **WAYSIDE SPRINGS FROM THE FOUNTAIN OF LIFE.** Sixth Thousand. Square 16mo, cloth, 1*s.* 6*d.*

4. **GOD'S LIGHT ON DARK CLOUDS.** Twenty-second Thousand. Cloth, 1*s.* 6*d.*

   "A literary gem of rare utility and beauty. It only requires to be known to be approved of, and then sown broadcast."—*Clergyman's Magazine.*

5. **HEART LIFE.** Nineteenth Thousand. Fcap. 8vo, cloth, 1*s.* 6*d.*

   "A most delightful and experimental little volume."—*Christian.*

6. **HEART CULTURE.** Twelfth Thousand. Fcap. 8vo, cloth, 1*s.* 6*d.*

   "The short and pithy papers are exceedingly good, and Dr. Cuyler's treatment of them is in every way admirable."—*Rock.*

7. **HEART THOUGHTS.** Fourteenth Thousand. Crown 8vo, 1*s.* 6*d.*

   "Short, pithy, and persuasive."—*Sunday School Chronicle.*

8. **THOUGHTS FOR HEART AND LIFE.** Containing "Heart Life," "Heart Culture," and "Heart Thoughts." Eighth Edition. Crown 8vo, 3*s.* 6*d.*

THE EPISTLE TO THE ROMANS. By HANDLEY
C. G. MOULE, M.A., B.D., Principal of Ridley Hall, Cambridge. Third Edition. Crown 8vo, cloth, 7s. 6d.

"Mr. Moule has made a very careful study of Paul's great doctrinal epistle, and has entered thoroughly into its spirit."—*Scotsman.*

"We do not hesitate to place it in the very front of the little group of volumes which are the best examples of this carefully edited work. It would be pleasant to linger upon this commentary, upon the clearness with which the great evangelical doctrines of the Epistle are explained and enforced, upon the earnestness of its personal appeal, and the charm which often marks its language; but the judicious student of the New Testament will obtain the book for himself."—*Record.*

BY THE SAME AUTHOR.

1. **VENI CREATOR.** Thoughts on the Person and Work of the Holy Spirit of Promise. Sixth Thousand. Cloth, 5s.

2. **TO MY YOUNGER BRETHREN.** Chapters on Pastoral Life and Work. Second Edition. Crown 8vo, cloth, 5s.

3. **LIFE IN CHRIST AND FOR CHRIST.** Fourteenth Thousand. 32mo, cloth, red edges, 1s.

A NEW CHRISTOLOGY.

THE VISIBLE GOD AND HIS RELATION TO MAN IN CREATION AND REDEMPTION. By the Rev. W. MARSHALL. Crown 8vo, cloth, 6s.

BY THE SAME AUTHOR.

NATURE AS A BOOK OF SYMBOLS. Second Edition. Crown 8vo, cloth, 3s. 6d.

A PRACTICAL COMMENTARY ON THE GOSPEL ACCORDING TO ST. MATTHEW. By JAMES MORISON, D.D. Ninth Edition. 8vo, cloth, 14s.

BY THE SAME AUTHOR.

1. **SHEAVES OF MINISTRY:** Sermons and Expositions. 8vo, cloth, 10s. 6d.

2. **A PRACTICAL COMMENTARY ON THE GOSPEL ACCORDING TO ST. MARK.** Seventh Edition. In One Volume, 8vo, cloth, 12s.

3. **ST. PAUL'S TEACHING ON SANCTIFICATION.** A Practical Exposition of Romans vi. 8vo, cloth, 4s. 6d.

4. **EXPOSITION OF THE NINTH CHAPTER OF THE EPISTLE TO THE ROMANS.** Demy 8vo, cloth, 7s. 6d.

TURNING POINTS IN SUCCESSFUL CAREERS.

By WILLIAM M. THAYER, Author of "From Log Cabin to White House." Second Thousand. Crown 8vo, cloth, 3s. 6d.

"For the rest we have little to say that is not in praise of a volume which is modelled somewhat on the lines of Dr. Smiles' 'Self-Help.' There is so much pernicious literature in circulation that it is always a pleasure to meet with books which confront the young ideas with golden deeds. Happily, Mr. Thayer writes with vivacity, and knows how to select the picturesque and salient incidents, and in the majority of instances he has likewise the good sense to let it speak for itself."—*Speaker.*

BY THE SAME AUTHOR.

THE WAY TO SUCCEED; or, the Secret of Success in Life. Fifth Thousand. Crown 8vo, cloth, 3s. 6d.

TACT, PUSH, AND PRINCIPLE. Seventh Edition, completing 20,000. Crown 8vo, cloth, 3s. 6d.

The Theological Educator.

Edited by the Rev. W. ROBERTSON NICOLL, M.A., LL.D., Editor of the *Expositor*. Fcap. 8vo, cloth, price 2s. 6d. each.

A MANUAL OF CHRISTIAN EVIDENCES. By the Rev. Prebendary C. A. ROW, M.A. Thirteenth Thousand.

"A veritable *multum in parvo*, clear, cogent, and concise, without being sketchy or superficial."—*Saturday Review.*

AN INTRODUCTION TO THE TEXTUAL CRITICISM OF THE NEW TESTAMENT. By the Rev. Professor B. B. WARFIELD, D.D. Fifth Thousand.

"A masterly survey of the whole subject."—*Expositor.*

A HEBREW GRAMMAR. By the Rev. W. H. LOWE, M.A. Second Thousand.

"A brief and masterly sketch of the Hebrew grammar."—*Literary Churchman.*

A MANUAL OF CHURCH HISTORY. By the Rev. A. C. JENNINGS, M.A. In Two Volumes.

Vol. I.—From the First to the Tenth Century. Third Thousand.

Vol. II.—From the Eleventh to the Nineteenth Century. Third Thousand.

AN EXPOSITION OF THE APOSTLES' CREED.
By the Rev. J. E. YONGE, M.A. Second Thousand.

"An able treatise."—*Church Times.*

THE PRAYER BOOK. By the Rev. CHARLES HOLE, B.A.,
Professor at King's College, London. Third Thousand.

"It is not overloaded with detail, and yet supplies in an admirably compact shape all essential information."—*British Weekly.*

AN INTRODUCTION TO THE NEW TESTAMENT.
By the Rev. Professor MARCUS DODS, D.D. Thirteenth Thousand.

"Dr. Marcus Dods has packed away an immense amount of information in a very small space."—*Methodist Recorder.*

THE WRITERS OF THE NEW TESTAMENT: Their
Style and Characteristics. By the Rev. W. H. SIMCOX, M.A. Second Thousand.

"One of the choicest productions of English scholarship in recent years." —*Manchester Examiner.*

THE LANGUAGE OF THE NEW TESTAMENT. By
the Same Author. Third Thousand.

"A book which deserves and will well repay the attention of all students of the New Testament."—*Athenæum.*

AN INTRODUCTION TO THE OLD TESTAMENT.
By the Rev. C. H. H. WRIGHT, D.D. Sixth Thousand.

"The work is of brief compass, and covers a vast field of study, but the necessary compression has been done with the skill of one experienced in the needs of students."—*Scotsman.*

OUTLINES OF CHRISTIAN DOCTRINE. By the
Rev. H. C. G. MOULE, M.A., D.D., Principal of Ridley Hall, Cambridge. Thirteenth Thousand.

"A compendium of Christian doctrine of the very highest excellence.'— *Sword and Trowel.*

THE THEOLOGY OF THE NEW TESTAMENT.
By the Rev. Professor WALTER F. ADENEY, M.A. Third Thousand.

"The salient points of the subject are for the most part well seized, and simply and effectively presented."—*Methodist Recorder.*

EVOLUTION AND CHRISTIANITY. By JAMES IVERACH,
D.D., Author of "Is God Knowable?' etc. Fourth Thousand.

"A thoughtfully acute and well-reasoned little book."—*Glasgow Herald.*

THE THEOLOGY OF THE OLD TESTAMENT. By
the Rev. Professor W. H. BENNETT, M.A.

The Household Library of Exposition.

THE PARABLES OF OUR LORD. FIRST SERIES. As Recorded by St. Matthew. By MARCUS DODS, D.D. Ninth Thousand. Crown 8vo, cloth, 3s. 6d.

"There is certainly no better volume on the subject in our language."—*Glasgow Mail.*

BY THE SAME AUTHOR.

THE PARABLES OF OUR LORD. SECOND SERIES. The Parables Recorded by St. Luke. Seventh Thousand. Crown 8vo, cloth, 3s. 6d.

"An original exposition, marked by strong common sense, and practical exhortation."—*Literary Churchman.*

ISAAC, JACOB, AND JOSEPH. Sixth Thousand, 3s. 6d.

"The present volume is worthy of the writer's reputation. He deals with the problems of human life and character which these biographies suggest in a candid and manly fashion."—*Spectator.*

THE LIFE OF DAVID, as Reflected in his Psalms. By ALEXANDER MACLAREN, D.D., of Manchester. Eighth Edition. 3s. 6d.

"Real gems of exposition."—*Expositor.*
"Just the book we should give to awaken a living and historical interest in the Psalms."—*Guardian.*

THE SPEECHES OF THE HOLY APOSTLES. By DONALD FRASER, D.D. Second Thousand. 3s. 6d.

"Exceedingly well done."—*Scottish Review.*

THE LORD'S PRAYER. By CHARLES STANFORD, D.D. Fourth Thousand. 3s. 6d.

"For spiritual grasp and insight, for wealth of glowing imagery, and for rare felicity of style, it will hold a first place in this valuable series of expository monographs."—*Christian.*

THE LAMB OF GOD. Expositions in the Writings of St. John. By W. ROBERTSON NICOLL, M.A., LL.D. Second Edition. 3s. 6d.

"Replete with the richest thought and finest feeling."—*Aberdeen Free Press.*

THE GALILEAN GOSPEL. By Professor A. B. BRUCE, D.D. Fourth Edition. 3s. 6d.

"We heartily commend this little volume."—*Spectator.*

THE LAW OF THE TEN WORDS. By J. OSWALD DYKES, D.D., Author of "The Beatitudes," "From Jerusalem to Antioch," etc. Fourth Thousand. Crown 8vo, 3s. 6d.

"Dr. Dykes' spiritual insight, and his thorough sympathy with contemporary life, enable him at once to catch the true application of the Ten Commandments to present-day needs; his style is a singular combination of strength and beauty."—*Literary World.*

THE PARABOLIC TEACHING OF CHRIST: A Systematic and Critical Study of the Parables of our Lord. By ALEXANDER BALMAIN BRUCE, D.D., Professor of Apologetics, Free Church College, Glasgow. Sixth Edition. 8vo, cloth, 12s.

BY THE SAME AUTHOR.

1. **THE MIRACULOUS ELEMENT IN THE GOSPELS.** Third Edition. 8vo, cloth, 12s.

2. **THE LIFE OF WILLIAM DENNY.** With Portrait. Second Edition. 8vo, cloth, 12s.

3. **THE CHIEF END OF REVELATION.** Fifth Edition. Crown 8vo, cloth, 6s.

4. **THE GALILEAN GOSPEL.** Fourth Edition. Crown 8vo, cloth, 3s. 6d.

———————

THE NEW LIFE OF CHRIST: A Study in Personal Religion. By the Rev. Professor J. AGAR BEET, D.D. Second Edition. Crown 8vo, cloth, 6s. 6d.

BY THE SAME AUTHOR.

THROUGH CHRIST TO GOD. A Study in Scientific Theology. Second Edition. Crown 8vo, 6s. 6d.

DR. BEET'S COMMENTARIES ON ST. PAUL'S EPISTLES.

1. Romans. Eighth Edition. 7s. 6d.
2. Corinthians. Sixth Edition. 10s. 6d.
3. Galatians. Fourth Edition. 5s.
4. Ephesians, Philippians, and Colossians. Third Thousand. 7s. 6d.

DR. MACLAREN'S BIBLE TEXT BOOKS.

BIBLE CLASS EXPOSITIONS. Crown 8vo, cloth, 3s. 6d. each volume.

1. The Gospel of St. Matthew. 2 Volumes.
2. The Gospel of St. Mark.
3. The Gospel of St. Luke.
4. The Gospel of St. John.
5. The Acts of the Apostles.

28

THE CRITICAL AND EXPOSITORY BIBLE CYCLO-
PÆDIA. By the Rev. A. R. FAUSSET, D.D., Canon of York, Joint Author of "The Critical and Experimental Commentary." Illustrated by 600 Woodcuts. Cheap Edition, Unabridged. Eleventh Thousand. Cloth, red edges, 7s. 6d.

"This is a work of prodigious research, labour, and minute painstaking. The book is a rich and full storehouse of Scripture knowledge."—*Guardian.*

STUDIES ON THE EPISTLES. By F. GODET, D.D.,
Professor of Theology, Neuchatel. Translated by Mrs. ANNIE HARWOOD HOLMDEN. Crown 8vo, cloth, 7s. 6d.

"There is no other book in which the results of modern criticism are so conveniently accessible and so admirably sifted."—*Expositor.*

"It maintains the level of careful scholarship, critical sagacity, and practical piety on which all the writer's work stands. The mature and careful expression of his views on matters of such central importance, by one of the most highly and justly respected of living orthodox exegetes, will have great value for the theological student."—*Glasgow Herald.*

BY THE SAME AUTHOR.

STUDIES ON THE NEW TESTAMENT. Edited by
the Hon. and Rev. W. H. LYTTELTON, M.A., Canon of Gloucester. Tenth Edition. Crown 8vo, cloth, 7s. 6d.

"When he ascends into the higher regions of theology, as in the studies on the person and work of Jesus Christ, his insight is always profound, and his teaching weighty and suggestive."—*Spectator.*

STUDIES ON THE OLD TESTAMENT. Edited by
the Hon. and Rev. W. H. LYTTELTON, M.A. Sixth Edition. Crown 8vo, cloth, 7s. 6d.

"Unquestionably M. Godet is one of the first, if not the very first of contemporary commentators. We have no hesitation in advising all students of the Scripture to procure and to read with careful attention these luminous essays."—*Literary Churchman.*

THE APPROACHING END OF THE AGE, Viewed
in the Light of History, Prophecy, and Science. By the Rev. H. GRATTAN GUINNESS. Twelfth Edition. With Diagrams. Crown 8vo, cloth, 7s. 6d.

LIGHT FOR THE LAST DAYS. A Study, Historical
and Prophetical. By Mr. and Mrs. H. GRATTAN GUINNESS. Third Edition. With Diagrams. Crown 8vo, cloth, 7s. 6d.

FIRST THINGS FIRST. Addresses to Young Men. By the Rev. GEORGE JACKSON, B.A. Sixth Thousand. Crown 8vo, cloth, 3s. 6d.

"These addresses are short, full of force, and effectual in the lessons they convey. . . . He is no waster of words: he points a truth in a few brief, incisive phrases, and preaches a sermon in a paragraph. Above all, they are manly in tone, and have the sterling ring of sincerity."—*Dundee Advertiser.*

DAVID LIVINGSTONE. The Story of his Life and Labours ; or, The Weaver Boy who became a Missionary. By H. G. ADAMS. With Portrait and numerous Illustrations. Seventy-fourth Thousand. 8vo, cloth, 5s.

A.L.O.E.—A LADY OF ENGLAND ; or, Life and Letters of Charlotte Maria Tucker. By AGNES GIBERNE. With Illustrations. Third Thousand. Crown 8vo, gilt top, 7s. 6d.

CHRONICLES OF UGANDA. By the Rev. R. P. ASHE, M.A., Author of "Two Kings of Uganda." With Portrait and Twenty-six Illustrations. Second Thousand. 8vo, cloth, 7s. 6d.

REMINISCENCES OF ANDREW A. BONAR, D.D. Edited by his Daughter, MARJORY BONAR. With Photogravure Portrait, Fac-simile, and Illustration. Third Thousand. Crown 8vo, cloth, 6s.

ANDREW A. BONAR, D.D. DIARY & LETTERS. Transcribed and Edited by his Daughter, MARJORY BONAR. With Portrait. Third Edition. Seventh Thousand. 6s.

LIFE AND LETTERS OF JOHN CAIRNS, D.D., LL.D., Principal of the U. P. College, Edinburgh. By ALEXANDER R. MACEWEN, D.D. With Portrait. Second Edition. 8vo, cloth, 14s.

CHRIST, THE MORNING STAR, AND OTHER SERMONS. By JOHN CAIRNS, D.D., LL.D., Principal of the U. P. College, Edinburgh. Crown 8vo, cloth, 6s.

GREAT MISSIONARIES. By the Rev. C. C. CREEGAN, D.D. Crown 8vo, cloth, 3s. 6d.

HOLY MEN OF GOD. From St. Augustine to Yesterday. By the Rev. J. ELDER CUMMING, D.D. Crown 8vo, cloth, 5s.

EDWARD HOARE, M.A. A Record of His Life based upon a Brief Autobiography. By the Rev. J. H. TOWNSEND, D.D., Vicar of Broadwater Down, Tunbridge Wells. Second Edition. Crown 8vo, cloth, 5s.

SPIRAL STAIRS ; or, The Heavenward Course of the Church Seasons. Devotional Studies on the Christian Life. By the same Author. Crown 8vo, 3s. 6d.

THE BOOK OF KOHELETH, commonly called **ECCLE-SIASTES,** considered in Relation to Modern Criticism, and to the Doctrines of Modern Pessimism, with a Critical and Grammatical Commentary and a Revised Translation. By the Rev. C. H. H. WRIGHT, D.D., Ph.D. 8vo, cloth, 12s.

EASTERN CUSTOMS IN BIBLE LANDS. By H. B. TRISTRAM, LL.D., D.D., F.R.S., Canon of Durham, Author of "The Great Sahara," etc. Second Edition. Crown 8vo, cloth, 5s.

STUDIES IN ORIENTAL SOCIAL LIFE, and Gleams from the East on the Sacred Page. By the Rev. H. CLAY TRUMBULL, D.D., Author of "Kadesh-Barnea," "Teaching and Teachers," etc. With Thirty Illustrations from Photographs. Large crown 8vo, cloth, 6s.

BY THE SAME AUTHOR.

1. **TEACHING AND TEACHERS ;** or, The Sunday-School Teacher's Teaching Work, and the other Work of the Sunday-School Teacher. Fourth Edition. Crown 8vo, cloth, 5s.

2. **HINTS ON CHILD TRAINING.** Crown 8vo, cloth, 3s. 6d.

The Expositor's Bible.

EDITED BY THE

Rev. W. ROBERTSON NICOLL, M.A., LL.D.

Separate Volumes, 7/6. Price to subscribers for any single series, 24/- net, except the Eighth (7 volumes), the subscription price of which is 28/- net.

FIRST SERIES.

Colossians and Philemon. By ALEXANDER MACLAREN, D.D.

The Gospel according to St. Mark.
By the Very Rev. G. A. CHADWICK, D.D., Dean of Armagh.

The Book of Genesis. By the Rev. Professor MARCUS DODS, D.D.

The First Book of Samuel. By Professor W. G. BLAIKIE, D.D., LL.D.

The Second Book of Samuel. By the same Author.

The Epistle to the Hebrews. By Principal T. C. EDWARDS, D.D.

SECOND SERIES.

The Epistle to the Galatians. By Professor G. G. FINDLAY, B.A.

The Pastoral Epistles. By the Rev. A. PLUMMER, D.D.

The Book of Isaiah I.—XXXIX. Vol. I.
By Professor GEORGE ADAM SMITH, D.D.

The Book of Revelation. By Professor W. MILLIGAN, D.D.

The First Epistle to the Corinthians.
By Professor MARCUS DODS, D.D.

The Epistles of St. John.
By the Right Rev. W. ALEXANDER, D.D., D.C.L., Lord Bishop of Derry and Raphoe.

THIRD SERIES.

Judges and Ruth. By the Rev. R. A. WATSON, D.D.

The Prophecies of Jeremiah. By the Rev. C. J. BALL, M.A.

The Book of Isaiah. Chaps. XL. to LXVI. Vol. II.
By Professor GEORGE ADAM SMITH, D.D.

The Gospel of St. Matthew. By J. MONRO GIBSON, D.D.

The Book of Exodus.
By the Very Rev. G. A. CHADWICK, D.D., Dean of Armagh.

The Gospel of St. Luke. By the Rev. H. BURTON, M.A.

FOURTH SERIES.

Ecclesiastes, or the Preacher. By SAMUEL COX, D.D.

The Epistles of St. James and St. Jude.
By the Rev. ALFRED PLUMMER, D.D.

The Book of Leviticus. By the Rev. S. H. KELLOGG, D.D.

The Book of Proverbs. By the Rev. R. F. HORTON, D.D.

The Acts of the Apostles. Vol. I.
By the Rev. Professor G. T. STOKES, D.D.

The Gospel of St. John. Vol. I.
By the Rev. Professor MARCUS DODS, D.D.

The Expositor's Bible—*continued.*

Separate Volumes, 7/6. Price to subscribers for any single series, 24/- net, except the Eighth (7 volumes), the subscription price of which is 28/- net.

FIFTH SERIES.

The Epistles to the Thessalonians.
By the Rev. JAMES DENNEY, D.D.

The Gospel of St. John. Vol. II.
By the Rev. Professor MARCUS DODS, D.D.

The Book of Psalms. Vol. I. By the Rev. ALEXANDER MACLAREN, D.D.

The Acts of the Apostles. Vol. II.
By the Rev. Professor G. T. STOKES, D.D.

The Book of Job. By the Rev. R. A. WATSON, D.D.

The Epistle to the Ephesians.
By the Rev. Professor G. G. FINDLAY, B.A.

SIXTH SERIES.

The Epistle to the Philippians. By the Rev. Principal RAINY, D.D.

The First Book of Kings.
By the Very Rev. F. W. FARRAR, F.R.S., Dean of Canterbury.

The Book of Joshua.
By the Rev. Professor W. G. BLAIKIE, D.D., LL.D.

Ezra, Nehemiah, and Esther. By the Rev. Prof. W. F. ADENEY, M.A.

The Book of Psalms. Vol. II. By the Rev. ALEXANDER MACLAREN, D.D.

The Epistles of St. Peter. By the Rev. Prof. J. RAWSON LUMBY, D.D.

SEVENTH SERIES.

The Epistle to the Romans. By HANDLEY C. G. MOULE, M.A., D.D.

The Second Book of Kings.
By the Very Rev. F. W. FARRAR, F.R.S., Dean of Canterbury.

The Second Epistle to the Corinthians.
By the Rev. JAMES DENNEY, D.D.

The Books of Chronicles. By the Rev. Prof. W. H. BENNETT, M.A.

The Book of Numbers. By the Rev. R. A. WATSON, D.D.

The Book of Psalms. Vol. III. By ALEX. MACLAREN, D.D.

EIGHTH AND FINAL SERIES.

The Book of Daniel.
By the Very Rev. F. W. FARRAR, F.R.S., Dean of Canterbury.

The Book of Jeremiah. Chaps. xxi.-lii.
By the Rev. W. H. BENNETT, M.A.

The Book of Deuteronomy.
By the Rev. Professor ANDREW HARPER, B.D.

The Song of Solomon and the Lamentations of Jeremiah.
By the Rev. W. F. ADENEY, M.A.

The Book of Ezekiel. By the Rev. JOHN SKINNER, M.A.

The Minor Prophets.
By the Rev. Professor GEORGE ADAM SMITH, D.D. In two vols.

The Devotional Library.

Handsomely printed and bound, price 3s. 6d. each, cloth.

1. THE KEY OF THE GRAVE. A Book for the Bereaved. By W. ROBERTSON NICOLL, M.A., LL.D. Third Edition.

"Dr. Robertson Nicoll has produced a unique, exquisite, and most edifying book. We are much impressed by the delicate and profound spiritual insight manifested on every page of this beautiful little volume. Many a familiar passage in the Bible shines with a new, unexpected, and immortal light. It is difficult to know what to quote from a volume so full of delightful and memorable passages. It is pre-eminently a book to put into the hands of the refined, sensitive, scholarly, and devout, when they feel the awful pressure of the greatest bereavement."—*Methodist Times.*

2. MEMORANDA SACRA. Py Professor J. RENDEL HARRIS, M.A., Fellow of Clare College, Cambridge. Second Edition.

"Two gifts, both of the very highest, are marvellously united in Professor Rendel Harris, and here we have the ripe fruits of one, in most delicious flavour and most wholesome nourishment. It is not possible to review such a book as this. Words about it do not tell us what it is. Nor will a selection of words from it half convey its incommunicable fragrance."—*Expository Times.*

THE GENERAL GORDON EDITION.

3. CHRIST MYSTICAL. By JOSEPH HALL, D.D., Bishop of Norwich. Reprinted, with General Gordon's marks, from the Original Copy used by him, and with an Introduction on his Theology by the Rev. H. Carruthers Wilson, M.A.

"Hall's treatise is in itself an excellent example of the best kind of devotional literature, and it will contribute to its appreciation by the modern reader that its sacred teachings and appeals formed part of the spiritual nourishment of the English 19th century hero and saint."—*Christian World.*

4. RUYSBROECK AND THE MYSTICS. With selections from Ruysbroeck. By MAURICE MAETERLINCK. Authorised Translation by Jane T. Stoddart.

"It does much to make intelligible and attractive a powerful religious thinker, from whom most readers would turn aside on account of the perplexities and vagueness of his manner."—*Scotsman.*

LONDON: HODDER & STOUGHTON, 27, PATERNOSTER ROW.